DISHONOUR

KERRY KAYA

B
Boldwood

First published in Great Britain in 2025 by Boldwood Books Ltd.

Copyright © Kerry Kaya, 2025

Cover Design by Colin Thomas

Cover Images: Colin Thomas

The moral right of Kerry Kaya to be identified as the author of this work has been asserted in accordance with the Copyright, Designs and Patents Act 1988.

All rights reserved. No part of this book may be reproduced in any form or by any electronic or mechanical means, including information storage and retrieval systems, without written permission from the author, except for the use of brief quotations in a book review. This book is a work of fiction and, except in the case of historical fact, any resemblance to actual persons, living or dead, is purely coincidental.

Every effort has been made to obtain the necessary permissions with reference to copyright material, both illustrative and quoted. We apologise for any omissions in this respect and will be pleased to make the appropriate acknowledgements in any future edition.

A CIP catalogue record for this book is available from the British Library.

Paperback ISBN 978-1-83751-299-7

Large Print ISBN 978-1-83751-298-0

Hardback ISBN 978-1-83751-297-3

Ebook ISBN 978-1-83751-300-0

Kindle ISBN 978-1-83751-301-7

Audio CD ISBN 978-1-83751-292-8

MP3 CD ISBN 978-1-83751-293-5

Digital audio download ISBN 978-1-83751-295-9

This book is printed on certified sustainable paper. Boldwood Books is dedicated to putting sustainability at the heart of our business. For more information please visit https://www.boldwoodbooks.com/about-us/sustainability/

Boldwood Books Ltd, 23 Bowerdean Street, London, SW6 3TN

www.boldwoodbooks.com

For Daniel

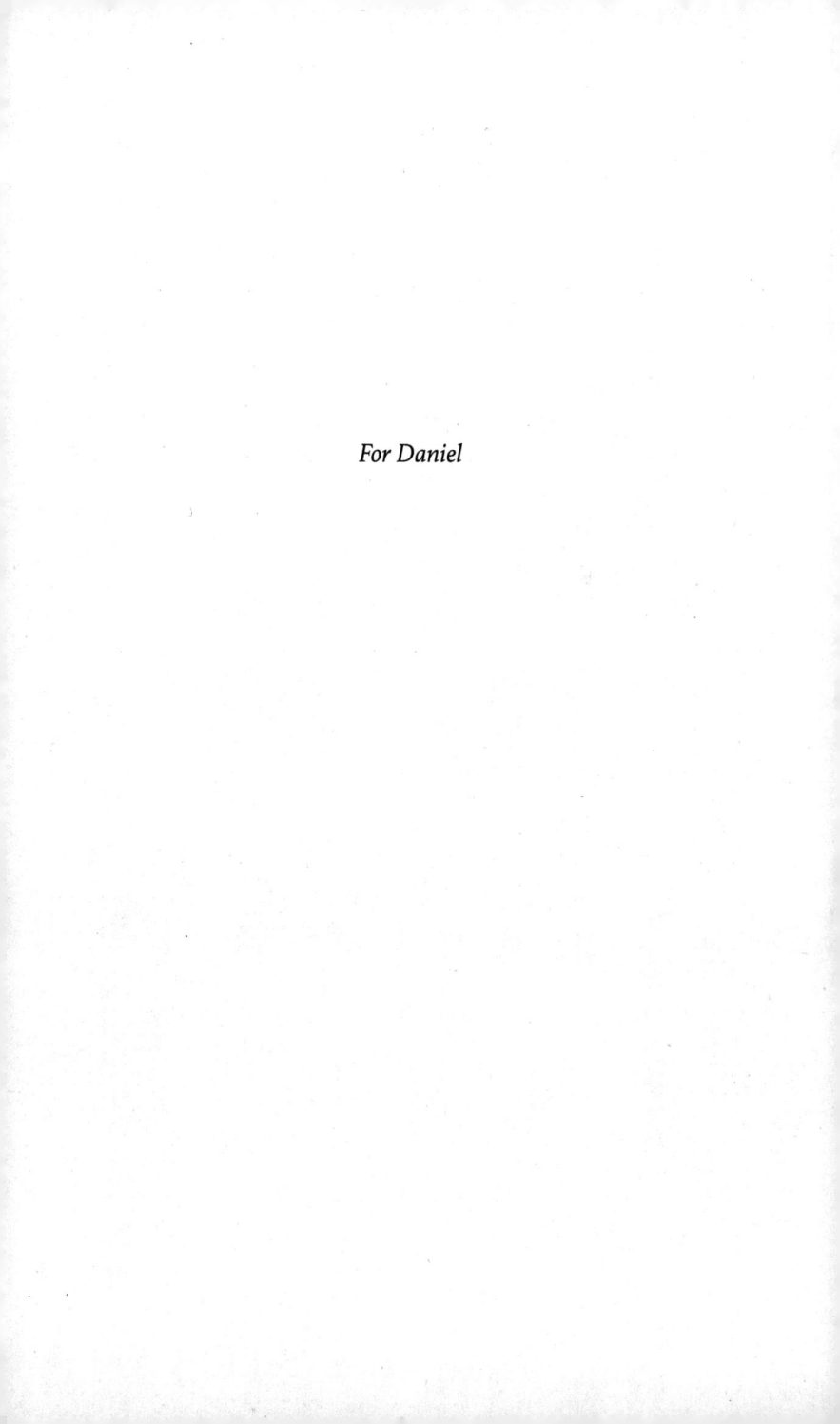

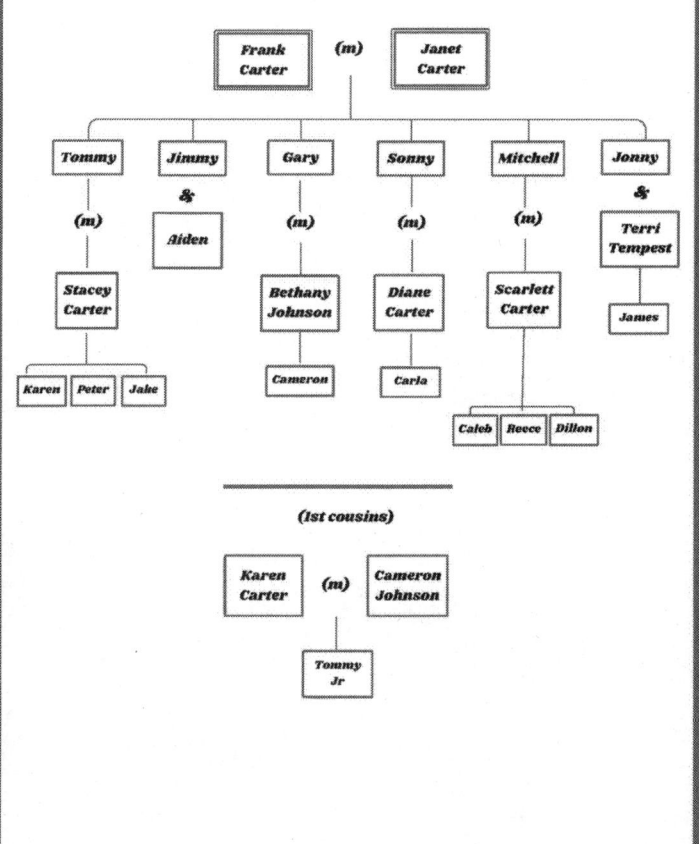

1

Switching off the ignition, Damien Vickers leaned back in the driver's seat, his elbow resting casually against the window frame and his hard stare fixated on the scrapyard across the street from where he'd parked.

Beside him in the passenger seat, Winston Baptiste unclipped his seatbelt and shifted his large frame in an attempt to make himself more comfortable. 'Well?' he asked with a lift of his eyebrows. 'Are we getting out of the motor or are you planning to just sit here shooting daggers at the gaff?'

Damien sighed and pinched the bridge of his nose. He had so many questions buzzing around his brain and knew without doubt that they could be answered by the family who owned the scrapyard, or at least one of them. Whether or not he was actually ready to hear what had gone down in Pentonville prison, though, was another matter entirely. As desperate as he was to learn the truth surrounding the murder of his younger brother, Dylan, he had a sinking feeling that hearing the grisly details first hand was going to break his heart in two, perhaps even irrevocably destroy him.

Winston shook his head and, sparking up a joint, he inhaled a lungful of smoke before exhaling languidly through his nostrils. 'Damien,' he tried again, holding out the spliff. 'We didn't come all this way just to sit here doing fuck all.'

Damien almost laughed and would have done too if he'd actually had a laugh inside of him. It wasn't as though they'd had far to travel. The journey from South London to the outskirts of East London had taken them less than twenty minutes. Waving away the spliff Winston held out to him, Damien returned his gaze back to the scrapyard. It had barely turned 9 a.m. and from his position, he noted several cars parked on the forecourt, indicating that the yard was already a hive of activity. Not that it mattered in the great scheme of things; he'd been more than prepared to wait all day if needs be. Taking a deep breath, he unclipped his own seatbelt and rolled his neck from side to side, his shoulder blades as taut as the muscles across his back and biceps.

'D,' Winston groaned. 'Come on, man. What are we waiting for?'

'Yeah,' Damien's cousin Vinnie piped up from the back seat. 'I didn't come here just to stake the place out.'

'Then maybe you shouldn't have come,' Damien growled back. 'In fact, and correct me if I'm wrong, but weren't you the one who insisted on tagging along?' Snatching the joint from out of Winston's fingers, Damien took a deep toke, hoping that the cannabis would somehow help him to relax. Despite his best friend and cousin egging him on, he just needed a few minutes to gather his thoughts, to give himself a moment or two to calm down before he went in all guns blazing and started throwing punches, or maybe even committing murder which, under the circumstances, was more than just a probability. A familiar sense of rage rippled through his veins and no matter how far down he tried to push it away, it wouldn't leave him. He wanted to hurt someone, to slam his fists into someone's face and not stop pummelling until he was out of breath and his knuckles were grazed and bloody. And even more than that, he wanted revenge, to maim and torture the bastards who had so cruelly taken Dylan's life, starting with the bastard who'd supposedly been his friend whilst inside; his only friend, might he add.

'You've got to remember,' Vinnie continued to goad as he jerked his thumb towards the yard, 'that if it wasn't for him then Dylan could still be alive. He did fuck all to help him and you know it.'

Damien's lips curled into a snarl. As much as he didn't like to admit it, Vinnie was right. Dylan hadn't stood a chance. The attack he'd endured had been so brutal, so heinous, that he would never have been able to fight back however much his life may have depended on it. Reaching out for the door handle, he shoved the door wide open.

'Now we're starting to get somewhere.' Winston grinned as he eagerly followed suit and swung open the car door.

Damien's hand shot out and, grasping onto Winston's arm, he shook his head. 'Wait here for me. And that goes for you an' all,' he added, looking over his shoulder at Vinnie, his expression deadly serious.

Winston's eyebrows shot up, his mouth dropping open as he looked from Damien's face then to the scrapyard. 'D...' he began.

From the back seat, Vinnie sprang forward. 'Leave it out,' he bellowed, a flicker of something that Damien couldn't quite decipher sweeping across his features. 'Dylan was my cousin...'

'And he's my brother,' Damien spat back. As he collapsed back in the seat, the enormity of what he'd just said hit him like a ton of bricks. His kid brother was gone. No matter how much he didn't want to believe it, it was true. A wave of emotions engulfed his entire being and, rubbing at his eyes, he took a series of deep breaths in an attempt to keep the tears at bay, not that they were ever far away. He'd cried so much over the recent weeks that he didn't know whether he was coming or going. He could barely even begin to comprehend the pain Dylan must have suffered; he didn't want to imagine it. Bringing his fist to his lips, he swallowed deeply, pushing the sickening images of his brother's last moments far from his mind. 'Just wait here for me,' he reiterated, his voice hard.

'Damien.' Speaking slowly as though he were addressing a child, Winston gave a look of warning. 'From what I've heard they're no pushovers,' he said, nodding towards the yard. 'They've got reputations.'

A small smile tugged at Damien's lips, a smile that until now he would never have believed he had inside of him. Like Winston, he had heard the rumours circulating about the Carter family. They were well known amongst the criminal fraternity, and not only did they have a lot of connections but they were also highly respected in their own right, and by all accounts they were handy with their fists. Well, two could play at that game. He too came from a renowned family. His surname was notorious in South London; he'd even go as far as to say that it was feared, exactly as it should be when you took into account who his father was. 'I don't need a bodyguard,' he declared. 'And unless it's escaped your notice I do know how to take care of myself.'

'Yeah,' Winston agreed. 'And that's exactly what I'm afraid of. At the best of times you've got a short fuse. All it's gonna take is for one of that lot,' he said, nodding back towards the scrapyard, 'to look at you the wrong way and all hell will break loose.'

'Give me some credit. I do know how to control myself.' As agitation rippled through Damien's veins, he rolled his eyes.

Although to be fair, Winston did have a point. It wouldn't take much for him to lose his rag, not that he actually needed an excuse under the circumstances. 'It's gonna be fine,' he lied with a wave of his hand. 'All I want to do is have a nice, friendly little chat and nothing more than that.'

Against his better judgement, Winston gave his best friend a knowing look before slumping back in the seat and throwing his arms up into the air. 'Fine,' he grumbled. 'We'll give you ten minutes and if you're not out by then, we're coming in.'

It was more than Damien could have hoped for seeing as Winston could be a stubborn bugger when the mood took him, not to mention loyal. They'd known one another since childhood and were more like brothers than best mates. And as much as Damien was grieving, he knew for a fact that Winston had been as equally affected by Dylan's death. As for Vinnie, as much as he may have grated heavily on Damien's nerves, they shared the same blood; they were family, kin, more's the pity. 'Make it twenty,' he answered, stepping out of the car and slamming the door firmly closed behind him before either Winston or Vinnie had the chance to protest.

As he strolled across the forecourt, Damien's strides were long and purposeful and his expression a mask of anger. Every fibre of his being screamed at him to keep calm, to keep a level head, not that it did him any good, he noted. If anything, he was even more irate, the need to cause significant harm so strong that he could almost taste it. This was to be payback, he told himself. Even thinking about the injuries his brother had sustained made him want to both weep and empty the contents of his stomach in equal measures.

As he shoved open the door to what he assumed was some kind of office, Damien's lips were curled into a snarl. He'd obviously taken the occupants by surprise and as several heads snapped in his direction, he pulled himself up to his full height. Standing at five foot eleven, he wasn't a particularly tall man but what he lacked in height he certainly made up for in notoriety. He was well known for having a quick temper, and even more widely known for being at loggerheads with his father, the high and mighty Jason Vickers, a man many would go out of their way to avoid upsetting in any way, shape, or form.

Before the men in front of him could open their mouths to question who he was or what he wanted, Damien clenched and unclenched his fists in rapid succession. This wasn't the time for pleasantries, neither was it the time to officially introduce himself. He'd come for one reason and one reason only and that was to smash the living daylights out of the bastard who'd stood idly by whilst his younger brother was being slaughtered like a pig. 'Which one of you bastards,' he hissed, 'is Tommy fucking Johnson?'

2

As an eerie silence fell over the office, Tommy Johnson, or Tommy Jr as he was more commonly known amongst his family, swallowed deeply, his stomach twisting up into knots. Around him he could sense the tension brewing, each of his family members on red alert as their spines straightened and the muscles across their shoulder blades became taut. Trouble was on the horizon and he knew instinctively that the next few moments would determine exactly how the situation was going to pan out. Either World War Three was about to erupt, or, and it was a very big or considering trouble had a nasty habit of following both him and his family around, they would somehow find a way to defuse the situation.

'Well?' the man who had burst into the office growled. 'Which one of you cunts is Tommy Johnson?'

'Who wants to know?'

Whipping his head around to look at his great-uncle Jonny, Tommy inwardly groaned. At the best of times Jonny was a loose cannon, as they all were, a family trait that had well and truly been passed down through the generations.

'I am.' Pulling himself up to his full height, Tommy Jr gave a nod all the while ignoring the look of warning that Jonny shot towards him. 'And I'm guessing that you're Dylan's brother.' It wasn't a question as such. He'd taken note of the similarities between his late friend and the man the moment he'd set foot through the door; they were too great for him not to. The same build, same colour hair, same colour eyes; they even shared the same faint smattering of freckles across their nose and cheeks. Although Dylan had been slightly taller, he noted.

For the briefest of moments the man faltered, as though Tommy had somehow taken him aback before his expression once again became one of fury and his hands curled into tight fists.

Casually tapping a biro pen against his teeth, Jonny Carter swivelled the office chair he was sitting on from side to side. 'I asked you a question,' he barked out. 'Who the fuck are you?'

The man snarled, animosity radiating off him as he tore his gaze away from Tommy Jr and aimed his glare in Jonny Carter's direction. 'Damien Vickers.'

Despite the flicker of recognition that spread across Jonny's face, he gave a nonchalant shrug. 'Is that supposed to mean something to me?'

'Jonny.' Giving a slight shake of his head, Tommy lifted his eyebrows. So much for them defusing the situation, not that he should have expected his great-uncle to back down. It wasn't in Jonny's nature for a start and seeing as he was now the head of the family despite having two elder brothers who by rights should have been handed down the reins to the family business, Jonny had a lot to prove.

'Because believe me, pal,' Jonny continued, purposefully ignoring the look of warning that came from his great nephew as he came to a halt, tossed the biro pen aside then rested his forearms on the desk, 'coming in here shouting the odds isn't going to end well for you. So why don't you do us all a favour and get to the chase, starting with who you are and what the fuck you want.'

In that instant Damien Vickers glanced around him, as if assessing the situation. It didn't take a genius to tell him that he was heavily outnumbered, six to one. Not that he appeared bothered or concerned by this fact. If anything, he looked even more determined, his fists clenching even tighter. 'It's because of you my brother is dead,' he spat, his nostrils flaring as he turned his hard stare back to Tommy Jr.

Tommy's mouth fell slightly open, his forehead furrowing. He hadn't been responsible for Dylan's death; in fact, he'd done the complete opposite and done his utmost to try and save his life. Unconsciously he looked down at his hands and turned them over, as though recalling how Dylan's blood had stained his skin and the scent of iron had assaulted his nostrils. 'I...' He swallowed again, the hard lump in his throat preventing him from answering. Still he could hear Dylan's screams as he'd been doused in boiling water before being repeatedly stabbed. They haunted him every time he closed his eyes, so much so that he'd begun going to bed with ear phones in, music blaring, in an attempt to drown out the memories of that fateful day. 'I...' He cleared his throat, pushing the hard lump down. 'It wasn't like that...'

The words had barely left his mouth when Damien's fist collided with his jaw, sending him hurtling backwards. Within a matter of seconds it was all over and as his family pulled Damien away, his uncle Jonny leapt out of the chair and rounded the desk.

'Oi,' he roared, stabbing his finger in Damien's direction.

'That's enough.' Turning his head slightly, he gave Tommy Jr a sidelong glance. 'Are you good?'

Regaining his balance, Tommy Jr nodded. As much as the punch had taken him unawares, a part of him had been expecting Dylan's brother to lash out. It was only natural that he would want to seek revenge for Dylan's death. Rubbing at his jaw, he opened and closed his mouth, checking that everything was still in working order. Maybe he'd deserved the slap. Perhaps he could have done more; exactly what he could have done, though, he didn't know. God only knew how much he'd tried to stem the bleeding. There were just too many stab wounds for him to contend with. And if that hadn't been enough, there were also the burns. Within a matter of seconds huge blisters had begun to form across Dylan's face, head, and neck, his face melting as the scalding-hot liquid had penetrated through skin, muscle, and tissue, burning him beyond recognition. 'I think I'm gonna throw up,' he muttered, bending forward and taking several deep breaths as he clasped onto his knees.

Jonny groaned and, taking a step to the side, he motioned towards another of his nephews, Reece. 'Get him out of here, will you.'

'No... I'll be all right.' As he slowly straightened back up, the colour returned to Tommy's cheeks. 'I just need a couple of minutes.' It was a lie, one that he had a feeling they could all see through, Damien Vickers included. Dylan's murder had hit him hard, to the point where he hadn't been able to bring himself to discuss the grisly details, not with his dad, his great-uncle Jonny, or even Reece, who wasn't only his cousin twice removed but also his best mate. Rubbing his hand over his clammy face, he gave a sad shake of his head. 'He used to talk about you,' he said, turning to give Damien a cautious look. 'A lot. He looked up to you.'

There and then, Damien's shoulders sagged and as he heaved in a ragged breath, his fists began to uncurl.

'And in a way you're right. I was there. I was a witness. But there was nothing I could have done to help him. It all happened too fast.' Glancing at his hands again, Tommy Jr turned them over as if expecting to still see Dylan's blood ingrained under his fingernails. 'He was too badly injured. The burns...' Shaking his head, Tommy Jr stuffed his hands into his pockets, the compulsion to inspect them too strong for him to bear. It had become a habit of his, something he'd tried to hide from his family although on the odd occasion he'd caught them shoot him a puzzled look, especially his dad and Reece. But when he was alone he would lose track of time as he stared at his hands for what felt like hours, recalling every speckle of Dylan's blood that had tainted his skin. His dad had even suggested he might need some form of counselling, claiming that he'd been through a traumatic situation. He'd laughed at that. Why the fuck would he need counselling? The only thing he needed was to see those responsible for Dylan's death brought to their knees and then he'd be fine, or at least this was what he hoped. 'The burns were too severe,' he continued. 'He wouldn't have been able to come back from something like that. I'm not even so sure he would have wanted to.'

Lifting his face to the ceiling, Damien closed his eyes, his expression one of pure devastation, and as he pinched the bridge of his nose, Tommy felt a moment of pity for him.

'I'm sorry, man,' Tommy continued. Taking a step forward, he tentatively placed his hand on Damien's shoulder and gave it a comforting squeeze. 'If I could have saved him then believe me, I would have done. He was my pal; we were there for one another.' Shifting his weight, he gave a helpless shrug, his cheeks flushing red. 'I dunno, having a mate inside, someone who understood what it was like to be banged up, made it that bit easier I suppose...'

As the door to the office swung open and two men walked through, the words died in Tommy's throat.

'Is this him?' one of them growled. 'Is this the bastard who stood idly by while Dylan was being butchered?'

Letting his hand fall to his side, Tommy shot Jonny a look. Like the rest of his family, he'd never been one to back down from a fight and unless he was very much mistaken, the two men who had walked through the door were more than spoiling for a ruck, they were downright baying for blood to be spilled, or at least one of them was, and unless he was even more mistaken, it was his blood they were after.

'I told you to stay in the car,' Damien spat.

'What and miss out on all of the fun?' the mouthier of the two answered. 'What are you waiting for?' he asked, pulling out a blade. 'Do the bastard.'

The fine hairs on the back of Tommy's neck stood up on end and as Reece tensed beside him, he swallowed deeply. 'There's no need for that,' he said, inching slightly forward, his arms outstretched. 'Put the knife down.'

The man's lips curled into a snarl. 'Not a chance,' he replied with a hint of a smirk. 'This is payback.'

'Vinnie,' Damien warned, the tone of his voice enough to warn those around him that he was in grave danger of losing his temper. 'Get out. This is fuck all to do with you.'

'It's got everything to do with me,' Vinnie continued to shout as he waved the knife in front of him. 'Dylan was my cousin and this fucker is going to pay for what he did to him.'

Anger flashed in Damien's eyes. 'I'm not going to tell you again,' he snarled. 'Get out before me and you have a big problem.'

As though weighing up his options, Vinnie momentarily studied his cousin. 'Nah, fuck this.' Bounding forward, he pulled back his arm, the blade pointing straight ahead of him.

In that moment Tommy froze, his brain sending him so many mixed signals that he wasn't sure how to respond. He should run, he knew that as well as he knew his own name. Only there was another part of him, a more dominant part of his brain, that wasn't prepared to back down. He was no coward and despite moving out of harm's way, that being the sensible thing to do, his legs wouldn't cooperate. Instead he screwed his eyes shut tight and braced himself for the blow, the sting as the tip of the blade plunged into his flesh tearing through muscle and tissue in its wake.

In the commotion that followed, Tommy peeled one eye open. Much to his surprise the blow hadn't come; instead, he'd heard a loud thud, then his family spitting out expletives as they dragged an unconscious Vinnie from the office. But what shocked him even more was that it was Damien Vickers who was shaking out his fist.

'He always was a mouthy bastard,' Damien scowled as he stared at the door his cousin had been hauled through.

Tommy Jr nodded, unsure of how best to answer, and as he tore his gaze away from the sight of his family giving Vinnie a kicking he wouldn't forget in a hurry, he gave a small smile. 'I meant what I said. If I could have saved Dylan then I would have.'

Damien sighed and as he rubbed the palm of his hand over his face, he turned to look at the second man and jerked his head towards the door. 'Do me a favour and break it up before they end up murdering the tosser,' he said, motioning to where the Carters were currently acting out their revenge. 'Chuck him in the motor, the boot preferably,' he added as an afterthought.

'The less I have to see of him the better it will be for all concerned.'

The man gave a light chuckle, his dark brown eyes sparkling with amusement. 'It's been a long time coming, D,' he said, motioning to the door, his voice deep and gravelly. 'Too fucking long if you ask me.'

'Yeah, you can say that again,' Damien agreed, and as the man made his way outside, Damien turned his attention back to Tommy Jr. 'Who was responsible? Who murdered my brother?'

For a moment Tommy Jr was taken aback. He'd assumed that Dylan's family would have already been given the low down, that they would have known who the murderers were, or at least this was what he'd been told by one of his fellow inmates. 'There were two of them,' he finally answered. 'They'd had some kind of beef with him from the get-go.'

Narrowing his eyes, Damien screwed up his face. 'Why?'

'I dunno,' Tommy answered. And it was true. Dylan had never given him any kind of explanation. He wasn't so sure that Dylan himself had known why the men had singled him out. 'I just assumed it was something to do with your old man.'

Damien visibly stiffened, his expression becoming one of anger as his lips curled into a snarl. 'What makes you say that?' he spat.

'I don't know,' Tommy repeated with a shrug. 'I'm just putting two and two together I suppose. I mean, Dylan let slip one day that your old man was a face and I just guessed it was something to do with that, that there had been some kind of trouble between them and your dad. You know what it's like inside; it's a breeding ground for scores to be settled, especially when the screws are partial to turning a blind eye.'

As he chewed on his bottom lip, Damien nodded, his expression becoming closed off again. Finally he glanced around the office as though only just seeing the upturned chairs that had been toppled over in the Carters' haste to reach Vinnie before he'd caused significant, perhaps even irreversible damage. 'I'll see myself out.' He cleared his throat then gestured around the office. 'If there's any damage caused I'll...'

'It's fine,' Tommy reassured him as he too took in the upturned furniture. 'It's all shit anyway,' he said, kicking out at one of the chairs. 'And about time my uncle put his hand in his pocket and replaced it with something decent.' Which was no lie in his opinion. As far as he was aware, the furniture had been there for decades, and he was pretty certain that the rickety leather sofa placed against the far wall was even older than he was, maybe even older than his mum. How the sofa was still standing was a mystery, not only to himself but to the rest of the family too.

Damien nodded and as he stepped outside the office, Tommy Jr sucked in a collective breath, his thoughts once again wandering back to the day of Dylan's murder. Resisting the urge to study his hands again, he shoved them deep into his pockets. He was okay, he was fine. Only deep down he knew this wasn't entirely true. Bearing witness to Dylan's murder had irrevocably changed him, and not for the better either. He'd become harder, colder, and a lot more conniving than he'd been previously. Making his way over to the window, he observed Damien Vickers walk to where he'd parked his car. He felt no ill will towards Dylan's brother despite the fact he'd clocked him one. How could he, when if the roles had been reversed, his family would have done exactly the same as Damien. They would have left no stone unturned in their pursuit to find the person who'd caused him harm. As for the men who'd carried out the murder, Tommy was as determined as Damien to get to the bottom of the matter. The attack hadn't been random, it had been a calculated, well thought-out execution. The question was, though, who had been the brains behind it? Because he had a niggling suspicion that it hadn't been the men who'd actually carried out the deed. No, they had been nothing more than foot soldiers carrying out an order. But whose order that might have been, he had no idea.

Heaving out a sigh, he moved away from the window, yanked a chair upright and took a seat, his mind going into overdrive as he tried to think back on his and Dylan's conversations. The answer was there somewhere, he knew it was. Dylan had loved to talk and as much as he hadn't particularly discussed his or his family's involvement in the criminal underworld, he had let slip on the odd occasion.

By the time the rest of the family made their way back into the office, Tommy was still deep in thought.

'So, that's Damien Vickers, eh,' Tommy Jr's father, Cameron, stated as he eyed the upturned chairs.

'Could have been worse,' Jonny retorted. 'Could have been his old man, Jason.' He stabbed his finger towards Tommy. 'Now that's one nutter you don't want to get on the wrong side of. Come to think of it,' he added, scratching his jaw, 'his business partner Arthur Brennan isn't much better because take it from me, that is one nasty, vicious, little bastard.'

Tommy glanced up. He'd heard the name Arthur before, he was sure he had, and he was pretty certain that Dylan had referred to him as Uncle Arthur. Giving a shrug, he went back to thinking the situation through and pushing all thoughts of both Jason Vickers and Arthur Brennan far from his mind. The answer was staring him in the face, he knew it was.

* * *

Stepping out of the scrapyard office, Damien had never been more livid, not only with his cousin Vinnie but also with himself. He'd been fully prepared to immediately lay into Tommy Johnson, to smash his fists into the bastard's face and not stop until he was out of breath and spent, or at least this had been his original intention. Only when the time had come and he'd found himself face to face with his brother's friend, he'd been unable to follow through with his plan. Oh, he still wanted to hurt someone, just not the kid who'd been standing in front of him, and in Damien's eyes he was a kid, same as Dylan had been in that respect.

As he reached his car and placed his hand on the door handle, Damien momentarily squeezed his eyes shut tight. Exactly what he'd been afraid of happening had come true. He hadn't wanted to hear the grisly details of his brother's murder; he could barely even begin to imagine Dylan's final moments, let alone hear about them. All he wanted was a name for the men responsible for the attack, a valid reason as to why they had singled his brother out. It wasn't as though Dylan had ever gone out looking for trouble, and unlike their cousin Vinnie who tended to use their surname to intimidate others, that hadn't been Dylan's style. Of course he could look after himself when he needed to, he was a Vickers after all, but he'd never actively been the aggressor, nor had he ever had a tendency to bully anyone.

A familiar sense of agitation curled around his insides as he cast his gaze upon the rear of the car. Winston had done exactly as he'd asked and dumped Vinnie in the boot, the best place for him as far as he was concerned. In his opinion, Vinnie was nothing more than an irritation, an itch that he couldn't quite reach. Even when they'd been kids Damien had viewed his younger cousin as a nuisance, or to be more precise, a lairy little bastard. Vinnie had a way about him that would make Jesus Christ himself curse, and over the years Damien had lost count of how many times he'd warned Dylan to steer clear of their cousin, not that it had ever done him any good. As far as Dylan was concerned, the sun had shone out of Vinnie's arse; he'd gravitated towards him in a way that Damien for the life of him had never been able to understand. And to top it off, Vinnie was a sly fucker. He'd failed to mention that he'd been tooled up. But at the end of the day, that was Vinnie all over, whereas Damien had never been a fan of using weapons, had never needed to use them to be fair. Vinnie on the other hand was a different breed altogether. He may give it all the mouth but when it came down to it, he was fuck all, hence his need to use a blade.

'You all right?'

From the passenger seat, Winston gave his friend a cautious glance.

'Not really,' Damien answered as he climbed behind the wheel and lounged back in the seat. 'I've been better, put it that way.'

Winston nodded and, taking a spliff from out of his pocket, he placed it between his lips and flicked his lighter. Inhaling the smoke deep into his lungs, he followed suit and relaxed into the seat. 'You know what you need, don't you?' he said, passing across the joint.

'What's that?' Taking a deep toke, Damien closed his eyes and exhaled through his nostrils.

'To learn how to chill the fuck out.' Winston chuckled. 'You're wound up so fucking tight man,' he said, his voice becoming serious, 'that you're going to end up doing yourself some damage.'

Damien couldn't help but laugh. It was true. He was wound up tight, and who could blame him? Not only had his kid brother been murdered, but also he and his father were at loggerheads, his mother was an addict, his sister was married to one of the biggest pricks he'd ever had the displeasure to meet, and then to top it off he had Vinnie and his antics to contend with. 'I will do,' he answered. 'As soon as I've found the bastard responsible.'

Winston sighed and, giving a shake of his head, he took the joint back and placed it between his lips. 'And what are you planning to do with him back there?' he asked, gesturing behind him in the direction of the car boot.

Giving a shrug, Damien ran his hand over his face. He knew what he wanted to do, what he should have done years ago, and that was to beat the living daylights out of his cousin and then promptly kick him to the kerb, or maybe even go that one step further, kill him and then dump his lifeless body in the Thames. Nothing would give him greater satisfaction. Only he couldn't do that, could he. Whether he liked it or not they were family and in his book that meant something. 'I don't know,' he finally answered as he turned the key in the ignition and pulled out onto the road. 'Drop his arse off home, I suppose.'

'Don't you think you should let him out first?' Winston asked with a rise of his eyebrows as the sound of Vinnie frantically kicking at the car boot reached their ears.

Damien grinned, his first genuine smile in weeks, and as he momentarily took his eyes of the road to look at his friend, he shook his head. 'Nah, it'll teach the little prick a lesson.' He winked. 'Put the fear of God into him and, with a bit of luck, it might even calm him down a bit, not that I'm holding out much hope of that ever happening.'

Winston laughed even harder and, turning on the car stereo in a bid to tune out Vinnie's cries, he took another deep toke then passed the joint across. 'I couldn't have said it any better, my friend,' he said, holding out his fist for Damien to bump it.

A moment of silence followed and after clearing his throat, Damien gave Winston a sidelong glance. 'I'm going to pay my old man a visit.'

Winston snapped his head around, his eyes narrowed into slits. 'Is that a good idea?' he asked with a shake of his head. 'The last time the two of you were together I had to physically drag you out of the house before you ended up doing him some damage.'

Damien sighed. The memory of that night was still fresh in his mind. Just hours earlier he'd been given the news that his brother had been murdered, and understandably emotions were running high. Naively he'd thought that maybe he and his dad would be able to bury the hatchet, that for a short while they would be able to come together as a family united in their grief, even if it was more so for his mother and sister's benefit than because he and his dad had truly put their dislike for one another behind them. He should have known that the evening wouldn't pan out the way he'd envisioned it would, especially when you took into account the history between them. As soon as Damien had stepped foot through his parents' front door, his old man had begun running his mouth. And before he'd even slipped his coat off or given his mother a comforting hug, the atmosphere had turned decidedly frosty, as it always did whenever he and his father were forced to spend any length of time in one another's company. 'Yeah, well.' He shrugged. 'It's about time I put the old bastard in his place, isn't it.'

Winston blew out his cheeks. 'I hope you know what you're doing because believe me, I can see this going tits up,' he groaned.

Flicking the indicator, Damien ignored the comment. In a

way he could understand Winston's concern. He and his dad had never had what he would call a healthy father and son relationship. Even as a young boy he'd hated the fucker; was hard not to, he supposed. Most days he'd dreaded hearing his father's car pull onto the drive, and no matter how much his mother would warn him to stay out of his dad's way, he couldn't help but do the complete opposite. They had a knack of antagonising one another, and the older Damien became the more he would retaliate and deliberately push his dad's buttons. Even the threat of his dad's belt or fists had done nothing to deter him; if anything, it had spurred him on even further. 'I can tell you right now,' he said, turning his head, 'if I find out my old man is the reason my brother was murdered, I'm going to end the bastard.'

'Yeah,' Winston answered with a grimace. 'I had a feeling you were going to say that.'

* * *

Clenching his jaw, Jason Vickers gave an irritated sigh, his hard stare directed at his only daughter's husband. In his opinion, Gio Ferrari was a waste of space, or more to the point a waste of oxygen. And if anyone's mother should have swallowed the night they were conceived then he could hand on heart state that it was Gio's old girl.

Even now as he watched Gio scroll through his mobile phone, chuckling at some cheesy meme he'd found on social media, Jason had to fight the urge not to pull back his arm and fell the tosser to the floor. Everywhere he looked, the lanky streak of piss, better known as his son-in-law, was there. He wasn't even able to escape to his office for a bit of peace and quiet without Gio trying to follow on behind, as though he were too afraid he was going to miss out on some juicy gossip.

'Haven't you got any work to do?' he spat.

Gio looked up, his dark eyes wide and his mouth hanging open as though he'd been deeply offended.

'Dad,' his daughter, Demi, chastised, forever defending her husband. 'Do you have to be so bloody rude.'

Sighing again, Jason ever so slightly relented, his shoulders sagging. Perhaps he was being a little harsh. And as much as Gio may not be everyone's cup of tea, especially not his own, his daughter loved him. Why, he had no idea. It wasn't as though Gio had much going for him. No, he was more than content to spend his day running errands, pretty much doing fuck all other than sitting on his arse and sponging off his wife or father-in-law all so that he could gamble away their hard-earned cash, and unless Jason was very much mistaken, Gio also had a particularly nasty, not to mention expensive, habit of snorting Charlie up that big hooter of his too. The signs were all too obvious even if Demi refused to acknowledge them.

Flicking her head towards the door, Demi motioned for her husband to leave the office. 'Will you give us a minute,' she asked, jerking her thumb in Jason's direction. 'I want a word in private with my dad.'

As Gio opened his mouth as if to refuse the request, the glare Jason shot towards him was enough to make him bolt out of his seat, the colour draining from his face.

'Dad,' Demi said a few moments later once her husband had gently closed the office door behind him. 'You're not the only one who misses him, you know,' she said as she slipped her arms around her father's neck and lightly pressed a kiss to his stubbled cheek. 'Dylan was my brother.'

Jason closed his eyes and, clenching his fists in an attempt to stop himself from shoving his daughter away from him, he withdrew from her embrace, sank back in the seat and rubbed at his temples. The effort of that small action alone was enough to make him feel exhausted. He was more than just grieving; his entire world had been blown apart and as much as he'd screamed, shouted, and sworn to maim and torture those responsible for harming his son, the outcome, much to his dismay, could never change. His boy was gone; the only son he'd been close to, the only one who had shown any interest when it came to one day taking over the reins of the business.

'Dad,' Demi said again, breaking his thoughts, her voice gentle. 'Why don't you try and make amends with Damien...?' Her voice trailed off slightly as though she expected her father to erupt into a fit of fury which, under normal circumstances, wouldn't have been unheard of. 'Just try and talk to him.'

Jason scoffed. 'Why would I want to do that?'

'Because he's your son.'

Waving his hand dismissively, Jason got to his feet. He had no desire whatsoever to speak to his eldest son, or even lay his eyes upon him for that matter. Damien had more than made his feelings known the last time they had come face to face. And then there was the resentment he felt towards his eldest son. In his mind, Damien was as much to blame for Dylan's death as those who had actually carried out the deed. Damien had been the last one to visit Dylan, and surely to God, he must have realised that something was amiss. His boys had been close, or at least this was what he'd been led to believe, and if Dylan had been in trouble then he would have told his elder brother, surely. So why had Damien done nothing? Why had he left his brother at the mercy of those who had gone on to slaughter him like a pig?

'Dad, please,' Demi pleaded. 'Just speak to him. It's about time this feud of yours came to an end, isn't it, if not for my sake then for Dylan's.'

Jason turned his face, his expression a mask of fury, and the anger he'd been trying so hard to swallow down bubbled to the surface. 'Don't,' he growled, stabbing his finger in his daughter's direction. 'Don't you fucking dare pull that crap with me. Your brother...'

Demi's cheeks turned red. 'Do you know what your problem is?' she spat, cutting her father off. 'The reason why you and Damien can't see eye to eye?'

As he breathed heavily through his nostrils, Jason's eyes were narrowed into slits. Instinctively, he knew what was going to come out of his daughter's mouth next, the same words he'd heard a hundred times before.

'It's because the two of you are so alike,' she hissed. 'You're both pig-headed, both have to be right all the time, and neither one of you know how to back down and admit when you're in the wrong.'

Jason shook his head. It wasn't the first time he'd been told that he and his eldest son shared the same traits, that Damien was like the spit out of his mouth. Not that Jason believed this to be true; how could it be when from the very moment of his birth Damien had been nothing but trouble. As a baby he'd screamed nonstop, his cries piercing enough to induce a headache. Colic, his wife had said was the cause for his constant wailing. They'd even taken it in turns to walk the length of the bedroom, bouncing the baby on their shoulder, hoping, praying, that the motion would somehow help him to settle. Not that it ever did; if anything, Damien would scream even louder, hellbent on making his presence known. 'I don't want to see him,' he finally muttered. 'In fact, the further away we are from one another the better.'

As she stood with her hands on her hips, Demi's eyes flashed with annoyance. In that moment she looked so like his wife that

Jason's breath caught in the back of his throat. Or at least a younger version of his wife before the booze and drugs had sucked the life out of her. His Carmen was still a beautiful woman, always would be in his eyes, but even he couldn't deny that her addictions, or her demons as he preferred to call them, had taken a toll on her body. It shouldn't have come as a surprise, not really. He'd known from day one when he'd picked her out of the gutter that she had an addictive personality, only he'd stupidly believed that if he loved her enough she wouldn't have been tempted to return to her old life. He'd been so foolish, so gullible back then that he'd really thought that if he gave her everything she'd ever desired then she wouldn't want to seek out the dealers from her past, the ones who had contributed to her downfall. The very same ones he had hunted down and whose lives he had brutally ended. Hindsight was a wonderful thing, he decided. Perhaps he should never have married her; perhaps he should have used and abused her body as so many others had before him and then moved on without a backward glance. And finally, maybe they should never have had children; maybe he'd been asking too much of her. He'd known of her struggles; she'd never tried to conceal them from him, at least not in the beginning anyway. He'd thought that having a child, a family of her own, would somehow help her to settle down, would give her a reason to want to turn her life around. And if he was being even more truthful, the only reason he'd deliberately set out to impregnate her was so that she would forever be cemented to him.

'Dad,' Demi huffed, breaking his thoughts. 'You can't avoid him forever. Whether you like it or not, he is your son.'

As he gave an irritated sigh, Jason rubbed at his eyes all the while forcing himself to keep a lid on his temper. He could hardly blow up at his daughter. He'd lost one son, was estranged from the other. Demi was all that he had left, and even then they had their moments all thanks to his dislike of her ponce of a husband. 'I'll think about it,' he grumbled. Which of course he had no intention of doing. Why should he when in his mind Damien was equally to blame for their turbulent relationship, if not even more so?

Demi gave a satisfied smile and as she wrapped her arms around him again, she rested her head on his shoulder and gave a soft sigh. 'He's hurting as much as we are, Dad,' she said quietly. 'He loved Dylan.'

Jason fought the urge to roll his eyes. He very much doubted that. Damien thought of no one but himself. Even as a youngster he'd been nothing but a selfish, disobedient, cocky little bastard, one he could have happily choked the life out of, and would have done too if it wasn't for his wife's love of the boy. 'Like I said,' he reiterated, giving a small smile, 'I'll think about it.'

'Make sure you do.' Straightening up, Demi chewed on her bottom lip. 'After all,' she said after a moment's thought, 'the two of you coming together has to be a lot better than being enemies.'

The smile slid from Jason's face. His daughter had made a point, and a valid one at that. Damien had become more than just his enemy over the years. The two were barely able to spend more than a few moments at a time in the same room together without one of them, if not both, exploding into a fit of fury. And as much as he'd tried to keep tabs on his eldest son's business interests, he hadn't managed to get very far. Damien was as tight-lipped as his business associates were when it came to the activities they were involved in, which in Jason's opinion made his son a downright dangerous individual.

Getting up from the chair, he made his way over to the drinks cabinet and poured himself a generous measure of whiskey. After knocking the alcohol back in one large gulp, he wiped the back of his hand over his lips. He would have never said it outright, but he couldn't help but feel somewhat wary of his son. Damien had grown up amongst the criminal underground. He'd made connections up and down the country, many connections if the rumours were anything to go by, perhaps even more than he himself had. Not only did Damien have the power to become the top dog of South London, but he also had the means, not to mention the backup from other criminal families should he need them which, knowing Damien, he didn't. He'd always been a lone wolf, and the only person he'd ever needed or truly wanted in his life was his best mate Winston. The two of them together were a powerful combination, far more powerful than Jason and his business partner Arthur could ever hope to be.

As his daughter left the office, Jason made his way back over to his desk and, slumping down onto the chair, he closed his eyes, not for the first time wishing that Damien and Dylan could have traded places. And as wicked as those thoughts may have been, he didn't care, not one iota. The wrong son had died, and nothing and no one would ever be able to sway his mind on that matter.

3

Exiting his car, Damien glanced up at his father's casino. It had been years since he'd last stepped foot inside; he'd had no need to, and even if he had, it wasn't as though his dad would have welcomed him with open arms. If anything, he would have promptly thrown him out on his ear, as he'd done on more than one occasion.

'You all right?'

Damien turned his head. It was becoming somewhat of a habit for Winston to ask him if he was okay, and as much as he appreciated the sentiment, the words were beginning to grate heavily on his nerves. He didn't need babysitting, and Winston better than anyone should have known that.

'Yeah, of course I am,' he answered, all the while ignoring the look of concern that Winston shot towards him. 'Why wouldn't I be?'

Winston lifted his eyebrows, and as he tore his gaze away from his best friend, he looked towards the casino and blew out his cheeks. 'It's been a long time,' he remarked, gesturing to the building before them. 'And as we both know, the last time the two of you were together didn't end so well.'

No it hadn't, not that this was enough to deter Damien. Bollocks to his old man. He hadn't turned up at the casino because he was at a loose end and wanted to pass the time of day, neither had he come to enquire about his dad's wellbeing. The only thing he wanted from the man was answers, to find out exactly what he knew surrounding Dylan's death, and he had to know something, he was bound to. His dad had enough people on his payroll to ensure he was the first to know everything that was going down.

'Best get it over and done with, eh,' he said as he made his way towards the entrance. 'The quicker we get away from this shithole the better.' Although it would be fair to say that his dad's casino was anything but a shit hole. No expense had been spared when it came to the fixtures and fittings, and the slot machines were some of the best on the market. As for the roulette tables cossetted away in a private members' area towards the back of the property, they could easily rival those that were housed in some of the best casinos in Las Vegas.

As soon as he stepped across the threshold, the scent of furniture polish assaulted his nostrils and the patterned carpet below his feet was so dense that his shoes sank into the fibres. Momentarily he paused, taking in his surroundings. As far as he could tell, nothing much had changed during his absence, at least not on the surface anyway. As he stepped further into the casino, he glanced around him, taking note of the fact that it was still early evening and other than the diehard regulars already taking up residence in front of their favourite machines, the casino was empty.

Moving further into the premises, Damien narrowed his

eyes, his steps coming to a halt. Up ahead of him was his dad's business partner Arthur Brennan, and his sister's husband Gio, their heads bent together as though they were deep in conversation. 'I've seen more fat on a fucking chip,' he commented as he nodded towards his brother-in-law's slim frame. 'For the life of me I don't understand what my sister sees in the prick.'

Beside him Winston chuckled. Their mutual dislike of Gio was the one and only sentiment they shared with Damien's father.

As though sensing their presence, Arthur looked up, surprise momentarily etched across his face.

A sense of unease snaked its way down Damien's spine. He'd never been a big fan of Arthur. He couldn't quite put his finger on what it was but there was something he didn't like about him.

'Damien.' Arthur grinned and as he covertly shoved Gio away from him, he took a step forward, his arms outstretched as though ready to pull Damien into his embrace. 'This is a surprise.'

'Yeah.' Stuffing his hands into his pockets, Damien made a point of keeping his distance. 'It's been a while.' Although this wasn't strictly true seeing as Arthur had been present when he and his dad had last come face to face just weeks earlier.

Arthur's expression became pained and, running his hand through his greying hair, he shook his head. 'I still can't believe it,' he stated, each word said with clear enunciation, a dead giveaway to the fact he'd been born with what most people would consider to be a silver spoon in his mouth, which in all honesty was a stark contrast when you considered the vicious, spiteful nature that bubbled underneath the surface and made Arthur Brennan so feared amongst his peers.

'No.' Damien swallowed deeply and pressed his lips together

in an attempt to stop himself from becoming a blubbering wreck and embarrassing himself. He offered a weak smile, all the while studying Arthur's reaction. 'Dylan was harmless. Why would someone even want to target him?'

Giving that same pained expression, Arthur shook his head. 'The prison system is a breeding ground for rats,' he answered. 'And you,' he added with a knowing nod, 'should know that better than anyone.'

Damien nodded, his cheeks turning slightly red. Like his brother, he'd also served time. Only in his case, the punishment he'd received had been well and truly deserved. He'd lost his temper, had lashed out, and as a result had come close to ending a man's life. Still to this day he felt ashamed of his actions, of what he'd caused. If it hadn't been for Winston pulling him away, he would have been charged with murder rather than a lesser charge of manslaughter, which in its own right still carried a hefty sentence. It was only by some miracle that he'd been sentenced to ten years, of which he'd served just over half of the term. The man he'd assaulted hadn't got away from the altercation quite as easily; he'd been left with irreversible brain damage, and although he was still able to function to a certain degree, he was unable to work or live what many considered to be a normal life. 'Yeah, well,' he began after clearing his throat. 'That was a long time ago.'

Amusement sparkled in Arthur's eyes. 'You're right.' He smirked with a flap of his hand, his gaze once again raking the length of Damien's body. 'No need to drag up the past. What's done is done.' Stepping to one side, he spread open his arms and gestured to where the offices were situated. 'Your dad is in his office, but I have to warn you,' he said, 'he isn't in the best of moods.'

'When is he ever,' Damien muttered. Glancing over his shoulder, he nodded for Winston to follow him and had barely taken two steps forward when Arthur's hand clamped down on his wrist. 'A little dickie bird told me that you paid the Carter family a visit.'

Ever so slightly, Damien's eyes widened. Not that he should have been entirely surprised. He'd been aware for quite some time that his old man had been keeping tabs on him, or had at least tried to. 'Don't tell me,' he growled. 'It was Vinnie who opened that big trap of his.'

Neither confirming nor denying the comment, Arthur laughed. 'You should know me better than that.' He grinned, tapping the side of his nose. 'I'm not in the habit of revealing my sources.'

Damien rolled his eyes, agitation once again getting the better of him. He didn't need Arthur to confirm what he already knew. Vinnie was a snake, always had been. No wonder he'd been hellbent on accompanying him to the scrapyard; he'd wanted to relay his movements back to his old man, and Arthur, perhaps even earning himself some much-needed kudos in the process. Tugging his arm free, Damien shot his brother-in-law a hard stare, taking a moment of great satisfaction to see Gio promptly avert his gaze, his usual smug smirk instantly dropping from his face.

'Damien.'

As he turned his head, Damien's shoulders relaxed as his sister walked towards him and offered a small smile.

'How are you doing?' she asked as she pulled him in for a hug.

'The same as you I expect.' Damien shrugged as he took note of how tightly his sister clung to him.

Demi nodded. 'He's not in a good way,' she said, gesturing

behind her to their father's office. 'He's been on the whiskey pretty much the entire afternoon,' she sighed.

As he took the warning on board, Damien groaned. His dad was bad enough without drink inside of him, but with it he became a downright nightmare.

'Maybe now isn't a good time,' she added, chewing on her bottom lip, her eyes filled with concern.

'When is it ever a good time,' Damien answered. As he continued on his way, he paused and spun back around. 'Have you seen Mum?'

'This morning,' Demi answered.

'And?'

'She's up and down mostly. She was out of it when I popped round this morning. She barely knew what day it was let alone what was going on around her.'

Damien screwed up his face. 'Bit early for her to be wasted, isn't it, even by Mum's standards.'

Demi shrugged. 'Apparently not, at least not any more. I don't think it's even registered yet that Dylan's gone, or that he isn't coming back. She was talking about throwing a party. She even asked me to look up a couple of caterers.'

Damien clenched his jaw. It wasn't the first time his mum had been what could only be described as wasted; in fact, he could barely remember a time when she wasn't as high as a kite. Growing up he'd often found the stash of booze or pills that she'd closeted away. In the beginning he'd either hid them from her or dumped them in the nearest rubbish bin, until he'd eventually cottoned on to the fact that she had a never-ending supply courtesy of his father. Perhaps this was where the resentment for his dad stemmed from. As far as he was concerned, his dad should have done everything within his power to help her get clean, rather than do the complete opposite and enable her addictions. And on the rare occasion when Jason had threatened to send his wife to rehab, nothing had ever changed. Why would it when all along she'd known it was nothing more than an empty threat and that her husband would never have allowed her out of his sight for any length of time? 'I blame him for this,' Damien spat as he jerked his head towards the office. 'He did this to her. The only reason she's a junkie is because he allowed her to become one.'

'No.' Taken aback, Demi screwed up her face. 'You're wrong. Dad loves her.'

Damien gave a low, humourless chuckle. 'He's got a funny way of showing it. You know as well as I do that he should have put her in rehab or found another way to help her. But no, not him, the big I am Jason fucking Vickers. He couldn't bear to let her out of his sight. Why else do you think he supplies her with that shit? It's another way for him to control her.'

As Demi opened her mouth to protest, the door to the office behind her sprang open and standing at the threshold was the man in question, Jason Vickers, one hand curled around a glass of whiskey, the other clenched into a tight fist at his side. 'What the fuck do you want?' he spat at his eldest son, his eyes as hard as flints.

Momentarily taken aback, Damien narrowed his eyes. The all too familiar desire to lash out at his father was temporarily pushed aside. His dad had seemingly aged overnight. Not only was his face drawn and his once brown hair peppered with grey streaks, but he also appeared smaller, as though his once large, muscular frame had suddenly become frailer.

'I asked you a question,' Jason snarled. 'What the fuck do you want?'

'Dad,' Demi cried, throwing up her arms. 'Will you please stop?'

With his face set like thunder, Jason took a step forward, ignoring his daughter's request. 'Look at you,' he hissed, addressing his son. 'Coming in here acting the Billy big bollocks. Well let me tell you something for nothing,' he roared, stabbing his finger forward. 'You're fuck all.'

In that instant Damien knew with a finality that their relationship was beyond help. That nothing either one of them said or did would ever be enough to paper over the cracks let alone make amends. 'I can't talk to him when he's like this,' he said, turning to look at his sister, his shoulders taut. 'I'll only end up losing my rag and swinging for him.'

'Damien, please,' Demi cried as she looked between her brother and father. 'This needs to end. For all of our sakes. We're family for crying out loud.'

'Since when?' Damien shot back. 'That bastard has hated me from day one.' Pulling himself up to his full height, he squared his shoulders and looked his father dead in the eyes. 'And trust me when I say this,' he added, glaring at his dad. 'The feeling is more than mutual.'

'Yeah, you've got that much right,' Jason countered. 'You've got some fucking front showing your face here. My boy is dead. My fucking boy,' he roared. 'He was my legacy, the only son worthy of the Vickers surname. I should have ended you when I had the chance. I should have made sure you were ripped out of your mother's womb and flushed down the toilet where you belong, because believe me I would have been doing myself and everyone else for that matter a fucking favour.'

Damien swallowed. The words shouldn't have hurt. It wasn't as though he hadn't heard them a hundred times before. Only deep down they did. Whether he liked it or not Jason was his dad, and to be told that he meant nothing to him, fuck all, stung. And then there was the humiliation. Casting both Arthur and

Gio a surreptitious glance, he took note of the familiar smirk spread across his brother-in-law's face. Anger began to spread through Damien's veins. Never had he wanted to hurt his father as much as he did in this very moment. Involuntarily, his hands clenched into tight fists and as the muscles across his biceps became taut, he forced himself to count to ten, all the while taking deep breaths, knowing instinctively that if he threw a punch he wouldn't be able to stop, not until he was panting for air and his knuckles were smeared with blood regardless of the fact it would be his father's blood smeared across his skin. 'And if you'd have been any kind of decent father,' Damien shouted back, 'then maybe Dylan wouldn't have been banged up. Just maybe he would have had a chance at life.'

Jason's expression hardened, his eyes narrowing into slits. Without warning, he hurled the whiskey glass and as the sound of breaking glass filled the air, he bounded forward, hellbent on causing his remaining son some considerable harm.

In the moments that followed, all hell broke loose as father and son threw punches at one another. Even the terrified scream that came from Demi wasn't enough to deter either man from punching the living daylights out of one another. Within a matter of minutes it was all over, although it would be fair to say it had been a struggle to pull the two apart.

'Do you know what,' Damien panted through gritted teeth as Winston physically dragged him away from his father. 'You're not worth it.'

With those parting words, Damien shrugged Winston away from him and then stormed back through the casino, his entire body trembling with rage.

'D,' Winston called after him. 'Wait up, man.'

Outside on the street, Damien's face was a mask of anger.

The desire to hurt someone was still so strong that he could virtually taste it.

'He was out of order,' Winston panted once he'd caught up with him. 'The man's a prick, you know that.'

Damien could barely bring himself to answer. He knew better than anyone what his dad was like. He'd been raised by the man, after all, and he could barely remember a time when the two of them had been close. Oh, they had had their moments, of course, the odd occasion when they had been able to put their differences momentarily behind them, but those times had been few and far between.

'Look,' Winston continued as he leaned casually against the car, dug his hand into his jacket pocket and pulled out a pack of cigarettes. 'You must have known this was coming,' he said, nodding in the direction of the casino. 'It's not like he was going to welcome you with open arms.'

'I already know that,' Damien growled as he gingerly touched the slit across his eyebrow and hissed at the sting which no doubt had been caused by the heavy, solid gold signet ring his father wore on his pinky finger. Wiping the blood smeared across his fingertips down the length of his dark blue jeans, he took the cigarette offered to him, lit up, then inhaled a lungful of smoke. 'I just thought...' Pausing for breath, he pinched the bridge of his nose, the fight leaving him. 'I don't know,' he continued. 'I just thought this time it would be different. That we shared a common goal. That together we'd want to find out who'd murdered Dylan or why they'd targeted him. And there must have been a reason,' he said, screwing up his face. 'You know as well as I do that this wasn't over some petty feud.' Swallowing deeply, he shook his head. 'Sugar and boiling water,' he continued, giving Winston a helpless look. 'That type of punishment is dished out to nonces and I can tell you right now that my brother was no nonce.'

'You don't have to tell me that,' Winston was quick to answer. 'I knew Dylan, I loved him like a brother and I know for a fact that he was a good kid.'

'I just can't get my head around it,' Damien added, huffing out a breath. 'To go to those lengths, to cause him that much damage...'

'You don't think it could have been used as a way to disable him, do you?' Winston interrupted. 'He was a Vickers after all. One on one, Dylan would have stood a good chance.'

'I don't know.' Damien sighed. 'No matter which way I look at the situation, it doesn't make any sense to me.'

Winston lifted his eyebrows and as he turned to look at the casino, he jerked his thumb towards the premises. 'And you reckon your old man has the answers?'

Damien shrugged. 'Maybe. Let's face it, he seems to know everything else that's going down.'

'Yeah,' Winston agreed. 'You've got a point there.'

A few moments of silence followed and, pushing himself away from the car, Winston sighed. 'D...' he began.

'You don't have to say it,' Damien groaned, cutting him off. 'I already know what you're going to say. That I should have known better.'

As he shook his head, Winston took a deep drag on the cigarette. 'This is me you're talking to,' he said, exhaling a cloud of smoke above his head. 'And we both know there's only one reason you turned up here tonight. You wanted to have it out with your old man. You've been spoiling for a fight ever since Dylan died. Not that I blame you,' he added, holding up his hands. 'Let's face it, it's been a long time coming between you and your dad.'

'Yeah.' And as much as what Winston had said was true, Damien couldn't help but feel deflated. He'd allowed his father to humiliate him, and even worse than that he'd allowed him to have the upper hand – the cut to his eyebrow alone was testament to that fact. 'I'm going to head off home,' he said, flicking the cigarette butt across the pavement.

'What about your old girl? You don't want to check up on her, make sure she's all right?'

Damien paused and, rubbing his hand across his face, he thought the question over before shaking his head. 'What would be the point? She'll more than likely be tripping off her nut or have drunk herself into a stupor. I doubt she'll even know who I am let alone be coherent enough to have a conversation.'

As he gave a sad smile, Winston clapped Damien on the back. 'Tomorrow then.'

'Yeah.' Pulling out his car keys, Damien gestured to his motor. 'Do you want a lift home?'

'Nah, you're all right,' Winston answered. 'The night's still young,' he said, rubbing his hands together and flashing a cheeky grin in a bid to lighten the mood. 'And you never know.' He winked. 'Luck might be on my side where the ladies are concerned.'

Damien couldn't help but laugh. 'You're one dirty bastard.' He chuckled. 'If you're not careful that dick of yours will end up dropping off.'

Winston grinned. 'It's gotta be better than living like a hermit,' he said, his voice becoming serious. 'I'm starting to worry about you,' he added sincerely. 'It's about time you found yourself a bird and had a bit of fun. When was the last time you actually went out?'

'I don't know.' Damien shrugged. 'Before Dylan died, I suppose.'

Winston lifted his eyebrows. 'It was long before then. It's been fucking months. I'm telling you, man.' He grinned. 'You need to get yourself out there.'

'Yeah, maybe.' Damien shrugged, his cheeks flushing red as he unlocked the car. Keen to change the subject, he climbed behind the wheel and started the ignition. 'Vinnie's becoming a problem,' he declared a few moments later.

'Tell me something I don't already know,' Winston groaned as he lightly tapped the car roof before setting off down the street.

As he drove in the direction of his home, Damien was deep in thought. In the grand scheme of things Vinnie was the least of his problems, he supposed. What with his brother's murder, and then the long-standing feud between himself and his dad, he had more than enough to contend with. And if that wasn't enough then there was the fact that his mother was an addict and that his sister was married to one of the biggest pricks this side of the water.

A short time later he pulled up outside his house, climbed out of the car, then made his way down the pathway. Unlocking the front door, he stepped across the threshold, not bothering to turn on the lights as he headed for the kitchen, and tossed his car keys onto the dining table. Pulling open the fridge, he sighed. Other than some cheese, which was more than likely out of date, the shelves were empty.

Slamming the fridge door closed, he straightened up, his body involuntarily tensing as the sound of a floorboard creaking came from directly behind him. It wasn't until slender arms wrapped around his waist, and the unmistakable scent of coconut body cream invaded his nostrils, that he allowed himself to once again relax.

'You're home late,' a woman said, her voice soft. 'I was beginning to get worried.'

Turning around, Damien smiled, his hand automatically reaching up to hide the split across his eyebrow. Not that he should have bothered. If nothing else, Natasha was observant and if the slight grimace she gave was anything to go by then she'd already spotted the injury.

'What happened?'

'Nothing.' Damien shrugged dismissively. 'At least nothing I couldn't handle.'

The look Natasha gave in return was enough to tell him that she wasn't amused.

'It's nothing,' Damien reassured her. 'You've seen me with a lot worse over the years.'

'Were you with Win?'

Damien paused before nodding.

'And,' Natasha urged.

Averting his gaze, Damien sucked in his bottom lip. 'It wasn't the right time,' he muttered, unable to look her in the eyes. Which was true considering what had gone down, not only between himself and the Carter family, but also with his father.

Natasha rolled her eyes and pulled the short, thin, satin robe around her slim frame as she crossed her arms over her chest. 'You can't put it off forever,' she declared.

'You know it's not that simple...'

'Of course it is,' Natasha retorted. 'Sooner or later you're going to have to tell him about us.'

'That works both ways, darling,' Damien fired back. 'And you're a fine one to talk about keeping secrets, because you've been keeping a pretty big one yourself, haven't you.'

Before Damien could finish the sentence, Natasha gently pressed her finger to his lips, cutting him off. 'Don't spoil it,' she commented with a knowing look. 'As for Winston, he's my brother,' she said, taking hold of his hand and pulling him in the direction of the bedroom. 'Not my keeper, and the quicker the two of you realise that fact the easier it will be for all of us.'

As he allowed himself to be pulled along, Damien fought the urge to sigh. His life was a mess and to top it off he'd been betraying his best mate for the best part of six months. A betrayal that he had a sinking feeling Winston was never going to forgive him for.

4

Early the next morning, Vinnie Vickers let himself into his uncle's home and made his way through the house. Having spent the majority of his life living under his aunt and uncle's roof, the layout was familiar to him, and his uncle Jason's home was impressive. Boasting six bedrooms, an indoor swimming pool, state of the art kitchen, and furnishings that would have been best suited on the front cover of a magazine, it would be easy to assume that the lady of the house would have a great deal of input into the upkeep. And although this may have been the case once upon a time, those days were long gone. Nowadays Carmen Vickers preferred to spend her days either pissed out of her nut or as high as a kite, sometimes even both.

'Is that you, Vinnie?' a voice called down from somewhere upstairs.

'Yeah,' Vinnie called back as he took in the state of the kitchen. Just days earlier, littering the island positioned in the middle of the large room had been several vases filled with fresh flowers and an abundance of condolence cards from well-meaning friends and associates. Now there was nothing but empty wine bottles, used glasses complete with lipstick stains, and an overflowing ashtray. Bringing a glass to his nose, he screwed up his face and immediately reeled back, the strength of the alcohol enough to knock him on his back. Returning the glass to the table, he then wandered across the kitchen and threw open the door that led out to the patio in a bid to let some fresh air into the house.

All the while Vinnie's mind was working overtime. His uncle had worked hard to ensure that his wife's addictions, were well concealed from outsiders, and that the house remained immaculate – even if this was all thanks to a housekeeper who came in on a daily basis. Glancing around him again, Vinnie shook his head. What the hell was going on?

'Hello, my darling.'

Vinnie spun around, thankful at least to see that his aunt looked her usual self. As much as there might have been a slight slur to her voice, she looked alert, her clothes relatively clean, her makeup nothing less than perfect, other than the smudge of mascara underneath her left eye, and her hair was pulled up into a messy bun, although he had a feeling it was more accidental than styled. Ignoring the mug clutched in her hands, knowing full well that it contained more than black coffee, he pulled his aunt into a one-armed hug, his free hand gently patting her back. Even through the exuberant amount of perfume she'd sprayed on he could smell a hint of stale alcohol seeping through her pores. It clung to her, no matter how often she showered, changed her clothes, or doused herself in perfume.

'Have you been fighting again?' she scolded as she pointed out the bruise on her nephew's cheek.

Vinnie shook his head. He could hardly tell her it was her

own son who'd caused the damage. 'Nah.' He laughed. 'You know that's not my scene.'

Carmen lifted her eyebrows. And just as she was about to argue the case, he hastily changed the subject.

'No Joanie today?' he asked, referring to his aunt and uncle's housekeeper.

Carmen waved her hand dismissively and, climbing onto a stool at the kitchen island, she gripped onto the sticky countertop so tightly as she attempted to stop herself from toppling to the floor that her knuckles turned white. Once seated, she pushed loose strands of hair from out of her face, leaned her elbows on the counter, and offered a bright smile, one that immediately made her look at least ten years younger.

'Where's Joanie?' Vinnie asked again.

As she lifted the mug to her lips, Carmen paused. 'I got shot of her.' She shrugged before swallowing down a large mouthful. 'Every time I turned around the old bat had her eyes on me, judging me. And if I so much as dared pour myself out a small glass of wine, well.' She rolled her eyes. 'There'd be murders. Anyone would think I'd committed a crime the way she carried on.' Giving an involuntary shudder, she took another sip of her coffee that had more than likely been laced with vodka or brandy. 'That's not a way to live, Vin,' she said, reaching over and patting his hand. 'And I told her as much and to her face an' all.' She nodded. 'I told her how it is, that if she got a life of her own and stopped being so concerned with mine then she might actually find something to smile about for once. I was sick to the back teeth of looking at her miserable boat race. Same goes for the rest of this family, you're all the bleedin' same, all of you sitting there judging me like your own shit doesn't stink.'

Vinnie narrowed his eyes and, tilting his head to side, he studied his aunt. In the circumstances there hadn't been much to smile about of late what with Dylan's murder. And seeing as Dylan had been her youngest son, he'd assumed his aunt would still be in a state of grieving, same as the rest of them. Then there was his uncle. He would have never dismissed the housekeeper; he relied on her too much to keep Carmen under control during his absence, or rather to keep her safe and not burn the house down while she was tripping off her nut. 'Does Uncle Jason know about this?'

About to take another sip of her coffee, Carmen paused again, her eyes flashing dangerously. 'I don't need my husband's permission,' she scolded, banging her hand down on the counter. 'And unless it's escaped your notice, I'm a grown woman, not a child.'

Holding up his hands, Vinnie dropped the subject, knowing full well that his aunt could be feisty at times, especially when it came to her independence. 'Yeah, of course you are,' he answered in an attempt to placate her, all the while making a mental note to inform his uncle about the situation. And that was another thing, he decided while taking another sneaky glance around him. Where the hell was his uncle and how the fuck had he let the house get into such a state? Just as he was about to voice his concerns, the doorbell rang.

'Get that will you, darling,' Carmen asked as she popped a cigarette between her lips and began searching the island for a lighter.

Vinnie nodded and, hopping off a stool, he casually made his way towards the entrance hall.

Within seconds of opening the front door, his back collided with the wall, and a hand was wrapped tightly around his throat, cutting off his air supply. 'Hello, Damien,' he managed to croak out.

Damien's lips were curled into a snarl and as he applied

further pressure around his cousin's neck, he leaned in even closer. 'I should fucking end you,' he growled before roughly shoving his cousin away from him.

Straightening up, Vinnie rubbed at the indentations Damien's fingers had left around his throat. 'Fucking hell, Damien,' he wheezed. 'It's nice to see you an' all.'

As Damien's hand curled into a fist, Vinnie lifted his eyebrows, cocked his head to the side and shouted out to his aunt. 'Guess who's come to see you,' he said in a sing-song tone. 'It's Damien.'

Almost immediately, Damien's hand dropped to his side, and as he pushed past his cousin, his expression was one of pure rage. 'This isn't over,' he hissed. 'And you'd better believe it, because sooner rather than later I will have you.'

'Yeah.' Vinnie couldn't help but smirk back as he still rubbed at his neck. 'If you say so, cuz.'

* * *

Pausing at the kitchen door, Damien took a deep breath before entering, his heart heavy. It was the unknown, he supposed, an irrational, or maybe not so irrational fear that one day he would find his mum unresponsive on the floor, in a pool of her own vomit, after she'd OD'd on whatever shit she'd snorted, smoked, or swallowed this time.

'Hello, sweetheart.'

As he exhaled a breath, Damien relaxed. The fact his mum was talking had to be a good sign; even the slur to her voice was minimal compared to the last time he'd seen her. Coming forward, he wrapped his arms around her and kissed the top of her head.

'You look well, Mum,' he said with a soft smile.

Despite basking in the compliment, Carmen waved her hand dismissively. 'You're just like your father.' She chuckled as she puffed on her cigarette. 'He can be a sweet talker an' all when the mood takes him.'

The smile slid from Damien's face. The less talk of his father the better, and as he unconsciously dabbed at the scab that ran through his eyebrow, he glanced around him, taking note of just how many empty wine bottles were lined up on the kitchen island. As he snapped his head around to look at his cousin, Damien's forehead was furrowed. 'Where's Joanie?'

Vinnie lifted his eyebrows and as he discreetly nodded in Carmen's direction, he crossed his arms over his chest and leaned against one of the cabinets. 'Your mum got rid of her.'

'Do what?' Damien's eyes widened. Joanie had worked for the family for years. And to be honest most sane people would have resigned on the spot if they'd witnessed the things she had during her time working for the Vickers family. But not Joanie. Not only had she embraced the family as her own, but she was also loyal and trustworthy. You could even go as far as to say she was one of the family herself. And the fact she'd accepted his mother's dismissal without making a fuss or arguing the case, especially at a time like this, didn't sit right with him.

'Mum?' he said with a hint of trepidation as he pulled out the stool beside her and took a seat. 'What have you done?'

'What do you mean?' Carmen was quick to answer, her tone defensive. 'I haven't done anything.'

'What about Joanie?'

Stubbing out her cigarette in the already overflowing ashtray, Carmen licked her lips. It was a nervous reaction, one that Damien had seen her exhibit a thousand times before.

'Mum.' Grabbing hold of her hand, he gave it a gentle squeeze. 'Answer the question. Why did you get rid of Joanie?'

Right there and then Damien could see the cogs turning in his mother's head. She wouldn't give him a straight answer; she rarely ever did, especially when she was trying to hide something from him.

As if on cue, Carmen snatched her hand away and, climbing off the stool, she gripped onto the island, her eyes flashing dangerously. 'I don't answer to you,' she spat. 'Just who do you think you are? You've barely shown your face here in years. You've avoided this house, me included, like it's the fucking plague. And now all of a sudden,' she continued, placing her hand on her hips, 'you want to come in here throwing your weight around. Well, newsflash, sunshine. I don't owe you, or anyone else for that matter,' she growled, nodding in Vinnie's direction, 'an explanation as to what I do or don't do, thank you very much. Are we clear on that?'

Damien swallowed deeply. A large part of him wanted to throw her words back in her face; they both knew the reason why he'd avoided visiting his parents' home. And it was for her benefit more than anyone else's; he didn't want her to bear witness to the constant conflict between himself and his father, knowing full well that it upset her. And if he didn't visit then at least she would be oblivious to the ever-growing animosity between them.

'I said,' Carmen hissed, 'are we clear on that?'

Damien nodded. What else was he supposed to do? And as his mother left the kitchen none too steadily on her feet, he chewed on the inside of his cheek before glancing towards Vinnie, who gave a helpless shrug in return, his lips downturned.

As Damien made his way back through the house, he paused at the front door and looked towards the grand staircase that led up to his parents' bedroom, his forehead ever so slightly furrowing as he tried to think back on the conversation he'd had with his mother. Not once had she mentioned his younger brother, neither his death nor even to say that she missed him. In fact, if he didn't know any better, he would assume that his mother was unaffected by Dylan's murder, or that maybe she didn't care.

* * *

Twenty minutes later, Damien pulled up outside a block of maisonettes. The entire estate was so rundown that it was in need of bulldozing in his opinion, especially the maisonette where his parents' housekeeper, Joanie, lived.

Locking the car, he took a quick glance around him. In the distance he could see a couple of kids kicking a ball about, and loitering at the entrance of the maisonettes was a group of teenagers. The heady scent of cannabis hung heavy in the air, instantly making him wrinkle his nose. And yeah, he'd be the first to hold his hands up and admit that that made him a hypocrite seeing as he and Winston weren't averse to the odd spliff, but at the end of the day that wasn't the point. Joanie lived here and he didn't want her subjected to that kind of shit on her doorstep.

'Nice car,' one of the boys commented amid sniggers from his pals as Damien made his way past.

As he turned around, Damien's eyes were hard. 'Yeah,' he agreed as he glanced to where he'd parked his motor. 'And it had better stay fucking nice.' Taking a step closer, he stared the boy down, seventeen at the most, his skin littered with spots and his light brown hair slick with either grease or too much hair gel. 'Do you understand what I'm telling you, because if I find so much as a scratch on my car I'll hunt the lot of you down.'

An uncomfortable silence followed and it wasn't until the boy broke eye contact that Damien took a step back and continued on his way to the communal stairwell. Not that he would have actually hunted the kids down, and as much as he would have been pissed off should anything have happened to his car, he wasn't in the habit of hurting kids. Still, he reasoned sending the boys a stark message wasn't going to hurt, and if anything he had a feeling that all thanks to his word of warning, his motor was probably one of the safest on the entire estate.

A short time later, he banged his fist on Joanie's front door and as he glanced up and down the desolate walkway that looked down onto the car park below, he could hear her padding down the hallway, her footsteps heavy.

'Fuck me,' Joanie declared once she'd pulled open the front door. 'You've got a knock like a bleedin' copper. Has anyone ever told you that before?'

'Funnily enough, no.' Damien couldn't help but chuckle. 'And let's face it, I'm one of the last people on the planet who'd ever be accepted into the police force, not that I can say I've ever been inclined to join up.'

'Blue's not your colour, eh?' Joanie chuckled.

'Nah, you've got that much right.'

'Well, come on in,' Joanie beamed. 'You're letting all the bleedin' heat out. And I'm not made of money, you know.'

As he followed Joanie through to the living room, Damien took a quick glance around him. She may not have had much, at least compared to what his parents had, but Joanie's home was welcoming, cosy and well cared for. Alongside a large photo frame on the mantelpiece were several porcelain knickknacks, and although the furniture was well worn it seemed to suit Joanie's personality. There was nothing flash or fancy about her and he liked that. Joanie was just Joanie, no airs or graces, and she swore like a trooper too.

'So to what do I owe this pleasure?' Gesturing for him to take a seat, Joanie settled herself onto her favourite armchair. 'Or is that a daft question?'

Avoiding the question, Damien jerked his head towards the front door. 'Is it safe for you to live here?'

Joanie lifted her eyebrows. 'Of course it bleedin' is. I've lived here for the majority of my adult life.'

'And what about that lot loitering around downstairs?' he asked, narrowing his eyes. 'They don't give you any trouble, do they?'

Joanie waved her hand through the air. 'They're nothing but kids. And believe me,' she said, stabbing a finger in Damien's direction. 'If I was able to put up with you and your brother's antics while you were growing up then I can take on anyone.'

Damien laughed again. There was some truth to Joanie's words. Both he and his brother had been a nightmare as kids, as well as his sister. And although they would never have been disrespectful, they had pushed their luck on occasion. 'Yeah, maybe you've got a point there.'

'Too right I bleedin' do.' Joanie smiled. She took a moment to study him, and her expression became serious. 'Well, come on, spit it out. Because I've got a feeling you didn't turn up here today just to ask after my wellbeing or talk about the weather.'

As he shook his head, Damien sank back in the chair. 'I went to see my mum today.'

Joanie nodded. 'I thought as much,' she sighed.

'What the fuck is going on?'

Taking a deep breath, Joanie took a few moments to think through her answer. 'I've known your mum for years,' she finally said. 'Long before you were even a twinkle in your dad's eye.

And sometimes people can't be helped. They don't want to be helped.'

'But...' Damien began.

Joanie lifted her hand in the air as if to quieten him down before patting her silver hair, a clear indication that the conversation was making her feel uncomfortable. 'Your mum,' she sighed, 'was so beautiful once. Oh, I know she still is,' she continued, holding up her hand again. 'As much as she was a free spirit, she also had a vulnerability about her that made everyone fall in love with her, me included, although not in that way before you start thinking otherwise,' she hastily added. 'She had this way about her that made people want to look after her, your dad being one of them. But...' Taking another deep breath, she gave a small shrug. 'Like I said, some people can't be helped, no matter how much you might want to. Sometimes the past runs through their veins a little too deep. And no matter how much they might want to, they can't change that fact.'

'I don't understand,' Damien began.

Leaning forward, Joanie patted his hand. 'And maybe it's a good thing that you don't understand. I know that you and your dad haven't always seen eye to eye...'

'Yeah, and that's an understatement,' Damien cut in with a roll of his eyes.

'But,' Joanie carried on regardless, 'in his own way he's done the best he can to help her.'

'What, by enabling her to become an addict?' Damien spat. 'How the fuck is that him helping her?'

Joanie sighed and as she rested her elbows on the arm of the chair, she steepled her fingers, her lips pursed. 'Your dad isn't the villain you make him out to be. Don't get me wrong, he's no angel and I'm sure that people have their reasons to be wary of him, but when it comes to your mum, she's his weakness, always has been, and dare I say it perhaps the only person he truly loves, unconditionally. Oh, I know you don't quite understand,' she said as she glanced up at the photo frame on the mantelpiece, a soft smile tugging at her lips. 'But maybe one day you'll find yourself a nice girl and then you'll know exactly what I mean, what I'm trying to get at.'

Damien let out a hollow laugh. 'I doubt it.' Although that wasn't strictly true. He got it all right. How could he not? Natasha meant the world to him; he'd kill for her if he had to, without even giving the matter a second thought.

A moment of silence followed, each of them lost in their own thoughts. 'So, is that it then?' he finally asked. 'You're just going to give in and stop working for the family?'

'I don't know,' Joanie sighed. 'Maybe it's time I retired.'

'Leave it out.' Damien laughed. 'You've got years left in you yet.'

'Give over.' Joanie laughed back. 'I'm almost seventy, I'm hardly a spring chicken. And if truth be told I haven't done much work in years, other than potter around, straightening things up, and keeping an eye on your mum of course. A couple of years ago your dad hired a cleaner to come in a few times a week, nice woman, Portuguese. Well, it's her who does all of the heavy work now.'

Damien's eyes widened. 'I didn't know that.'

'You wouldn't do, would you?' Joanie retorted, her lips pursed. 'Seeing as you rarely visit your mum.'

As he gave a sheepish grin, Damien averted his gaze. 'Yeah, and you know why.'

'Yeah,' Joanie agreed. 'I do. And I wish I could bang your bleedin' heads together.' She gave a sigh. 'Once everything has blown over I'll go and see your mum, give her a bit of time to cool down first. Like I said, I've known her for a long time and it isn't in her nature to let things fester.'

Damien nodded. At least that was something to be thankful for. Getting to his feet, he bent down and planted a kiss on Joanie's cheek. 'I'll see myself out.' Just as he was about to turn around, he paused. 'Oh, one more thing I wanted to ask you.'

'What's that?' Joanie smiled up at him.

'How has my mum been since Dylan died?'

'How do you think?' Joanie flung back. 'She's devastated. He was her son, her baby.'

'Yeah, I know he was. It's just, I don't know.' He shook his head, debating within himself whether or not he should voice his concerns. 'It just seems as though she got over it pretty quick.'

'Got over it quick,' Joanie seethed. 'She hasn't even started grieving yet. And let me tell you something now,' she added, pointing her finger forward. 'Your mum might have had her problems over the years but she loves her kids, all of you, so don't you dare start with all this "she got over it quick" rubbish.'

'Yeah, I suppose.' Feeling foolish for even doubting his mum, Damien stuffed his hands into his pockets and gestured towards the front door. 'I'll see you later.'

In return, Joanie nodded and as Damien made his way down the hallway, he missed the look of concern that creased her face.

* * *

Carmen Vickers was a creature of habit and as she downed her mug of coffee, or rather coffee laced with vodka, her fingers were itching to drag the crack pipe from out of her pocket. Already she could feel her body begin to tremble. The shakes, they called it. Well, she was more than just shaking; her entire body was vibrating, so much so that she had to hold the mug with two hands for fear that she would drop it.

Placing the mug on the island, she gave the clock on the wall a surreptitious glance, wishing that Vinnie would hurry up and leave. He never usually stayed this long, most days it was an hour or two at the most.

'So what do you reckon then?'

Carmen glanced up, her forehead furrowing. What did she think about what? She'd tuned Vinnie out a while ago, her thoughts consumed with her little pipe.

'Carmen?'

'Yes.'

Vinnie gave an irritated sigh. 'I said, what do you think about Damien turning up here out of the blue?'

As she fought the urge to tell him to leave, Carmen frowned. She hadn't realised she was expected to have an opinion. 'I don't know,' she finally answered. 'I didn't really think much of it.' She shrugged. 'It was a bit odd I suppose.'

'Yeah, that's what I thought.' As he sucked in his bottom lip, Vinnie tapped his fingers on the island. 'Really fucking odd. He didn't stay long either, did he.'

'No,' Carmen snapped. Unlike someone else she could mention.

'I mean, it just seemed a bit pointless really, him turning up like that.'

Carmen gritted her teeth, her need for a fix so strong that she was in half a mind to pull her pipe out here and now. Delving her hand into her pocket, her fingers skimmed over the smooth glass and then the rough edges of the tiny, chalky, white rock nestled beside it. Just one hit, that was all she needed, one hit and then she would be as right as rain. 'Look, Vin,' she said, getting to her feet, 'I think I'm going to go upstairs and have a lie down.'

Vinnie narrowed his eyes.

'I didn't sleep too well last night,' she added, faking a yawn. 'And I've got a blinding headache.'

When he still made no attempt to move, Carmen was ready to pull her hair out from the roots. 'Vin,' she repeated, her voice rising and becoming tinged with hysteria. 'Will you just fuck off home and give me a bit of peace and quiet?'

Without saying a word, Vinnie got to his feet. She'd hurt him, she could see it written across his face. She'd never thrown him out of the house before and after the death of his parents at a young age, she and Jason had pretty much raised him, or rather Joanie had. As much as she so desperately wanted to take her harsh words back, she couldn't. Her need to get high far outweighed her desire to make things right with her only nephew.

'I'll get going then.' Grabbing his jacket from where he'd draped it across the back of the stool, he slipped it on, his movements still not fast enough in Carmen's opinion. She was practically climbing the walls at this rate, her fingers wrapped around the crack pipe in readiness of his departure. As he reached the kitchen door, he came to a halt and turned around. Opening his mouth as if to say something, he quickly snapped it closed again and shook his head before making his way out to the grand hallway, his footsteps heavy across the marble floor.

As soon as she heard the front door softly shut behind him, Carmen pulled out the pipe, her fingers still trembling as she searched for the rock. The anticipation was more than she could bear and, licking at her dry lips, she concentrated on the task at hand, her tongue ever so slightly poking out as she pushed the rock inside the glass bowl.

By the time she began searching for her lighter, Carmen's heart beat so wildly that she wouldn't have been surprised if the organ jumped out of her chest. Within a matter of seconds, panic began to set in. Where the hell was the lighter? It had to be here somewhere, she knew it did, she'd used it that morning. Tears of frustration sprang to her eyes and as she pushed the empty bottles and used glasses aside, her body felt as though it were on fire, the craving inside of her becoming more and more intense with each passing minute. She wanted to scream at the top of her lungs, to kick out at something, to swipe her arm across the island and push everything to the floor. It was the latter that won out and as the glasses and bottles smashed to smithereens on impact, she fought the urge to sink to her knees and cry her eyes out.

Vinnie must have taken the lighter. How or when he'd swiped it from underneath her nose she had no idea, but he had; there was no other explanation as to how it had gone missing. 'You bastard,' she roared. 'You bloody bastard.'

'Well, this is a fine way to behave.'

Carmen whipped her head around, tears still streaming down her face. 'What do you want?' she spat out.

As she surveyed the kitchen, or rather the mess that Carmen had made, Joanie puffed out her chest. 'I had a visitor,' she said as she placed her handbag on the island and then proceeded to roll up her sleeves. 'And let me put it this way,' she added as she pulled open a cupboard and took out a dustpan and brush. 'He isn't stupid.'

A shiver of fear ran down the length of Carmen's spine. Instinctively, she knew who Joanie was referring to, she was only annoyed that she herself hadn't guessed that Damien would pay Joanie a visit.

'He's going to find out the truth,' Joanie continued as she swept up the glass. 'And then what, eh? What happens then?'

'He won't,' Carmen croaked out, her need for a fix temporarily taken over by the terror building in her gut. 'He can't.'

'He can and he will,' Joanie retorted. 'If anyone was stupid then it was us for thinking that we could conceal the truth from him. He's too astute,' she said, tapping her temple. 'Always has been.' Emptying the glass into the waste bin, Joanie returned the dustpan and brush to the cupboard then placed her hands on her hips. 'You should know yourself what he's like; you were the one who gave birth to him. He's like a dog with a bone once he sets his mind to something, and let me tell you now, lady,' she said, pointing towards Carmen. 'He's more than a little suspicious, I could see it in his eyes.'

The colour drained from Carmen's face and as she attempted to swallow, her throat was dry. Joanie was right. If anyone had been foolish then it was them. Damien was going to learn the truth, a secret that she had been holding close to her chest for so long that it had become easier to pretend that it wasn't true. Except it was true and it was only a matter of time until everyone around them also learned the truth. And once that happened there would be no stopping World War Three from erupting.

5

Tommy Johnson was feeling restless. Not only was Damien Vickers' visit still fresh in his mind, but he was also unable to shake off the feeling that the answers to Dylan's murder were staring him in the face.

Time and time again he'd gone over his and Dylan's conversations in his mind and each time he'd come up empty handed. Dylan had given nothing away, at least nothing that had stuck out anyway. They'd mostly talked about football, or the first things they were going to do the very moment they got out of the nick. There'd been a lot of banter too, each of them taking the piss out of the other. Rarely though had they spoken about their backgrounds or their upbringing. And other than mentioning the family members they were particularly close to, their private lives had remained just that – private. There'd been no need for them to have known the ins and outs of each other's lives; there would have been nothing for either of them to gain from it.

'Are you actually planning to do any work today?'

Tommy jerked his head up. Already it was on the tip of his

tongue to fling back a retort until he noted that it was one of his elder cousins who his great-uncle, Jonny Carter, was referring to.

Caleb Carter groaned. 'Yeah, and what about him?' He scowled, nodding towards Tommy Jr. 'How come he gets away with doing fuck all?'

'I'm talking about you, not him,' Jonny countered as he scooped up a metal stapler and pulled back his arm.

Scrambling to his feet, Caleb ducked down, narrowly missing the stapler that Jonny threw towards him.

'Oi,' Caleb yelped. 'That nearly hit me.'

'Yeah, and next time I won't miss,' Jonny shouted. 'Go on, get to work. I don't pay you to sit on your arse doing fuck all.'

As Caleb left the office still grumbling, Tommy Jr couldn't help but laugh. Just months earlier he'd been the one on the receiving end of Jonny's tongue. It was funny how times changed. His stint inside had somehow made him grow up, not that he could say he'd really had any choice in the matter. He was about to become a father and whether he liked it or not it was time to knuckle down.

'Lairy little bastard,' Jonny commented once Caleb was out of earshot.

'A true Carter then, eh?' Tommy grinned.

Jonny huffed out a breath. 'Did he look stoned to you?'

Tommy stared after his cousin. 'I suppose so,' he answered with a shrug. But then again it wasn't anything unusual. Caleb had been smoking weed for years, and considering he'd only just turned twenty-one, that was saying something. 'Do you want me to have a word with him? Or maybe ask Reece to?' Although Tommy had a feeling that it wouldn't go down too well if Reece was to pull Caleb up on his behaviour. The two barely got along as it was, and Tommy knew for a fact that it went beyond the usual sibling rivalry. The brothers had a genuine dislike for one another. They rarely interacted and when they did it was a guarantee that fists would end up flying.

'Nah, not yet,' Jonny sighed. 'I'll keep an eye on him. Speaking of work though,' he said as he leaned back in his seat, lifted a mug to his lips then took a sip of his coffee. 'What are your plans for the day?'

'I dunno,' Tommy answered as he glanced towards where his car was parked on the forecourt. 'I was kind of thinking of paying Damien Vickers a visit.'

Jonny almost choked on his drink, and reeling forward, he slammed the mug down onto his desk then wiped away the coffee that dribbled down his chin. 'Look at what the fuck you've made me do now,' he shouted as he jumped to his feet and gestured to the front of his pale blue shirt, which was now stained with coffee.

Tommy laughed even harder. 'How the fuck was that my fault?'

Grabbing a tea towel, Jonny ran the stiff cloth over his face. 'Are you all right in the head?' he asked. 'Because sometimes I seriously do wonder about you.'

Tommy rolled his eyes.

'It was only a couple of days ago that Vickers tried to top you.'

'That wasn't him, it was his cousin,' Tommy declared. 'And you know it.'

'Same thing, ain't it?' Jonny fired back. 'They're all the same, those Vickers. They're nutcases, the whole bloody lot of them.'

'They're villains, same as us lot,' Tommy protested, referring to the fact that the scrapyard was merely a cover for their real line of work – armed robberies. 'That doesn't necessarily make them nutcases.'

'I take it you've met the old man, Jason Vickers, then have you?'

Tommy shook his head. 'You know I haven't.' Other than the rumours he'd heard about Dylan's father, he knew nothing else about him. In fact, he could pass him by in the street and he'd be none the wiser.

'Look,' Jonny said, his tone softer as he unbuttoned his shirt, shrugged it off his shoulders then reached out for the fresh one he kept for emergencies. 'Don't get involved. Trust me, it's not worth the aggro. I know that Dylan was your pal, but you only knew him for a short time and you weren't responsible for his death. Regardless of the shit that went down, it had nothing to do with you, or any of us for that matter. Believe me, we're better off staying well out of it.'

'Yeah, maybe.' As he chewed on the inside of his cheek, Tommy Jr couldn't help but think his uncle was wrong. No matter how much he might not want to be involved, he was. He'd been there the night Dylan had been murdered. He was a witness, and nothing and no one could change that fact.

* * *

As he studied himself in the mirror, Jason Vickers grimaced. Not only was he beginning to look old, but his skin was sallow and his eyes red rimmed and bloodshot. The booze he was guzzling down on a daily basis was beginning to take its toll, not forgetting the pain in his back all thanks to him spending his nights sleeping on the sofa in his office. It made no sense really seeing as he had a solid oak, king-sized bed waiting for him at home, the mattress so thick and comfortable that it was a struggle to wake up in the mornings. But that was the problem. He didn't want to go home; he couldn't bear to look Carmen in the face, knowing that he'd let her down. That if it wasn't for him, their boy would still be alive. Damien had been right to blame him. If he hadn't have encouraged Dylan to join the business then he would never have been sent down, would never have been in Pentonville Prison, and would never have been subjected to a gruesome, horrifying, painful death.

Pushing the thought from his mind, Jason walked over to the drinks cabinet. It was far too early to start on the booze, and as he lifted the bottle to his lips, he momentarily closed his eyes before screwing the lid back on and putting the bottle down. Sometimes he envied his wife, envied the fact that she was so often out of her nut that she didn't even know what day it was let alone feel any real emotion. Her only real thought or concern was that of her next fix.

From behind him, the door opened a crack and, turning his head, Jason hastily smoothed down his hair before his daughter walked inside, her high heels clip-clopping across the floor.

'Are you okay, Dad?' she asked as her gaze automatically went to the sofa, the crumpled blanket a dead giveaway that he hadn't been home again.

Jason nodded, wondering when exactly the roles between them had changed. Shouldn't he have been the one looking out for her welfare, not the other way around? 'Got a busy day,' he said, motioning to the desk. 'Thought I'd get an early start.' Even as the words left his mouth he could tell that she knew he was lying, and if the little huff of breath she exhaled was anything to go by then he had a feeling she was about to tell him so.

'Dad.' As she rubbed at her temples, Demi sighed. 'This isn't healthy. Not for you or for Mum.'

For the briefest of moments it crossed Jason's mind to lie again. To tell his daughter that he had no idea what she was talking about, but what would have been the point? She wasn't daft. He'd been wearing the same shirt for three days, hadn't showered or shaved, and to top it off his office was beginning to smell like a teenage boy's bedroom. He was actually starting to wonder if he could be depressed. Dylan had been his and Carmen's golden boy. He could do no wrong in their eyes, unlike Damien, who had a knack of leaving a trail of destruction behind him everywhere he went. Even Demi could be a moody cow at times.

'When was the last time you went out?' Demi prodded. 'Got some fresh air.'

Jason shrugged. It had been days since he'd ventured outside the casino, and even then he preferred to spend his time couped up in the office, alone, wallowing in his grief.

'For crying out loud,' Demi chastised. 'This isn't you, Dad. Wake up, will you? Where's your fight gone? You were hellbent on getting justice for Dylan and other than sit on your arse day in and day out getting blind drunk, you've done fuck all. Thank God Damien's out there searching for answers,' she shouted, motioning towards the door. 'Because if it was left down to you, the bastards who killed him would get off scot-free.'

At the mention of his eldest son, Jason's lips curled up into a snarl. He should have known that Damien would be mentioned somewhere. The bastard had a nasty habit of sticking his nose in where it wasn't wanted.

'Please, Dad,' Demi continued. 'It would break Dylan's heart to see you like this.'

'All right, all right.' Lifting his hand up, Jason shook his head. 'You've made your point loud and clear.' As he looked around him, he took in a deep breath. The office stank. Lifting his arm in the air, he bent his head closer to his armpit. Yeah, just as he suspected, he stank too. Maybe it was time he headed home, had a shower, and got his life together. Demi was right, he wouldn't be able to seek out his son's murderers from the comfort of his office. It was about time he put in an appearance and started asking questions, by force if needs be.

Scooping up his car keys, he kissed his daughter on the cheek. Maybe this had been exactly what he needed; a pep talk, or to be more precise, a kick up the backside. As he exited his office, Arthur was making his way towards him.

'What's going on?' he asked, his voice holding a hint of caution as he looked from Jason to Demi.

'Exactly what I should have done weeks ago,' Jason answered. 'I'm going to find the cunts who tucked up my boy.'

Somewhat taken by surprise, Arthur nodded and after hastily clearing his throat, he quickly regained his composure. 'Good.' He cleared his throat a second time and gave a small smile. 'It's about time.'

'Yeah, too right it is,' Jason answered as he slipped on his jacket. 'I'm going to nip home, have a shower, have a bit of grub and then I'll be back.'

Arthur nodded and, giving another awkward smile, he took a step to the side so that his business partner could slip past him. 'I'll be here,' he said. 'You know me, I'm ready whenever you are.'

'Cheers, pal.' Gripping hold of Arthur's hand, Jason pumped it up and down. 'I'll be back as soon as,' he called over his shoulder as he made his way through the casino.

Turning her head to look at Arthur, Demi nodded after her dad. 'This is exactly what he needs,' she said. 'To get back to business, to get some normality back.'

'Maybe,' Arthur answered, his gaze still locked on Jason's retreating back. 'Depends on whether he ends up running into that brother of yours along the way.'

As she chewed on her bottom lip, Demi snapped her attention back to her dad. 'I didn't even think of that.'

Arthur lifted his eyebrows. 'No, but it's a good job that at least one of us did.'

* * *

Pulling open his front door, Damien nodded a greeting.

'Tea?' he asked, lifting his mug in the air.

Winston shook his head. 'I'd rather coffee, and as strong as possible.'

Damien stifled a laugh. 'Sounds like someone had a good night.'

'Yeah, from what I can remember of it,' Winston answered as he entered the lounge. Sniffing the air, he tilted his head to the side. 'And maybe I wasn't the only one.' He grinned. 'Have you had a bird in here?'

Damien froze. 'No. What makes you say that?'

'Perfume,' he answered, sniffing the air again.

'Nah.' Damien laughed off the comment. 'It's probably my aftershave.' Which of course it wasn't and only a fool would be stupid enough to believe that. There was only one reason his gaff would smell like perfume and that was because Natasha had doused herself in pretty much an entire bottle before leaving his house to go to work that morning.

Winston narrowed his eyes. 'There's something seriously wrong with your hooter if you're buying shit like that. What are you trying to do, smell like a fucking tart?'

Waving the comment away, Damien padded into the kitchen. Flicking the switch for the kettle, he retrieved a mug from out of the cupboard. 'Sugar?'

'Nah, sweet enough.' Winston winked. 'I'm gonna use your khazi,' he said, nodding towards the staircase.

Absentmindedly, Damien nodded. Seconds later, the hairs on the back of his neck stood up on end. Glancing up at the ceiling, he swallowed deeply. What if Natasha had left something in the bathroom? He'd only just got away with passing the perfume off as his aftershave, and there wasn't a chance in hell that he'd be able to do the same if Winston was to stumble across a pair of her discarded knickers. Moments later, he heard the toilet flush, then the sound of running water, before Winston finally made his way back down the stairs, his hands, much to Damien's relief, empty.

'So what's the plan then?' Winston asked as he took the mug of coffee and leaned against the worktop.

'I don't know.' Damien rubbed at his temples. 'I just need a lead, anything that will point me in the right direction. I was thinking maybe have another pop at this Tommy Johnson kid. There's gotta be something he can tell us.'

'Or...' Winston jiggled his eyebrows up and down.

'Or what?' Damien frowned.

'We take a trip to Pentonville nick, have a little word with my cousin, see if there's anything he can tell us.'

Damien's eyes widened. 'The visit was accepted?'

'Yeah.' Winston nodded and, pulling out his mobile phone, he opened the email app and turned the device around so that Damien could see for himself that a visit to the prison had been booked for that afternoon. 'I told you it would be, didn't I.'

'Why the fuck didn't you say something earlier?' Damien asked as he playfully punched Winston's shoulder.

'What, and miss the look on your face?' Winston grinned back. 'It was fucking priceless, mate.'

As he rolled his eyes, Damien sipped at his tea. As much as a visit to Pentonville Prison would stir up painful memories of when he'd last seen his brother, it was also a necessity. Winston's cousin Cain Daly was residing in the nick and although he hadn't actually been transferred there until a few days after Dylan's murder, he was bound to have some inside knowledge; after all, cons talked. It was one of the only things they had to pass the time away.

Placing his empty mug in the sink, Damien glanced at his watch and took note of the time, calculating how long it would take them to get to North London. 'What are we waiting for then?' He grinned. 'Let's fucking do this.'

* * *

On Joanie's orders, Carmen had taken a hot bubble bath. And with a white towelling robe pulled around her slim frame, her freshly washed hair had been brushed, pulled up on top of her head and wrapped inside an equally white fluffy towel. With her face scrubbed of all makeup, it was hard to believe that she had been an addict for the majority of her life.

'There you are.' As Carmen walked into the kitchen, Joanie offered a gentle smile. 'You look better already.'

Carmen nodded. She didn't feel any better. She was exhausted, not to mention feeling highly irritable. The craving for a hit was all she could think of. Pulling out a stool, she hopped on then rested her elbows on the now spotlessly clean island that had been cleared of any clutter and begun chewing on her fingernails.

'I made you a cuppa, nice and sweet, just how you like it.'

Carmen mumbled her thanks and as she wrapped her hands around the teacup, savouring the warmth, she was debating whether or not to add a shot of vodka to the milky liquid just to take the edge off her cravings. The sound of a key turning in the lock made her sit bolt upright, her anxious gaze instantly snapping towards Joanie.

As she too stared warily towards the kitchen door, a flash of worry was reflected back in Joanie's eyes.

Very few people had a key to the house. Herself, Joanie so that she could come and go without disturbing them, Jason of course, Vinnie, Demi, and then the final key had belonged to Dylan.

'Just act normal,' Joanie whispered as she turned back to the sink, turned on the tap then rinsed the used teaspoon underneath.

Moments later, Jason entered the kitchen, his large frame dominating the space. He looked tired, Carmen noted, and dare she say it also unkempt, which in itself was highly unusual. In fact, she would go as far as to say that in all the years she had known him she had never seen him look anything but smart. In that instant her heart felt heavy. Ever since Dylan's death she had sensed a growing distance between them. He hadn't been home in days, and as much as she had relished the freedom of not having him constantly watching over her, she couldn't help but wonder if this was to be their new reality. If her behaviour, or rather her lifestyle, coupled with the loss of their youngest son, had finally pushed him over the edge and away from her.

To her surprise and despite his outward appearance, Jason appeared to be in high spirits and as he rounded the island and pulled her into his arms, he lovingly planted a kiss on her forehead. 'You look good, darling.' He beamed. 'And you as well, Joanie.' He winked towards the older woman.

Basking in the compliment, Joanie patted down her silver hair and smiled back.

'I could do with a bit of grub,' he said, rubbing his stomach, one arm still placed protectively around his wife's shoulders.

'How about I rustle you up some bacon and eggs?' Joanie called over her shoulder as she opened the fridge and began rummaging around. 'And a nice fried slice, with a couple of fried tomatoes.'

'Sounds good to me.' Taking a step back, Jason scrutinised Carmen's face. 'How about you, sweetheart? You look like you could do with some food inside of you, you're nothing but skin and bone.'

Food was the last thing on Carmen's mind; she had little to no appetite, but as her husband stood studying her, she found herself nodding along. If for no other reason than to placate him, knowing full well that sometimes it was far easier to agree with him.

As soon as he left the kitchen, Joanie was beside her. 'Buck yourself up,' she whispered in a warning, her voice harsh. 'Just eat whatever I put in front of you without any complaint,' she added as she kept one eye on the kitchen door. 'The last thing we want is for him to start worrying, because you know what'll happen then. He'll start asking questions. And the last thing either of us want is for him to start digging around.'

Carmen opened her mouth to protest. She didn't need Joanie to tell her how to behave. She'd been married to the man for almost thirty years and knew him inside and out.

'Carmen,' Joanie warned again, her eyebrows almost touching the ceiling. 'For both of our sakes will you please do as I ask, just this once.'

'Fine,' Carmen relented. And maybe Joanie was right. If Jason was to start digging too deep then perhaps he might find out that she had been relieved to see her youngest son sent to prison, and why, may God forgive her, there was a tiny part of her that was thankful Dylan would never be coming home.

6

Pentonville Prison, home to the dregs of society. Or at least this was what the media wanted the general public to believe. Damien, however, knew differently. Not only had he himself spent time there, but even Winston had done a short stint in the Ville, as it was more commonly known.

Taking their seats at their allocated table, Damien glanced around him, his gaze roaming over the faces of the other visitors. There was a buzz in the air, an excitement that he too had once been swept up in. Now he felt nothing but emptiness and anger.

Beside him, Winston elbowed him in the ribs, and as he jerked his head towards the door that the prisoners were entering through, he got to his feet.

Cain Daly was huge, not only in height, but also in build. And other than the fact he and Winston shared the same Jamaican grandparents, there were no other similarities between them. They certainly didn't look alike. The two men were, however, close, and as Cain pulled his cousin in for a bear hug, Damien couldn't help but smile before he too went on to shake Cain's hand.

Once they were seated, Cain leaned back in the chair, his frame appearing far too large for the small seat. 'I was sorry to hear about your bro. From what I've heard he was a good kid. Kept himself to himself, didn't cause any aggro.'

This was exactly what Damien had suspected. Dylan hadn't been a troublemaker, neither inside prison nor out of it. 'Yeah.' He rubbed his lips together. 'For the most part he was a good kid, which is why none of this makes any sense.'

Cain nodded and as he swiped his hand over his chin, he waited for a prison officer to pass by their table before continuing. 'What I've heard though is that he was known to the bastards who topped him.'

Damien screwed up his face. 'Who are they?' he growled.

'A couple of nobody's.' Cain shrugged. 'By all accounts it was a planned target. From the get-go your brother had a price on his head.'

'Nah.' As Damien looked from Cain to Winston, he shook his head. 'That can't be right. You just said yourself that he kept himself to himself so why the fuck would he have had a price on his head?'

Cain shrugged. 'I was hoping you would know the answer to that.' Leaning forward, he lowered his voice. 'This wasn't over some petty feud. The order came from the outside. It was just pot luck that he ended up in the same nick as the two who did him over.'

'But...' Damien was still shaking his head as his mind whirled. 'I don't understand. I mean...' His voice trailed off. 'So you're saying that it was an execution. That this was planned?'

Cain nodded again and after a quick glance around him to see where the screws were, he gave a chilling smile. 'You don't have to worry about the bastards responsible, or rather dumb and fucking dumber as I prefer to call them. I've got their number; they were hardly discreet about what they did and let's just say that they'll get their comeuppance, or rather they'll find a welcoming committee waiting for them when they're least expecting it. At the moment they're swanning around without a care in the world. They think they're the dog's gonads. Like I said,' he added, tapping the side of his head, 'they're not firing on all cylinders. They've more than likely been given a load of old pony and think that they have protection. Well let me tell you now, there ain't no protection in here, not for the likes of them.'

Damien nodded, his mind still reeling from the information he'd just been given. Perhaps Tommy Johnson had been onto something when he'd said that he'd assumed Dylan's murder had something to do with their dad. And even then it made no sense, not really. Dylan hadn't been in the game long enough to have made enemies, at least not to the extent that they would want to kill him.

All too soon the visit was over and after saying their goodbyes, Damien and Winston made their way to where they had parked the car.

'So, what are you thinking?' Winston asked.

Unlocking the car, Damien paused and, resting his forearms on the car roof, he blew out his cheeks. 'Probably the same as you. That my old man has got himself into something, and that by taking Dylan out, a message was either being sent or...' He paused and rubbed at his temples. 'Unless it was a case of retaliation: you touch one of mine and I'll touch one of yours sort of thing.' Even as the words left his mouth, Damien wasn't so sure this was the truth. If nothing else his dad had loved Dylan. He would never have willingly put him in danger.

Winston sighed. 'I can't help but think it's all a bit too convenient.'

'What do mean?'

Heaving himself onto the passenger seat, Winston turned his head. 'Say for argument's sake it was a hit, how the fuck did they manage to ensure that Dylan ended up in the same nick as the two who did him over? That's gotta be more than just a coincidence, hasn't it?'

Damien was thoughtful for a moment. He could see what Winston was getting at. No one had that kind of sway, not unless they had friends in high places, of course. The problem was, who? Just who could his dad have been dealing with that had enough power to influence a judge?

* * *

Arthur Brennan was deep in thought as he tapped his fingers absentmindedly on the desk and chewed on the inside of his cheek. Despite his reputation, a knot of worry had begun to form in the pit of his stomach. On a good day, Jason wasn't the kind of man to be crossed, but fuelled with a need for revenge, he was a downright menace to society. That wasn't to say that Arthur hadn't been expecting this day to come, because he had. All along he'd known that it was only a matter of time until Jason stopped wallowing in self-pity and actually took action.

After a quick glance at his Rolex, he pushed back his chair, stood up and made his way across to the window. Standing at six feet, he was a tall man, his greying hair giving him the appearance of what some might call a silver fox. As far as looks went, it would be fair to say that he was average looking; there was nothing about him that stood out. The only aspect of his appearance that was notable was his attire. His suits were made to measure and his leather shoes Italian. Only the finer things in life were good enough for Arthur. He was a product of his upbringing. Boarding school, skiing lessons, polo, university, all of which had been wasted on him. Even from an early age he'd had the mind of a criminal. At school he'd dabbled in selling drugs, had made quite a bit of money too until he'd finally been caught and expelled. And despite walking away from university with a first-class honours degree in business, it was the connections he'd made along the way that were more valuable to him than the education he'd gained.

From an outside perspective it might seem odd how he and Jason Vickers, a man from a council estate with little to no prospects, had ever managed to cross paths let alone become business partners. But that was the beauty of having contacts. Jason was a man of his own heart. He was ruthless, conniving, and above all else ambitious.

Together they had built an empire of sorts. Their combined reputations were widely known up and down the country. Their casino alone was a goldmine and that was without the more illegal aspects of their business. On top of the casino, money laundering had given them a nice steady income, and then there were the favours they rolled out, all for a decent sum of money of course. A safe house here, a tip off there; they'd even been known to hide the proceeds of an armed robbery, a rather infamous robbery that had dominated the front pages of every newspaper in the country. But above all else they were trusted, respected, and in their game that went a long way.

'So old man Vickers finally got his head out of his arse, eh?'

Arthur turned his head. The scowl across his face was enough to warn Gio that he'd overstepped the mark. Not that he expected the man to take heed of his warning; he was too much of an imbecile for that to ever happen.

'Bet there's gonna be a lot of people quaking in their boots.' Taking the seat that Arthur had vacated, Gio put his feet up on the desk. 'What do you reckon?' he asked, quirking an eyebrow. 'Am I right or am I wrong?'

'Is there a point to this visit of yours?' Arthur growled.

Gio shrugged. 'Maybe.' Glancing down at his hands, he inspected his fingernails. 'How much cash do you reckon Jason would hand over for a name? I mean, there's got to be some sort of a reward, right?'

Arthur narrowed his eyes.

'Hypothetically of course. Or...' He lifted a finger in the air as if the idea had just occurred to him. 'How about Damien? He's not short of a bob or two. How much do you reckon he'd be willing to give for the right information? Dylan was his kid brother, after all.'

A snort of laughter left Arthur's lips. 'Fuck off, Gio.'

'You can't blame a man for trying.' Gio grinned and just as he began to take his feet down from the desk, from out of nowhere, his head was slammed cheek first onto the polished wood.

'Don't ever,' Arthur hissed in his ear, 'try to blackmail me again.' As he pushed the side of Gio's face even further into the desk, spittle flew out of Arthur's snarled lips. 'Because we both know what happened to the last lairy little cunt who tried to fuck me over.'

Terrified, Gio could only grunt in return, and as sweat broke out across his forehead, he screwed his eyes shut.

'Are we clear on that?'

As best as he could, Gio nodded and as Arthur released him, he slowly straightened up and rubbed at the side of his face. His cheek was on fire and already a red mark had formed.

'Now get out,' Arthur hissed.

Gio didn't need telling twice and in his haste to escape the office, he knocked over a chair.

Arthur sighed and, heaving the chair upright, he smoothed

out his shirt, readjusted his cufflinks and then resumed his position in front of the window. There was nothing more he detested in the world than a grass, and even more than that, a grass who had the front to try and extract money from him.

* * *

An hour later, Jason and Arthur entered The Bull Tavern, a pub situated just off Tooley Street in South London.

Within a matter of seconds they found who they were looking for. It would have been hard not to considering he stood head and shoulders above the majority of patrons.

John, or rather Geordie John as he was more widely known, was at the bar. With the looks of a typical thug – cropped hair, tall, muscular body, tattoos running up and down the length of both arms – John was often given a wide berth. Which in itself wasn't very unusual when you considered what John did for a living. As an enforcer it went without saying that John knew how to handle himself. Luckily for him, and those around him, his sheer size and reputation were usually enough to ensure that any debts owed were paid up on time. Just a glance in the man's direction was often enough to make people feel uneasy and for those stupid enough to try and take him on, just one look from the man made their bowels turn to liquid.

'John.' Jason stuck out his hand. And as John shook the proffered hand, he gestured towards the bar. 'Drink?'

If John was surprised to see them, he didn't show it and as he nodded, he held up his glass towards the waiting barmaid, indicating that he wanted the same again.

'So what brings you here?' he asked, eyeing both Jason and Arthur.

Jason couldn't help but laugh. John was a man of few words,

but when he did engage in conversation he was a straight talker; it was just one of the many reasons why he was so respected amongst the criminal underworld. There wasn't much that John didn't know; after all, his livelihood depended on him knowing where to find people, or at least have the means to.

Once their drinks had been ordered, John leaned against the bar, his eyes slightly narrowed.

'Your boy was in here just over a week ago.'

Involuntarily, Jason's spine stiffened. He was irritated not only by the fact his son had been brought up in the conversation but also that Damien was ahead of him. 'And what did he want?'

John paused and, taking a moment to assess the situation, he reached out for his pint glass, then swallowed down a large mouthful of the lager before answering. 'He was after an address,' he said, lowering his voice slightly, 'same as you I expect.'

Jason grinned. 'There are no flies on you, are there, pal.'

'You'll have to get up early to get one over on me.' John chuckled in agreement.

'So, are you gonna fill me in on the details or am I supposed to guess?'

As if thinking the question over, John took another long pause before answering. 'It's no big secret,' he said with a shrug. 'Otherwise you'd be getting fuck all from me. You know what I'm about, that I don't open my trap for the fun of it.'

Jason nodded. That went without saying; John was one of the best in the business.

'He wanted to know where he could find Tommy Johnson.'

Immediately, Jason's ears pricked up. The name was as good as ingrained into his brain. Tommy Johnson had been a witness to his son's murder; in fact, other than those responsible for the vicious attack, he had been the *only* witness. Hastily taking a sip of his drink to compose himself, he swallowed the liquid down. 'Well, that's hardly rocket science. He's banged up in the Ville.'

'Was,' John answered. 'He got out about a week or so ago.'

This was news to Jason and as he gave Arthur a sidelong glance, there was a tiny part of him that wondered if his business partner was aware of this new development, and if he was then why the fuck hadn't he filled him in? 'And what did you tell him?'

John gulped down another mouthful of lager then wiped the back of his hand across his lips. 'I told him to look up the Carter family from over in Barking. If anyone will know where to find him it will be them.'

Unsure of the connection between Tommy Johnson and the Carter family, Jason frowned. 'I'm not following. Where do the Carters come into this?'

'They're related,' John answered. 'Tommy Johnson is a Carter, or rather his dear old mum is,' he said, cocking his head to the side as he tried to work out the family dynamics. 'Or maybe it's his father?' he finally added with a wave of his hand. 'Either way, somewhere along the lines this Tommy Johnson is a Carter.'

Taken aback a second time in as many minutes, Jason gave Arthur another surreptitious glance. How was this the first time they were hearing about Johnson's connection to the Carter family? 'And you're sure about that?' he asked, still unconvinced.

'Of course I am,' John replied, tapping the side of his nose. 'You should know me better than that. I'm no Billy bullshitter.'

Jason nodded and as he downed his drink, a familiar churning began to build in the pit of his stomach. Fucking Damien. Why the fuck hadn't the little bastard shared that vital piece of information with him? Conveniently, he chose to ignore the fact that the last time he and his son had been in close proximity to one another it had come to blows between them, and if the grazes across his knuckles were anything to go by then it would be fair to say he'd got his share of punches in too.

Thirty minutes later, he and Arthur were back in the car.

'So where now?' Arthur asked as he started the ignition.

As he fought the urge to shrug, Jason sighed. As much as he despised himself for even thinking it, even he had to admit that he and Arthur were doing nothing more than revisiting old ground. Damien, the fucker that he was, was one step ahead of them. The thought was enough to make him feel depressed all over again.

* * *

As Tommy Jr unclipped his seatbelt, he took a sneaky glance around him before opening the car door and stepping outside. As far as meeting points went, the area that Damien Vickers had chosen to meet was highly unusual.

Crossing the road, he momentarily surveyed the shop in front of him before pushing open the door and stepping over the threshold.

Almost immediately a wave of warmth hit him, mingled with a scent that brought back memories of being a kid when his nan used to take him to Roman Road market on a Saturday afternoon. And what's more, luckily for him he was a huge fan of pie, mash, and liquor.

Spotting Damien and his pal towards the back of the shop, he raised his arm in a greeting then quickly gave over his order. Just moments later, and with a steaming plate in his hands, he made his way over to them.

'You all right?' he asked in a greeting as he slid into a booth.

Damien nodded and, sliding the condiments across the

table, he went back to tucking into his food. After a few moments, he took a swig of his tea and gestured down at Tommy Jr's plate.

'Thank fuck you didn't order gravy,' he said with a straight face. 'Because you would have been sitting as far away from me as possible if you had.'

'Nah, fuck that.' Tommy Jr chuckled at the obvious banter. 'It's liquor all the way.'

Damien lifted his eyebrows and, jerking his head, he indicated towards Winston's plate, which much to his displeasure was swimming in dark brown liquid.

'What?' Winston claimed between mouthfuls. 'Don't knock it until you try it. And trust me, the pair of you don't know what you're missing out on.'

Tommy Jr couldn't help but laugh and as he went back to his food, his shoulders relaxed. He had a sneaky suspicion this was the main reason Damien had suggested the eel shop for their meet, and as far as strategies went it had worked a treat.

Once the meal had been eaten, Tommy Jr leaned back on the wooden bench and snapped open a can of cola.

'Did Dylan ever mention my cousin Vinnie?' Damien asked.

'Who, the nutter that tried to stab me?' Tommy asked before taking a sip of his drink.

'Yeah, that's the one.'

'Not that I can remember.'

'What, not even once?'

Thinking back on his and Dylan's conversations, Tommy drummed his fingers on the table. 'He might have mentioned him once or twice. I think one time you and your cousin were coming in for a visit. He could barely keep still he was that excited. He said that he hadn't seen either of you for a while.'

Damien nodded. 'Yeah, that sounds about right. But other

than that did he ever mention him? Did he ever say that the two of them were involved in something?'

'I don't think so.' Tommy shrugged. 'But then again he rarely said much about his personal life. He could be a closed book at times.' Taking another sip of his drink, he cocked his head to the side. 'He did mention an Arthur though. Uncle Arthur.'

'Arthur Brennan. My dad's business partner.'

'Yeah, he said they were close.'

'I suppose so,' Damien answered with a shrug.

'And he did mention Liverpool a few times.'

Damien frowned. 'What about Liverpool?'

'That he was a frequent visitor there. He gave me the impression it was business related.'

The crease between Damien's eyes deepened and, turning his head to look at Winston, confusion was clearly evident across his face. 'Why the fuck would he have been going to Liverpool?'

Just as Winston shrugged, a name sprang to Tommy's mind.

'He mentioned someone called Cal. Cal, or Calvin maybe.'

'Calvin Rivers?' Winston volunteered.

'I dunno,' Tommy answered. 'Could be.'

Sinking back in his seat, Damien rubbed at his temples. 'Why would Dylan have had business dealings with Calvin Rivers?'

'You tell me,' Winston sighed. 'Calvin Rivers is bad news. And if he and Dylan were doing business together then I can guarantee you right now that it was something big. I'd bet my fucking knob on it, and I don't say that lightly.' He grimaced as he nodded down at his nether regions. 'You know exactly how fond I am of that part of my anatomy.'

'Yeah,' Damien groaned. 'That's exactly what I'm afraid of.'

7

As Jason made his way back through the casino, his face was set like thunder. If anything, he wanted to berate himself for not taking action sooner. After all, he had the rest of his life to grieve for his son. Not only had he allowed those responsible for his boy's murder to walk away without so much as a backwards glance, but he'd also allowed himself to appear weak, and in his line of work that was as good as signing his own death warrant.

On seeing him approach his office, Gio quickened his pace as he began to make his way towards him.

'Not now,' Jason barked out.

'Yeah but...'

'I said not fucking now,' Jason roared before slamming the door to the office firmly closed behind him.

Shrugging off his jacket, he tossed it onto a chair then unbuttoned the top button of his shirt and slid his fingers around the inside of his collar. He felt as though he were being suffocated. Gio was beginning to get on his last nerve, not that he could say he'd had a lot of patience for the man to begin with. Placing his hands on his hips, he took a series of deep breaths before pinching the bridge of his nose.

He needed a plan of action, something proactive that would actually help to ease the ball of anger inside his chest that seemed to grow bigger and bigger by the day. Problem was, he didn't know where to start. Of course, he could pay the Carter family a visit but seeing as Damien had already beaten him to it, he'd end up looking even more of a fool then he already did.

As though on autopilot, he walked over to the bar, unscrewed the lid of the whiskey bottle then poured himself out a generous measure. Before Dylan had been murdered, he'd never been what he would call a heavy drinker. Even on an evening out he'd never have more than a couple of drinks. He preferred to keep his wits about him which, when in the company of likeminded villains, was always a wise move. Many a time he'd seen a man laughing and joking one moment then ready to commit murder the next. In those circumstances it went without saying that it was imperative to stay on your guard; in some cases it was a matter of life and death.

A commotion coming from outside the office caught his attention and, taking a quick glance at his watch, he inwardly groaned. The casino had barely been open an hour and from the sound of it the punters were already kicking off. No doubt blaming everyone but themselves for the reason they had just blown a week's wages on the slot machines. Downing the whiskey in one large gulp, he slammed the glass down then, placing his palms on the desk, he breathed heavily through his nostrils. He'd had a gutful, he knew that much, not only of the casino and everything it entailed, but also of Gio and his need to constantly follow him around like a lost sheep. And as if that wasn't enough, to top it off, he also had Damien to contend with.

The shouts from outside became even louder and, banging

his fist down on the desk, Jason straightened up and stormed across the office, more than prepared to lay into the culprit. Within seconds of opening the door, he staggered backwards, his hand automatically reaching up to clutch at his jaw.

'Right from the start I knew you were involved, that you were the reason my brother is dead.'

Jason's eyes almost bulged out of his head, and before he could even open his mouth to answer, a second punch sent him reeling across the desk.

'Does Liverpool ring any bells?' Damien seethed as he shook out the tension in his fist. 'Or how about Calvin fucking Rivers?'

Still splayed across the desk, Jason brought his thumb up to his lip and dabbed at a droplet of blood, smearing it across his chin as he did so. He was too stunned to speak let alone answer the question. He knew nothing about Liverpool let alone Calvin Rivers, other than that he was a cocky little bastard who needed bringing down a peg or two.

'What have you done, eh?' Damien continued to roar. 'What the fuck have you done?' Pulling back his fist again, he was just about to lunge forward when Winston pulled him back.

'Enough, man,' Winston warned as he glanced warily in Jason's direction. 'You're gonna end up killing him.'

At this Jason snorted out a laugh. He was Jason Vickers, not some prick his son had encountered in a boozer someplace. Gingerly, he sat up then, easing himself into a standing position, he straightened out his shirt. To his shame the altercation had brought some unwanted attention. Arthur and Gio, both of whom had done nothing to intervene other than stare at him with their mouths agape, but also a few of the bar staff who no doubt would spread his humiliation around the casino and beyond like wildfire.

'A bit of privacy wouldn't go amiss,' he snapped.

Moments later the door was hastily closed, leaving just himself, his son, and Winston alone. Perhaps not so much a wise move considering just seconds earlier Damien had been hell-bent on battering the life out of him.

Dabbing at his lip again, Jason rounded his desk, picked up a packet of cigarettes and fished one out. Sliding the packet across the desk, he popped the cigarette between his lips and lit up. 'Do you want to explain to me what this is about?' he asked, exhaling a cloud of smoke above his head, his voice strong and unwavering.

Damien's lips were curled into a snarl, his stance very much that of a man ready to explode. 'I knew you were low,' he spat, 'but not this low. Dylan was a kid; he'd only just turned nineteen for fuck's sake. He knew sod all about the life and yet you sent him out doing your dirty work.'

Jason held up his hand, his eyes hard as he fought to keep a lid on his temper. 'He was keen to learn. He had a good head on his shoulders, not that I would have expected any different to him; he was a Vickers after all. But as for dirty work, you've got that much wrong. For the most part he worked here,' he said, gesturing around him. 'Do you honestly think that I would send him out if I didn't think he could handle it?'

In that instant, Jason could see that his words had hit home. As much as his and Damien's relationship was strained, and that was putting it mildly, he had never been in the habit of putting his sons in danger, Damien included. Or at least this had been the case when his eldest son had first set out, when he'd had little to no experience of what being a member of the criminal underworld entailed.

Damien sighed and, as his shoulders began to relax, he reached down, scooped up his father's cigarette packet, and took two cigarettes out, passing one to Winston then placing the other between his lips. 'So, where does Liverpool come into this?'

As he shook his head, Jason's mind reeled. To his knowledge Dylan had never visited Liverpool, and he knew with certainty that he'd never sent him there. He'd had no need to. It had been years since he'd last had any business dealings in the area. And even then it had been to arrange a safe house for a diamond smuggler, rather than because he himself had any actual business there. 'I don't know,' he finally answered. 'There has to be a mistake.'

'There's no mistake. It came from Dylan himself. He told Tommy Johnson that he was a frequent visitor to the area and that he dealt with someone called Cal or Calvin, who I'm guessing is Calvin Rivers.'

Jason nodded. He could see how Damien had come to that assumption. Calvin Rivers was notorious in Liverpool. His name preceded him and he was feared by many. 'And is this Tommy Johnson a reliable source?' he spat as anger once again began to build inside of him. 'The bastard left your brother to die alone on a concrete floor,' he added, stabbing a stiff finger forward. 'All to save his own fucking skin.'

Damien shook his head. 'It didn't go down like that.' Momentarily, he closed his eyes and took a deep breath. 'Dylan...' clearing his throat, he began again. 'Dylan didn't stand a chance. He was as good as dead the moment those cunts burst into his cell. There was nothing Johnson, or anyone else for that matter, could have done to save him.'

Listening to the reality of his son's death was Jason's undoing and as much as he was loathe to show any form of vulnerability, especially in front of his eldest son, he was unable to stop himself from turning his body and grasping on to the edge of his desk so tightly that his knuckles turned white. As he swallowed down the hard lump in his throat, he was aware of Damien taking a step closer.

'I'm going to take a trip to Liverpool, see what I can find out.'

Jason turned his head, and as a shard of ice-cold fear ran down the length of his spine, he swallowed again. Never would he have imagined himself feeling any form of concern for his eldest son, and yet for some reason he did. He was unable to recall the last time he and Damien were civil to one another, let alone be able to hold a conversation without at least one of them kicking off or throwing insults at the other.

'If Dylan was travelling to Liverpool then I need to know why, and by all accounts it wasn't a one off; he was a frequent visitor.'

It was on the tip of Jason's tongue to argue the case. He'd already lost one son and if there was a chance that Calvin Rivers was somehow involved in Dylan's murder, then one way or another it was inevitable that he would lose his remaining son, whether that be by death or a lengthy prison sentence. 'I'll come with you.'

An incredulous laugh escaped from Damien's lips. 'Like fuck you will. The last thing I need, or even want for that matter, is you tagging along with me.'

Almost immediately, Jason's back was up and as he spun around, he was just about to fling back a retort when Damien continued.

'It's been a long time since I've needed my dad to hold my hand, and you know that as well as I do.'

Jason sighed. As much as he didn't like to admit it, he could see where Damien was coming from. Even from a young age Damien had been too independent, too defiant, too knowing, especially when it had come to his mother's addiction problems no matter how much he'd initially tried to conceal them from him. Perhaps this was why he'd poured everything he had to give into his youngest son. The reason why he'd considered Dylan to be his golden child, his legacy. He'd been able to hide his imperfections from him, but in Damien's eyes he was nothing but a failure as both a husband and a father. And as much as he may have pretended not to give a flying fuck about his son's opinion, deep down it had bothered him. As a result he'd retaliated the only way he knew how, which in turn had led to the bad blood between them. That wasn't to say however that his son was faultless; Damien had given as good as he'd got, hence why people often commented on how alike they were.

'Fine, do it your way.'

Damien nodded and as he jerked his head towards Winston, indicating it was time for them to leave, Jason's heart felt heavy.

'You'll keep me updated?'

Coming to a halt, Damien turned his head, his mind in turmoil as he weighed up his options. He could either take the olive branch offered to him or he could laugh in his father's face. A large part of him wanted to refuse the request. Jason could see it in his son's eyes. Eventually, and much to Jason's surprise, Damien nodded and as he and Winston left the office, for the first time in a long time, Jason felt as though a heavy weight had been lifted from his shoulders.

* * *

Tommy Jr resisted the urge to roll his eyes and as he glanced towards his great-uncle Jonny, he shook his head. As far as excuses went he'd heard them all during his time working for his family's debt-collecting business, so much so that he could see them coming from a mile away. 'Is this prick having a bubble?'

'I swear to you,' Ashton Miller said, the words tripping out of his mouth so fast that spittle had gathered at the corner of his lips. 'I was just on my way to you.' He gave a high laugh, his wild gaze flicking between Tommy and Jonny. 'You know me, you know what I'm about. I'd never try to tuck you up; I'd have to be some kind of idiot to do that, wouldn't I.'

Leaning casually against an iron railing that ran the length of the alleyway where they had had Ashton trapped, Jonny Carter flashed a jovial grin. 'Is that why I've personally spent the best part of a week tracking you down?'

Ashton swallowed, the colour draining from his face. 'I was on my way to you,' he repeated, his beady eyes scanning the immediate area for an escape route. 'I swear I was.'

The smile slid from Jonny's face. 'Smash him up,' he said with a nonchalant wave of his hand in Tommy Jr's direction.

Before Tommy even had the chance to lift his arm, Ashton let out a squeal of fear.

'No, no, no!' he cried. 'I've got the money.' Digging his hand into his pocket, he pulled out a handful of crumpled notes and shoved them into Jonny's chest. 'Take it,' he pleaded. 'Take all of it.'

'See, that wasn't so hard, was it.' Counting out the cash, Jonny grinned before stuffing the money into his pocket. 'Next time, make sure you pay up on time.' Tapping the side of Ashton's face, he took a moment of satisfaction to see him flinch. 'Because next time I won't be so generous, I'll set him on you,' he said, flicking his head in Tommy's direction. 'And believe me, his bite is a lot worse than his bark.'

Ashton's face paled as he scuttled away as fast as his feet could carry him. Tommy couldn't help but laugh. 'Tosser,' he said, nodding at Ashton's retreating back. 'He must think we were born yesterday.'

'They always do,' Jonny sighed. Tossing across his car keys, he nodded to where they had parked the car. 'You can do the honours and drive us back to the yard.'

Catching the keys with one hand, Tommy's free hand slipped inside his pocket and, pulling out his mobile phone, he took one look at the caller ID and came to an abrupt halt. 'I'll catch you up,' he said, gesturing down to his phone. 'It's Aimee,' he added, referring to his girlfriend. 'She more than likely wants to chew my ear off over something or other.' It was a lie of course and it wasn't until his uncle had walked a safe distance away from him that he pressed answer.

A few minutes later, he ended the phone call and chewed on the inside of his cheek. The fact Damien Vickers had called him at all should have been enough to tell him that something big was about to go down, but the fact he'd invited him along for the ride was even more surprising.

Breaking out into a jog, he caught his uncle up.

'All sorted?' Jonny asked as he motioned down to the phone still clutched in Tommy's hand.

'Yeah.' Tommy gave a small laugh that, even to his own ears, sounded false and as he climbed behind the wheel, pushed the key into the ignition, then stepped his foot down on the accelerator, the only thing on his mind was his upcoming trip to Liverpool. And more than that, how the hell he was going to disappear for the day without causing suspicion amongst his family?

* * *

Natasha Baptiste slipped her handbag over her shoulder and exited the building where she worked. Having waved goodbye to a colleague, she frowned then glanced up and down the street before making her way across the road to where Damien had parked his car.

'What are you doing here?' she asked after taking another furtive glance around her before climbing inside. 'I didn't think I was seeing you today.'

'You're not,' Damien answered. Slipping his hand into his pocket, he took out a pack of cigarettes, took one out then placed the box on the dashboard. 'At least not technically anyway,' he added as he wound the window down a couple of inches before lighting up and inhaling a lungful of smoke.

'Okay.' Natasha tilted her head to the side as she looked at him. 'So do you want to fill me in on what this is about, or is this a case of what I don't know can't hurt?'

'Pretty much,' Damien sighed. He glanced towards the building Natasha had exited just in time to witness a police car drive through a set of iron gates. 'After all, once a copper always a copper, right.'

'Don't be a dick,' Natasha retorted. 'My chosen career isn't an issue when we're in bed together, is it.'

'I suppose not.' Damien sighed again. 'I was given some information about Dylan.' Holding up his hand as if to stop her from interrupting, he continued. 'It could turn out to be fuck all but either way I need to find out. Me and Win are gonna to take a trip to Liverpool.' He glanced at his watch. 'We're leaving in a couple of hours.'

Natasha's eyes widened. 'Jesus Christ, Damien.' Snatching up the cigarette box, she took one out for herself and paused. 'Do you know how hard it's been for me to quit?' she asked as she waved the cigarette in the air.

Shaking his head, Damien passed his lighter across.

'No, of course you don't,' she said as she placed the cigarette between her lips and lit up. 'Because you're so consumed with Dylan's murder and seeking revenge that—'

Anger flashed in Damien's eyes. 'He was my brother.'

'I know he was.' Taking a deep drag on the cigarette, Natasha screwed up her face as she blew out a thin stream of smoke. 'This is vile,' she stated as she pushed open the car door and tossed the cigarette onto the tarmac. 'You need to let the police do their job...'

Letting out a snort of laughter, Damien shook his head. 'Leave it out, Tash.'

'Taking the law into your own hands isn't going to help anyone,' Natasha continued. 'The only thing you're actually going to achieve is to fuck up the entire investigation.'

'What investigation?' As Damien turned in his seat, the anger across his face was more than visible. 'There is no fucking investigation and you know that as well as I do. They couldn't give two shits about Dylan. As far as the filth are concerned he was just some con, some low-life scumbag who was banged up and who got what he deserved, his comeuppance.'

'That's not true.'

'Isn't it?' Damien growled.

'No, and you know it isn't.' As she grabbed hold of his hand, Natasha's voice became more gentle. 'Damien, please... stop this. I understand, really I do, but—'

'But what, Tash?' Snatching his hand free, Damien leaned back in the seat, the muscles across his shoulder blades becoming rigid. 'How about,' he said, flicking his head towards the police station, 'we both go and have a look at this big investigation for ourselves. Have a little nosy around the investigation room or whatever the fuck you call it, because I can guarantee you right now we're gonna come away empty handed. I tell you what, while we're at it you might as well let the cat out of the bag and introduce me to your boss.'

As she glanced towards her workplace, Natasha swallowed deeply and shook her head. 'You know I can't do that.'

'Why not?' he shrugged. 'You stick the kettle on and I'll grab the biscuits, then we can sit down together and fill him in on all of the gory details, starting with my criminal past. I'm not so sure it'll score you any brownie points but at least there'll be no more sneaking around. Let's face it, you're quick enough to have a pop at me when it comes to telling Winston but you're not so quick off the mark when it comes to your poxy job.'

For the briefest of moments a look of hurt flashed across Natasha's face before she shook her head and reached out for the door handle. 'Fuck you.'

'Wait.' Gritting his teeth, Damien pulled her back towards him. 'I'm sorry,' he admitted. 'I was bang out of order.'

'Yeah, you were,' she answered, her lips set into a thin line. 'I know it might not mean much to you but I've worked my arse off to get to where I am today. And I'm already treading a thin line all thanks to Winston's past convictions. Time and time again I've had to prove myself; I'm hardly what you would call an ideal candidate for the force, am I? Brought up on a council estate, my brother has been in and out of prison the majority of his life, my mum cleans toilets for a living and as for my dad, well,' she shrugged, 'it would help if we even knew where the bastard was. And that,' she continued, 'is just my immediate family. What about my cousins? How many of those have been nicked or done time? Because off the top of my head I can think of at least three.'

'Yeah.' Damien nodded, his cheeks flushing red. 'I know.'

'Do you?' Natasha snapped. 'Have you honestly got any idea about the shit I've had to put up with in the past? The snide comments, the sly looks that went around every time the estate I grew up on was mentioned. Or how about when I walked in one day to find a mugshot of my brother pinned to the board, that supposedly,' she said, using her fingers as quotation marks, 'was a joke, a bit of banter, something that I should have took on the chin and laughed off.'

Damien's gaze snapped towards the police station, his eyes flashing with fury. 'Who did that?' he growled. 'Point the bastard out to me and I'll have a word with him.'

Natasha threw her arms up into the air. 'And that, right there, was the reason I never said anything. I handled it.' Taking a deep breath, she reached out for his hand. 'I'm a bloody good copper, Damien, and I'm ambitious, I'll do whatever it takes to get to the top and I'm not prepared to let anyone get in my way, not you, not Winston, or any of that lot,' she added, jerking her head behind her to the police station.

'Yeah.' He gave a small chuckle in an attempt to lighten the mood. 'You've always gone after what you want, I'll give you that.'

Natasha smiled. 'Look,' she said, becoming serious again. 'Forget my job for a moment. I'm asking you this as your girlfriend, your partner. How dangerous is this trip to Liverpool likely to be?'

As he shrugged, Damien rested his head on the headrest and gave her a sidelong glance. 'It could get a bit hairy.' He gave another smile then, leaning forward, kissed her gently on the forehead. 'You don't need to worry about me. If I haven't learnt how to handle myself by now then somewhere along the lines there's a serious problem.'

'That doesn't exactly help,' Natasha retorted as she settled into his embrace.

Damien laughed and, easing out of her arms, he turned the

key in the ignition and motioned to the road up ahead of them. 'I'll give you a lift home.'

'I've got my car,' she protested.

'And?' Damien retorted as he gave her a wink. 'You can get an Uber in the morning and pick it up.'

Moments later he flicked the indicator then pulled out into the road, completely oblivious to the driver of the car that had slowed down to let him out, a driver who had the means to rip his entire world to pieces.

8

As Jonny Carter swivelled his chair from side to side, he couldn't help but take note of how often his great nephew Tommy Jr glanced down at his hands, often appearing to study them for long minutes at a time. And what's more, it wasn't the first time he'd noticed Tommy's strange habit. Clearing his throat, he brought the chair to a halt and rested his forearms on the desk. 'You good?'

Tommy Jr looked up, his expression one of confusion. 'Yeah, of course I am. Why wouldn't I be?'

Jonny shrugged. 'No reason.' And as he began to swivel the chair again, he caught the look Tommy's father shot towards him. Something wasn't right, that much was evident. In fact he'd go as far as to say that Tommy Jr hadn't quite been himself since he'd been released from prison a few weeks earlier. In a way he supposed it was only natural that there would be a change in him; after all, he'd gone to prison a boy and come out a man. But in Jonny's mind it went deeper than that. It was almost as though a switch had been flicked. Gone was the nephew who'd been reckless, irresponsible, and at times hard to control and in his place was a man who was calculated, scheming, and downright frightening. In fact, if he didn't know better he would have assumed he was working alongside his late brother, Tommy Jr's grandfather, Tommy Snr. The similarities between the two were uncanny and he was pretty sure that he wasn't the only one to have noticed.

'I'm going to shoot off.' As he got to his feet, Tommy Jr slipped on his jacket.

Jonny narrowed his eyes and, taking a quick glance at his watch, he looked back up. 'Bit early isn't it?'

As he busied himself pocketing his mobile phone, Tommy lifted his shoulders. 'I promised Aimee that I'd take her shopping. And, well, you know what it's like, she's been on at me about buying the baby some bits.'

Jonny nodded. As a new father himself he understood what it was like to prepare for a new baby. Only there was something about Tommy's explanation that somehow didn't ring true. 'Can't she go with her mum?'

In that instant Jonny could see the unease in Tommy's eyes. It may have only been slight but he'd seen it, nonetheless. The truth was Tommy had never been a good liar; it was this fact that had got him into endless trouble as a kid. When his cousins had got away with murder, Tommy Jr was often the one to have been caught out and then subsequently punished.

'Nah,' he answered, averting his gaze. 'It's getting a bit late and I'd rather drive her there myself than her take the bus.'

It was a plausible answer, Jonny supposed, and one that he would have believed if he hadn't known Tommy as well as he did. He gave another nod and as Tommy left the portable cabin that the family used as their office, Jonny was deep in thought. Chewing on the end of a biro, he absentmindedly twirled the chair. After a moment or two he looked up and nodded towards his nephew, Caleb. 'Follow him and see where he goes.'

Tommy's father, Cameron, threw up his arms. 'Is that really necessary?' he barked out.

'Yeah, it is,' Jonny countered as he flicked his head towards Caleb, reaffirming his order. 'Something isn't right with him, and you know it.'

Cameron was about to protest before slumping back in the seat. Like Jonny, he too had seen a change in his son, one that he wasn't so sure was for the better. 'He's no idiot,' he finally answered.

'Maybe not,' Jonny replied. 'But he's young and he has far too much Carter blood running through his veins for my liking. And that makes him dangerous.'

Unable to argue the case, Cameron rubbed his hand over his jaw. He and his wife were first cousins; their fathers had been brothers. Which in turn meant that their son, their only child, had more Carter blood inside of him than the rest of the family combined. Getting to his feet, he came to stand in front of the window that overlooked the forecourt just in time to watch Tommy drive through the iron gates. 'Prison fucked him up,' he declared as he turned back to look at Jonny.

Jonny lifted his eyebrows. If you took prison out of the equation, there was always a high chance that Tommy Jr was going to become a law unto himself. Tommy Snr had been the one to set the family on the road of armed robbers. He'd not only been well respected amongst the criminal underworld but also feared. And then there was his third elder brother, Gary, Tommy Jr's paternal grandfather. Like Tommy Snr, Gary had been calculated, only whereas Tommy Snr had only ever put his family first, Gary's only priority had been for himself and Cameron's mother, a cold, deceitful, spiteful woman called Bethany Johnson. She had not only been obsessed with Tommy Snr but had also been the one to have manipulated Gary into carrying out the heinous act of murdering his own brother in cold blood.

'Look,' Jonny sighed. 'I'm not denying that he's a good kid, or at least he is most of the time anyway,' he said with a smile to soften his words. 'But even you, as his dad, have to admit that it could be down to him to run this place one day,' he said, gesturing around the office. 'Not that I'm planning to hang up the gloves for a good few years yet.' He laughed. 'But one day, when that time comes, someone will need to lead the family, and being Tommy Snr's grandson, it would make perfect sense for Tommy Jr to take over the reins.'

As he exhaled a breath, Cameron glanced back towards the window. 'You know that Karen,' he said of his wife, 'won't like it. As it is she still thinks of him as her little boy. If she had her way she'd have him suited and booted and working up the city in some poncy office.'

'Karen won't have a say on the matter,' Jonny was quick to answer. 'Whether she likes it or not he's a Carter, or a Johnson,' he hastily corrected seeing as Cameron had been given his grandfather, Dean Johnson's, surname rather than his father's surname of Carter. 'And when the time comes I've got a sneaky suspicion that nothing and no one is going to stand in his way. Which is why,' he added, 'he needs to be watched or guided, whichever way you want to look at it.'

'Yeah, I suppose.'

'No suppose about it,' Jonny answered. 'If he even has just a small part of my brother, Tommy, inside of him, then let me tell me you now...' As he glanced down at his mobile phone, the words died in his throat. 'What did I tell you?' he growled, tossing the device back onto the desk. 'I knew he was lying. So much for taking Aimee shopping, the little bastard is heading towards South London.'

The colour drained from Cameron's face, and as he inhaled a deep breath, he lifted his eyes to the ceiling. 'This kid is going to be the death of me,' he groaned.

'Yeah, you and me both,' Jonny retorted with a grimace.

* * *

As Winston Baptiste leaned up against Damien's car, he crossed his arms over his chest. 'Remind me again,' he asked, 'why you've invited this Tommy Johnson kid along for the ride?'

Damien gave an agitated sigh. He'd already explained himself once and still Winston wasn't satisfied with his answer. 'You know why.'

'Yeah.' Winston gave a brief nod. 'Something about Dylan telling him he'd been to Liverpool,' he grumbled.

Tossing his jacket onto the back seat, Damien straightened up, his expression hard. 'If you've got something to say then just come out and say it instead of pussy-footing around, we both know that's not your style.'

'All right.' Dropping his arms to his sides, Winston pushed himself away from the car. 'I don't trust him, not one little bit. Firstly,' he said, holding up a finger, 'he's a Carter...'

'Johnson,' Damien corrected.

Winston gritted his teeth. 'And secondly,' he said, holding up two fingers, 'I think your old man could be on to something. If you want my opinion I think that the little bastard has spun us a load of old pony just to cover his own arse. For all you know it could have been him who stuck the blade into Dylan. I mean,' he said, spreading open his arms, 'he had the opportunity. Come on, bro, even you have to see where I'm coming from, that it's more than a little bit suspicious.'

'Hence why I invited him along,' Damien interrupted a second time.

Throwing up his arms, Winston shook his head. 'And that's your plan, is it?' he snapped. 'Take him on a day trip and hope that by some miracle he'll confess to murder?'

'Listen.' Motioning to the car that was pulling in behind them, Damien lifted his eyebrows. 'If he was lying then believe me, the sly bastard won't be returning from Liverpool. In fact the only place he'll be going is to the bottom of the Mersey.'

'I don't like this,' Winston groaned as Tommy Jr climbed out of his car. 'You're playing a dangerous game. If the Carters get wind of it, they're gonna hunt the pair of us down and trust me, the bottom of the Mersey will be nothing compared to what they're capable of.'

Damien chuckled. 'Do you honestly think he's told them where he's going?' He winked. 'From what I've heard they're a close-knit family. There isn't a chance in hell they would happily allow him to skip halfway across the country without at least one or two of them in tow, especially after what went down with that prick Vinnie.'

Still unsure, Winston reluctantly walked around the car, yanked open the front passenger door and climbed inside. 'We'll see,' he muttered. 'But don't say I didn't warn you.'

* * *

With his face set like thunder, Jonny Carter jabbed at the redial button on his mobile phone. 'I'm gonna muller him,' he growled, slamming the device down on the desk when the call once again rang off. 'I'm seriously starting to think that he's not right up here,' he said, tapping his temple. 'That he's got a screw loose. I know that I might have pulled some stupid shit when I was his age but I wasn't this dense.'

Mitchell Carter, Jonny's elder brother, raised his eyebrows. 'That's debatable.'

'What do you mean?' Jonny argued. 'I know I wasn't a saint but I definitely wasn't hellbent on getting myself killed either.'

'Like I said,' Mitchell retorted, 'that's debatable. You and Tommy Jr are like two peas in a pod. Neither of you think before acting,' he said, ticking the list off his fingers. 'You're both reckless, both cocky. And neither of you have ever listened to reason. Do I need to go on?'

'Yeah, all right,' Jonny groaned. 'You've made your point.'

Mitchell's son, Reece cleared his throat. 'I don't know why you're all getting so worked up. You don't even know for certain that he went to see Vickers.'

'What do you mean I don't know?' Jonny roared as he stabbed his finger in his nephew's direction. 'I'm not fucking stupid. What other reason would there be for him to head towards South London?'

Reece shrugged. 'I dunno, but whatever it is he must have his reasons. Didn't you say,' he added as he looked around at his family for confirmation, 'that he said he was going to take Aimee shopping? Or...' He clicked his fingers as though the idea had just occurred to him. 'He could have gone to see the Bannerman brothers. South London is their neck of the woods an' all, ain't it.'

'Leave it out,' Jonny shouted. 'There's no reason for him to be anywhere near the Bannermans and if he is then he's even more stupid than I thought he was.' Narrowing his eyes, he studied his nephew. 'You better not be covering for him,' he warned. 'The two of you are tight and more often than not joined at the hip.'

When Reece didn't answer, Jonny continued to glare at him.

'Well?' he snapped.

'Nah, of course I'm not.' Averting his gaze, Reece chewed on his thumbnail. 'I've barely even seen him since he came out of the nick and when I do see him he ends up having a pop at me.'

Jonny sank back in his seat and laced his fingers together. 'I don't understand what goes through that head of his sometimes,' he sighed. 'It was only a few days ago that Damien Vickers tried to iron him out and that was without the other nutcase trying to slice him up.'

'If you're that concerned,' Mitchell said as he looked between Jonny and Cameron, 'take a trip over to South London yourselves. It's not like he'll be hard to find, is it. You know where Jason Vickers' casino is, it's only twenty minutes or so down the road if you put your foot down.'

'I could do without this,' Jonny groaned. 'Haven't I got enough on my plate without him adding to my problems?'

Mitchell leaned back in the chair, his lips curled up into the faintest of smirks. 'This is what you wanted, remember,' he said, motioning around the scrapyard office. 'By rights it should have been me and Sonny,' he said, referring to his twin brother, 'who took over the reins. We were next in line. Not that you gave a flying fuck or gave us a look in. The minute Jimmy said that he was thinking of retiring, you were on his case.'

'Yeah, all right, you don't have to rub it in,' Jonny grumbled. As much as he hated to admit it, Mitchell was right. He'd badgered his elder brother Jimmy something chronic, determined that he would be the one to lead the family into the future. What he hadn't envisioned, however was just how much of a handful his nephews were, particularly Tommy Jr. How Jimmy had managed to keep the boys on such a tight rein, for the life of him he couldn't work out.

'What do you want to do?' he said as he flicked his head towards Cameron. 'We can either go out looking for him or wait for him to show back up and then read him his rights, give him a bollocking that he won't forget in a hurry. You're his dad. It's your call.'

'What do you think?' Cameron got to his feet and dug his hand into his pocket, pulling out his car keys. 'It's about time he grew the fuck up. He's about to become a father for fuck's sake and he's still pulling stupid stunts like this.'

Blowing out his cheeks, Jonny got to his feet and slipped on his jacket before heading for the door. 'Like I said,' he muttered underneath his breath out of Cameron's earshot, 'the kid's not all the ticket.'

* * *

Stopping every now and again to say hello to the die-hard regulars that he recognised, Jason Vickers made his way through the casino.

Finally he came to a stop before a set of double doors that led through to where the poker tables were. Or rather where the more private tables were housed and large amounts of money would exchange hands, and not just through the game being played. More often than not the casino was considered a safe sanctuary. Deals would be made, highly illegal deals of course, and not only would crimes be plotted, but on the odd occasion murders too.

'You all right, boy?'

Startled, Vinnie Vickers turned his head. 'Yeah,' he said as he straightened up and grasped his uncle's hand in a firm handshake. 'You?'

Jason nodded. 'Anyone notable in there I should know

about?' he added as he scanned the room, his hard gaze falling upon his son-in-law, Gio.

'Nah.' Vinnie shook his head. 'No one of importance.' Turning to look at his uncle again, he motioned towards the red mark on his jaw. 'Looks like someone's had a crack at you.'

Jason groaned, and as he absentmindedly lifted his hand to prod at his jaw, he grimaced. 'I'm surprised you haven't heard already. You know what this lot are like,' he said, motioning to the bar staff.

Vinnie shook his head and as he too glanced across to the bar, he frowned. 'I've only just got here. What happened?'

Jason gave an irritated sigh. A part of him was embarrassed to admit that it had been his own son who'd marked him. Still, he reasoned it wasn't as though Vinnie was a stranger; he was family.

As he leaned slightly back to study his uncle, Vinnie's eyes ever so slightly widened. 'Let me take a guess. Damien paid you a visit.'

'Got it in one.'

Whistling softly, Vinnie shook his head again. 'Yeah, he had a pop at me a couple of days ago as well,' he said as he smoothed his thumb over the outline of a bruise on his cheek, one of many bruises as a matter of fact, all thanks to the Carter family. 'He's definitely on one, eh.'

'Yeah, you can say that again.'

Just as Vinnie was about to answer, he turned his head in the direction of two men who were approaching. 'We've got company,' he said, his shoulders tensing as he pulled himself up to his full height.

Jason looked over his shoulder. As far as he was concerned the men needed no introduction. And although it would be fair to say that he was unable to recall if he'd ever met the two in question before, immediately he could see that they were Carters. They had a presence about them, a confidence that could only come from being a part of a notorious family, not to mention they were all walking clones of one another. Each of them well over six feet tall, with mops of thick dark hair and piercing blue eyes.

As Jason went on to shake the men's hands, a wave of unease spread throughout his body. Call it intuition, but he had a sneaky suspicion they hadn't travelled from East London just for a game of poker. And considering his eldest son had also recently paid them a visit, he had a nasty feeling that they hadn't returned the sentiment out of the goodness of their hearts.

'I'm looking for my nephew,' the elder of the two announced, cutting to the chase. 'Tommy Johnson.'

Jason gave Vinnie a surreptitious glance. As far as he was aware the Johnson kid had been nowhere near the casino. 'And what makes you think he'd be here?'

Ignoring the question, the elder Carter directed his hard stare towards Vinnie. 'And seeing as you tried to top him the last time we met then you'd best start talking, and fast before I end up losing my rag. Because believe me,' he growled, placing his thumb and forefinger an inch apart, 'I'm this far away from erupting.'

As Vinnie rubbed at the back of his neck, his cheeks flushed red. 'That was a misunderstanding,' he muttered.

'Misunderstanding or not,' the younger of the men barked out, 'you still tried to run my son through with a fucking blade.'

'Hold up.' Jason held up his hand. 'Before tempers start to flare can we all calm the fuck down for a minute and someone explain to me what the fuck is going on here?'

A moment of silence followed. 'Well, come on,' Jason spat as he glared at his nephew. 'Do as the man says and start fucking talking.'

'Nothing happened.' Shifting his weight from one foot to the other, Vinnie could barely look his uncle in the eyes. 'Things just got a bit out of hand, that's all.'

'Yeah, and that's an understatement,' the older of the two men barked out.

'What did you expect me to do?' Vinnie hastily added as he turned back to look at his uncle. 'I did it for Dylan, and if you'd have been there you'd have done the same.'

Resisting the urge to fell his nephew to the floor, Jason shook his head. The fact he was clueless to what had gone down was enough to make him look like a fool, yet again. 'Why is this the first time I'm hearing about this?' he growled.

Vinnie shrugged, the action coming across as sheepish. 'Take it up with Damien. It was nothing to do with me,' he lied. 'I just tagged along for the ride.'

Jason narrowed his eyes. As much as he believed his son to have had a large part to play, he knew that Vinnie wasn't quite as innocent as he made himself out to be. For a start he had too much of his father inside of him, and if there was one thing Jason knew about his late brother Colin, it was that he'd never shied away from causing aggravation. Before he could even think the situation through, Jason's arm shot out and, grasping Vinnie by the front of his shirt, he pulled him close, so close that their noses were almost touching. 'Are you trying to take me for a mug?' he bellowed into his nephew's face.

Blinking rapidly, Vinnie shook his head, his expression one of shock. 'No...' he stammered. 'You know I wouldn't do that.'

Unsatisfied with Vinnie's answer, Jason yanked him even closer. 'Because you've just made me look like a fucking muppet,' he hissed in his ear. 'Do you hear what I'm saying? A fucking muppet.'

Vinnie nodded and as Jason shoved him roughly away from him, he staggered several paces back, his shirt a crumpled mess. 'I'm sorry.'

'Yeah, you will be,' Jason snarled.

'Regardless of who did what,' the elder man snapped, 'my great nephew is still on the missing list.' Which was a slight exaggeration considering it had been less than two hours since they had last seen Tommy Jr. 'Jonny Carter,' he said, motioning to himself. 'And this is my nephew Cameron Johnson,' he said, jabbing a finger towards the second man. 'Tommy Jr's old man.'

Jason nodded. He'd already guessed who they were. As for Cameron Johnson, he'd met his grandfather once, Dean Johnson, a hard bastard in his own right, and one that not many people were stupid enough to take on, at least not single-handed anyway. 'Your boy hasn't been here,' he said before eyeing Vinnie a second time. 'At least that I'm aware of anyway.'

As all eyes turned to look at Vinnie, he squirmed underneath their hard stares. 'What are you looking at me for? I haven't seen him. I've only just got here myself.'

'There's your answer,' Jason said. 'He hasn't been...' Suddenly, the words died in his throat. Vinnie may not have been at the casino, but Damien had. In that instant his mind began to reel and as he rubbed his hand across his jaw, he lifted his eyes to the ceiling and exhaled noisily. 'Get Damien on the blower,' he ordered Vinnie. 'Now.'

'Me?' Vinnie exclaimed. 'He's not gonna answer the phone to me. I'm not exactly his favourite person, am I.'

'And you think I am?' Jason snapped. 'Do as you're told and get him on the phone.'

'What's going on?' Jonny asked as he shot a glance towards Cameron and indicated for him to try calling Tommy Jr again.

Debating within himself just how much information he should divulge, Jason snatched the mobile phone out Vinnie's hand. 'Come on,' he growled as he brought the device up to his ear. 'Answer the fucking phone.'

'What's going on?' Jonny demanded a second time, concern clearly audible in his voice. 'Because I swear before fucking God if a single hair, just one single fucking hair,' he shouted, holding up a finger, 'has been harmed on my nephew's head then I'm going to tear this place apart,' he continued to roar as he motioned around him. 'Have you got that?'

Jason shook his head. 'No harm will come to him, or at least it shouldn't do.'

'What the fuck is that supposed to mean?' Cameron spat.

Still debating within himself exactly how much he should give away, Jason paused. He'd never been in the habit of telling tales, firmly of the belief that a grass was nothing more than a rat, the lowest of the low. Yet he couldn't help but imagine how he would feel if the shoe had been on the other foot and it had been Dylan on the missing list. He would have torn the Carters to pieces he knew that much. 'He could be on his way to Liverpool.'

'Do what?' Jonny yelled.

'My eldest son, Damien,' Jason hastily explained. 'He drove up there looking for answers. By all accounts, your boy,' he said, flicking his gaze towards Cameron, 'gave him some information. They've gone looking for Calvin Rivers.'

Jonny screwed up his face. 'I am going to seriously kill that little bastard when I get my hands on him,' he seethed, referring to Tommy Jr. Turning to look aimlessly around him, he rubbed at his temples. 'I can't believe this, I can't fucking believe it.' As he glanced down at his watch, his entire body bristled. 'Try him one last time,' he said, motioning down to the mobile phone in Cameron's hand.

Doing as he'd been asked, Cameron pressed redial and when the call rang off yet again, he shook his head. 'Still not picking up.'

'It's going to take us at least four hours to drive up to Liverpool.'

'If we're lucky. And they've got, what,' Cameron added as he too glanced at his watch, 'an hour or two on us.'

Giving a shake of his head, Jonny let out an irritated sigh. 'I take it that I won't need to tell you to put your foot down then.'

Cameron shook his head. 'What do you think,' he answered, pulling out his car keys.

Jonny heaved out a breath. The fact he'd spent the majority of his life acting as the family's getaway driver hung heavy in the air. 'Better still, let me drive,' he said, holding out his hand.

Without argument, Cameron handed over his car keys.

Unconsciously, Jason's hand slipped into his pocket, his fingers curling around his own set of car keys. The last thing Damien would want was for him to turn up unannounced and if truth be told, he didn't blame him. What would even be the point? His eldest son didn't need him and was more than capable of looking after himself, and then there was Carmen to think about. He rarely strayed too far away from her, too afraid of what she would get up to in his absence. She was nothing but skin and bone of late. The death of their youngest son had taken a toll on her already fragile body. What would happen if she were to lose a second son? In that instant, Jason's mind was made up and as he pulled out his keys, he nodded towards the exit. 'I'll be right behind you.'

If the Carters were surprised, they didn't show it, Jason

noted. And as the men made their way out of the casino, Vinnie clasped him on the shoulder.

'I'm coming with you.'

'No...' Jason began.

'I said I'm coming with you,' Vinnie reiterated.

Before Jason could open his mouth to protest, Vinnie flashed a cheeky grin. 'I'm interested to see what this Calvin Rivers has to say for himself,' he said before shooting a glance towards the poker tables.

Jason frowned and as he too turned to follow his nephew's gaze, he scowled at the sight of Gio sitting casually at one of the tables as though he didn't have a single care in the world.

'I'll wait for you outside.'

Turning his head, Jason nodded. By rights he should have informed Arthur of the unexpected turn of events and maybe once upon a time he would have done. But as of late, he and Arthur hadn't been as close. And the strange thing was he didn't know why. They hadn't argued or fallen out; it was more to do with the fact that they seemed to have become distant with one another. Perhaps their business ideas and goals had changed, or perhaps they had everything they needed and so were no longer thirsty for power in the way that they had been as young men.

After giving Gio one final glare, Jason followed on in his nephew's footsteps, oblivious to the fact that Gio had been intently watching the interaction and that before Jason had pulled away from the kerb, Arthur would have been made aware of his departure.

* * *

Tommy Jr shifted his weight. The car he was travelling in was by no means small but after almost four hours of sitting in the same position, his backside was beginning to feel numb.

'Do you even know where to find this Calvin geezer?' he asked, resting his forearms on his knees and leaning slightly forward.

Damien looked over his shoulder. 'He won't be hard to find, put it that way. He's a cocky cunt who thinks he's untouchable. He likes to show his face, likes people to see him. The prick thinks it makes him look all the more powerful.'

Tommy nodded. He'd come across similar men before. The type who liked to give it the big 'un in front of their pals. 'I take it you've met before then.'

'Yeah,' Damien answered as he gave Winston a sidelong glance. 'Let's just say we've had one or two run-ins over the years.'

Lifting his eyebrows, Tommy slumped back in the seat. How or why Dylan had become involved with someone like Calvin Rivers he had no idea. Surely he must have been aware of the bad blood between him and his brother. Clearing his throat, he looked between the two men. 'You said that Rivers was into some bad shit.'

'He is,' Winston answered.

'Like what?'

Damien gave a hard chuckle. 'You name it and the bastard has his grubby little fingers poking around in it. Drugs, protection rackets, pimping out women.' He screwed up his face. 'The bloke is pure scum.'

'Sounds like it,' Tommy mumbled. Sucking in his bottom lip, he stared out of the window for a few moments before finally turning his head again and speaking what was on his mind. 'Why would Dylan have involved himself with someone like that?'

As Damien fell silent, the atmosphere in the car became notably tense.

Eventually, Damien looked over his shoulder. 'That's exactly what I plan to find out,' he growled.

9

The moment Damien stepped foot across the threshold of The Admiral, in Kirkdale, Liverpool, his presence had been duly noted. It was a fairly small boozer, full of locals, and somewhat cliquey. The type of pub where strangers were not particularly welcome, or at least this was what he assumed if the punters' reactions were anything to go by. As he'd made his way inside, every single head had turned in his direction, their beady little eyes scrutinising the newcomers, more than likely looking for any signs of there being trouble on the horizon.

But there was only one pair of eyes Damien was interested in and he knew for a fact that Calvin Rivers had clocked his arrival. The silence that fell across the pub had been the first indication, that and then the whispers and knowing looks that followed.

Making a show of ordering their drinks, Damien leaned casually against the bar. Outwardly he appeared at ease, perhaps even friendly as he chatted amicably with the barmaid as she set to work pouring out their drinks. Inside, however, he was raging. There was nothing he wanted more than to steam across the pub and smash his fist into Rivers' smug face. Just the mere sight of the bastard was enough to make Damien's blood boil. Forcing himself to stay calm, he pocketed his change then lifted the glass up to his lips, swallowing down a large mouthful of the alcohol.

Beside him, Winston's large frame was tense, not that Damien was entirely surprised. It wasn't the first time they had come across Calvin Rivers. And this time around Damien wouldn't be leaving until he had the answers he craved, no matter what he had to do to get them. He was more than prepared to smash the entire pub to smithereens if needs be, Calvin Rivers and his scummy little pals included.

Once their drinks were finished, Damien placed his glass down on the bar and then took a deep breath, more so to remind himself not to entirely lose the plot than for any other reason. Finally, he shot Winston a look and as the two locked eyes, he jerked his head in the direction of Calvin, the movement so slight that many people would have missed it.

Taking the lead, Damien then began to weave his way through the pub and as a hush fell, people stepped out of his way, creating somewhat of a pathway. He could see the intrigue written across their faces, knowing for a fact that whatever was about to go down would be the main topic of conversation for the days and weeks to come.

As he neared closer, a large dog that he assumed was some kind of bull breed mixed with what looked like an Akita and which had previously been laying contentedly at Rivers' side sprang to its feet, its heckles raised and its teeth bared as it let out a low, menacing growl that resonated around the pub.

Warily, Damien kept one eye on the dog. All it would take was for Rivers to let go of the thick metal chain wrapped around his fist and then the dog would be set loose, and no doubt in a position to cause a great deal of damage. The dog had to weigh at least sixty kg, the majority of which was pure muscle, and judging by the size of both its canines and muscular jaw, he had a feeling the dog's teeth would easily be able to rip through flesh and bone.

To Damien's surprise, however, Calvin Rivers yanked the animal back, and as its growls soon turned to a low whine, the dog once again settled itself at his master's feet, resting its large, muscular head on the floor.

It was then that Calvin Rivers leaned back in his seat and gave them a grin wide enough to show off several gold teeth nestled towards the back of his mouth.

'I was wondering how long it would take for the replacements to show up.'

* * *

As Arthur Brennan chewed on the inside of his cheek, his forehead was furrowed.

Opposite him, Gio lounged back in the chair, his eyes sparkling with excitement. 'Didn't I tell you,' he said, speaking fast, 'that heads were gonna start to roll.'

The nerve at the side of Arthur's eye twitched and as he drummed his fingers on the desk, his mind began to reel. It was unlike Jason not to keep him informed, and considering they had been business partners for the best part of thirty years, it would be safe to say that he knew the man inside and out, or rather he knew exactly how his brain worked. As for the Carters, for what reason had they turned up, and more importantly, why had Jason and Vinnie left with them in such a hurry?

Sinking back into the seat, he steepled his fingers across his chest. 'Have you paid that bitch a visit yet?'

Gio's face paled. 'Not yet,' he admitted. 'Not since Dylan... I mean, to be honest I've been kind of avoiding the place. Even before Dylan was topped the house was like a morgue. It's too fucking big and too fucking quiet for my liking.' He gave an involuntary shudder. 'The place gives me the creeps.'

As Gio spoke, Arthur's eyes narrowed into slits.

'Well, don't you think you should?' he barked out. 'All it would take is one word from her and it'll be game fucking over for the both of us.'

A craftiness settled over Gio's face. 'You're not worried, are you?' he goaded with a smirk. 'Scared that someone will tell Jason exactly what his—'

Before Gio could finish the sentence, Arthur was out of his seat and rounding the desk. 'You never fucking learn, do you?' he snarled as he gripped hold of Gio's jaw and wrenched his head back so that he could look him in the eyes. 'You and that big trap of yours are pushing me to the limit and believe me, I've killed men for far less.'

Gio swallowed and as his Adam's apple bobbed up and down, fear began to get the better of him. 'I'm sorry,' he whimpered. 'I wasn't thinking.'

'You never fucking are,' Arthur roared, spraying Gio in spittle before roughly shoving him away from him. Straightening out his shirt, Arthur took a step back then ran his hand over his head, smoothing down his greying hair. 'Think of this as a warning,' he snarled, stabbing a stiff finger in Gio's direction. 'Your last warning.'

Shamefaced, Gio averted his gaze.

'We need to make sure that bitch Carmen keeps her mouth shut.' Wandering back around the desk, Arthur briefly paused before fishing a key from out of his pocket and then opening the desk drawer. Pulling out a small plastic bag, he tossed it onto the middle of the table. 'Give her that. And while you're there, remind her that there's plenty more where it came from.' He snorted out a laugh. 'With a bit of luck the bitch will end up killing herself, and not before fucking time either. The amount of shit the cunt has put into her body over the years I'm surprised she's even lasted this long.'

Gio eyed the bag and before he could reach down and grab it, Arthur grasped hold of his wrist. 'Make sure that you give it to her,' he added, gesturing towards the bag. 'And I mean all of it, Gio, are we clear on that?'

Still eyeing up the bag, a layer of cold sweat broke out across Gio's top lip, and snaking his tongue across his teeth, he nodded.

'Because if I'm capable of getting rid of one junkie,' Arthur said with a menacing grin as he none too gently tapped the side of Gio's face, 'then disposing of two will be a piece of piss.'

Taking the warning on board, Gio nodded again and as Arthur released his wrist, he snatched up the bag and stuffed it into his pocket.

'Oh, and one more thing,' Arthur said as he returned to his chair. 'Make sure that nosey old cunt Joanie isn't around when you hand over the goods. She's another one that's got a bit too much to say for herself.'

'Yeah, all right.' Gio nodded as he inched towards the door, keen to make his escape. 'I'll make sure that she's not around.'

Satisfied, Arthur sat down and as soon as Gio left the office, he rested his elbows on the desk, steepled his fingers together, and then chewed on the inside of his cheek. The fact Jason had left with the Carters concerned him far more than he'd been prepared to let on. Ever since Dylan's death, he'd sensed a change in Jason; it was to be expected, he supposed. He'd lost his son after all. Only he'd wrongly assumed that Jason would be fairly easily to influence, that with little to no effort he would be able to guide him in a different direction, hence why he'd suggested they take a visit to The Bull and have a word with Geordie John. Right from the start he'd known that John would remain tight lipped and other than let slip that Damien had paid the Carter family a visit, he'd said fuck all else. And as far as he was concerned, that should have been the end of it, a dead end. But what he hadn't banked on was for the Carters to turn up unannounced at the Casino, neither had he imagined that Jason would up and leave with them, at least not without informing him of where he was going first.

Irritation curled around his insides, and thumping his fist down on the desk, he slumped back in the chair and wearily rubbed at his eyes. He was losing control, a notion that was as new to him as it was alien. He needed to get a grip and fast, needed to take back his power, because if he didn't he had a sinking feeling that the empire he'd built from the ground up was going to topple down before his very eyes and once that happened, there would be no stopping the destruction that followed.

* * *

A look of confusion swept across Damien's face and, as he shot a glance towards Winston, he narrowed his eyes. Of all the things he'd been expecting, it would be safe to say that this wasn't one of them.

'When I heard the news it cut me like a dagger to my heart,' Calvin Rivers continued as he placed his fist on his chest, then brought it up to his lips before placing one finger in the air. 'He was like a brother to me and will be sadly missed.'

Damien's lips curled in disgust. 'What the fuck are you talking about?' he snapped.

Warily, Calvin eyed the three men. 'Dylan. He was a top lad.

One tough bastard.' He turned his head to look at his minions, his eyes gleaming with excitement as he retold a story. 'Do you remember the time he smashed that bastard's face down on the bar? There was blood and glass everywhere, claret pissing out of the prick.' He laughed as he used his hands to describe some sort of fountain. 'And your brother,' he continued, his chest puffed up with pride. 'Do you know what he did?'

Damien shook his head and as he glanced over his shoulder at the bar, he wasn't so sure he even wanted to know.

'The geezer was screaming, and bleeding out.' Calvin chuckled as though the entire story was hilarious to him. 'And Dylan, still covered in the geezer's claret, just calmly ordered himself another drink as though nothing had even happened.'

Nausea washed over Damien. This wasn't the brother he knew. Dylan hadn't been violent; fair enough, he hadn't been an angel either, but he'd never gone out of his way looking for trouble. There'd been a mistake; there had to be. A case of mistaken identity, perhaps. At a loss for words, Damien could only stare at Calvin, his mind numb.

'D.' After a few moments had passed, Winston cleared his throat, and with a rise of his eyebrows, he flicked his head in Calvin Rivers' direction.

As though brought back to reality, Damien shook his head. He'd barely heard anything else Calvin had said let alone allowed the impact of his words to register in his brain.

'And that's why I've been waiting.'

Damien narrowed his eyes. 'Waiting?' he repeated, having no idea as to what Calvin was actually talking about. 'For what?'

'For a replacement.' For the first time since their arrival, Calvin glanced warily between the three men. 'I mean, he said there'd be a replacement, that he'd send someone to take care of business.'

'Who did?'

Waving his hand dismissively, Calvin leaned back in the seat. 'What do you mean who?' He laughed. 'You know who.'

Damien's jaw was clenched so tight that he could feel the muscles across his neck flex. 'I asked you a question,' he growled.

The smile slid from Calvin's face and as he gripped onto the chain wrapped around his fist even tighter, he yanked the dog to a standing position. 'Stop fucking with me, man.'

'I'm being deadly fucking serious,' Damien continued to growl. 'Who told you there would be a replacement?'

As the two men eyed one another, the atmosphere around them became tense. No matter which way he looked at the situation, it was more than obvious to Damien that they were outnumbered. Not that this bothered him. If anything it only made him all the more determined to get his point across, to show Calvin Rivers that he wasn't the kind of man to back down.

'I'm going to ask you one more time,' he snarled, 'before I smash your fucking face in. Who told you that?'

And there it was, the smirk that Damien had been waiting for, and as Calvin waved his hand dismissively through the air, he took that as his cue to lunge ahead, his fists already curled into tight balls as he swung them forward, feeling nothing but satisfaction as they hit their intended target. Even the dog, barking and snarling as it fought to protect its master, did nothing to deter Damien. He'd been waiting for this moment for so long that he could barely feel the dog's teeth slicing into his flesh, could barely feel the pain as he himself began to bleed out. The only thing that mattered to him was that he obliterated Calvin Rivers. The man had been a thorn in his side for far too long and the fact he had dragged his brother, his dead brother might he add, into his sick game was more than enough of a reason to end his life.

Finally, after what felt like an age, he was being pulled away. And it wasn't until he heard his father's voice that he actually turned to see who it was that was holding him back.

'Fuck off,' Damien snarled as he fought to free himself.

The grip around his waist tightened. 'You're bleeding out,' Jason snapped back at him, although even to Damien's ears he could hear a sense of concern in his father's voice. It was so unfamiliar to him that for a moment or two he was taken aback.

It was then that he glanced down at his arm. His old man was right, he was bleeding out. Pulling out his shirt, he wrapped the material around his forearm, hoping it would stem the blood flowing from the puncture wounds.

'Do you want to tell me what the fuck is going on?' Jason asked, his voice low so that only Damien could hear.

Momentarily, Damien paused. And as he watched the scene before him unfold, he shrugged his father away from him. 'Fuck off, Dad.'

'Damien.' There was almost a pleading to Jason's voice. 'Don't do this.'

As he snorted out a laugh, Damien shook his head. 'Don't do what exactly?' he asked, squaring up to his father. 'Drop the fucking act, because believe me it's far too late to pretend you care now.' With those parting words, Damien stormed back out of the pub and it wasn't until he came to where he'd parked his car that he allowed his shoulders to slump. And as he pulled the shirt away from his arm to inspect the damage, he hissed at the sting. Yeah, it was bad all right, not that he'd expected anything else. The sheer size of the dog should have been enough to tell him that any damage caused would more than likely need hospital attention.

And then there was Dylan, his kid brother, the one who had looked up to him when they were younger and followed him around like a lost puppy. It couldn't be true, it just couldn't. Only at the back of his mind there was a niggling doubt. One that told him anything was possible. And Dylan had become a lot more secretive in recent years. If truth be told, they'd rarely ever hung out together. He couldn't even recall meeting any of his brother's friends, especially any he'd made since leaving school. Could it be that he'd never even known his brother?

'This is bollocks,' Winston shouted as he walked towards him, shaking out his fist as he did so. 'There ain't no way that Dylan was involved with that nutcase.' Pausing for breath, he glanced down at Damien's forearm. 'Do you need to go to hospital?'

'Nah.' As he too glanced down, Damien moved his wrist from side to side, ignoring the stab of pain that was so severe it was almost enough to make his eyes water. 'I'll be okay,' he lied. 'If it gets too much then I'll get it seen to.'

Winston nodded and as he looked over his shoulder in time to witness not only Jason and Vinnie but also Tommy Johnson and his family exit the pub, he sighed. 'How the fuck did your old man know exactly where to find us?'

'I dunno,' Damien lifted his eyebrows. How had his dad known where to find them?

'If I find out that Johnson kid had something to do with it I'm gonna muller the life out of him.'

'It wasn't him,' Damien groaned. 'The kid's all right. And he's no grass, I know that much. Think about it logically. We knew exactly where to find Rivers. He's hardly in the habit of making his whereabouts a secret, is he?'

'No, I suppose not,' Winston reluctantly agreed. Walking around the car, he paused before climbing onto the passenger seat. 'Are you sure you don't need to get that seen to?' he said, nodding towards Damien's arm. 'That mutt of Rivers' really went for you?'

Damien paused. As much as he had a feeling he might need one or two stitches, he shook his head. The last thing he wanted was to be sat in A&E all night, and then he'd have to explain how he came by the injuries, and no doubt some nosey old bastard would want to call in the filth to report a dog attack. 'Nah, I'll be all right.' Keen to change the subject, he lifted his eyebrows. 'What do you reckon the chances are of any of that lot in there calling the old bill?' he asked, referring to the pub's customers, all of whom had been witness to him hammering the life out of Calvin Rivers.

Winston chuckled. 'No chance at all. It's more than likely a daily occurrence, a bit of entertainment for the locals. And I bet it's not often they witness Calvin Rivers get a battering he won't forget in a hurry.'

'Probably not,' Damien muttered as he too climbed into the car.

'It was all bullshit. You know that, right?' Winston continued, his voice becoming serious. 'Dylan was a good kid.'

Damien turned his head. 'Was he?' he sighed. 'Because let's face it, Win, I can't help but wonder if there's a ring of truth to what Rivers said. Did either of us know Dylan? I mean, really know him. Did we actually know what was going on up here?' he said, tapping his forehead. 'Because I know for a fact that I didn't know what he was getting up to on a daily basis, and not once did it ever enter my head to keep tabs on him. I didn't think any of us needed to.'

As he thought the question through, Winston shook his head. 'Come on, D, you can't tell me you actually believe Rivers,' he asked with narrowed eyes. 'You know how much of a prick he is; he was trying to mess with your head and nothing more than that.'

Collapsing back in the seat, Damien rubbed at his eyes. 'I don't know what to believe,' he admitted. 'And to be honest with you, Win,' he sighed, 'if my brother was in front of me right now I'd happily throttle the life out of him for the shit he's caused.'

Winston narrowed his eyes. 'You don't mean that, man.'

For a moment Damien was quiet. Of course he didn't mean it. If his brother was in front of him he'd hug him so tight that he'd more than likely squeeze the life out of him. 'I miss him,' he said as he cleared his throat to rid himself of the hard ball there. 'And to answer your question, no, I don't believe Rivers. Dylan wasn't all bad; if he was I'd have known about it. We grew up together, for crying out loud. I would have seen the signs.'

'Exactly.' Slamming the car door closed, Winston pulled across his seatbelt then slid his hand into his pocket, pulling out a zoot. 'How about a quick smoke before we head off?' he asked, flashing a cheeky grin.

'Yeah, go on.' Damien grinned back. 'We might as well.' If nothing else, the cannabis might help to numb the pain radiating across his arm.

***

As the colour drained from Arthur Brennan's face, he sat forward in the chair, one hand clutching a mobile phone to his ear and the other massaging his temples. He should have guessed that this day would come. And if he hadn't been so arrogant, so cocksure of himself, then he would have known that the lies and deception he'd spun could only stay hidden for so long before the truth eventually came to light.

Abruptly, he ended the call and tossed the device onto the

desk. Calvin Rivers' irate screams down the phone were beginning to give him a headache. Dylan had never struck him as the type to tell tales or feel the need to boast about the business he was involved in. Neither had he been the kind of man to seek anyone's approval. He did exactly what he wanted regardless of whether or not his actions were deemed appropriate, or if they fit into society's expectations. He'd also had no qualms when it came to breaking the law and had in fact been fast on his way to making a name for himself when he'd been arrested and then subsequently handed down a ten-year prison sentence. All through the police interviews and then the court trial, Dylan had remained tight-lipped. And yet for some unknown reason as soon as he'd reached Pentonville Prison he'd begun to talk, whether it had been to impress someone or not Arthur didn't know, nor did he care to know for that matter. Dylan had meant nothing to him; in fact, he'd barely given him a second thought since his murder. Even the fact he'd watched him grow from a babe in arms to a man meant absolutely nothing. The only thing that did matter was that Dylan had said something, and it didn't take a genius to tell him that it was the Johnson kid he'd opened his mouth to. Why else would Damien have gone looking for Calvin Rivers? And if that wasn't enough, why would Jason and the Carters have then gone tearing after him?

Unease wrapped its way around Arthur's insides. Perhaps Damien was closer to learning the truth than he'd first thought. And if Damien was close then Jason wasn't too far behind him.

Snatching up the phone again, he began to scroll through his contact list. Gio, the useless prat that he was, needed to move, and fast. Carmen was one of his biggest concerns. She knew far too much for his liking and considering she'd been as high as a kite for the majority of her life, when it came to her kids she didn't miss a trick. She'd sensed a change in Dylan.

She'd even pleaded with him to see the error of his ways. Not that Dylan would have listened. Knowing him, he would have laughed in her face, and would have probably got a kick out of seeing her so distraught. Talk about loyalty. Dylan hadn't even known the meaning of the word. To him, family meant nothing. Even his dad, the man who'd raised him and taught him everything he knew, was considered fair game in Dylan's eyes.

Perhaps it had all come down to greed, although Arthur had a feeling it went a little deeper than that. Dylan hadn't only wanted his father's business; he'd wanted the power that came along with it too. And once he'd found a way to get rid of his father, who would have been next? Carmen, Damien, or maybe even Demi. And what did that mean for himself? He was Jason's business partner, and in the event of Jason's death he would still own 50 per cent of their business. It was inevitable that sooner rather than later he would find himself on Dylan's radar, and then before he knew it Dylan would have begun planning his murder too, just as he'd begun to plan out his own father's. And being the sadistic fucker that Dylan was, Arthur had a feeling his demise wouldn't have been pretty or for the faint-hearted.

Could anyone blame him for getting in first? It had to be better than looking over his shoulder morning, noon, and night for fear of his life. At the end of the day, it was a dog-eat-dog world. A case of only the strongest survive, or should that be the wisest? In the end, Dylan had to go. There was no two ways about it. He couldn't be trusted and it had been no lie when he'd told Gio that he'd witnessed Dylan smile just moments before thrusting a blade into someone's gut, because he had. He'd been as unpredictable as he was savage, a dangerous combination.

The call to Gio rang off and, pushing back his chair, Arthur wearily got to his feet. Gio was another problem. Like Carmen, he knew far too much, and if put under pressure Arthur had a sinking feeling that he'd become loose-lipped, and as the old saying went, loose lips sunk ships. Gio was hardly discreet as it was and had on more than one occasion attempted to blackmail him, even if he had then brushed it off as nothing more than a bit of banter. Well, banter or not, Arthur didn't take too kindly to being threatened, and like Dylan, Gio was about to find that out the hard way.

As he contemplated his latest problem, an idea sprang to Arthur's mind, and as a small smile tugged at his lips, he gave an incredulous shake of his head. The solution to his worries had been staring him in the face all along. At the best of times Gio was nothing more than an irritation, and Arthur knew for a fact that he grated heavily on Jason's nerves. So much so that on Demi's wedding day, Jason had tried his utmost to persuade her to reconsider her choice of groom, and had even offered her a large sum of cash not to show up at the church. Not that Demi had listened; she'd likened herself to being in love, much to Jason's disgust.

Lounging back on the seat, he lifted his head towards the ceiling and closed his eyes as calmness once again washed over him. Perhaps there was more than one way to skin a cat after all.

10

Tommy Jr had never been more livid, and as he stared at his uncle's back, he shook his head.

'Well, come on,' Jonny bellowed. 'I told you to get in the car.'

Tommy's lip curled up into a snarl. All thanks to Damien Vickers ditching him, he had no other choice but to get a lift back to London with his family. But that wasn't the main cause of his anger. The fact that his dad and uncle had even turned up was enough to make him want to scream obscenities at them. He wasn't a kid any more, and the quicker his family realised that fact the better it would be for all of them.

'Did you hear what I said?' Jonny continued to roar. 'Get in the fucking motor.'

'Or what?' Bounding forward, Tommy came to a halt just inches away from his great-uncle. 'Well, come on,' he hissed. 'Or fucking what?'

'Tommy...'

Tommy ignored his dad's warning. He'd never squared up to Jonny before; he'd been too afraid to do so if truth be told. Jonny Carter, along with the rest of his great-uncles, had reputations and not only had they once had promising boxing careers ahead of them, but it was also a well-known fact that they weren't in the habit of allowing others to mug them off.

'What did you just say to me?' Jonny growled.

'You heard what I said,' Tommy Jr answered, his face pale and his shoulder blades rigid. 'I'm not a kid any more and I won't have either of you telling me what I can or can't do.'

'Nah.' Jonny screwed up his face. 'Rewind a bit,' he said, taking a step even closer. 'Because I'm going to ask you one more time and only fucking once. What did you just say to me?'

Under normal circumstances it would have been the calmness in his uncle's voice that would have terrified Tommy all the more. But the days of him backing down were long gone. He'd watched someone he classed as a friend die. And if his uncle thought he would be able to intimidate him into towing the line then he had another thing coming. 'And I'm not going to ask you again,' Tommy hissed. 'Or fucking what?'

'Why don't we all calm down, eh,' Cameron pleaded as he came to stand between his son and uncle. 'Tempers are beginning to flare and that isn't going to get us anywhere.'

'Nah,' Tommy spat, shoving his dad out of his way. 'Let's have this out here and now. If you want to order the rest of them about,' he said, referring to his cousins, 'then fine, you do that, act the big man if that's what you need to do, but leave me the fuck out of it.'

'Tommy,' Cameron reiterated, his eyes wide. 'I said that's enough.'

'Enough?' Tommy gave a hard chuckle. 'I haven't even started yet.'

Jonny clenched his fists. 'No, it's all right,' he said, his eyes narrowed into slits. 'Let him say his piece before I batter the life out of him.'

'I don't think so,' Tommy answered, coming forward so that their noses were almost touching. 'You need to remember something,' he hissed, his voice low. 'I've got, what, twenty something years on you. Do you honestly think you'll be able to bounce me around this car park?' He laughed as he motioned around them. 'Leave it out! One punch and I'd send you to sleep before you even think about swinging for me.'

For the first time in his life, Jonny faltered. That wasn't to say that he was afraid, because he wasn't. Jonny, along with his brothers, had never been scared of anyone or anything. It was more the shock of his great-nephew's words that had made him hesitate. Standing his ground, Tommy Jr continued, his voice low and menacing. 'Let's get one thing straight. I'm Tommy Carter's grandson, not some fucking muppet off the street, and it's about time people acknowledged that fact. I'm no idiot, I know exactly what I'm doing. Dylan was my pal, and yeah, fair enough, I hadn't known him for very long, but I was still there to witness his murder. I was the one who heard his screams and I was the one who had his blood on my hands. And if I can help his family get justice for him then I'm more than prepared to do that, with or without your approval.'

For a long moment there was nothing but a strained silence as the three men stared at one another. Finally, Jonny sighed. 'You've made your point. Get in the motor,' he said as he jerked his head in the direction of the car.

Still not satisfied, Tommy Jr lifted his eyebrows.

Jonny sighed again. 'I said you've made your point. And I don't know about you but all I want to do is to get off home rather than stand here freezing my nuts off arguing over which one of us is going to iron the other one out first.'

Tommy gave a small laugh. In that instance he was more than aware that this was as much as Jonny was ever going to back down. Taking the olive branch offered to him, he opened the rear passenger door and climbed in, all the while taking note of the wary glance his father and uncle shared. It also didn't escape his notice that there had been a shift in power, however slight it may have been.

* * *

Demi Ferrari, as she was now known, was the image of her mother, Carmen. Standing at just five foot one, she was petite, with bright blue eyes and long blonde hair that framed a pretty face. Given her tiny stature, many would wrongly assume that Demi was the more docile of her siblings, until she opened her mouth that was. If nothing else, Demi was a straight talker who took no nonsense from anyone, which probably wasn't so unusual when you took into account who her father was.

Slipping her designer handbag off her shoulder and placing it on the kitchen island, Demi studied her mother. From as far back as she could remember, her mum had only been what could be described as delicate, so much so that it was hard to believe she'd once been considered a free spirit by those who knew her.

'Are you all right, Mum?'

Carmen snapped her head up, her shoulders becoming rigid and her movements jerky, reminding Demi of a small, frightened bird. 'Yes, why wouldn't I be?'

Demi sighed. The black rings underneath her mother's eyes told a very different story. 'Have you been sleeping well?'

Carmen waved her hand dismissively. 'So, so.'

A wave of frustration swept over Demi, not that she could say the feeling was anything new. As much as she loved her mum, there were days when she wanted nothing more than to take her by the shoulders and shake some life into her. She was still a relatively young woman and had only recently turned fifty and yet to look at her, at how thin and fragile she'd become in recent months, and at how far she had let herself go, it would be easy to assume she was a lot older. How her dad was unable to see just how far down his wife had sunk was beyond her. Surely he could see that she was nothing but skin and bone, and not only was her hair often greasy and lank but she had lost the sparkle in her eyes too. It was almost as though she'd given up on life.

'Have you eaten?'

In the process of lighting a cigarette, Carmen paused, a flash of annoyance sweeping over her face. 'What is this?' she barked out. 'Fifty questions?'

'I'm just worried about you,' Demi answered, her voice becoming gentle as she gave Joanie a surreptitious glance. 'You need to eat, Mum.'

'I do eat,' Carmen growled back. 'Tell her, will you,' she snapped at Joanie. 'Tell her what I had for dinner.'

Demi glanced towards Joanie again, who lifted her eyebrows in return, her lips pursed as she gave a slight shake of her head. It was the exact reaction Demi been expecting. Her mum may have been able to pull the wool over her father's eyes but with Joanie watching her every move the truth always came out in the end.

'Mum,' Demi sighed. 'You're going to end up making yourself ill. Is that what you're actually trying to achieve?'

Stubbing out her cigarette in an overflowing ashtray, Carmen bristled. 'I've eaten,' she hissed. 'How many more times do I need to tell you that.'

'And when was the last time you showered?'

'Oh, I see,' Carmen snapped. 'You and her,' she said, jerking her thumb in Joanie's direction. 'The pair of you ganging up on me. Did your father put you up to this?' she added as an afterthought. 'Did he send you over here just so you could spy on me?'

'Leave it out, Mum. I came because I wanted to see how you are. I'm worried about you and I know that Dylan wouldn't want to see you like this.'

On hearing her youngest son's name, Carmen flinched and in that instant, Demi's heart softened towards her. She couldn't ever imagine losing a child, let alone have to actually live through something so traumatic. 'I'm sorry,' she said, grasping her mother's free hand. 'But it's the truth, Mum. He wouldn't want this, it would break his heart.'

Carmen snatched her hand free, her expression so unreadable that for a moment it was as though Demi were looking at a stranger. 'I don't want to talk about your brother.'

'I know but...' Before she could finish the sentence, the doorbell rang.

'I'll get it,' Joanie said as she made her way past, stopping briefly to give Demi's shoulder a reassuring squeeze.

Moments later, Gio entered the kitchen, his strides long and his stance bordering on cocky, before he came to an abrupt halt, shock etched across his face. 'What are you doing here?'

'What do you think I'm doing here?' Demi snapped back. Narrowing her eyes, she stood back slightly to look at him. Gio had always had a shiftiness about him. When they had first started dating she'd likened it to him being mysterious. Talk about love being blind. There was nothing mysterious about him whatsoever; in fact, a more apt way to describe him would be sly, something she'd begun to increasingly notice about him. 'More to the point, Gio, what are you doing here?'

'What do you think?'

There was an arrogance about him too, Demi noted, one that she didn't particularly like very much. 'Funnily enough I don't know, which is exactly why I'm asking.'

Ignoring the question, Gio pulled out a stool and sat down. 'You all right, Carmen, girl?' He winked, his voice loud as he swiped an apple from the fruit bowl then proceeded to sink his teeth into it and chew noisily before using his thumb to wipe away a drop of apple juice from his chin.

He was far too over friendly with her mother too, Demi observed. Something her dad would go ballistic over if he were to ever witness the way Gio often spoke to Carmen. He'd view the interaction as a form of disrespect, and there was no one in the world, not even his children, who were able to disrespect his wife and live to tell the tale.

'Gio,' Demi said between gritted teeth. 'Answer the question. What are you doing here?'

Just as he'd been about to take another bite of the apple, Gio turned to look at his wife. The smile he'd put on for Carmen's benefit slid from his face. 'Your dad sent me.'

'What for?' Narrowing her eyes, Demi crossed her arms over her chest. Her dad wasn't in the habit of sending anyone to check up on her mum, and on the odd occasion that he did, it certainly wouldn't have been his son-in-law. After all, her dad had made his thoughts on her choice of husband well known, and as much as he may have tolerated Gio, he certainly didn't like him.

'I don't know.' He shrugged. 'Maybe he was too busy to come himself. I mean, it's not as though he sits on his arse doing sweet FA all day, is it. He does have a casino to run amongst other things,' he added with a knowing grin.

Demi nodded. At least that much was true. The casino was the equivalent of a goldmine and always busy, especially of an evening. And then there were her dad's other business interests to contend with, more so the illegal side of his business. As far back as she could remember, her dad had dabbled on the wrong side of the law, or at least this was what he'd told her. It was only as she'd grown older that she'd discovered her dad did a lot more than just dabble. Not only was he successful, respected by the criminal fraternity, and extremely wealthy, but he was also feared by those who knew him.

'Besides.' Gio smirked. 'If Dylan had still been alive then your old man would have sent him instead, wouldn't he.'

Demi's gaze snapped towards her mum. Dylan was already a sore subject and the last thing she wanted to do was upset her mum any more than was necessary. Although at some point her brother's death would need to be addressed. Surely it wasn't healthy to block out everything relating to him. 'Yeah, I suppose so.' Wearily, she pulled out another of the stools and hopped on.

The kitchen had always been the heart of her parents' home despite a grand sitting room, with several overly stuffed sofas and a large fireplace, complete with a thick plush carpet, situated directly next door. As children, her, her brothers, and cousin, Vinnie, had all congregated in the kitchen. They'd not only eaten their meals there but they had also completed their homework while sitting at the island, more often than not overseen by Joanie rather than their mum. Even back then Carmen had often been too spaced out to look after her children. Drugs had always been her number-one priority.

Sometimes Demi wondered why her parents had even bothered to have children, especially when they'd made it so abundantly clear that they had neither the time nor commitment to actually raise them. And yet despite all of this they had adored their mother, had worshipped the ground she walked on, and still did to a certain degree. As for their father, both she and

Dylan had been close to him. It was only Damien who, for whatever reason, seemingly despised him. And even now, all these years later, Demi wasn't so sure of the reason why.

Jason had been strict, but he'd never beat them and had taught them right from wrong and to respect others. Nowadays it was a different story altogether. Both Damien and their dad had swung for one another more times than she could count. The animosity between the two had become so heated, and was so deep-rooted, that they were unable to be civil to one another let alone spend any length of time in one another's company. Sometimes she wondered how or when it was all going to end.

'When are you going to get off home?'

Her thoughts broken, Demi looked up.

'I said it's getting a bit late,' Carmen repeated. 'When are you going home?'

Taken aback, Demi glanced at her watch. It had only just gone 9 p.m. 'Cheers for that, Mum,' she huffed. 'Talk about make me feel welcome. I've only just got here.'

Carmen rolled her eyes. 'Well, fancy turning up at this time of the bleeding night. You've had all day to come and see me.'

Refusing to be drawn into an argument, Demi hopped back off the stool and slipped the strap of her handbag over her shoulder. 'How about I give you a lift home,' she said to Joanie. 'I don't want you getting a bus this time of night.'

'I'll be all right, girl,' Joanie answered, waving her hand dismissively. 'I'm used to getting the bus.'

Demi lifted her eyebrows. 'I won't take no for an answer.' She smiled. 'Grab your coat and I'll take you home.'

Joanie hesitated and, as she glanced between Carmen and Gio, she sucked in her bottom lip.

'For God's sake,' Carmen barked out. 'What's the matter with you? Let her take you home.'

'As long as you're sure,' Joanie said as she began to gather her belongings.

'Of course I am,' Demi replied. Turning then to look at her husband, she motioned towards the kitchen door. 'Well, come on, don't just sit there. My mum isn't going to want to sit looking at you all night, is she.'

'She might do.' Gio smirked. 'Ain't that right?' he added, giving Carmen a wink.

'Gio,' Demi warned with a lift of her eyebrows.

'All right, keep your bleeding hair on,' Gio grumbled as he dropped the apple core onto the island then slid off the stool. 'I'm gonna use the khazi if that's okay with you,' he asked with a hint of sarcasm. 'And then I'll get off.'

'Yeah, all right,' Demi answered. 'But don't be too long.' Turning then, she kissed her mother on the cheek. 'We'll see ourselves out. Love you, Mum.'

'I'll see you in the morning, love,' Joanie chimed in as she heaved her handbag up onto her shoulder. 'And if you get a bit peckish there's some leftover chicken drumsticks in the fridge.'

As her right knee bobbed uncontrollably up and down, Carmen chewed impatiently on her thumbnail and nodded.

It wasn't until they were outside the house that Joanie turned to look at Demi. 'Do you not think you should wait for Gio?'

Demi screwed up her face. 'What for?' she called over her shoulder as she marched across the driveway to where she'd parked her car. 'He's a big boy. I'm sure he can find his own way out.'

Still unsure, Joanie glanced towards the front door before following on behind.

'Be honest with me,' Demi asked as she unlocked the car. 'How do you think she's doing?'

Joanie paused before answering, and as she looked up at the

house, she gave a small shrug. 'It can't help her being cooped up in this place all day. I can't remember the last time she actually ventured outside.'

'I think it was when we went to see Dylan in Pentonville,' Demi volunteered. 'I remember the day well. I had to virtually force her out of the car. She didn't want to budge. It's funny really,' she sighed. 'Her and Dylan had always been so close but on that day for whatever reason she didn't want to see him.'

'Well…' Choosing her words carefully, Joanie gave a shrug. 'You know what your mum is like. She isn't so keen on new environments, is she. They make her feel uneasy.'

'Yeah, maybe.' Unlocking the car, Demi paused. 'Do you fancy a drink?'

'Who, me?' Joanie asked, taken aback.

'Yes, you.' Demi chuckled. 'Who else do you think I'm talking to.'

'Well.' Joanie patted her grey hair into place. 'I've hardly got me glad rags on, have I.'

'And?'

'I don't know.' As Joanie's cheeks flushed red, there was a coyness about her. 'You don't want to be seen out with an old woman like me.'

Demi rolled her eyes. 'Get in,' she said, gesturing to the car. 'Because I don't know about you but I could do with a large glass of wine.'

Joanie beamed, her eyes twinkling. 'I wouldn't say no to a lager shandy.'

'Well, come on then.' Demi laughed. 'What are we waiting for?'

* * *

On hearing the front door close after his wife, Gio descended the stairs, one hand in his pocket toying with the polythene bag nestled there, the other resting casually on the winding banister rail. As much as he'd been telling the truth when he'd said that his in-laws' house gave him the creeps, he couldn't help but wonder how it must feel to own the vast property. Which one day he would. With Dylan gone, that only left Demi and Damien, and considering the relationship between Damien and Jason, he had a sneaky suspicion that Damien wouldn't figure in Jason's will, meaning that everything would be passed down to his wife – not only the house and the acres of grounds that it sat on, but also the casino and whatever else Jason had invested in over the years.

Barely able to contain his excitement, Gio rubbed his hands together. One day he was going to be rolling in it, or rather Demi would, but seeing as she was his wife, what was hers was his, that was his right. And he couldn't wait for the day when Carmen and Jason kicked the bucket. If truth be told it was the only reason he'd stuck around for so long.

From day one Demi had been nothing more than a means to an end. He'd known exactly who she was when he'd chatted her up, and as much as she may have been a stunner, the only thing that had interested him was gaining an in to her father's world. In truth, Demi was a little too independent for his liking. He liked his women to be pliable; to do exactly as he asked without question. In the beginning he'd thought that he might be able to mould Demi, and that with time she would learn to do his bidding, with the help of a backhander every now and then of course to show her exactly who was the boss in their marriage. But he'd not countered on just how feisty she was. The very moment he'd attempted to lay down the law she'd squared up to him, her eyes hard. But it had been her words that had chilled him to the very core, and he had more than just a sneaky suspicion that she'd meant every word she'd spat at him. He gave a small shiver, his lip curling into a snarl as he recalled the words she'd used. 'You've just made the biggest mistake of your life. Because believe me, Gio, from now on you'd best learn to sleep with one eye open. If you even think about laying a finger on me again then trust me when I say this, I will end you. You'd be surprised just how much damage can be caused by a tiny little nick here,' she'd said, pressing her thumb to the inside of his wrist. 'Or here,' she'd added lightly, tracing the length of the artery at the side of his neck.

Still, he reasoned there were some perks to being married to her. He was Jason Vicker's son-in-law and the amount of kudos that brought him was unbelievable. Rarely did he have to pay for a meal when out, and more often than not his drinks were bought for him. Above all else, he had respect. People wanted to be near him, especially the women, and the fact he wore a thin gold band on his wedding finger did nothing to deter them. If anything, it made them slip their knickers off even quicker. They all wanted a piece of him much more than his own wife ever had.

As much as Demi may have come across as a pampered princess with her designer handbags, manicured fingernails, and flashy outfits, she'd never been afraid to put her father or brothers in their place. Not only was she prepared to fight like a man, but she thought like one too and had a business acumen that at times made him both astounded and wary of her in equal measures.

As he entered the kitchen, there was a cockiness to Gio's swagger. Unlike her daughter, he had a feeling that Carmen would be like putty in his hands. She was so desperate for a fix that she was bound to do anything he asked her to, including dropping to her knees if that was what he wanted. Slipping his hand into his pocket, he pulled out the small polythene bag containing the crack and dangled it in front of his mother-in-law's face. Just as Carmen reached out for the bag, he pulled his arm back, his eyes gleaming with malice.

He loved toying with her, loved having a sense of power over the mighty Jason Vickers' wife. He was playing a dangerous game and was more than aware of that fact, and yet he couldn't bring himself to stop. He got a kick out of seeing her beg, and as he dangled the bag in front of her a second time, a ripple of elation shot through his veins. Dylan had been the one to introduce her to crack; before then she'd been more than content to shove pills down her throat on a daily basis, or guzzle down bottles of vodka. In his opinion, Dylan had been nothing short of a genius; he'd known exactly how to keep his mother under control and had taken the opportunity with both hands. As a result, Carmen had become so dependent on her son, or afraid of him, whichever way you wanted to look at it, that all Dylan had needed to do was threaten to tell his father about her crack addiction and she would have done whatever he asked of her.

'Please, Gio.'

There was a softness to Carmen's voice, and a vulnerability about her that pleased Gio no end. Gone was the agitated tone she'd used when speaking to her daughter or Joanie. It was as though she were his puppet, her eyes filled with longing and just enough desperation that made Gio want to laugh out loud. Of course he'd give her the bag, eventually. He had no other choice – Arthur had ordered him to do so – but until then, he could have a bit of fun.

As he smirked to himself, Gio's hand shot out and, wrapping a lock of Carmen's hair around his fist, he gave her a chilling grin before abruptly tightening his grip. Using his free hand to unzip his trousers, he then shoved her down on to her knees, ignoring the startled yelp that escaped from her lips as she desperately tried to recoil away from him, her feet slipping on the marble floor in her haste to stay upright. Yeah, he may be playing a dangerous game, but at the end of the day he wasn't the only one. Damien had been keeping a secret, a rather large secret, that if discovered was bound to ruin his reputation. He'd be known as a rat, or worse than that if it was even possible, a police informant. After all, what other possible reason could there be for him to engage in what looked to be an extremely cosy chat with the filth? And not just any filth, but his best mate's sister, nonetheless. He'd always had a feeling that Winston couldn't be trusted. How could he be when his own flesh and blood was a copper? Just how much information had he plied her with over the years, and how many arrests had been made all thanks to him opening that big trap of his? It was definitely food for thought.

A wicked smile made its way across Gio's face, and it took everything within his power not to rub his hands together again. Oh, this was going to be so good. He had the power to destroy each and every member of the Vickers family. As for Arthur Brennan, well, just maybe the old bastard wasn't quite as clever as he thought he was. In fact, he'd go as far as to say that Arthur had made a cock up of epic proportions. Although in all fairness he'd been right not to trust Dylan. Not only had he been unhinged, but he'd also not given a flying fuck about anyone, his own family included. Hence why he'd come up with the masterplan to kill his own father, and being the sick bastard he was, Dylan had wanted to be the one to personally do it. He'd even fantasised about how, each version of the deed becoming all the more gruesome.

And when it came to himself, they'd all underestimated him.

Not only Arthur but also Jason, Damien, Vinnie, Demi, even Dylan. They all treated him as though he were an imbecile, a joke, someone who was worthless. Well, little did they know that he was a lot more astute than they'd ever given him credit for. He'd been biding his time, waiting for the right moment to bring them all down. It was exactly what they deserved, their comeuppance for treating him like he was some kind of mug. At the end of the day, none of them were squeaky clean, not even his wife, and yet the way she carried on anyone would think that she'd never put a foot wrong in her life.

Shoving Carmen away from him, he kissed his teeth, then tucked in his shirt before zipping up his trousers. She was a mess. Her eyes were red-rimmed, and her mascara streaked across her cheeks from the silent tears she'd wept. Taking out his mobile phone, he aimed the camera towards her, feeling nothing but glee as she held up a hand in an attempt to hide herself.

'Look at you,' he snarled as he dug his hand into his pocket and pulled out the polythene bag containing the crack. 'You're a fucking state, a disgrace, a dirty skank.' His expression twisted with hatred, he tipped out a couple of the rocks, stuffed them deep into his pocket then tossed the bag on top of her. 'No wonder your own son couldn't stand the sight of you.'

With those parting words, Gio walked out of the house to the sound of Carmen's sobs echoing through the air behind him.

11

Settled at a table, Joanie took a sip of her drink. 'Oh, I needed this,' she said, smacking her lips together.

Demi nodded. 'Tell me about it,' she agreed.

About to take a second sip, Joanie paused and, tilting her head to the side, her forehead was furrowed. 'How's everything with you?'

Giving a shrug, Demi sighed. 'Exactly how you'd expect I suppose. It's been a tough few weeks.'

'Yeah, it has.' Placing her glass on the table, Joanie leaned back slightly and crossed her arms over her chest. 'But that wasn't what I meant.'

Demi frowned.

'You know what I'm talking about,' Joanie continued. 'You're not daft. You and Gio. I know it's none of my business but I could sense some tension between the two of you. Is everything okay?'

Briefly, Demi looked away before lifting her shoulders again. 'You know what it's like. We live together, work together, we're bound to drive one another around the bend at times.'

'Yeah,' Joanie agreed. 'And I'd believe it if that were the case,' she added. 'But I know you too well and I can tell you're not happy, darling, not really, not deep down in here,' she said, placing her hand on her chest.

Demi laughed the comment off. 'Show me a married couple who are happy.'

Joanie lifted her eyebrows. 'Me and my Alan were. May God rest his soul. Thirty years married and barely a cross word between us.'

The smile slid from Demi's face. 'Like I said, it's just been a tough few weeks,' she reiterated. 'My mind has been all over the place what with Dylan and everything.'

Joanie nodded. She knew when to let the subject drop. Even when she'd been a little girl Demi could be a stubborn mare when the mood took her, and Joanie knew from experience that it was better to sit it out and wait for Demi to talk when she was good and ready rather than push her. Taking a sip of her drink, she hastily swallowed the liquid down, her eyes widening. 'Is that Natasha?'

Demi turned her head. 'Tash,' she called out. 'Over here.'

Moments later, Natasha Baptiste joined them at the table, her smile wide as she took a seat.

'What are you doing here?' Demi asked.

Natasha nodded across the pub. 'One of my colleagues is having a leaving do. I've only popped in for a couple of drinks just to show my face.'

An awkward silence followed and as Joanie glanced in the direction of Natasha's colleagues, she pursed her lips. It still made no sense to her why a nice girl like Natasha would want to join the police force. Maybe she was getting old, that was the trouble. Girls nowadays were all about having careers. Back in her day you worked to keep a roof over your head and put food on the table and nothing more than that. And for those who had

had aspirations of mapping out a career of sorts, they'd chosen to become hairdressers, secretaries, nurses, or teachers. Certainly not coppers.

As Natasha cleared her throat, her expression became solemn. 'How's your mum doing?'

Demi's shoulders tensed. 'Exactly how you'd expect,' she answered with a lift of her eyebrows. 'And I know for a fact she'd be a lot better if your lot took their fingers out of their arses for once and actually solved my brother's murder.'

'Demi...' Natasha began.

'No,' Demi snapped back. 'I don't want to hear any excuses. I'm sorry, Tash,' she said, holding up a hand. 'I know it's not your fault but surely you can see where I'm coming from. If it had been Winston...'

'I get it,' Natasha interrupted, reaching out to clasp hold of Demi's hand.

'Do you?' Demi retorted.

Natasha nodded. 'Look,' she said, lowering her voice as she glanced towards her colleagues. 'It's like I told Damien. Sometimes things are going on behind the scenes that you're not aware of. Investigations take time, we need evidence, it's not always as straight forward as you might think, and there are protocols to follow, sometimes even an enquiry...'

Demi narrowed her eyes. 'When did you speak to my brother?'

For a moment Natasha appeared flustered. 'I don't remember exactly,' she said, waving her hand dismissively, her cheeks reddening. 'A few days ago, I think.'

Joanie narrowed her eyes and as Demi fell silent beside her, she continued to study Natasha. It hadn't escaped her notice how cagey she'd become. Perhaps Natasha knew a lot more than she was letting on, or maybe... Sinking back in the seat, she went over the conversation in her mind. It wouldn't have been entirely unusual for Damien and Natasha to have been in contact. It wasn't as though they were strangers. Being Winston's sister, she'd known Damien since her childhood. Only the moment Damien's name had been mentioned, Natasha had become somewhat nervous, as though she were trying her utmost to hide something from them.

Her mind working overtime, Joanie continued to sip at her drink. She was no fool; she'd worked for the Vickers family for the best part of thirty years and knew that Jason hadn't earned his vast fortune by merely running a casino. No, Jason had taken part in more than his fair share of illegal activities, Damien too. And she knew that because Damien had once asked her to stash away a holdall filled to the brim with cash. And that was without the blood she'd often washed out of his shirts whenever he'd been out fighting. Of course he'd only been young then, eighteen at the most. In recent years she had no idea what he'd been getting up to, but judging by the fact he'd bought his house outright and that he drove about in a flashy motor, it would be safe to say he was doing all right for himself, no matter how he may have come by the money.

The burning question, though, was whether or not Natasha was aware of how her brother and Damien earned a living. And if she was then what did she plan to do with that information? After all, Natasha was a copper and it was a well-known fact that they were never off duty. Wasn't there even some laws or guidelines in place that stated they had to be prepared to arrest their own family members if needs be?

Unease snaked its way around Joanie's insides, and as she gave an involuntary shiver, she gulped down the remainder of her drink. She was only grateful that Demi hadn't picked up on Natasha's vagueness too because the last thing either of them needed was for Demi to have an actual reason to kick off, which no doubt she would. She'd always been protective over her brothers, and who could blame her? Growing up, all they'd had was one another, and as a result they'd been closer than most siblings. All in all, if it hadn't been for herself making sure that their meals were cooked and their clothes were freshly washed and pressed, they would have been left to fend for themselves.

She'd have a word with Damien, she decided. After all, it didn't hurt to be on your guard especially where the police were concerned. And as much as she may have liked Natasha, there was a niggling doubt at the back of her mind, something she couldn't quite put her finger on. Whatever it was, she didn't like it. All she could do was hope and pray that her instincts were wrong because the family were already at breaking point and one more incident could well and truly push them over the edge.

* * *

Underneath a jet of steaming water that was so hot it was almost at boiling point, Carmen scrubbed at her skin. She'd already brushed her teeth so vigorously that she'd drawn blood. And yet she couldn't bring herself to stop scrubbing. She felt dirty, used. Tears sprang to her eyes and as she continued dragging a rough loofah over her arms and torso, she allowed the tears to fall freely onto her cheeks. Her skin was red raw, and yet she could barely feel the pain. She needed to erase the memory of Gio's hands upon her.

Eventually, she collapsed back against the tiles. Dropping the loofah, she looked down at her body. She could still smell Gio; his scent was ingrained upon her. Until now she'd never noticed just how pungent it was – cheap aftershave mixed with fresh sweat, and a hint of cannabis. A wave of nausea washed over her, and with one hand covering her mouth, she darted out of the shower and dropped to her knees in front of the toilet.

Heaving, she emptied the contents of her stomach and it wasn't until she was spent that she finally sank back on her haunches and allowed herself to gulp down large lungfuls of air. Gooseflesh covered her skin, and wrapping her arms around herself, Carmen got to her feet, her teeth chattering as she began to shiver uncontrollably.

For a few moments she stood stock-still before reaching out for a towel and covering herself with it. She stared at herself in the large mirror above the sink, her hands trembling as she scrutinised every inch of her appearance. Fear began to engulf her. Jason would kill for her – he already had in the past – and if he were to ever find out about what Gio had done, then son-in-law or no son-in-law, Jason would tear him apart limb from limb. And then what would become of them? Would her daughter blame her for the death of her husband? Would her remaining son spiral out of control if he was to learn about what she had been subjected to? And finally, Jason – would he look at her differently? Would he think of her as soiled goods?

Perhaps she should have stood up to Gio, only her need for a fix had won out, as it always did. Her gaze fell to the pile of clothes that she had torn off in her haste to climb into the shower and scrub away every lingering trace of her son-in-law. She stumbled from the ensuite bathroom, feeling both dazed and confused. Until now, Gio had never laid a hand on her. He'd been cruel, yes, but no more than her own son, Dylan, had been.

She gave another shiver, then, shrugging off the towel, she climbed into bed, not giving one iota that her hair was still wet. The cool Egyptian cotton sheets were like a balm against her scalded, sore skin, and as she lay on her side, she brought her knees up to her chest and squeezed her eyes shut tight, praying for sleep to take her. At least then she wouldn't be forced to relive the scenes that had taken place, neither would she be tempted to crack open a fresh bottle of vodka in a bid to block out the assault she'd endured. Not once had she given Gio any indication that she was prepared to hand out sexual favours. She was a married woman, and as much as he may have driven her crazy at times, she loved her husband. Jason had been there by her side through thick and thin. He was her rock. He'd stood by her when so many other men would have given up and walked away.

Fresh tears sprang to her eyes and, swiping them away, she let out a ragged breath. Jason must never find out, not ever. She would rather kill then allow her husband to discover something so despicable, so heinous. A newfound determination swept over her. She'd never had anything to fight for before. Oh, she had her kids, of course, but they'd never needed her, not really, not when they'd had Joanie to take care of them. The most she'd done was waltz in and out of their day, more often than not with a glass of alcohol in one hand and a cigarette or a spliff in the other. Huge chunks of their childhoods were missing from her memory, and she could barely recall their birthdays, Christmases, or when they'd lost their first teeth and she'd been supposed to leave a coin under the pillow for the tooth fairy. The only stark memories she had was craving her next fix and shooing the children away from her so that she could get high in peace. In that instant, shame engulfed her and as a lone tear slipped down her cheek, she gently patted it dry. Was it any wonder that Dylan had despised her? Because she was under no illusions that this had been the case. He'd told her so to her face enough times, but it had been his actions that had truly confirmed his hatred. She had been so afraid of him, her own son. She'd birthed him and yet he'd become nothing more than a stranger to her. He'd not only been cruel, but he'd also been devious and had played games with her mind to the extent that she'd often wondered if she were actually going crazy. But worse of all had been the threats. Every day she had lived in fear, terrified that Dylan would actually tell his father about the crack that he himself had introduced her to.

As she placed her hands over her face, Carmen's cheeks flushed red, the humiliation all too real. If only she'd said no, if only she'd put Dylan in his place from the get-go. Hindsight was a wonderful thing. If she could turn back the clock, she would do things very differently. She would never have allowed her son to have the upper hand, that was for sure; neither would she have taken the crack pipe and brought it up to her lips no matter just how tempted or curious she may have been.

Turning on to her back, she stared up at the ceiling. She wouldn't allow Gio to destroy what was left of her life. She would rather die than give him the opportunity to place his hands on her a second time. Her mind made up, she turned back on to her side and resumed her position. One way or another Gio had to go, there were no two ways about it.

* * *

With one hand on the steering wheel, Jason used his free hand to rub at his eyes. He would never have admitted it out loud, but he was beginning to wonder if maybe he was too old to be traipsing up and down the country, at least not without taking a lengthy break in between trips.

Beside him in the passenger seat, Vinnie turned his head. 'Are you sure you don't want me to take over?' he asked, nodding towards the steering wheel.

As tired as he was, Jason shook his head. What would even be the point? He'd come this far and with only fifty or so miles to go before reaching London, he may as well soldier on.

'Do you want me to drop you off home?' he asked as he reached down for the cup filled with coffee that he'd picked up at a service station.

Stifling a yawn, Vinnie shrugged. 'Yeah, you can do, or I could crash at yours. I'm easy.'

Jason nodded. It would probably make more sense for Vinnie to stay over, seeing as his house was nearer and that he had plenty of guestrooms. Taking a sip of his coffee, he grimaced. Not only was it lukewarm but it was also bitter. It had cost him an arm and a leg too. Daylight robbery as far as he was concerned, and he'd told the cashier as much too. A spotty teenager who'd looked bored out of his nut. Not that the kid had argued the case. He'd simply shrugged and called out 'Next', leaving Jason to silently seethe and shoot daggers at him.

At the sound of Vinnie clearing his throat several times, Jason gave his nephew a sidelong glance. 'You okay?'

'Yeah,' Vinnie answered as he shifted his weight before kicking out his legs. 'I was just...' Clamping his lips together, he shrugged again. 'Nah, don't worry about it,' he said, waving it off. 'It doesn't matter.'

Jason's forehead was furrowed. 'No. Come on, out with it. What's up?'

Vinnie was quiet for a few moments. 'I was just...' Snaking his tongue across his top lip, he shrugged again, clearly stalling for time.

'For fuck's sake, Vin,' Jason barked out. 'Will you just spit it out. I'm really not in the mood for playing guessing games right now.'

Lifting his eyebrows, Vinnie inhaled a breath. 'I was just

thinking about my mum and dad, that's all,' he answered, turning to look at his uncle.

As he too fell silent, Jason rubbed his hand over his jaw. 'Yeah, well...' He gave a slight shake of his head. 'I mean...' Looking up at the rearview mirror, he desperately tried to find the right words. 'It's only natural that you'd think about them. They were your parents.'

'Yeah.' As Vinnie turned to look out of the window, an uncomfortable silence followed until Jason finally followed suit and also cleared his throat.

'They thought you were dead too, did you know that?'

Snapping his head around, Vinnie narrowed his eyes. 'No.'

'Yeah,' Jason continued. 'They found you in the footwell behind the front passenger seat. It's a miracle that you even survived the crash let alone come out of something like that with barely a scratch on you.'

Vinnie gave a hollow laugh. 'I was a tough kid.' As soon as the words left his mouth, he glanced away, his smile instantly fading. 'I don't remember.'

'You wouldn't do,' Jason answered as he flicked the indicator before switching lanes. 'They reckon you must have been asleep at the time of the accident. They said it explained how you survived with nothing more than a few minor injuries. Something or other about the muscles being relaxed. I don't know.' He shrugged. 'Whatever the reason I'm thankful for it.'

Swallowing deeply, Vinnie shook his head. 'I meant that I don't remember them. My mum and dad.'

At a loss for words, Jason momentarily took his eyes off the road. Never had it crossed his mind that his nephew may not remember his parents. Admittedly, Vinnie had only been young at the time of the accident. He'd barely turned three when the crash had taken place. But even so he'd always assumed that

Vinnie was able to recall something, whether it be a vague memory or perhaps the sound of his parents' voices.

'And you never talk about them,' Vinnie continued. 'No one does.'

'No.' And it was true, he didn't. He'd spent so many years being angry with his brother, and not only because he'd died in such a careless and avoidable way. But because he'd also had his wife and son in the motor with him when he'd decided to get behind the wheel of a car pissed out of his nut. It had been so out of character for Colin to drink and drive. He rarely drank if truth be told. He was very much like himself in that respect. The two of them had preferred to keep their wits about them when they were out and about. But for some unexplainable reason, that night Colin had been well over the drink-drive limit. He'd ended up losing control of the car and crashing head-first into a tree, killing both himself and his wife on impact.

'But I remember once, I was only a kid, probably about eight or nine,' Vinnie continued, 'and you said that I'd been the apple of my dad's eye.'

'You were,' Jason agreed. 'He was chuffed to fucking bits when you were born.'

For a moment or two, Vinnie fell silent again. 'So then why the fuck would he have done what he did?'

As he thought through the answer, Jason stared straight ahead of him. What was he supposed to say? He himself didn't have the answers, and Colin had been his brother. 'I wish I knew what to say,' he said, giving Vinnie a sad smile. 'But I don't. At the time I'd been adamant that the old bill had made a cock-up. Your dad idolised both you and your mum, and I know for a fact that he would never have put either of you in unnecessary danger.' Gripping onto the steering wheel, Jason sighed. 'But you can't argue with the evidence and it was there in black and white. Your dad was more than three times over the drink-drive limit.'

Vinnie sucked in a breath.

'I'm sorry, mate,' Jason added as he patted Vinnie's shoulder. 'I'd give anything for things to have been different.'

'Yeah,' Vinnie mumbled back. 'So would I.'

As Vinnie went back to looking out of the window, Jason turned onto the tree-lined avenue where his house was situated. And after giving his nephew one final weary glance, he eased his foot off the accelerator and pulled on to his driveway.

The house was lit up, as it always was of an evening regardless of whether or not they were home. The electricity bills were through the roof but compared to the reassurance he was given, it was a small price to pay.

Moments later he was exiting the car, striding across the driveway and then letting himself into the house. Stuffing his car keys into his pocket, Jason gestured around him. 'You know where everything is. Help yourself to whatever you want.'

Vinnie gave a yawn. 'I'll probably head straight to bed.'

Jason nodded and, pausing at the bottom of the stairs, he jerked his head towards the ceiling. 'Well, you know where your old room is.' Halfway up the stairs, he came to a halt and looked over his shoulder. 'And Vin?'

'Yeah?' Vinnie answered.

'I know it's not quite the same, but no matter what, I've always treated you as though you were one of my own.'

'Yeah.' Vinnie swallowed deeply. 'I know that.'

Jason nodded. 'That's good to know.' And he meant it too. As angry as he may have been with Colin, he owed it to his elder brother to make sure that his only child was well cared for. Making his way into the bedroom, Jason paused at the threshold. In the dim light he could just about make out the outline of his wife's body. He gave a soft smile then began to undress, tossing his clothes onto a chair before stepping over the pile of clothes Carmen had discarded on the floor. Careful not to disturb her, he slipped underneath the covers and snuggled in closer, his hand automatically curling around her body. As his fingers skimmed over her stomach, his forehead furrowed, and he fought the urge not to recoil. She was nothing but skin and bone. He'd already known that she'd lost weight, but it wasn't until now that he'd come to realise just how much. Her hip bones were protruding and her stomach caved in on itself. In that instant, Jason wanted to jump out of the bed and shake her awake, to demand answers from her for once and for all.

Perhaps he'd become lack when it came to watching over her. Before Dylan's murder he'd watched her every move like a hawk, or at least he'd tried to. Of course there were long periods throughout the day when he was unable to physically be near her, hence why he paid Joanie to come over and oversee the house. She'd been his eyes for the best part of thirty years and knew Carmen almost as well as he himself did. So, where exactly had it all gone wrong? How had his wife managed to get herself into such a state without at least one of them noticing the extent of her weight loss?

Against his better judgement, Jason decided to let Carmen sleep. He'd speak to her in the morning, he decided once he'd calmed down a bit. If he woke her now he'd only lose his temper with her, and that was the last thing he wanted to do, especially when he took into account just how delicate she was.

* * *

The next morning, Vinnie woke with a start and, bolting upright, he looked around him, feeling momentarily disorientated. For a few moments there was nothing but an eerie silence, then the sound of his uncle's irate shouts echoing through the house.

Jumping out of bed, he pulled a T-shirt over his head then made his way out of his childhood bedroom and across the landing. Outside his aunt and uncle's bedroom, he paused, one hand suspended in the air, ready to knock on the door.

The sound of something being thrown against the wall was all it took for Vinnie to throw caution to the wind and shove open the bedroom door, his eyes immediately becoming wide as he took in the scene.

His aunt and uncle's bedroom was in a state of disarray. The duvet a crumpled heap on the floor. The dressing table upturned, and his aunt's expensive perfume bottles scattered around the room. But what shocked him even more was the state of his aunt. Carmen was huddled in the corner with a bedsheet wrapped around her, her eyes red-rimmed, her expression one of absolute terror.

'What the fuck is going on?'

Jason turned his head, his lips curled into a snarl.

It was then that Vinnie saw the crack pipe that his uncle was holding, and as his eyes grew even wider, he snapped his gaze in Carmen's direction. 'Jesus fucking Christ,' he groaned before shaking his head and pinching the bridge of his nose. On top of everything else that was going on, this was the last thing any of them needed.

12

Jason and Vinnie weren't the only ones to have received a shock. Joanie too had been on a mission of sorts and as she made her way down Damien's pathway, she couldn't help but smile. He'd done all right for himself, that much was evident. As a sense of pride engulfed her, she patted down her hair then knocked on the front door.

Moments later, the door was opened and, lifting her eyebrows, she shook her head. 'You do realise what time it is?'

Damien was dressed in just a long-sleeved T-shirt, a pair of boxer shorts, his hair tousled as though he'd only just crawled out of bed, and a look of confusion creased his face.

'It's gone nine,' she said, glancing down at her watch for confirmation. 'Shouldn't you be up and about by now? Because I know for a fact that I didn't bring you up to be a lazy bastard.'

Looking over his shoulder, Damien stepped out of the house, gently closing the front door behind him. 'What are you doing here?' he asked, glancing from Joanie to the pathway.

'What do you think I'm doing here?' Joanie snapped back at him with a roll of her eyes. There was a hint of unease in his voice, she noted, as though he'd been caught out. It reminded of her of when he'd been a child and she'd caught him with his hand in the cookie jar. 'I wanted to have a word.' Pushing past him, she was still shaking her head as she shoved open the front door and entered the house. Almost immediately, she came to an abrupt halt, her mouth falling open as she looked Natasha up and down, her eyes widening as she took in her state of undress. 'What the bloody hell is going on here?' she asked, averting her gaze while Natasha hastily pulled on her clothes.

As Damien rubbed at the back of his neck, his cheeks were red. 'What do you think?'

Joanie snapped her head around. 'Don't you get smart with me,' she scolded, pulling herself up to her full height and placing her hands on her hips. 'I used to change your shitty nappies, so do yourself a favour and show me a bit of respect, because believe me, you're not too old for a slap.'

As his cheeks flushed even redder, Damien gave Natasha a coy glance.

Noting that her words had had the desired effect, Joanie continued. 'Now, I asked you a question. What the hell is going on here? And as for you,' she added, directing her hard stare towards Natasha, 'does your brother know you're here?'

Natasha glanced towards Damien before answering. 'I'm not a child, Joanie,' she answered gently. 'I'm allowed to see who I want with or without Winston's permission.'

'Is that so.' Joanie pursed her lips. 'So he's aware then, is he? About this, I mean,' she said, wagging her finger between them.

As Damien gave her a sheepish look, Joanie crossed her arms over her chest. 'No, I didn't think so,' she said, shaking her head. 'What the bleedin' hell is wrong with you, eh? He's your best mate and this is how you repay him, by shagging his sister.'

'Jesus Christ,' Damien groaned. 'That's one way of putting it.'

'What other way is there?' Joanie bristled. 'I knew you were acting bloody shifty last night.' Joanie continued motioning towards Natasha. 'As soon as his name was mentioned,' she said, jerking her thumb in Damien's direction, 'you started stuttering and muttering. And that's another thing,' she turned now to look at Damien, 'you do realise she's one of that lot, don't you?'

Both Damien and Natasha shared a glance.

Joanie threw her arms up into the air. 'She's a copper. They'd arrest their own bleedin' mothers if they had to.'

'Leave it out.' Slumping onto the sofa, Damien rubbed his hand over his face. 'No one is going to be arresting anyone. Tasha knows the score, and,' he said, glancing towards his girlfriend, 'as long as we're careful, and as long as neither of us brings our work home with us, then there won't be an issue.'

'Then you're bloody naïve, that's what you are, the pair of you.' As she too slumped down on the sofa, Joanie sighed. 'I've never taken you for a fool, but right now,' she said, shaking her head, 'I'm seriously beginning to wonder. And what about Winston, eh?' she said, placing her hand on Damien's arm. 'What's he going to think about this...'

The hiss that escaped from Damien's lips made Joanie reel back in horror, the words dying in her throat. 'What's the matter?' she all but screamed at him.

'Nothing.' Jumping up, Damien turned his back to them, screwed his eyes shut tight and clamped his lips together. 'It's nothing, okay?' he finally answered.

Wide-eyed, Joanie glanced towards Natasha and, seeing a look of concern in her eyes, she slowly got to her feet.

'Damien...'

'I said it's nothing,' Damien snapped.

'Doesn't look like nothing,' Joanie answered, nodding towards his arm.

For a moment Damien was quiet, as though he were debating how much he should divulge. 'I said it's—'

'Yeah, I heard what you said,' Joanie interrupted. 'Now stop with the bullshit and tell me what's going on.'

As he took a deep breath, Damien's shoulders slumped, and he inched up his sleeve, letting out another hiss.

A look of horror creased Joanie's face. 'What on earth is this?' she shrieked as she inspected what looked to her untrained eyes to be puncture wounds.

'That looks like a dog bite,' Natasha remarked as she too took a closer look.

Damien nodded. 'Yeah, it is. And it was a big fucker an' all.'

'You need to get that seen to,' Joanie gasped. 'You might need a tetanus jab.'

Yanking down his sleeve, Damien shrugged. 'I'll see how it goes.'

'You're one stubborn bugger.' Placing her hands on her hips, Joanie lifted her eyebrows. 'What are you waiting for... your arm to fall bleedin' off? Or how about wait until it turns septic and you have green pus oozing out of it?'

'Leave it out,' Damien groaned. 'I said I'll see how it goes.'

Just as Joanie was about to argue the case, her mobile phone began to ring. 'It's your father,' she said with a frown.

Moments later, she pulled the device away from her ear and as Jason continued to bellow down the phone, her face paled.

Damien's gaze snapped from Joanie's face to the phone clutched in her hand. 'What's going on?'

Joanie shook her head. She suddenly didn't feel very well, and as she placed her hand on her chest, the room began to swim. How on earth had Jason discovered that his wife had a crack addiction? If nothing else, Carmen was discreet. She'd never left the crack pipe laying around; it was always well hidden, more often than not in the pocket of whichever outfit she had chosen to wear that day.

Coming forward, Natasha guided Joanie back onto the sofa. 'Get her some water.'

Shaking her head again, Joanie brought her hand up to her face, taking note of how clammy her skin was. She didn't need water, nor anything else for that matter. If anything, she was afraid, not so much for herself but for Carmen.

'I need to go.' Clambering to her feet, Joanie headed for the front door.

'Joanie,' Damien called after her. 'What's going on?'

When he received no reply he turned to look at Natasha.

'Go after her,' she mouthed.

Damien glanced down at his boxer shorts, then, bolting for the stairs in order to get dressed, he shouted over his shoulder, 'If anything's happened to my mum I'm gonna go absolutely garrity.'

* * *

Jason's heart was pounding. He'd always known that his Carmen was a troubled soul but not for a single second had he believed that she could stoop so low. When it came to the booze and the weed he'd turned a blind eye. In his mind it had been a lot better than the sniff or pills that she'd once favoured. But crack... now that was a whole different ball game, something he could neither accept nor turn a blind eye too. Crack was for the real junkies, the ones you saw begging on the streets, or who went out shoplifting in order to feed their habit. In other words, the type of junkie that couldn't be trusted as far as you could throw them. And that was another thing – how had she even come by the drug? She rarely ventured outside the house, and when she did she was never alone. So who had been supplying her? He knew for a fact it wasn't the kid who dropped off the cannabis on a weekly basis, because he'd been personally vetted by himself, and what's more, he'd given the boy strict instructions as to what he could and couldn't supply.

Pacing the length of the kitchen, Jason tilted his head to the side, his ears strained. From upstairs he could hear Vinnie gently coaxing Carmen into getting washed and dressed. As far as he was concerned it was a battle his wife had already lost. No matter how much he may have wanted to help her, and no matter how much he loved her, she didn't want his help. She'd made that abundantly clear. And if he was being entirely honest, he had a feeling she was more than content to waste her life as an addict, a junkie.

Breathing deeply through his nostrils, Jason came to a halt and as he gripped onto one of the kitchen stools, he bowed his head. Perhaps he should have walked away from her after all. Maybe Arthur had been right all those years ago when he'd said she was no good, and that she would end up bringing him down.

He and Arthur had got into a fight that night, the one and only time either of them had ever squared up to one another and gone toe to toe. Blood had been drawn, and as fists had begun to fly, the only thing on his mind had been to avenge the woman he planned to marry.

Aware of his nephew standing at the kitchen doorway, Jason turned his head.

'She's in the shower.'

Jason nodded. A tiny part of him didn't want to know. He could barely bring himself to look at her let alone take an interest in what she was doing. And then there was another part of him, an even greater part, that loved her so much he would die for her.

'Is she okay?' As much as he hated himself for asking the question, Jason had to know.

'I think so,' Vinnie answered. 'She was a bit shaken up.'

Jason nodded again. He'd laid into her, not physically of course, but verbally he'd called her every name under the sun. He hadn't meant any of it; it had been the anger talking, the shock of finding the crack pipe as he'd scooped up the clothes she'd dumped on the floor the previous evening. The glass pipe must have fallen out of one of her pockets and it had taken him a few moments to comprehend what he was actually looking at. But once he had, once it had finally registered, that was when the bottom had fallen out of his world.

From behind Vinnie came a movement and, kissing his teeth, Jason straightened up, his lips curled up into a snarl as Joanie came into view.

'Where is she?'

For a moment, Jason remained silent. As angry as he may have been, Joanie showed no fear. She stood tall, her head ever so slightly tilted to the side and her eyes hard.

Finally, he flicked his head towards the ceiling and as Joanie retraced her steps and began ascending the stairs, he let out a deep breath before digging his hands into his pocket and pulling out a pack of cigarettes. Taking out two, he placed one between his lips and passed the other across to Vinnie. Words eluded him, and as he lit up, he inhaled a lungful of smoke before noisily blowing it back out. He needed to get away, needed some air, and pulling out his car keys, he left the kitchen without saying another word. In the hallway, he glanced upwards. He could hear mumbled words being spoken, and he took a wild guess that his wife was now out of the shower.

His heart heavy, and his shoulders slumped, Jason left the house. He had nowhere in particular to go. Of course there was always the casino, or maybe he could pay Arthur a visit, neither of which appealed to him. Climbing into the car, he pulled his seatbelt across and, after giving the house a final glance, he turned the key in the ignition then sped away, oblivious to the dust and pebbles that became dislodged in his haste to escape.

* * *

Joanie shook her head. She'd long given up despairing over Carmen. There was a saying that her old dad had often used, and never had she found it more appropriate than she did right now. *You can't force a horse to drink water.* That was Carmen all over. She had so many resources at her fingertips and not only that, but she also had the money to pay for them. Rehab, counselling; she could even have a stint at a private health farm if she so wished. But that was the problem. Carmen wasn't interested; she was more than happy to carry on as she was. A waste of life as far as Joanie was concerned.

Entering the master bedroom, Joanie paused. Carmen sat on the edge of the bed, her head bowed and her long hair obscuring her face.

'Carmen, love.'

There was no reply, and stepping even further into the room, Joanie took a look around her. The usually pristine room was in a mess, the duvet crumpled and the dressing table upturned.

'Carmen...'

It was then that Carmen glanced up, her eyes full of unshed tears and her bottom lip quivering.

'Oh, love,' Joanie cried as Carmen dived into her arms and held on for dear life. 'It's okay, darling. Everything will be okay.' Even as she said the words, Joanie wasn't so sure this was the case. Jason was on the war path, so much so that she'd never seen him so angry. And as for Carmen, she looked completely and utterly broken.

Call it instinct or intuition, but she had an inkling that there was a lot more going on here then met the eye. As much as Carmen wanted to keep her addiction a secret, she would never have been this upset all because Jason had found the crack pipe. She would have shrugged it off and then got on with her day regardless of how much he'd screamed and shouted at her.

'Carmen,' she tried again. 'What's going on, darling?'

It was then as Carmen looked up at her that it took everything in Joanie's power not to rock back on her heels. In that instant, her stomach began to churn. She'd seen that same look once before and no matter how long ago it may have been, it was something that Joanie had never forgotten.

'Gio…' Carmen whispered, her voice wavering.

There was no need for Carmen to utter another word of explanation. Joanie could see it in her eyes as plain as day. The hurt, the fear, the desperation, and dare she say it, the shame.

'Oh, love,' Joanie repeated as she pulled Carmen towards her. 'The bastard, the no-good bloody bastard.'

Tears slipped down Carmen's cheeks and as she began to sob, Joanie held on even tighter. She wanted to kick herself. If only she'd have waited around, if only she'd never left Carmen alone with Gio. At the time, she'd had her concerns, she hadn't trusted him, hence why she hadn't initially wanted Demi to give her a lift home. But not for a single second had she thought that Gio would take his cruelty to another level. Oh, she'd heard his smart arse remarks; she'd even heard him speaking to Carmen as though she were nothing but a piece of dirt on the floor, all habits that he'd no doubt picked up from Dylan. After all, if Dylan could get away with treating his mother as though she were the lowest of the low, then others were bound to follow suit.

'Does Jason know?' As soon as she asked the question, Joanie had already known the answer. Of course he didn't. If Jason had just an inkling of what his son-in-law had done then he would have torn out of the house ready to commit murder.

Carmen vehemently shook her head, her eyes wide with fear. 'He can't ever find out,' she cried. 'Please, Joanie.'

Joanie hesitated. 'What about the police? You should report him for what he did...' She momentarily paused. She didn't exactly know what Gio had done, other than it had been something horrific. She had a good idea of what might have taken place, not that she allowed her mind to wander too far. If truth were told, she didn't want to know the grisly details; just to know that something had happened in the first place was enough to make her want to string Gio up by his gonads. 'What he did to you was wrong.'

'No, no, no,' Carmen cried as she rose to her feet and wrapped her arms around herself. 'I can't do that. Please, Joanie,' she whispered. 'If I go to the police then Jason will find out and I can't allow that to happen. Please...' she pleaded.

Against her better judgement, Joanie found herself relenting. What other choice did she have? And Carmen had made a point. Jason was bound to find out if the police became involved, and then there was the question of court. Was Carmen strong enough to give evidence? Joanie wasn't so sure. Besides, the last thing she wanted to do was open up a can of worms, because once that happened so many other secrets would come tumbling out. Secrets that perhaps were better left buried. Secrets that if discovered were bound to destroy the Vickers family for once and for all.

13

Of all the places Jason Vickers could have driven to, he found himself parked up outside the Carter family's scrapyard. He wasn't even so sure why he'd been compelled to come. He barely knew the Carters, and though he'd perhaps recognise one or two of them, the rest he wouldn't have been able to name if his life depended on it.

Except deep down that wasn't quite true. He did know why he'd come. The last person to have ever seen his youngest son alive worked from the scrapyard. He'd caught a glimpse of Tommy Johnson the previous evening, but with so much going on he hadn't had the chance to introduce himself. But more than anything he wanted a distraction. Something, anything that would stop him from thinking about his wife and the discovery he'd found this morning.

Tapping his fingers on the steering wheel, Jason sucked in his bottom lip. It was unlike him to be hesitant. From an early age he'd known what he wanted from life and had taken it with both hands. He'd been an opportunist; still was, he supposed. Perhaps it was this that had made him so successful. It had also helped that he'd feared no one, and that he'd been more than prepared to fight for what he wanted.

Swinging open the car door, he stepped outside, adjusted his shirt then crossed over the road. From the outside, the scrapyard was nothing special, although it was fairly large, he supposed, considering there was enough room to fit several cars on the forecourt. As he walked through the gates, he glanced around him. He'd heard a rumour once that the cars piled high on top of one another were worth a small fortune, or rather the contents of the cars were. The very same person had also told him that the cars were often used to hide the proceeds of armed robberies. He chuckled to himself; yeah, somehow he couldn't quite see that as being true. He may not have known the Carter family on a personal level, but from what he did know of them it would be safe to say that they weren't fools. Unless that was exactly what they wanted people to think. Out of curiosity, he eyed the cars before giving a hollow laugh. Nah, it had to be a rumour and nothing more than that.

A short time later, he stepped inside the cabin that the Carters used as an office. Well aware that his arrival was unexpected, he gave a small smile in an attempt to put them at ease.

'I'd like a quiet word,' he said, gesturing to Tommy Jr.

Jonny Carter lifted his eyebrows and as he glanced towards his great-nephew, he relaxed back in his seat and steepled his fingers. 'Are you all right with that?'

Tommy Jr nodded. 'Yeah.' Getting to his feet, he slipped his mobile phone into his pocket and made for the door.

'Oi, Tommy,' Jonny called after him. 'Use my car so that I can keep an eye on you.' Tossing across the keys, he jerked his head to where his car was parked on the forecourt. 'Just in case,' he added before casting a glace in Jason's direction. 'No offence, mate, but the last time one of your lot turned up they tried to run him through with a blade, and seeing as he's family, we get a bit touchy about things like that.'

Jason lifted his eyebrows. He hadn't been aware of what had taken place at the time. But if he had been, he wasn't so sure he would have stopped Vinnie, not when he'd been under the impression that Tommy Johnson had left his son to bleed out on a concrete floor.

As Tommy Jr led the way outside, Jason followed until they came to a dark grey, brand spanking new Mercedes-Benz S class saloon.

'Nice motor,' he said, climbing inside.

'Yeah,' Tommy answered as he looked the car over. 'It's all right I suppose. Not really my cup of tea but my uncle seems to like it.'

Once they were seated, an awkward silence followed until eventually Jason cleared his throat. It was pointless asking if his boy had suffered in the final moments leading up to his death because he'd known for a certainty that he had. How could he not have? He'd been doused in boiling water before being stabbed. It didn't take a genius to tell him that it would have been enough to cause excruciating pain.

'Did...' Jason cleared his throat again. 'Did he say anything before he... before he, well, you know...'

Tommy Jr shook his head. 'No.'

'Good.' Jason nodded more so for his own benefit than for Tommy Johnson's. In a way it was a relief that Dylan had had no final words. If he'd have been calling out for his mum or dad, Jason didn't think he would be able to take the pain of knowing that he hadn't been there when his son had needed him the most.

'And how about leading up to that day? Was he okay? Was he worried about anything, or maybe wary of anyone?'

Tommy Jr took a deep breath, and for the first time since they'd entered the car, Jason turned to look at him, really look at him. He was nothing but a kid. Roughly the same age as Dylan had been.

'He was, erm...' Tommy Jr paused and as he swallowed, he glanced down at his hands. 'He wasn't worried about anything, at least that I know of.' He stared out of the windscreen as though thinking the question over. 'I mean, he wasn't happy about being locked up but at the same time he definitely wasn't worried about anyone having a dig at him.'

It was exactly what Jason had expected. Neither of his sons were weak. They took after their old man in that respect. And as much as Dylan hadn't been the type of man to cause trouble, he'd also known how to have a ruck, something that Jason had instilled into both of his boys from an early age.

'And the cunts who did it,' he asked, screwing up his face. 'Have you got a name for them?'

Tommy Jr shook his head. 'I was told they were being taken care of.'

'That wasn't what I asked.'

'Yeah, I know.' As he glanced out of the window again, Tommy Jr sighed. 'One was called Hobbs; he was the mouthier of the two. The other was Reid, or something like that.'

Pushing open the door, Jason placed one foot outside. 'One more thing. I wanted to apologise on behalf of my nephew. He's...' He gave a small smile, as though to take the edge off his words. 'He's somewhat hot headed and he and Dylan were close.'

Tommy Jr shrugged. 'It's water under the bridge. At the end of the day no harm was done. It's not the first time that someone has tried to run me through, and I doubt it'll be the last,' he sighed. 'Especially when you take into account the family I come from.'

Jason gave a small chuckle. 'Yeah, we've all been there.' Stepping out of the car, he nodded towards the office. 'Thanks for the chat. If nothing else it's helped put my mind at ease.'

'No worries.' Stuffing his hands into his pockets, Tommy Jr glanced down at the floor. 'If it's any consolation,' he said, looking up, 'I did everything I could to help him.'

'I know.' Jason nodded. 'Damien told me.'

With those parting words, Jason walked back to where he'd parked his car, his heart somewhat lighter, or at least as light as it could ever be under the circumstances.

* * *

As Tommy Jr stood watching Jason Vickers as he climbed into his car, he was aware of a presence behind him. Looking over his shoulder, he acknowledged his great-uncle.

'Everything okay?' Jonny asked with a nod towards the gates.

'Yeah,' Tommy answered.

Jonny narrowed his eyes. 'So why do you look like someone pissed in your cornflakes this morning?'

Tommy Jr groaned, and as he rolled his eyes, he continued to watch as Dylan's father drove away. The truth was he was feeling a bit embarrassed. Last night, for the first time in his life he'd squared up to his uncle, and what's more he was still alive to tell the tale. But the problem was after he'd given his great big speech about Dylan being his pal and wanting to find out exactly who'd murdered him, he'd had the time to calm down a bit, to actually think the situation through. And yeah, Dylan had been his pal and he did want to find out who'd killed him and why. But the thing was, he was beginning to think he'd never known Dylan, at least not the real Dylan. Not once during their time spent inside had Dylan ever spoken about what he'd been involved in. Tommy himself was no saint, but not once had it ever crossed his mind to pimp women out, or deal drugs, or even beat the crap out of random people. And yeah, he knew that made him a hypocrite of sorts seeing how he and Reece had got into plenty of rucks over the years. But not once had he ever walked up to some innocent bystander and then smashed them in the face just for the sheer fun of it. That wasn't what he was about. And yeah, he might like the odd spliff every now and then, but he had no inclination to actually go out and become a dealer.

'Yeah, well, as long as you're sure,' Jonny said as he turned to make his way back to the office.

'Yeah, I am,' Tommy replied as he glanced over his shoulder a second time. For a few moments he stood just thinking. Whether he liked it or not, he was involved and there was no walking away from that fact. But there was another part of him that was beginning to think that Jonny had been right all along. It wasn't their fight, and just maybe him and his family would have been better off staying well out of it.

* * *

Damien could scarcely breathe by the time he brought the car to a screeching halt on his parents' driveway.

Jumping out, he thumped his fist on the front door, growing all the more impatient as the seconds ticked by.

Finally the door was flung open and on seeing his cousin in the doorway, Damien scowled as he pushed past him.

'Where's my mum?' he shouted as he poked his head into both the kitchen and the lounge and finding both rooms empty.

'She's upstairs,' Vinnie answered.

Damien spun around. The fact there wasn't a hint of cockiness to Vinnie's voice concerned him all the more, and taking the stairs two at a time, he charged up to his parents' bedroom.

By the time he'd reached the door, Joanie was waiting for him.

'Where is she?' he asked.

Joanie shook her head. 'Now isn't the right time.'

'What the fuck do you mean now isn't the right time?' Damien roared as he attempted to peer around her.

'Exactly what I said.' As she placed her hand on his chest as though to stop him from coming any further, Joanie's expression was serious. 'Let your mum rest.'

Damien's mouth fell open. 'I don't understand.' On hearing footsteps behind him, he turned his head. 'Vinnie. What the fuck is going on here?'

Vinnie took a deep breath and as he gave a helpless shrug, he glanced towards Joanie. 'Your dad found a crack pipe this morning.'

Damien's eyes widened. 'What do you mean he found a crack pipe?'

'Exactly what I said. And I'll give you two guesses as to who it belongs to.'

'Nah, I don't believe this. I mean...' The words died in his throat. How could he not believe it? His mum was an addict. She'd been an addict the entirety of his life. Even before his birth she'd been popping pills like they were going out of fashion. Although from what he could remember, she'd become far worse after Dylan had been born.

'Where's my dad?'

Vinnie gestured behind him, and as the sound of a key

turning in the lock reached their ears, Damien bolted down the stairs.

'I blame you for this,' he roared as he ignored the pain in his arm and shoved his father against the wall. 'You should have got her help years ago. Instead you did fuck all.'

As Jason's back collided with the wall, he curled his fists into tight balls. 'You know nothing,' he said, pushing his son away from him, his voice surprisingly calm. 'Don't you think I tried to get her help? She's ill.'

Damien screwed up his face. She wasn't ill, she was an addict. Big difference.

'What did you expect me to do?' Jason continued. 'Have her committed into rehab against her will? She's my wife. I couldn't have her locked up.'

'And she's my mum,' Damien spat back. 'You should have done whatever you had to do for our sake. For me, Demi and Dylan. We deserved to have a mum who could at least function without the need to down half a bottle of vodka or shove pills down her neck just to get out of bed in the morning.'

'Yeah,' Jason agreed. 'Maybe I should have, but she didn't want that. If you kids weren't a good enough reason for her to get clean then nothing and no one would have ever come before the booze and drugs. That's just how it is and whether we like it or not, we have to accept that.'

'You're lying,' Damien snarled as he pushed his father back against the wall. 'You were the one who stopped her from getting help. You couldn't bear for her to be out of your sight.'

Jason shook his head. 'No matter what you might think of me, that's not true. I tried. And I'll tell you something else for nothing,' Jason said as he pointed his finger forward. 'I did everything in my power to try and protect you from witnessing the things you saw. You were a kid. Do you honestly think I wanted my children exposed to that shit, that I wanted you to know what drugs even were?'

Years of pent-up rage engulfed Damien. The familiar hatred he'd had for his father growing up rushed to the fore. In his mind, his dad had enabled his mum and nothing and no one would ever be able to make him think differently. His dad was the one who'd supplied her with booze, an entire cellar filled to the brim with expensive bottles of alcohol that she would help herself to on a daily basis. And when it came to the pills, he'd turned a blind eye. He'd even made excuses for her erratic behaviour. It was only as Damien had grown older and met his friends' mothers that he'd realised his mum was different, and that other mums didn't slur their words or sway from side to side when they poured out their drinks. As he pulled back his arm, the only thing on Damien's mind was to obliterate the man he had the misfortune to call Dad.

'Stop.'

As he sucked in a breath, Damien's fist stopped just inches away from his father's face.

'Please,' Carmen begged as she ran down the remaining steps. 'Both of you, stop. Enough of this.'

Damien turned his head, the sight of his mother stopping him dead in his tracks.

As she came to stand between father and son, Carmen's body trembled. 'Your dad is right.'

'No.' Damien shook his head. 'He's wrong. I know he is.'

'Your dad is right,' Carmen reiterated. 'I've had many chances over the years. More than I care to admit and far more than I deserved. I didn't want help; and more to the point, I wasn't ready to be helped. I don't expect you to understand, either of you,' she added, glancing towards her husband. 'So please stop this. For my sake will you please stop blaming one another. If anyone is to blame, it's me.'

'I don't understand,' Damien began.

'I know,' Carmen answered as she rested her hand over his heart. 'And I don't want you to understand. It's better that way.'

Damien shook his head. 'You're talking in riddles, Mum, as per fucking usual.'

'Oi,' Jason warned, his eyes flashing with anger as he stabbed a finger forward. 'Watch your mouth. That's your mum you're talking to.'

'Nah, something's not right about this.' As he shook his head again, Damien's eyes were hard. 'Did he put you up to this?' he demanded of his mother.

'Leave it out,' Jason shouted. 'What do you think I fucking am? Your mum's not a fucking puppet, she's got a mind of her own.'

'Yeah, that you just love to control,' Damien shouted back as he tapped his forehead. 'You must think I was born yesterday, that I don't know what you're trying to do. Who's gonna be next, eh? Demi, or how about him?' he snarled, jerking his thumb in Vinnie's direction. 'Because one by one you'll push everyone away until she's so isolated that all she has left is you. That's what this is all about, isn't it? In fact, it wouldn't surprise me if you were the one who plied her with the crack to begin with.'

The colour drained from Jason's face and as much as Damien knew he'd gone too far, he was unable to stop himself.

'What did you just say?'

'Jason, please,' Carmen begged of her husband. 'He didn't mean that.'

'Yes, he did,' Jason growled. 'And you know that as well as I do.' Shrugging his wife's hand away from him, Jason took a step forward. 'Well, come on, tough man,' he goaded. 'Say it again and see what happens.'

'It was Dylan.'

A deathly silence fell and as all eyes turned to look at Vinnie, Damien's jaw dropped.

'Do fucking what?'

Vinnie took a cautious step back. 'Think about it,' he said, pointing to his head. 'It's the only thing that makes any sense. Because I know for a fact that I didn't supply the crack, and if everyone here is also denying it then that leaves only one other person, doesn't it.'

'I'm gonna fucking kill him,' Damien hissed, bounding forward.

Slamming his eyes shut tight, Vinnie brought his arm up to protect his head. 'Think about it logically,' he yelled. 'Who else could it have been?'

Before Damien could throw a punch, Jason's hand gripped onto his forearm, his skin ashen and his eyes wide. 'Is he right?' he asked, turning to look at his wife.

There was a notable tremble to Carmen's hands, and as she brought her hands up to her chest, she looked to be in grave danger of collapsing. 'He wasn't who you thought he was...'

'What?' Jason cocked his head to the side, as though the motion would help him to hear her better. 'What did you just say?'

Carmen swallowed, and as she looked up at Joanie, tears sprang to her eyes.

'She said that Dylan wasn't the person you thought he was,' Joanie repeated. And with her head held high and her back ramrod straight, she descended the stairs. 'And before either of you even think about arguing the case,' she added, 'I know that to be a fact because I was there. I was a witness.'

14

There was a cockiness to Gio's swagger as he made his way through the casino. Not only was he untouchable but he was also fast on his way to having everything he'd ever desired. Stopping at one of the roulette tables, he greeted those he recognised and was just contemplating whether or not he should try his luck and have a game when Arthur beckoned him over.

As he cursed under his breath, a smile remained plastered across Gio's face. He had to appear in control even if he wasn't. That was how the game was played, and if there was one thing that his wife had taught him, it was to learn to smile through any issues thrown at him. Take their marriage, for example. It was all but over, had been for years, and yet when they were in front of an audience, he and Demi still pretended to be happy and in love. It was sickening really, especially when the only thing he'd love to do was put the bitch in her place.

'Yeah, you wanted me.' There was a hint of boredom in Gio's voice as he tapped his knuckles on the door to Arthur's office.

'Yes. Come in and shut the door.'

Resisting the urge to roll his eyes, Gio did as he was told.

'I've got a little job for you.'

'Yeah, and what's that?' Gio asked as he perched on the edge of the desk and picked up a heavy gold paperweight before turning it over in his hand as though inspecting it.

Plucking the paperweight out of Gio's hand, Arthur returned it to his desk before offering a grin. It was a maniacal grin, the type that under normal circumstances would have put the fear of God into Gio.

'I want you to find someone for me.'

Gio cocked his head to the side. 'How am I supposed to do that?'

Arthur chuckled, and sitting forward in the chair, he rested his elbows on the desk. 'Let me rephrase that,' he said. 'I already know where he can be found. What I want you to do is go and collect him and then bring him straight to me.'

A look of confusion creased Gio's face, and blowing out his cheeks, Arthur shook his head.

'It's not rocket science,' he barked out. 'Drive over to the Carters' scrapyard in Barking, find that little scrote Tommy Johnson and then bring him to me.'

His forehead furrowed, Gio narrowed his eyes. 'But what if he doesn't want to come?'

Arthur gritted his teeth. 'Then use your imagination.'

'Yeah but—'

'For fuck's sake, Gio,' Arthur roared. 'It's a simple fucking request, one that Dylan would have been able to do with his eyes closed.'

Arthur's words had the desired effect and as Gio's lips curved into a snarl, he got to his feet. 'I didn't say I couldn't do it. I was just checking, that's all,' he lied. 'I wanted to see how much force I was allowed to use.'

Arthur laughed, a huge belly laugh that almost had him

doubled over, and as he slapped Gio on the shoulder, he wiped the tears of laughter from his eyes. 'That was a good one. And, might I add, exactly what it is I like about you so much.' He chuckled. 'Just when I think you can't possibly be any more of an imbecile, you come out with an absolute cracker.'

Gio gave a nervous smile, unsure if he should be pleased or insulted. 'I'll get off then, shall I?'

'You do that.' Arthur nodded. 'Oh, and Gio. Make sure you're discreet. The last thing either of us wants is the entire Carter clan to turn up on our doorstep. Because somehow I've got a feeling that their bite is far worse than their bark.'

Gio's face paled. And as he left Arthur's office, beads of cold sweat broke out across his forehead. He hadn't signed up for this. Not once had he actually made it known that he was willing to get his hands dirty. Because as far as he was concerned, dropping off a little bit of crack to Carmen once in a while was his limit. As much as he may have given it all the talk, he wasn't a tough man and when it came down to it, he had absolutely no idea how to force a man into his car. Especially one who was more than capable of breaking his jaw with one punch if needs be.

Giving an involuntary shiver, Gio made his way outside the casino. Perhaps he could pretend that he couldn't find the kid? Or maybe, and it was a very big maybe in his opinion, he could tell Tommy Johnson that Arthur wanted a little chat and then hope that he willingly got into the car. Somehow though, he couldn't quite see that happening.

As he chewed on his thumbnail, Gio contemplated how he was going to execute the deed. He needed a plan of action, something concrete, or rather something fool proof. Problem was, what?

Starting the ignition, he pulled out onto the road, dread

curling around his insides. He didn't even want to imagine what would happen if he failed. Arthur would hang him out to dry, he knew that much. And as it was he had a feeling that he was already skating on thin ice, especially if Carmen opened her mouth and told someone about what he'd done to her. Of course he could always turn it around and put the blame onto her. He could say that she'd put it on him, that she'd handed it to him on a plate. And at the end of the day, who'd be daft enough to believe her version of events? She was a junkie, a dirty skank. Whereas he was a married man; he had a job, of sorts. He loved his wife; again, a slight exaggeration. But no one else needed to know that. From the outside looking in, he was an upstanding member of society. He paid his taxes, or at least he thought he did. Either way, it was her word against his, and he had a sneaky suspicion that no one would believe a woman who'd spent the majority of her life as high as a kite. Or at least this was what he hoped.

* * *

Carmen's hands shook so violently that she could barely light her cigarette. Once it was lit she took several short, sharp puffs, then exhaled the smoke through her nostrils. Sitting on the edge of the armchair, she shivered. She was always cold of late, but it wasn't the temperature of the room that had made her shiver, it was the circumstances, and as her husband, son, and nephew stared at her, she could feel her cheeks burning under their scrutiny.

She wasn't even so sure that they believed her. Dylan had been the baby of the family, the golden boy. He'd had everything his heart could ever desire and yet there was another side to him, a cruel, wicked side that so few people saw. Although

Carmen had noticed that the older he became, the harder it was for him to conceal his true identity. He'd been a good actor too, or liar, whichever way you wanted to look at it. In his father's company, he'd pretended to be the perfect son, and when he'd been with his siblings, he'd acted out the role of the lovable kid brother, the one that they had both adored. But when they were alone, when it was just the two of them, that was when Dylan would show another side of himself. In the beginning he'd been careful to not let anyone else see, but towards the end he hadn't cared one iota if Joanie, or Gio, had been present.

'I don't believe this,' Damien cried, throwing his hands up into the air. 'This is Dylan we're talking about, not some monster.'

Carmen continued to chain-smoke, her movements jerky and her nerves all over the place. If ever she'd needed a hit, then it was now. She was on the verge of having a mental breakdown and it was on the tip of her tongue to scream at them all to leave her alone. But they wanted answers from her and she had a feeling they wouldn't leave her alone until she'd told them everything. Well, not quite everything; there was one thing she would never disclose. The one thing that no matter how far down she'd buried it, was always there, mocking her. Perhaps that was why Dylan had been so evil. And maybe that was why she hadn't loved him as much as she had loved his brother and sister.

'Mum,' Damien shouted. 'Will you say something?'

Carmen looked up at her son. Her firstborn. She loved him so much and as a fresh wave of shame washed over her, she fought the urge to look away. He deserved answers; they all did. 'Where's Demi?'

Damien threw his arms up again. 'Don't worry about where

Demi is,' he growled. 'Just start fucking talking. Finish what you started because you can't leave us hanging like this.'

No, he had a point, she couldn't leave them hanging, not after she'd dropped this bombshell on top of them. She took a deep breath. 'Dylan, he...' She shook her head, not wanting to say the words out loud. She wasn't even sure of when it had all gone so wrong. He'd been a lovely little baby, and an even nicer little boy, but once he'd hit puberty it had become glaringly obvious that there was a problem. In the beginning it had been a case of Dylan back-chatting, being rude, disobedient. Until finally he'd become physical, a push here, a shove there, and then one day he'd actually punched her full pelt in the stomach. It had been so unexpected, and as tears had sprung to her eyes, the shock of what he'd done had actually taken her breath away. It wasn't the last time he'd lashed out at her either; it became a regular occurrence. No matter what she did she seemed to make him angry. And then when he offered her the crack, she'd readily taken it, wanting an escape. Of course, she should have known it would become nothing more than another outlet for him to threaten and bully her, only this time he'd added blackmail to the list too. Whenever she didn't do as he asked, he would threaten to tell his father about the crack, and in Carmen's eyes it had been no idle threat. Dylan would have got a kick out of seeing her brought down even further.

'Mum, please,' Damien begged as he knelt down beside her and grasped her hand in his. 'You're killing me right now. I need to know.'

Carmen nodded, and as her free hand reached out, she smoothed a lock of hair away from her son's forehead. He was a handsome man, but as much as he shared his father's traits, she could see herself in him. All three of her children took after her in looks, especially Demi, although both her sons' hair was a shade or two darker than her own. As she gave her husband a small, hesitant smile, she took another shuddering breath. 'I think he was about twelve or thirteen when it all started, maybe even a year or two younger. At first I thought nothing of it. Thought he was just playing up, acting out because I'd been drinking and what not. But his behaviour became worse. Until eventually he'd threaten me or hit me if I refused to do his bidding.'

As he dropped his mother's hand, Damien sank back on his knees. 'No,' he said, looking behind him to his father. 'Dad, that can't be right. Dylan would have never...'

Jason's skin was ashen, his hands curling involuntarily into fists.

'It's true,' Joanie piped up. 'I saw the things he did, and on more than one occasion an' all.'

'Then why did you never say anything?' Jason hissed. 'That's what I pay you for.'

Joanie opened her mouth and before she could answer, Carmen spoke for her.

'Because I told her not to. Because I didn't want any of you to know what Dylan was capable of.'

As her husband rubbed at his temples, Carmen reached out for her cigarette packet. There was so much more. Dylan hitting out at her was only the tip of the iceberg. 'He'd wanted the combination code to your safe.'

Jason narrowed his eyes.

'I didn't even know you had a safe,' Carmen continued. 'I mean, I'd never seen one, at least not here at home. But it turned out he meant the one in your office at the casino.'

Damien snapped his head around to look at his father again, as though gauging his reaction.

'I...' Jason blinked several times before clearing his throat. 'I don't understand why he would have wanted to get into the safe. There is fuck all in it.'

Carmen shrugged. 'I don't know, he never explained himself,' she said, shaking her head. 'But for whatever reason he'd got it into his head that I would know the code. And then when I didn't, that's when he became really nasty. He frightened me.'

Damien turned his hard stare onto Vinnie. 'And are you saying that you never saw any of this?' he accused. 'You're always here. You and Dylan were joined at the hip.'

Vinnie gave an incredulous laugh. 'Is that what he told you?'

A look of confusion creased Damien's face.

'Maybe when we were ten,' Vinnie continued. 'But since then we haven't been particularly close. He might have been my cousin, my family, but we definitely weren't the best of mates.'

'I can't get my head around this,' Jason said. 'Are you telling me that my boy was a wrong 'un? That he was fucked up in the head?'

Carmen remained silent. Jason looked as though he was broken, and in that instant her heart went out to him. He'd always referred to Dylan as his boy; he'd been so proud of him. Nausea washed over her and, pressing her hand to her lips, she swallowed deeply.

'Carmen,' Jason bellowed. 'Is that what you're saying?'

This time, Carmen gave a small nod. It hurt to admit how much of a monster her youngest son had been. She'd wanted to hide Dylan's true identity from her husband. In a way, she'd convinced herself that she was protecting him from knowing just how wicked Dylan truly was.

'I don't fucking believe this.' His face twisted with anger, Jason began to pace the lounge. 'Is that it?' he roared. 'Or is there anything else I should have been made aware of?'

As she took a deep breath, Carmen shook her head before giving Joanie a surreptitious glance. There was more, so much more. Not that she was prepared to ever reveal what that was. Jason would never forgive her if she did, and to see the hurt and devastation written across his face would all but destroy her. Then there was the trouble her admittance would cause. Her husband would commit murder, and as much as it would have been warranted, she didn't want that. She didn't want to lose him, and either way, she would. He would either go to prison or he would leave her, there was no sugar coating that fact, and at the end of the day, who could blame him? Carmen certainly wouldn't.

* * *

There was a bounce in Tommy Jr's step as he exited the scrapyard. With a pocket full of cash, life was on the up. So much so that he was planning to surprise his Aimee. She had her eye on a particular designer handbag. As much as she hadn't actually hinted that she wanted it, he'd caught her eyeing it up more than once.

Unlocking the car, he tossed his mobile phone onto the passenger seat then climbed in. He might even treat her to a night out, he decided, a meal or something like that. He highly doubted that she'd fancy a night out boozing seeing as she was pregnant, although he supposed they could always pop into the pub for a drink or two on their way home before last orders were called.

Thirty minutes later, he glanced up at the rear mirror, taking note of a car that had been tailing him. Shifting his weight, he glanced up again. Yeah, it was still there. He was unsure of what to do as his gaze kept flicking up to the mirror. It could have been a coincidence, he supposed. It would soon be nearing rush hour, after all, and so traffic was bound to begin building up.

A few moments later, he spotted a parking space and, pulling in, he looked up again at the mirror. The car that had been behind him drove on and as it did so, he let out a laugh. He was becoming paranoid. Which considering he still had flashbacks of being arrested then subsequently imprisoned, who could blame him?

Jumping out of the car, he locked up, then took a quick glance at his watch before shooting off a text to Aimee telling her that they were going out for dinner. He couldn't wait to see her face when he presented her with the bag. And after the shit they had been through recently, she deserved to feel special. The death of her dad had hit her hard. Not that he could say it had affected him in any way, shape, or form. It was because of Aimee's old man, Kevin Fox, that he'd been banged up. And as far as he was concerned, good riddance to the no-good bastard. Not that he'd ever made his feelings known to Aimee; the less she knew the better, and considering he'd had a hand in her dad's death, maybe it was best she was kept in the dark.

Within fifteen minutes, he was back at the car and, placing the box containing the bag on the passenger seat, he was just about to climb in when he felt a tap on his shoulder.

'I thought it was you.'

Tommy Jr narrowed his eyes. He had no recollection of the man standing in front of him. 'Do I know you?'

'Gio,' the man said, pointing to himself. 'Jason Vickers' son-in-law.'

'Ah.' Tommy broke out into a grin. 'You all right, mate?' he asked, shoving out his hand. 'Sorry about that, I didn't recognise you.'

Gio nodded and as he wiped his hand across his clammy

forehead, he glanced up the road. 'You couldn't help me out, could you? I'm having a bit of car trouble.'

Tommy hesitated. He'd told Aimee he would be picking her up at five, and he still needed to get home, shower, shave, and then change his clothes. And if he didn't get a move on he'd be cutting it fine, especially if he ended up getting caught in traffic.

'You'd be doing me a massive favour.'

'Yeah, go on then,' Tommy relented. 'But I can't hang about for too long.'

'Cheers, pal. My car is this way.'

Hastily locking his car back up, Tommy fell into step beside Gio. After a few moments he glanced behind him as Gio led the way around the back of the shopping parade.

'How did you spot me if you were parked back here?'

Gio shrugged. 'By chance really.'

Tommy narrowed his eyes again. Yeah, it was a little too convenient for his liking that they both happened to be in the same place at the same time. A ripple of unease began to spread through his veins and he looked over his shoulder again.

'This is it.'

As he turned his head, the hairs on the back of Tommy's neck stood upright. It was the same car he'd thought was tailing him.

'We're you following me?' he growled.

Gio gave a nervous laugh.

'Oi,' Tommy hissed. 'Answer the fucking question. Were you following me?'

Again, Gio didn't answer and as he kicked out at a stone, Tommy took a good look at him. He could take him, easily. He was nothing more than a lanky streak of piss.

'Do you know what,' Tommy said with a dismissive wave of his hand as he turned away. 'Fuck you.'

He'd barely taken two steps forward when he heard a loud crack followed by what could only be described as excruciating pain across the back of his head. On instinct, Tommy brought his hand upwards and on seeing blood staining his fingertips, he stumbled forward, the edges of his vision turning black.

'What the fuck...' he began before sinking to his knees, and as he fell face forward, everything turned black.

15

'So, that's that then. Time to put it to bed.'

As Joanie's jaw dropped, she could only stare at Carmen in utter confusion. 'What do you mean that's that?' she hissed.

Carmen lifted her shoulders into a shrug. 'It's out in the open now. No more secrets. It's time to move on.'

Joanie shook her head. The calmness in Carmen's voice was making her feel uneasy. 'But what about—'

'I said no more.' Carmen was quick to answer. 'I just want to forget about everything else that's happened and get on with my life.'

'But you've given them half a story,' Joanie persisted. 'What about the rest? How Dylan—'

'I said no more,' Carmen cried. 'He's dead, and that should be the end of it.'

Joanie fell quiet. She knew it had been difficult for Carmen. Dylan had been a constant reminder of her past. A time in her life that she had tried so hard to block out. 'And so that's it then. You'll let them,' she said, referring to the family, 'continue grieving for him.'

After a moment's thought Carmen nodded, and as she looked up at the ceiling, Joanie caught the glinting of tears in her eyes.

'Maybe it wasn't entirely his fault. He couldn't help who he was. He was born like that,' she said, turning now to look at Joanie. 'I made him like that.'

'No.' Grasping Carmen's hand, Joanie pulled her roughly around to face her. 'Don't you dare start all of that and go putting the blame onto yourself. There is only one person to blame and you know it. How many other people start out in life the same way as Dylan did and turn out just fine?'

'One?' Carmen repeated. 'Don't you mean two? Because let's not forget his part in all of this.'

Sucking in a breath, Joanie took a step back. It was the first time Carmen had ever admitted out loud something that Joanie had always suspected. 'Carmen, love...' she began.

Carmen shook her head, and pulling herself away from Joanie, her voice was cold. 'Enough now. I don't want to talk about it any more. What's done is done,' she said, reaching out for the vodka bottle and pouring herself out a large measure.

'But...'

Downing the alcohol in one large gulp, Carmen poured herself a second glass. 'I said no more,' she said, lifting the glass up to her lips. 'My son is gone. It's time to let whatever happened in the past die with him.'

* * *

As Arthur stared at Gio, he was beginning to think he was even more of a fool than he'd first thought. No, he didn't just think it, he now knew it to be a complete and utter fact.

'How was I to know?' Gio grumbled, his bottom lip protruding like a petulant toddler.

'How were you to know?' Arthur roared, incredulous. 'How could you have not known?'

Pacing the pavement, he clutched at his forehead. Of all the things Gio could have done, this had to be up there with the most mindless, unintelligent, obtuse decision he could have ever made. Peering at the car again, Arthur could sense his blood pressure rising. Laid out on the back seat, dead to the world, was Tommy Johnson.

'Is he even alive?' he barked out.

Gio shrugged. 'I think so.'

Arthur glared. 'Well, don't you think you should check?'

Just as Gio was about to shrug again, a look of panic swept over his face. 'What if he's dead? I'll be done for murder.' Clambering into the car, he searched for Tommy Jr's pulse. 'I can't find it,' he called over his shoulder.

As irritation swept over Arthur, he closed his eyes. 'Maybe it would help if you looked in the right place,' he said, barging Gio out of his way. Placing two fingers against Tommy's neck, he gave a nod then backed out of the car. 'He's alive.'

'Thank fuck for that,' Gio remarked as he dragged a hand over his clammy forehead. 'My arsehole was proper flapping there for a minute.'

Wrinkling his nose in disgust, Arthur glanced at his watch. It still didn't erase the fact that Gio had brought an unconscious Tommy Johnson to the casino of all places, especially when he had a perfectly good lockup just a mile or so down the road.

'I take it you don't need directions on how to get to the lockup?' he asked with a hint of sarcasm. 'Or should I draw you a map?'

Gio's cheeks flushed red. 'I'm not an idiot,' he mumbled.

Arthur lifted his eyebrows. That remained to be seen. It was times like this that he actually missed Dylan. As much as he'd been a cocky little bastard, at least he hadn't needed instructions on how to carry out the simplest of tasks.

'I'll meet you there in an hour,' Arthur announced as he glanced at his watch a second time. 'And Gio, don't fuck it up this time.'

Walking away, he didn't wait around for Gio's response. To be perfectly honest, he had a more pressing issue on his hands. Jason had been on the missing list for the entire day. In fact, he'd not seen him since he'd left with the Carters the previous evening. Even his phone calls and text messages had gone unanswered. And if it wasn't for the fact that he knew his messages were definitely going through and that Jason's phone hadn't been turned off, he would have been even more concerned.

As he made his way towards his office, Demi was walking towards him. She looked so like her mother, a younger version of course. Dressed in what she liked to call her power suit and her high heels, Demi looked the part. Not only did she scream wealth, but she also gave the impression of being the boss.

'I was just looking for you,' Demi said as she came to stand beside him. 'My dad called. He said he won't be coming in tonight, something about a dicky tummy.'

The nerve at the side of Arthur's eye twitched. Jason was a workaholic. Even if he had been on his death bed he would have attempted to crawl into work. Pulling out his mobile phone, he stared down at the screen. He'd had no missed calls from Jason informing him that he wouldn't be at work, not even a text message.

He gave a stilted smile. 'I hope he feels better soon.'

'Yeah,' Demi answered as she looked into the distance. 'It's probably one of those twenty-four-hour things. You know what my dad is like, he'll more than likely be back at work tomorrow, as right as bleedin' rain.'

Arthur nodded. 'Actually,' he said after clearing his throat, 'do you think you can manage if I head home early?' He rubbed his hand over his stomach. 'I've been a bit off today too. Was probably something me and your dad ate.'

A look of concern creased Demi's face. 'Bloody hell,' she said. 'What with my dad and now you. What's going on?'

Screwing up his face as though he were in discomfort, Arthur rubbed at his stomach again. 'Like I said, I think it was something we ate.'

'Well, don't hang around,' Demi said. 'Get off home and put your feet up. Don't worry about this place. I can take care of everything.'

'Thank you,' Arthur said, patting her arm. 'I'll just grab my coat.'

Once he was safely tucked away in his office on the pretence of collecting his coat, Arthur fought the urge to swipe the contents of his desk to the floor. Something wasn't right, he could feel it in his gut. Never had Jason not kept him in the loop before. They were business partners, for crying out loud. Not only did they work together but they also made decisions together. It was just one of the many reasons as to why they were so successful.

By the time Arthur was making his way through the casino, he was all but ready to hurt someone, really hurt someone. And he could think of no one better to take his anger out on than Tommy Johnson.

* * *

Pulling back the net curtain, Aimee Fox stood on her tiptoes and, craning her neck, she looked up and down the street.

'Where the bloody hell is he?' she remarked to her mum, Melanie. 'He said he'd be here at five.'

Melanie looked up from her magazine. 'It is rush hour,' she answered as she glanced at the clock on the mantelpiece. 'And you know what the A13 is like this time of the night.'

Aimee chewed on the inside of her cheek. She supposed her mum was right, and her Tommy would have had to either drive down the A13 or across it, depending on which way he'd driven. Still, for some reason she'd expected him to go home first, rather than come straight from work, especially as they had arranged for him to stay the night.

'Give him a call if you're that worried.'

'Nah.' Aimee shook her head, and as she slumped down on the sofa, she rubbed her hand over her ever growing bump. 'I don't want to call him just in case he's driving.'

Melanie gave a small grin. 'That baby of yours is going to come out a nervous wreck the way you carry on.'

As much as Aimee rolled her eyes, she couldn't help but grin. She was so excited to meet her and Tommy's baby, and she just knew that despite what her mum had said, he or she was going to be just perfect.

* * *

Opening one eye, Tommy Jr immediately slammed it shut again. The lights were too bright and he had a blinding headache. Kicking out his legs, he screwed up his face. Everything seemed to hurt, even the back of his head. Gingerly, he made to lift up his arm, and on finding it hadn't moved, he attempted to lift it again. What the fuck was going on? Was he paralysed? Panic began to bubble within him and, opening both eyes, he looked down at his arm.

Almost immediately he tried to reel back. His wrist was being restrained by a thick plastic cable tie, and a quick peek at his other arm confirmed that that wrist had also been tied to the arm of the chair.

'What the fuck,' he shouted. 'What's going on?'

From behind him he could hear the sound of someone clapping. It was a slow clap, the kind that was more sarcastic than happy.

'Wakey, wakey, rise and shine. I was wondering how long it would take for you to wake up, and for a moment there I thought that perhaps Gio had hit you a little too hard.'

Tommy Jr turned his head to the side and glared at Gio. He remembered now. Gio had said that he'd had car trouble. After that, though, everything was a blur and until he'd woken up just now, he didn't have a clue what had happened to him in between, or even where he was. He could have been out of it for hours or even days for all he knew. 'What the fuck do you want?'

From behind him he could hear footsteps, and turning his head this way and that, Tommy grimaced at the pain across the back of his head. 'Stop fucking about,' he growled. 'And show your fucking face.'

Moments later, a man came into view. He was an older man, Tommy observed, and one that he was pretty certain he'd never met before.

'What do you want?' he asked again.

'What do I want? Now that is a question.' The man grinned.

Tommy Jr narrowed his eyes. He tugged at the restraints again and could feel the hard plastic rubbing against his skin.

'Save your energy. You won't break free.'

Tommy looked up. It was true. No matter how much he

tried, the cable ties wouldn't budge. 'Why are you doing this?' Tommy tried again. 'I don't even know who you are?'

The man straightened up, and placing both hands on his chest, he gave a look of surprise. 'Well, how rude of me.' He grinned. 'Of course you wouldn't know who I am. We've never had the pleasure of meeting before. Arthur Brennan,' he said, motioning to himself. 'And you and I, Tommy Johnson, have a mutual friend, or rather we did have a mutual friend.'

Tommy swallowed deeply. And as the hairs across the back of his neck stood upright, he glanced around him. He'd heard rumours about Arthur Brennan. People had said he was unhinged. Even his uncle Jonny had called him a vicious, spiteful bastard. 'I...' He snaked his tongue across his top lip, unsure of what to say. His mind had gone completely and utterly blank.

'Cat got your tongue?'

Tommy shook his head. 'I...' He swallowed again and shifted his weight. 'You won't get away with this. My family...'

'Your family,' Arthur repeated. 'The famous Carter family that I keep hearing so much about.' He shook his head. 'What makes you think your family will even find you?'

As Tommy opened his mouth to answer, Arthur began to laugh. 'I'm joking.' He chuckled. 'Forgive me. I have what some people might call a dark sense of humour.'

Tommy Jr narrowed his eyes.

'You see, Tommy...' Pausing, Arthur tilted his head to the side as though something had just occurred to him. 'Can I call you Tommy or would you prefer I call you by your given name, Thomas?'

'I don't care,' Tommy Jr spat out. 'Call me whatever the fuck you want.'

'Tommy it is then.' Arthur smiled. 'You see, Tommy,' he

continued. 'We have a small issue; you could even call it a problem of sorts.' He motioned towards himself. 'You've seen my face now.'

A shard of ice-cold fear jolted down the length of Tommy Jr's spine. He knew exactly what that meant. No matter what happened, he wouldn't be going home. How could he when, like Arthur Brennan had just stated, he already knew far too much?

16

Aimee was becoming increasingly concerned. 'Right, that's it,' she declared. 'I'm gonna phone his dad.'

Melanie nodded. Like her daughter, she too was worried. Tommy Jr wasn't in the habit of letting Aimee down; in fact, she would go as far as to say that he worshipped the ground she walked on. They were a match made in heaven and so in love that if it wasn't so sweet it would be sickening.

'You do that,' Melanie said as stood watch at the window, hoping, praying, that she would catch a glimpse of Tommy's car pulling up.

Moments later, Aimee ended the call.

'Well?' Melanie asked.

Aimee chewed on her bottom lip; her eyes filled with worry. 'His dad said that he left work hours ago. And that he should have been here by now. Oh, Mum,' she cried. 'What if he's been in an accident?'

Melanie took a deep breath. She'd never been in a situation like this before. Oh, her ex-husband had been on the missing list pretty much the entirety of their marriage; the only difference was she actually knew where he was most of the time and that was in the boozer propping up the bar. Should they start ringing around the hospitals? 'What did his dad say?'

Aimee wiped at her eyes. 'He said he was going to ring around the family and see if anyone had seen him.'

'Well, there you go,' Melanie said, faking a smile. 'I bet you any money he's with his cousin, Reece. You know what the two of them are like once they get together.'

'Yeah, I suppose.' Aimee nodded as she glanced towards the window again. 'It just makes no sense that he'd arrange to take me out if he was meeting up with Reece.'

'Yeah,' Melanie agreed. Aimee was right; it made no sense at all.

* * *

As Cameron Johnson switched off the call to his son's girlfriend, he glanced at his watch. It was nearing seven and his son had arranged to collect Aimee at five, meaning that he was more than two hours late. Knowing just how much Tommy Jr loved his food, that in itself was highly unusual, and when it came to Aimee he would never have stood her up. If something had come up or if he'd have made other plans, he would have let her know straight away. He certainly wasn't in the habit of letting her down, he respected her far too much to ever do that, and ever since he'd found out that she was carrying his child, Tommy had pretty much wrapped her up in cotton wool.

Something wasn't right, that much was evident. Scooping up his mobile phone, he began to scroll through his contact list, and after shooting off more than a dozen text messages asking if anyone had seen his son, he placed the phone beside him on the arm of the chair.

'Is everything okay?'

Cameron looked up.

'Was that Aimee on the phone?' Karen asked.

Cameron nodded. He could see the concern etched across his wife's face. Tommy Jr was their only child and his wife doted on him.

'Is Tommy okay?'

Cameron nodded again; he was too afraid to actually answer knowing full well Karen would be able to tell by the tone of his voice that he'd just told a lie.

Several notifications popped up on the phone screen, and snatching up the device, Cameron read the text messages, his heart ever so slightly sinking as he did so. No one had seen hide nor hair of his son.

Chewing on the inside of his cheek, he stared into the distance. His instincts had been right after all. Something was very, very wrong.

* * *

Closeted away in Jason's office at home, Jason, Damien, and Vinnie were all quiet, each of them lost in their own thoughts.

Finally Damien got to his feet, and digging his hand into his pocket, he plucked out his box of cigarettes. Taking one out for himself, he placed the box on his father's desk then lit up.

Following suit, Jason slid the box towards him, took two cigarettes out, one for himself and one for Vinnie.

'You know this is bollocks, right,' Damien finally barked out. 'Dylan was a good kid...' As his voice trailed off, he rubbed at the back of his neck as the words Calvin Rivers had used to describe his brother came back to haunt him. 'How could we have not known?'

Jason lifted his eyebrows. And as he inhaled a breath, he shook his head.

'He was a good actor,' Vinnie piped up. 'He must have been to have fooled everyone.'

Damien turned his head. Maybe. Or maybe it came down to the fact that he wasn't as good a judge of character as he'd always believed himself to be. Take Vinnie, for example. He couldn't stand the sight of his younger cousin, neither did he trust him, yet when it came to his mum, he couldn't fault him. Vinnie cared about her in the way that Dylan should have done.

'Maybe I spoiled him too much,' Jason admitted. 'I gave him everything. And when he'd been growing up I thought that I'd shielded him from seeing the shit your mum puts herself through on a daily basis. I thought...' He took a deep breath. 'I thought he was my chance at being a decent father.'

Damien bowed his head. Dylan had been his parents' miracle baby. With ten years between them, he'd been excited to have a kid brother. Only it was after his brother's birth that his mum had really spiralled out of control. His dad had blamed it on post-natal depression, not that Damien had even known what that was back then. All he'd known was that his mum was even more spaced out than usual.

'What's this about the safe?' Damien asked as he jerked his chin in his father's direction.

Jason shrugged. 'There's fuck all in it really. Some petty cash, some legal paperwork. That's about it.'

Damien was thoughtful for a moment. 'So if that is all that's in it, why was Dylan so determined to get in it?'

As Jason shrugged, Vinnie cleared his throat.

'This legal paperwork. It wouldn't happen to be the deeds to the casino by any chance, would it?'

Jason narrowed his eyes.

'Is he right?' Damien asked as he looked between his father and cousin. 'I mean, what else could he have been after? It couldn't have been the cash because I know for a fact you would have given him a decent wage.'

Jason nodded. 'He was doing okay for money.' As his forehead became furrowed, he gave a deep sigh. 'There has to be a mistake. Either your mum misheard Dylan or we're jumping to conclusions. Putting two and two together and coming up with five.'

'And you're still protecting him,' Damien muttered, throwing up his arms.

Jason rounded on his eldest son. 'He was my boy,' he shouted. 'I didn't spend the last nineteen years bringing up a stranger.'

'And what about the crack?'

Jason fell silent.

'I know I didn't believe it at first,' Damien continued. 'But Mum would have no reason to lie. Besides, it's the only thing that makes any sense. How else would she have come by it? You said yourself that she doesn't go out unless someone is with her.'

'You're forgetting something,' Jason said with a lift of his eyebrows. 'For the past six months your brother was banged up. So if it is true then who has been supplying her in his absence?'

Just as his father had moments earlier, Damien fell quiet. Yeah, he hadn't thought of that. If Dylan had been banged up and his mum was still receiving the crack, then that had to mean that Dylan had been in cahoots with someone else. The burning question, though, was who?

* * *

Gio had never heard a man scream before. And as Arthur brought the hammer down on Tommy Johnson's kneecap, he turned his face away.

He was starting to feel a little light-headed. Placing his hand on the concrete wall behind him, Gio attempted to keep himself grounded. And as he began to inhale deep breaths, he slammed his eyes shut tight. Maybe he wasn't cut out for this kind of life. God only knew that he could be cocky when the mood took him; he'd even strut around the casino as though he owned the gaff. But this, this was nothing more than barbaric.

The room began to spin, and as he felt himself slipping to the floor, Gio staggered forward. He needed some air, and even more than that he needed to be far away from the screams that came out of Tommy Johnson's mouth.

'Where the fuck are you going?'

Gio raised his hand in the air. He was going to vomit; he could feel the bile rising up into his throat. Slamming his hand over his mouth, he stumbled out of the lockup, gulping down lungfuls of fresh air. It wasn't enough, and leaning forward, he promptly emptied the contents of his stomach.

'What the fuck is wrong with you?'

Gio straightened up and, seeing Arthur at the door to the lockup with the claw hammer still clutched in his fist, he began to heave again. 'I can't,' he finally managed to get out as he motioned to the lockup. 'I can't do it.'

Arthur narrowed his eyes.

'I'm sorry,' Gio wailed as both terror and shame licked at his insides. 'I can't bear the noise. The screams.'

Arthur broke out into a laugh, or at least what Gio assumed was supposed to be a laugh. To Gio's ears it was nothing short of evil.

'It's not called torture for no reason, Gio.'

'I don't like it,' Gio complained. 'I can't handle something like that.' Looking around him for an escape route, he continued to take deep breaths. 'I thought I was gonna pass out, that I was gonna actually hit the deck.'

Arthur began to laugh again, and stepping aside, he gestured towards the lockup. 'Grow a pair of bollocks,' he commented as he motioned for Gio to go through the door.

Gio licked at his dry lips. 'I can't...' he began.

The smile slid from Arthur's face. 'It wasn't a request, Gio. Now get inside.'

Reluctantly, Gio took a step forward.

'Oh, and Gio,' Arthur said with a hint of amusement as he waved the hammer in the air. 'Try not to pass out. Because you never know, it might be your kneecap I start on next.'

Gio gulped. He wasn't sure if Arthur was playing with him or not, but the malice in the older man's eyes told him that just maybe it hadn't been a joke after all.

17

Jonny Carter placed his hands on his hips. Just like his brothers, he was a good-looking man who'd aged like a fine wine. His nephew Cameron had tracked him down to the pub that was part owned by his fiancée's brothers, Ricky and Jamie Tempest.

'And you've not heard from him at all?' Jonny clarified.

Cameron shook his head. 'If it wasn't for Aimee I probably wouldn't be as worried. But you know as well as I do that he would never willingly let her down.'

'No, you're right, he wouldn't,' Jonny confirmed. 'He idolises that girl.'

'And Aimee said that he was planning to take her out to dinner and you know as well as I do what he's like when it comes to food.'

'Yeah,' Jonny answered. Tommy Jr loved his grub so much so that he'd had to hide the biscuit tin they kept in the office otherwise the greedy little sod would eat the lot. 'All right, you've definitely got my attention,' Jonny said. 'And I agree with you, this isn't like him.'

Cameron nodded, and as he went back to flicking through his text messages, Jonny chewed on his bottom lip.

'You don't reckon he's been arrested again, do you?'

'Surely we would have heard by now if that was the case. He's allowed to have one phone call.'

'Yeah, that's true,' Jonny agreed. 'Maybe he took another trip over to South London.'

Screwing up his face, Cameron shook his head. 'He would have let us know.'

'He didn't yesterday,' Jonny pointed out.

'Yeah, but after the way he kicked off last night I can't see him keeping it quiet, he'd have no need to and you know what he's like, he would have said something even if it was just to prove a point.'

'Yeah,' Jonny sighed. 'He would have done an' all.' Gulping down the remainder of his lager, he fished out his car keys. 'I suppose we'd best call a meeting then. And try to find the little bugger.'

Cameron nodded and it wasn't until Jonny followed his nephew out of the pub that his expression became all the more serious. He was worried all right, really worried. It was one thing Tommy Jr lying to them about where he was going, but he would never have lied to Aimee, he was crazy about the girl. So for him to be on the missing list, something had to have happened. Something that had stopped Tommy Jr from fulfilling the plans he'd made with his girlfriend. What that could have been, though, he had no idea.

* * *

Tommy Jr's entire leg felt as though it was on fire. The pain surrounding his kneecap was so intense that he thought he might actually pass out, and he had a feeling that if it wasn't for the cable ties restraining him in place, he would more than likely have slipped off the chair and ended up on the floor, a crumpled mess. His knee was more than just broken, it had to be. He'd never felt pain like it, and even when he'd broken his arm as a kid it hadn't been as painful as this.

'Let's start from the beginning,' Arthur said. 'You and Dylan met inside Pentonville Prison.'

Tommy Jr could barely think, let alone answer, and as Arthur lifted the hammer in the air again, he hastily nodded.

'Yes,' he spat out. 'I've already told you this.' And it was true. He felt as though they were going around and around in circles. He'd answered the same questions so many times that he was sick and tired of giving the exact same reply over and over again. For the life of him he couldn't understand why Arthur didn't believe him. He and Dylan had never spoken about their families' business interests. They'd barely even spoken about their family full stop, and it wasn't until after Dylan's death that he'd found out his father was Jason Vickers.

Arthur narrowed his eyes. 'And the two of you had never met before that time?'

Tommy shook his head. He was exhausted, the back of his head still hurt, and he had a feeling he'd been bleeding too if the smears of blood on his collar were anything to go by.

'Bit of a coincidence that, isn't it?'

Tommy Jr glanced up. He didn't understand. What was a coincidence?

'I mean, two members from two different notorious families being placed on the same wing; that's more than a little bit odd, isn't it? Of course I know why Dylan was there, it was me who arranged his fate, but you,' Arthur said, tilting his head to the side as he studied Tommy. 'Who was responsible for having you shipped to Pentonville?'

Tommy screwed up his face. No one had been responsible. He'd been on remand. 'You're a fucking nut job,' he spat out.

Arthur's eyes hardened. 'You keep making this so easy for me,' he said, swinging the hammer through the air.

Another scream escaped from Tommy Jr's lips. He needed to find a way to escape before the nutter started to swing the hammer at his head. Because once that happened, he had a feeling he'd be as good as dead.

* * *

'All right you lot,' Jonny said as he tried his utmost to quieten the family down.

'Oi.' Sitting across from him, his niece Carla brought her fingers up to her lips and let out a piercing whistle. 'Shut up for a minute.'

Jonny nodded. 'Cheers, Carla.' Leaning against his desk, he flicked his head in Cameron's direction. 'Tommy Jr is on the missing list.'

'What, again?' Mitchell groaned. 'That's the second time in as many days.'

'Yeah,' Jonny agreed. 'But this time I'm actually worried, or rather more worried than I was yesterday.'

'So what makes this any different?' Mitchell's twin brother Sonny asked.

'Well,' Jonny sighed. 'He hasn't just wandered off. He was meant to meet up with Aimee, it was her who let Cam know that something was amiss.'

Sonny sighed. 'All right, I can see why you'd think it's a bit suspicious.'

'What should we do?' Reece asked.

Thinking the question through, Jonny glanced towards Cameron. As much as he didn't think Tommy Jr had actually taken a trip over to South London to meet with the Vickers family, surely it was the best place to start looking for him; at least then they could rule that scenario out.

'I'm gonna take a trip over the water and have a word with Jason Vickers.'

'I'll come with you,' Reece volunteered.

Jonny shook his head. 'We can't all go.' He nodded towards Mitchell. 'Me, you and Cam will go and have a word with the Vickers family. The rest of you can start searching the pubs, just in case he ended up having one too many sherberts and has lost all track of time.'

Once they were outside, Mitchell pulled on Jonny's elbow. 'I thought you said you didn't think he'd ventured over to South London.'

'I don't,' Jonny answered as he flicked his gaze towards Cameron. 'But there is nothing stopping the Vickers family coming over here, is there. And as we both know, one of them did try to run him through with a blade not so long ago.'

'So are you thinking that they might have come back for a second attempt?'

'I dunno,' Jonny sighed. 'But anything is possible, right?'

* * *

As Jason Vickers climbed the stairs, he took a deep breath. He'd put the inevitable off for long enough, but now he was eager to check in on his wife. Ever since she'd dropped her bombshell, Carmen had been closeted away in their bedroom. He wasn't even so sure she would want to see him.

Lightly, he tapped on the bedroom door before gently pushing it aside.

Joanie turned her head, and pressing a finger to her lips, she gestured down to Carmen's sleeping form.

'How is she?' he asked quietly.

Joanie sighed and as she glanced towards Carmen, she shook her head. 'She's been better.'

Jason nodded. Motioning towards the door, he jerked his head towards it. 'I want a few moments alone with her.'

Joanie hesitated.

'Just a few moments,' Jason reiterated.

Joanie nodded, and after glancing once more towards Carmen, she stepped outside the room.

Slipping off his shoes, Jason climbed onto the bed, and laying on his side, he ever so carefully wrapped his arm around Carmen's waist. It wasn't until she curled into his body that he closed his eyes tightly, biting back the tears. No matter what, he couldn't stay angry at her. She was the love of his life, always would be. He'd get her help, he vowed. And this time he meant it; she could kick and scream all she wanted but this time she would be going into rehab whether she wanted to or not.

* * *

It was no secret that Arthur Brennan had a vicious temper. Not only was he sadistic in his thinking but he also took great pleasure in causing others significant harm.

Taking a moment or two to rest, he sat on an upturned wooden crate, his hard stare fixed on Tommy Jr's unconscious form.

'I was around your age,' he said, turning to look at Gio, 'the first time I ever killed a man.'

As Gio nodded, he gave a nervous smile.

'I warned him about her. Did you know that?'

Gio cocked an eyebrow. Confusion etched across his face.

'Jason,' Arthur clarified. 'Not that he chose to listen of course. From the moment he set his eyes on the bitch she was all he could think about. She bewitched him with her tits and fanny and her free fucking spirit. Even back then she was on the gear. She even robbed him of twenty quid, all so she could pay off her dealer, and twenty quid in those days was a lot of money. And after all of that, after all of the shit she pulled, he still wouldn't listen to reason and get shot of the slapper.'

Narrowing his eyes, Gio swallowed. 'She's his wife,' he answered in a small voice.

'And?' Arthur snapped. 'I was his business partner.' Snapping his lips shut, he momentarily closed his eyes and rubbed at his temples. 'There was always someone else, always someone that little bit more important than me. He's never been able to see what's right in front of his nose, and that right there has always been one of his biggest problems. We were always a good team, even back when we were nothing more than a couple of kids. I told him that together one day we would build an empire.' Sweeping his arm around the lockup, he laughed. 'And I was true to my word even if he doesn't know about any of this yet.'

Gio nodded. 'Yeah,' he said with a nervous chuckle. 'You did it.'

'And do you know how?' Arthur asked as he got to his feet. 'Because I don't play fucking games. In fact, I eliminate anything and anyone that gets in my way.' Giving a wicked smile, he gripped onto Gio's arm, his fingernails digging into the delicate skin. 'Take Colin, for example,' he said of Jason's brother. 'He was a problem too once, a big problem. He had a bit too much to say for himself, exactly like that son of his, Vinnie. And Jason being Jason, well, he listened to everything Colin had to say; in fact. it would be fair to say he hung off his every word. If Colin had said jump, Jason would have asked how high. That was how it worked between them. Jason idolised his brother. He looked up to the big-mouthed fucker.'

Not liking where the conversation was going, Gio winced as he attempted to pull his arm free. 'I heard they were close,' he said, lifting his free arm up into a shrug.

'Close.' Athur screwed up his face. 'That's one way of putting it.' Giving a theatrical sigh, he tightened his grip around Gio's arm. 'Can you blame me for wanting to get rid of the bastard? At the end of the day, he had to go.'

Gio reeled back, his eyes wide. 'What are you talking about? Jason said that it was an accident. That he was smashed out of his nut, that he got behind the wheel of a car, lost control and then slammed into a tree.'

'Yeah.' Arthur chuckled. 'Or at least that was the coroner's conclusion. You'd be amazed at how desperate some people are for a bit of cash in their back pocket. They'd do anything if needs be, including tampering with evidence. The truth is, though,' he said, leaning his head closer as though they were fellow conspirators, 'Colin hadn't been drinking that night. As much as I hated the bastard, he did have some morals. And there wasn't a chance in hell he'd have attempted to drive if he'd been on the booze, especially not with his wife and kid in the car.'

Gio was too stunned to even answer, and his mind began to whirl. 'I don't understand...'

'And then there was Dylan,' Arthur continued. 'He had a lot of his old man inside of him, not that I need to remind you of what he was like.' He grinned. 'You know yourself that he was ruthless, and that he didn't give a shit about anyone other than himself. He'd stick a blade into you and smile while doing so, I even watched him do it once. But that was where he fucked up,' he sighed. 'He became too cocky, too sure of himself. And once he'd crossed that line of no return, there was only one way it was going to end,' he said, making a slicing action across his throat.

Fear began to get the better of Gio. 'Why are you telling me all of this?'

Arthur shrugged. 'I don't know,' he sighed as he heaved up a plastic container filled with water. 'To clear my conscious perhaps, or to confess my sins.' Unscrewing the cap, he doused Tommy Jr with the water, smiling to himself as he began to cough and splutter. 'Or maybe, Gio, it's because all of this,' he said, motioning around them, 'can only end one way.'

A cold shiver ran down the length of Gio's spine. 'What do you mean?'

'Well,' Arthur continued as he swung the hammer up onto his shoulder. 'Think about it. Do you really think that the Carters are going to sit back and do fuck all once they realise their blue-eyed boy over here,' he said, motioning to Tommy Jr, 'is on the missing list?'

Gio's throat was dry. He hadn't really thought that far ahead. Story of his life. 'I, erm...' he started. 'We could always let him go, dump him in the street somewhere.'

Arthur shook his head and laughed. 'He knows who we are. So no, we can't let him go,' he said as he came to stand just inches away from Tommy. 'As soon as he tells me exactly what it was that Dylan told him, I'll put him out of his—' Before Arthur could finish the sentence, Tommy Jr kicked out, his foot landing in the centre of Arthur's stomach, and as he fell backwards,

Tommy scrambled to his feet, his injured leg immediately giving way on him.

'Well, don't just stand there,' Arthur wheezed as he fought to catch his breath. 'Finish him.'

Gio's eyes were as wide as saucers. And as he glanced from Tommy Jr to the door, he debated whether or not he should make a run for it.

'Stop being a fucking imbecile,' Arthur roared. 'And kill him.'

Tommy Jr shook his head, his eyes beseeching Gio to do the right thing and let him go.

'I...' Gio turned to look at Arthur, and as the man began to heave himself up off the floor, he motioned for Tommy to make his escape, which was no mean feat when you took into account that he was restrained to the chair and that one of his kneecaps had been shattered.

'Come on, mate,' Tommy Jr screamed. 'Help me fucking out here.'

It was too late, and as Arthur got to his feet, his expression was murderous.

'I'm sorry,' Gio cried as he lifted his arms to protect his head. 'I panicked.'

'I'll give you fucking panicked,' Arthur yelled as he backed Gio into a corner.

Still continuing to cower, Gio whimpered. 'I won't do it again. I promise. It was all of this talk about Colin and Dylan, it threw me. I didn't know how to react.'

Arthur narrowed his eyes, and turning his head to look down at Tommy Jr, he began to slowly clap his hands together. 'Bravo. Bravo. A valiant effort even if I say so myself.'

Tommy Jr heaved out a redundant breath. He'd managed to

crawl five feet, and with the door to the lockup within touching distance, he'd almost made it. Flopping onto his back, he looked up at the ceiling then closed his eyes. It was no use; he wasn't going to come out of this alive no matter how much he wanted to.

18

Winston's eyebrows were pinched together, and as he shook his head, his lip curled upwards. 'Nah,' he said. 'I'm not having that. There's been a mistake, a huge fucking mistake, there has to have been.'

Damien sipped at a glass of whiskey. 'I wish I could say it was a mistake,' he admitted. 'But it isn't. My mum told us everything.'

Winston narrowed his eyes. 'I'm not being funny, mate,' he said, holding up a hand as if to ward Damien off, 'but was she pissed?'

Damien shook his head.

'Stoned then.'

Again, Damien shook his head.

'Well then she must have been buzzing off her nut.'

'She was sober as a judge. Probably the most coherent I've ever seen her.'

Winston blew out his cheeks. 'Fuck me, D, I didn't see that coming.'

'How do you think I feel? Dylan was my brother. I looked out for him. I loved him.'

'Yeah.' As he lifted his own glass up to his lips, Winston gestured around the lounge. 'I have to admit I never imagined this either. You and your old man in the same house without the pair of you kicking off.'

Damien let out a laugh. 'Stick around and I'm sure it'll go tits up at some point.' Swallowing down the remainder of his drink, he gave a sad smile. 'You know what we're like. It doesn't take much to get our backs up. Although I have to admit it's been kind of nice not being at each other's throats for once.'

Winston nodded. 'Yeah, I get that, man,' he said, patting Damien's shoulder.

Before Damien could answer, the doorbell rang. 'Let me get that,' he said, wandering out to the downstairs foyer.

'Oi, D,' Winston called out. 'Looks like you made yourself right at home.'

Damien chuckled. It was true. For the first time in years he actually felt welcome in his parents' home.

Moments later, he returned to the lounge with three men in tow.

'You remember Tommy Johnson's family,' he said, introducing the men.

'Yeah.' Warily, Winston got to his feet and as he shook the men's hands, he nodded.

'I'll give my dad a shout,' Damien said as he left the room.

Moments later, he tapped lightly on his parents' bedroom door, and on entering the room he took note of the soft snores that came from his dad. He gently shook his dad's leg to wake him up.

'The Carters are downstairs,' he said, making sure to keep his voice low so not to disturb his mother.

Rolling onto his back, Jason rubbed at his eyes then glanced at his watch. 'What do they want?'

Damien shook his head. 'I don't know,' he said, glancing towards his mum. 'There are three of them down there, though.'

'Okay.' Jason nodded as he sat up. 'Tell them I'll be down in a minute.'

Damien nodded again and before he could leave the room, Jason called after him.

'Are they tooled up?'

Damien narrowed his eyes. 'I don't know.' He shrugged, glancing towards the door. 'Why? Are you expecting trouble?'

'No.' Jason shook his head. 'Doesn't hurt to be careful, though,' he said as he climbed off the bed and began tucking in his shirt. 'Once upon a time, someone turning up on your doorstep unannounced would have had all the markings of a planned hit.'

Damien lifted his eyebrows, and on seeing his son's worried expression, Jason smiled. 'As far as I know the Carters aren't in the business of killing people. Tell them I'll be down in a minute.'

* * *

Five minutes later, Jason made his way into the lounge. And on seeing Jonny Carter, Mitchell Carter, and Cameron Johnson, he held out his hand. 'Can I get you a drink?'

All three men shook their heads, and it was Jonny who spoke, keen to get straight down to business.

'We're looking for my nephew, Tommy,' he said, glancing towards Damien and Winston. 'He's on the missing list yet again.'

Jason blew out his cheeks. 'I know for a fact that my son and nephew have been here all day,' he said, dipping his hand into his pocket and pulling out his mobile phone. 'I can give Arthur a bell and see if he's been at the casino.'

'He's not there,' Mitchell interrupted. 'We went there first and spoke to your daughter.'

Jason narrowed his eyes. 'You mean Arthur wasn't there?'

'Yeah,' Jonny answered. 'Or at least that's what your daughter said.'

That was news to him, and pulling up his daughter's phone number, Jason brought the device to his ear. A few moments later he ended the call, his expression remaining neutral despite the confusion that engulfed him. According to Demi, Arthur was suffering from the same bug that he himself had. Only, there was no bug; he'd made the entire thing up so as to not worry Demi when he didn't show up for work.

'Listen,' he said as he leaned casually against the arm of the sofa. 'I'll pop over to the casino and ask around, just to make sure he hasn't been there. If I find anything I'll give you a buzz.'

'Yeah,' Jonny answered as he got to his feet. 'It was a long shot anyway. Sorry to take up your time.'

'No problem. Kids, eh?' he said with a shake of his head. 'They'd drive you up the fucking wall if they could.'

'Yeah, tell me about it.'

As he walked the men out, Jason was all smiles and it wasn't until he'd shut the door behind them that the smile slid from his face.

'What was all that about?' Vinnie asked when Jason returned to the lounge.

'I don't know,' Jason replied as he slipped on his jacket. 'But something's not right, I know that much.'

* * *

About to climb into his car, Jonny looked over his shoulder at the Vickers' home.

'What do you reckon?' he asked.

Mitchell sighed. 'I dunno. I mean, he looked sincere enough to me but whether he is or not is another matter.'

'Yeah,' Jonny agreed. 'That's what I thought.' Resting his arms on the roof of the car, he toyed with his mobile phone. He'd hoped to have received a phone call by now from either Tommy Jr himself, or his brother Sonny, or one of his many nephews to tell him that his great-nephew had been located and that just as he'd originally predicted, he'd been found propping up a bar someplace. Only deep down, Jonny knew that wasn't Tommy Jr's style. He liked a drink, of course he did, what nineteen-year-old lad didn't, but he wouldn't have gone in the pub before collecting Aimee and he would never have risked driving her around while half cut.

As much as he hated to admit it, Jonny was worried, and as he tapped his thumb against his bottom lip, he was deep in thought. The night before he'd been spitting feathers, ready to come down on Tommy Jr hard. And as angry as he'd been with his great-nephew, he hadn't been as concerned as he was right now.

'Do you think we should report him as missing?'

Cameron stared at his uncle. 'Are you actually suggesting we go to the old bill?'

'I don't know.' Jonny blew out his cheeks. 'I've never been in a situation like this before. I mean, I've been responsible for plenty of other men going missing, but never a member of my own family. What are we supposed to do if he doesn't turn up?'

'We keep looking,' Mitchell suggested. 'He can't just disappear off the face of the earth. He's got to be somewhere.'

'Yeah, you'd think so,' Jonny answered while still deep in thought.

* * *

Gio moved around the lockup as though he were on autopilot. He couldn't bear to even look at the kid Tommy Johnson. His screams had soon quietened down to muffled groans, but for some reason Gio found those even harder to listen to. The kid's body was giving out on him, it had to be. No one would be able to endure what he had and live to tell the tale.

As for Arthur, Gio was beginning to think that he was stark-raving mad. He'd already killed twice that Gio knew of, and from the look of things, Tommy Johnson was next on his radar.

To make matters even worse, the kid still hadn't given Arthur the information that he wanted. He had to hand it to him though, because as far as Gio was concerned Tommy Johnson was one tough little bastard. If the roles had been reversed, Gio knew for a fact that he would have sung louder than a canary just to put an end to the beating. Or maybe the kid was a lot more astute than he looked. Either way, Arthur was going to kill him and he had a feeling that Tommy Johnson knew that.

Arthur's mobile phone began to ring, making Gio jump.

'Are you going to answer that?'

Glancing down at his phone screen, Arthur momentarily paused before running his hand through his greying hair then shaking his head.

Gio sighed. If he was being honest, all he wanted to do was go home. Only he couldn't quite see that happening, at least not until Tommy Johnson was dead and his body had been dumped in a ditch someplace. The mere thought of the work still to be done was enough to make him feel exhausted. Unlike Dylan, he wasn't cut out for this line of work. Dylan had got a kick out of harming others, as did Arthur.

He took a peek at his watch. They'd been here for hours and he was about to say as much when Arthur's mobile phone began to ring again. Just as he had before, Arthur ignored the call. By the time it had a rung a third time, Arthur was on the verge of erupting. It was on the tip of Gio's tongue to ask him who was calling. Whoever it was, they were persistent.

As Tommy Johnson began to groan again, Gio inadvertently rolled his eyes. Yeah, it was definitely going to be a long night, all right.

* * *

By the time Jason and Damien made their way into the casino, Jason was becoming all the more irate. Half a dozen calls he'd made to Arthur and each time the call had rung off.

'Dad. What are you doing here?' Demi asked as she hugged her father to her. 'I thought you were unwell.'

'I am. I mean, I was,' Jason answered.

'And what's this?' As she flicked her gaze between her brother and father, there was a twinkle in Demi's eyes. 'Are my eyes actually deceiving me or... No,' she said, giving Damien's arm a pinch. 'You're definitely here, and what's more the two of you aren't punching the living daylights out of one another.'

'Leave it out,' Damien chastised as he gently pushed his sister away from him. 'We're looking for Arthur.'

Demi narrowed her eyes. 'I told you that he went home feeling rough. He said that you and him had the same bug, either that or it was something you'd both eaten.'

Jason gave an irritated sigh and as he glanced down the corridor that led to their offices, he ran his tongue over his teeth. 'I need to collect something from his office. Some paperwork.'

'Yeah, okay.' Demi shrugged. 'I'll be in my office if you need me. Oh, and if you see Gio, tell him he's needed here tonight to help me lock up.'

'What do you mean, if I see Gio; where is he?' Jason snapped.

Demi paused, and just as she looked as though she was going to make up an excuse for her husband, her shoulders sagged. 'I don't know,' she admitted. 'I haven't seen him all day.'

Jason's mind began to whirl. It couldn't be a coincidence that both Arthur and Gio were on the missing list, could it? As he pulled himself up to his full height, his eyes were hard. 'If you see him before I do, tell him I want a word.'

'Dad...' Demi began before clamping her lips together and nodding. 'If I see him I'll let him know, okay.'

'Good girl.' Pulling his daughter towards him, Jason kissed the top of her head. 'You're too good for him, you know that, right?' he whispered in her ear.

Demi rolled her eyes. 'So you keep on telling me.'

A few moments later, both Jason and Damien were in Arthur's office. In a way it felt wrong to be rifling through his belongings, not that Jason actually expected to find anything of interest. They had been business partners for the best part of thirty years; they didn't keep secrets from one another, or at least Jason didn't think they did, and so when he came across the desk drawer that was locked, he had to admit his interest was piqued and he couldn't help but wonder what it was that Arthur was trying to hide.

'You could always prise it open.'

Jason looked up. 'Are you actually for real?' he spat. 'I'm not going to force it open. That might be the kind of partnership you and Winston have but...'

Damien shrugged. 'If it was Winston,' he interrupted, 'I wouldn't feel the need to be in his office in the first place.' He held up his hands. 'But obviously that is the kind of partnership you and Arthur have.'

Jason fell silent. His son had him there. The truth was, at the back of his mind there was a niggling doubt. He didn't even know how to explain what it was; it was just something off.

'Look,' Damien continued. 'You're here for a reason. And we can argue all day long about who has the better person beside them, but,' he said, nodding towards the desk, 'until you actually take a look, your mind won't be at rest; you'll always have that little voice in the back of your head asking what it is you might have found.'

His son had him there too. And it was true, Jason was more than a little intrigued; he actually had a bad feeling in his gut. 'Find me something I can use to jimmy it open.'

Damien began looking around the office. 'How about this?' he asked, holding up a metal ruler.

'That should do it,' Jason answered, holding out his hand.

Two unsuccessful attempts later, Damien pushed his father aside, then pulled up his sleeves.

Jason's eyes widened. 'Did you not get that seen to?' he said, motioning to the dog bites.

Damien shrugged. 'I'm okay. If it gets too bad I'll take some painkillers.'

Jason gave him a sceptical look but decided to keep schtum all the same. Even as a boy, Damien had been a stubborn bugger. Moments later, the drawer sprang open. And as both men stood back, they looked down at the contents inside.

As Jason cocked his head to the side, ever so slowly his eyes began to grow wider and his expression all the more horrified.

Beside him, Damien gave a low whistle. 'Is that what I think it is?' he asked as he took a step closer.

Too shocked to speak, Jason nodded. His intuition had been right. All along he'd known there was something wrong, he'd just been unable to state what the problem actually was. But now he was all too aware, and considering that the evidence was staring them in the face, there was no getting away from the fact that Arthur had been hiding a crack habit.

'The dirty bastard.'

The anger in his son's voice made Jason turn his head.

'The lowlife cunt,' Damien growled again. 'I'm gonna kill him.'

Taken aback, Jason narrowed his eyes.

'Oh, come on,' Damien roared at him. 'You're not stupid. Think, Dad. Open your eyes and actually look at what's in front of you.'

Jason turned back to look at the drawer. And it was only then that he felt the equivalent of a punch in the gut. 'No,' he gasped. 'No, no, no.' Stumbling backwards, he leaned his back against the wall, his skin ashen. It wasn't possible, it couldn't be. He and Arthur were as good as brothers. Nausea washed over him. Was he really so blind that he hadn't been able to see what had been going on under his nose this entire time?

'How could you have not seen any of this?' Damien implored. 'It was going on under your nose.'

'I...' As Jason rubbed at his temples, words failed him. He didn't know how to answer. He was still too stunned to string a sentence together.

'You still don't get it, do you?'

After giving his son a blank stare, Jason glanced back down at the drawer, his gaze raking over the contents again. He'd never been one for drugs; in a way, he guessed that Carmen had put him off for life. But even from what he could tell, there was a lot of crack, far too much for personal consumption.

Jason stood up a little straighter. 'Of course I get it,' he snapped. 'Dylan must have been getting the crack from Arthur. They both had a problem.'

Gritting his teeth, Damien threw his arms up in the air. 'How can you be so fucking dense?' Taking a deep breath, he nodded down at the narcotics. 'Dylan was the one who gave Mum the crack. And judging by the contents of the desk, Arthur was the one supplying it to Dylan. They were working together. They were a partnership.'

'No.' Jason's jaw dropped. 'What the fuck are you talking about? That's not possible.'

Damien continued. 'And if they were in a partnership, then Arthur was more than aware that Dylan was travelling to Liverpool. And the reason he knew that is because the two of them were doing business with Calvin Rivers.'

'No, no, no.' Moving across the office and away from his son, Jason held up his hand. 'You're talking bollocks. This is you all over. This is what you do. You love nothing more than to cause hag, to stir up shit everywhere you go. You're not content until you've riled everyone up. I've always said that you're poisonous, that you've got a destructive nature. And do you know fucking what?' he yelled. 'I was right all along, you're all those things and a lot more besides.'

Despite his father's words, Damien appeared calm; after all, it wasn't the first time his dad had berated him. 'Liverpool,' he said as he began to calmly tick the words off his fingers. 'Calvin Rivers knowing exactly who Dylan was. Dylan supplying Mum with crack. Dylan wanting to know the code to your safe. The crack that is in Arthur's desk. Come on, Dad,' he beseeched. 'I know you're not this stupid. They were in a partnership. How can you not see it?'

Jason heaved in a breath, and as his face drained of all colour, realisation finally took hold. His boy, his legacy, it had all been an act. A betrayal that cut him so deep he wouldn't have been surprised if he'd keeled over and had a coronary. Never would he have ever imagined that Dylan could be so disloyal. In a rare show of emotion, Jason pulled his eldest son into his embrace and held on for dear life. In all of his life, he had never been more sorry. He'd said such wicked, hurtful things, many of which could never be taken back or ever erased.

'It's all right.' As though he were reading his father's mind, Damien awkwardly patted his father's back. 'It's all right.'

Only it wasn't all right, and they were both well aware of that fact.

19

Cameron Johnson was deep in thought. His boy had been on the missing list for more than five hours and his wife was becoming increasingly suspicious. As it was she wasn't daft, and neither should she be seeing as she was a Carter through and through and that her father had been the head of the Carter family, the infamous Tommy Carter.

For the first couple of hours he ignored both her calls and subsequent text messages, hoping that by the time he did respond their son would have been located safe and well.

Eventually, Karen had turned up at the scrapyard, her eyes blazing with fury as she demanded to know where their boy was.

There had only been so many excuses he could give before it became blatantly obvious he was trying to put her off the scent. And even now as he could feel her shooting daggers into the side of his head, he was trying to think up yet another reason for their son's absence.

'I swear to God, Cam,' Karen seethed, 'I am this close to going ape shit,' she said, pressing her thumb and forefinger an inch apart. 'And believe me, you do not want that to happen. Because trust me when I say this, husband or not, your head will be one of the first to roll.'

Cameron sighed. She was telling the truth too. Karen had a wicked temper on her and it didn't take much for her to actually explode. The only exception was Tommy Jr, who could do no wrong in Karen's eyes. He was her baby, and despite Tommy being a nineteen, soon to be twenty-year-old man, she still liked to treat him as a child. Not that Tommy was happy with the way his mum babied him. Time and time again, until he was blue in the face, he would remind her that he wasn't a child. Not that Karen ever listened. Sometimes he couldn't help but think Tommy was equally to blame; like many other teenagers, he could be a lazy little bugger when he wanted to be. And the fact Karen still did his washing and ironing, and that she catered to his every whim, made him all the more lazier. Other than know where the fridge and food cupboard was, he was pretty sure that Tommy Jr had no idea how to navigate his way around a kitchen.

'Cameron,' Karen growled.

'All right, all right.' Throwing up his hands, Cameron could barely look his wife in the eyes. 'I don't know where he is.'

The colour drained from Karen's face. 'What do you mean, you don't where he is?' she shouted at him as she glanced frantically around the office as though thoroughly expecting Tommy Jr to pop up out of nowhere.

Cameron sighed. 'He was meant to pick up Aimee and take her out for something to eat but he didn't show up.'

'What in the ever loving fuck are you talking about?' Karen shouted. 'He was here, in the office. How on earth could he have just disappeared?'

Cameron gritted his teeth. This was exactly why he'd wanted

to keep schtum. The less Karen knew the better. Wearily, he watched her as she began to pace the portable cabin.

'I'm not stupid,' she finally barked out at him. 'You hear about this kind of thing on the news, young boys going missing, it happens all the time.'

Narrowing his eyes, Cameron frowned.

'Sex-trafficking,' Karen yelled as she threw up her arms. 'They even kidnap people for their organs now. And don't get me started on these grooming gangs, they target vulnerable people.'

Despite the seriousness in Karen's voice, Cameron couldn't help but snort out a laugh. 'Tommy Jr is hardly vulnerable, is he.'

'That's right, you laugh,' Karen seethed. 'But this kind of thing is going on up and down the country.'

Cameron shook his head and as his uncle entered the office, he lifted his eyebrows towards him. 'Kal has got it into her head that Tommy Jr has been sex-trafficked.'

Taken aback, Jonny could only stare at his niece.

'I didn't say that,' Karen gasped, slapping her husband on the arm. 'I said that the country is rife with these grooming gangs. And, well,' she bristled, 'my Tommy is a nice-looking boy...'

'Leave it out, Karen,' Jonny said with a hint of irritation to his voice. 'He's a tough kid, he knows exactly how to handle himself.'

'So where is he then, eh?'

Both Cameron and Jonny shared a glance. That right there was the million-dollar question. Where was Tommy Jr?

* * *

Tommy Jr inhaled a breath and held it in for a long second before slowly releasing it again.

He was tired. The pain throughout his entire leg was taking up every ounce of his energy. His wrists were red raw from how much he'd tried to free his hands. As far as he was concerned, that was all he needed, just one fist free, and then he would be able to defend himself, or at least try to.

Warily, he peeled his eyes open and took a surreptitious glance around him. The lockup had been fairly quiet for the past ten minutes or so, neither Arthur Brennan nor Gio uttering a single word. At one point he'd actually begun to wonder if they had left him. But no, much to his dismay they were still there.

Snapping his gaze in the direction of the door, he attempted to move his leg. The pain that ricocheted through him was enough to make him dig his fingernails into the palm of his hand just to stop himself from crying out. There was no other alternative; he either walked out of the lockup or he died here. And if there was one thing he knew about himself, it was the fact that he was no quitter. Tentatively, he moved his leg a second time and yet again another jolt of excruciating pain shot through him. He had roughly less than ten feet between himself and the door; just ten feet, that was all that stood between himself and freedom. Well, other than a busted kneecap that he was sure he wouldn't be able to walk on, and Arthur Brennan and Gio of course. Still, he reasoned. He'd worry about that when it came to it.

Closing his eyes, he took a few moments to once again concentrate on his breathing. He was pretty certain that the door to the lockup had been left unlocked. And in the commotion that had followed after his last attempt to free himself, not once had he seen either of the men move towards the door. Perhaps luck might be on his side after all. The only thing he needed to do was actually make it to the door in one piece.

Peeling open his eyes again, he took deep breaths. No matter how much it hurt, he was going to make a run for it. He'd even hop out of the lockup on one foot if he had to, which with the chair tied to his wrists might be more than a little awkward.

Slowly, he began to rock backwards and forwards just enough to give himself some momentum so that he could propel forward. With one eye still on the door, his knee bounced up and down, or rather his good knee did; the other just hung limp.

Finally he was ready, or at least as ready as he could ever be, and after a quick glimpse in the direction of Arthur and Gio, a roar that came from deep within his chest escaped from his lips, his expression one of pure and utter determination. And then he was up on his feet. Almost immediately his injured leg gave way, but Tommy Jr wasn't about to go down without a fight. Flinging himself against the wall, he managed to keep himself upright. And hopping several feet forward, he continued to scream, more so for the shock value than any other reason, although he had a feeling that if it wasn't for the adrenalin coursing through his veins, he would probably be screaming because of the pain.

The shock across Gio's face was even more of an incentive for Tommy Jr to keep going. Using every inch of his willpower to ignore the pain, he pushed his chin down onto his chest and charged forward, ramming head-first into Gio's chest and knocking him to the floor. Using the chair to his advantage, he barrelled his way through, not caring one iota as he trampled over Gio in his haste to reach the door.

There were only two things on his mind: the first to escape, no matter what he had to do to achieve his goal. And secondly, he needed to stay upright, because if his leg buckled underneath him a second time then it was as good as game over. There would be no other chances to escape. Arthur Brennan would kill him on the spot; he'd be daft not to.

The pain was excruciating, the injured leg so weak that the shattered kneecap was barely able to bear weight, if any at all. Still, Tommy Jr didn't give up. He'd worry about the damage later, and to be perfectly honest, spending months on end in a plaster cast had to be a lot better than the alternative.

From behind him he could sense Arthur Brennan's fury. The heavy breathing across the back of Tommy Jr's neck a dead giveaway to the fact that he was hot on his tail. Tommy Jr cried out even louder. He didn't dare look over his shoulder to see if Gio had got to his feet for fear that it would slow him down. From deep within he pushed himself even further. He didn't want to die. He wanted to live. He had to live. He was about to become a father and despite his initial reservations, he was excited to meet his child. And fair enough, he knew that he and Aimee were young, maybe even a little too young to think about settling down and having children, but at the end of the day Tommy Jr was 100 per cent sure that his Aimee was the only woman for him. She was the only girl that he'd ever loved and it had been a case of love at first sight. From the very moment he'd cast his eyes upon her, he'd been obsessed. His Aimee was stunning, and she had a lovely little figure on her too. But even more than that, she had a smashing personality. Everyone loved her and he'd never heard anyone have a bad word to say about her. She'd go out of her way to help anyone; she'd even go without herself just to help others.

The thought of Aimee spurred him on. He couldn't leave her, especially not when she was having his baby. He reached out his hand, his fingertips close enough to skim over the wooden door.

'You little cunt.'

The hatred in Arthur Brennan's voice chilled Tommy Jr to the bone.

Just a second or two more and he would make it. His fingers grasped the door and just as he was about to yank it open, his head jolted back, his neck straining under the pressure as Arthur clutched a handful of his hair in his fist.

Panic filled Tommy Jr. He'd come this close; he couldn't lose now. He allowed his upper body to become slightly limp, meaning that the grip Arthur had on him became more slack. He then flung his head forward and back again in quick succession. The sickening crunch of bone hitting bone was like music to Tommy's ears, and as Arthur screamed out a torrent of expletives, he released his grip upon Tommy Jr's hair.

Taking this as his chance to escape, Tommy sprang forward, his fingers grappling to pull open the door. After what felt like an age but what in reality was only a few moments, the door swung open, and using every last ounce of strength he had inside of him, he managed to hop just a couple of feet before losing his balance and collapsing to the floor directly in front of an unsuspecting dog walker.

Panting for breath, Tommy Jr lay on his side. He'd never felt more relieved and as the dog, an American Bulldog, let out a ferocious bark, he didn't know whether to laugh or cry.

'Mate, I need you to help me,' he pleaded. 'Because if you don't he's gonna kill me.'

The dog walker's expression was one of shock, and as he looked from Tommy Jr to Arthur, he puffed out his chest, his stance that of a man ready and willing to have a ruck. In his hand he clutched his mobile phone. And without missing a beat he hastily unlocked the device, began punching out several numbers, then brought the phone up to his ear.

Arthur's eyes were wide, and the bridge of his nose was

bloody from the collision with Tommy Jr's head. It didn't take a genius to tell him that he'd made a cockup of epic proportions, and as the dog walker lifted the phone up to his ear, he made the split-second decision to make a run for it with Gio hot on his tail.

Tommy Jr momentarily closed his eyes. He was alive. The mere thought made him laugh out loud. He'd honestly thought that his time was up, that his body would be dumped beside the side of a road or found floating in the Thames. 'Mate,' he said to the dog walker. 'I know I owe you my life but do me a favour, pal. Don't call the old bill. Just help me get out of this,' he said, motioning to the chair behind him.

Much to Tommy's relief, the man smiled, and turning his mobile phone around, he indicated to the blank screen. 'Trust me.' He grinned. 'I'm not in the habit of calling the old bill.' Crouching down, he pulled a small blade from out of his pocket and began the process of cutting the cable ties.

'Do you normally carry a knife on you?' Tommy Jr asked, his forehead furrowed.

Glancing up, the man chuckled. 'You never know who you might bump into,' he answered as he turned his head to survey the direction that Arthur Brennan and Gio had left by.

Once free, Tommy Jr gently rubbed at his grazed and bruised wrists then reached into his back pocket and took out his own mobile phone. Just minutes later after calling his dad to come and collect him, he lay on his back, staring up at the sky as he waited for his heart to once again return to its usual normal steady rhythm.

'Cheers, mate,' he said to the man as he sat up and shook his hand.

The man nodded in return and, keen to get on his way, he motioned towards the end of the alleyway. 'I'd best be off.'

'Yeah. Thanks again.'

As the man walked away, Tommy Jr narrowed his eyes. He'd looked familiar to him. Only he couldn't place where he might have seen him before. He was around his dad's age, dark skinned, and with a South London accent. 'Oi,' Tommy called after him. 'Do I know you?'

The man turned his head, a wide smile etched across his face. 'No.' He winked back. 'At least not personally. I don't venture over to your side of the water very often and when I do I try to avoid any areas connected to my old life.'

On hearing the cryptic answer, Tommy Jr's forehead furrowed, and flopping back onto his back, he blew out his cheeks. No matter how he did or didn't know the man, he was just grateful that he'd actually been there. He was alive and that was the only thing that mattered.

* * *

Gio had never run so fast in his life and didn't stop running until he was at least three streets away from his home. Looking over his shoulder, he came to a jog before finally coming to a halt. Bending forward, he rested his hands on his thighs and took several deep, shuddering breaths. He was knackered and so unfit it was unbelievable. Straightening up, he patted his gut, the slight pouch enough to tell him that he needed to cut back a bit. It was the booze, he guessed. And he did like to knock back shots of Apple Sourz or tequila on a nightly basis.

Another quick glance over his shoulder, then he carried on his way. He hoped that Demi wasn't home. The last thing he needed was her going on at him, giving him earache as per usual. If he thought he'd get away with it, he'd give her a slap; that might shut her up for all of two seconds. That big mouth of hers never seemed to stop, constantly telling him what to do as though he were a little kid instead of a grown man. Anyone would think that she was the boss the way she carried on.

Moments later he was walking down the pathway to his home, a modest two-bedroom, two-bathroom terraced house that had still cost over half a million. Jason had bought the house for them as a wedding present, although he was pretty certain the deeds were in Demi's name alone considering he'd never been shown them despite asking more than once to look at the legal paperwork. He'd actually been spitting feathers at the time. Apparently Demi had chosen the house herself, and instead of choosing a more substantial property, she'd opted for a house that was barely large enough to swing a cat in. Her explanation was that she'd grown up in a huge home and wanted something more cosy. He could have wrapped his hands around the stupid mare's throat and strangled her.

Glancing from one side of the pathway to the other, Gio was a nervous wreck. And who could blame him? Tommy Johnson was still alive and was bound to tell his family who it was that had held him captive. And then once his family knew, Jason Vickers would be informed. The mere thought of Jason turning up on his doorstep was enough to make him feel nauseous. He already knew that Jason wasn't very keen on him. In fact, if it wasn't for Demi, he had a feeling Jason would have told him to fuck off long ago.

Stepping into the house, Gio hastily closed the door behind him. A film of sweat covered his forehead, and his hair was damp. A quick sniff under his armpits told him that he stank. Not that he actually cared. He'd spray on some deodorant before climbing into bed. It wasn't as though his wife was going to come anywhere near him; she hadn't done so since their honeymoon four years earlier. The very same night that she had warned him of what would happen should he try to get lairy with her again. As a result they now had separate bedrooms. She'd chosen the larger one for herself and he was in the box room.

'Gio, is that you?'

Gio gritted his teeth. Who else did the bitch think it would be, unless of course she was giving out keys to all and sundry.

'Yeah,' he grumbled back.

Demi stepped into the hallway. Still dressed in her trademark suit, she placed a hand on her hip and tilted her head to the side. 'Where the fuck have you been? I had to close the casino on my own.'

Gio narrowed his eyes. Where was Jason? He gave a shrug. 'Not my problem. It's what you get paid for, ain't it?'

A laugh escaped from Demi's lips. 'It's also what you get paid for unless it's escaped your notice.'

Waving his hand dismissively, Gio shoved his way past and entered the lounge. Once there he flopped onto the sofa. 'I'm knackered. Rustle me up a bit of grub.'

Demi's mouth dropped open. 'You can't be serious.'

Gio shrugged again. He was actually being serious, not that she would cook him anything. Still, it had been worth the try.

'I'm going to bed,' Demi announced.

Not even bothering to answer, Gio closed his eyes, and as he kicked his legs up onto the sofa, he made himself comfortable. He was more than just exhausted. He felt absolutely drained. Within five minutes he was snoring his head off, his mouth hanging agape as drool gathered at the corners of his lips.

* * *

Demi stared up at the ceiling. Call it intuition, but she had a feeling that her husband was up to no good. Not that she could say she would be upset if he was. After all, adultery was grounds for a divorce, not that a reason was actually needed any more.

After tossing and turning for what seemed like an age, Demi threw the duvet away from her and sat up. Reaching for her dressing gown, she shrugged it on then as quietly as she could, she left her bedroom and made her way downstairs.

She heard Gio before she saw him, and wrinkling her nose, she looked down on him. Spread out on the sofa, with his mouth hanging open, he had never looked more repulsive than he did right now.

Beside him was his mobile phone. And for a reason that she was unable to explain, her gaze kept flicking towards it until she tentatively reached down and scooped it up. Wandering into the kitchen, she flicked the switch for the kettle to boil then took a seat at the breakfast bar. Surprisingly, Gio's phone didn't have a password, and she shook her head at how stupid he was. No doubt he had apps linked to his online banking too. If he should ever lose the phone and it was to fall into the wrong hands, they would have a field day.

Swiping the device open, she took a quick peek at his text messages. There was nothing there to pique her interest, just the usual crap that she'd been half expecting. Several codes to join various gambling sites, as if he hadn't joined enough already. Another from someone asking if he could get his hands on any cannabis for them. And then one from her brother Dylan telling him that something or other was still on for later that night. Her forehead furrowed. She hadn't even known that Dylan and Gio were on friendly terms. Or at least she'd never seen them interacting.

Closing the messenger app, she was just about to return his

phone when she paused and began scrolling to where his photo gallery was. Gio was a vain, arrogant prick and it wouldn't surprise her if he'd taken one or two dick pics of himself ready to try and impress some new tart.

Scrolling through the photos, which were mainly cars that he was probably interested in purchasing, her heart suddenly stopped. As her blood ran cold, she blinked several times, unable to comprehend what she was looking at. It was a photo of her mum, that much was obvious. But it wasn't just any photo. Her mum held one hand up in the air as though she were trying to hide herself. Lines of black mascara streaked her cheeks and her eyes were red rimmed and puffy.

Demi's head snapped in the direction of the lounge, a million questions buzzing through her mind. Why did Gio have a photo of her mum, and more to the point, when had it been taken? She looked back down at the image, taking note of the date and time displayed at the bottom of the screen. This was no snapshot of her mother having fun; she looked absolutely terrified.

Unease began to curl around Demi's insides. A part of her wanted to shove Gio awake and demand answers from him. Only deep down she already knew. Knew that the image hadn't been taken with her mother's consent and even more than that, something had happened prior to the photograph being taken. Without giving the matter another thought Demi left the kitchen, opened the front door and stepped out of the house.

As much as she loved her dad, she would never have considered herself a daddy's girl. She certainly had never relied on him to fix any problems for her; she was more than capable of taking care of things herself, and seeing as she had two brothers who would often rough house with her, she'd soon learned how to toughen up.

But even she knew that there was nothing she could do to Gio that would warrant what he had done to her mother. She could punch him, slap him, even kick out at him if she wished. But it wasn't enough. She wanted to hurt him, really hurt him.

Bringing her mobile phone up to her ear, she took a deep breath. She felt no remorse for what she was about to do. If anything, she was numb. Her husband may as well have been a stranger to her for how affected she was.

Finally, her father answered. It was then that a lone tear rolled down Demi's cheek. 'Dad,' she cried as she tugged at her hair and glanced over her shoulder at the house. 'I need you. It's Gio.'

20

In all of his life Jonny Carter had never driven so quickly. Even the times he'd acted as a getaway driver for the family during the armed robberies that they had partaken in over the years he didn't think he sped through the streets of London quite as fast as this.

In record time he'd reached South London. Cameron was beside him in the passenger seat, and both men were quiet.

Finally, Jonny cleared his throat. 'I fucking knew it,' he growled. 'I knew that this time was different and that we had every right to be worried.'

Cameron nodded. Tommy Jr hadn't actually said too much over the phone, as was typical of him. As much as he may have laughed and joked around, he could also be a dark horse at times. The only thing Tommy Jr had actually told them was that he was alive and that he needed picking up. Although from the sound of his son's voice, Cameron had been able to hear the weariness there and could only assume that his boy had been through some sort of ordeal.

Moments later, Jonny brought the car to a halt and before he could even switch off the ignition, Cameron was out of the car and crouching down beside his son.

'My fucking knee.' Closing his eyes, Tommy Jr screwed up his face, his voice wavering from the amount of pain he was in.

Leaning back slightly, Cameron raked his gaze over his son's injuries. 'Who the fuck did this?'

Tommy Jr shook his head and as he attempted to straighten out his knee, he sucked in a long breath, his eyes watering at the pain. 'I think my knee is fucked.'

Jonny could feel the anger within himself rising. 'Your dad asked you a question. Who did this to you?'

For a moment or two, Tommy Jr was quiet and after using his thumb to swipe away the tear that rolled down his cheek, he looked up. 'Arthur Brennan and Gio something or other.' His shoulders slumped. 'I don't know his surname. He introduced himself as being Jason Vickers' son-in-law, that's all I know.'

Jonny nodded. His blood was boiling. Right from the start he'd known that the Vickers family couldn't be trusted, and before he could make his thoughts known, Tommy Jr continued.

'Neither Jason nor Damien Vickers were involved.'

At this, Jonny narrowed his eyes. That couldn't be right. Jason Vickers and Arthur Brennan were business partners. Where one was, the other wasn't far behind. A bit like how his two elder brothers, Tommy Snr and Jimmy, had worked. The two had always been together. And if either one of them were after you, then you soon knew about it. They'd reminded him of a tag team. 'Are you sure about that?'

'Yeah.' Tommy Jr nodded. 'I'm positive.'

'Because that doesn't sound right to me...' Jonny began before Tommy Jr interrupted him.

'I need to speak to Jason Vickers. There's something I need to tell him.'

Screwing up his face, Jonny turned to look at Cameron. 'Are you sure he hasn't had a bump to the head as well? Because this is fucking madness.'

Tommy Jr groaned. 'My head is fine. Or at least I think it is,' he added, rubbing at the back of his head as he recalled the blow he'd taken. Maybe his uncle was actually onto something. He had been knocked out cold at one point. For all he knew he could be suffering with concussion. 'Either way it makes no difference. There's still something I need to tell Jason Vickers. Something important.'

Jonny rolled his eyes. Not that he could say he wasn't entirely convinced that Jason Vickers wasn't involved. 'And what about Arthur Brennan and this Gio geezer?' he growled.

As he shifted his weight, a hiss escaped from Tommy Jr's lips, and squeezing his eyes shut tight, he waited a moment for the pain to ease slightly before answering. 'I want them to pay for what they did. That bastard Arthur Brennan was gonna kill me.'

Jonny nodded. He'd thought as much. And seeing as Brennan was Jason Vickers' business partner, he took a wild guess that Dylan Vickers' death was somehow connected to the attack that Tommy had been subjected to. 'Yeah, well,' he answered with a scowl. 'You can't tell me that Vickers didn't know what was going on.'

'Listen,' Tommy said as he lifted his arms in the air and gestured for his dad and uncle to help him to his feet. 'You need to trust me on this.'

Helping his nephew up, Jonny screwed up his face as the howl of pain that came from Tommy echoed through the air. 'You're gonna need to go to hospital,' he said, taking a quick peek at the damage. 'Because I can tell you right now that doesn't look good.'

Tommy Jr shook his head. 'I will do, later,' he said. 'I need to speak to Vickers first.'

Jonny narrowed his eyes and as he helped Cameron to support Tommy Jr's weight as they slowly made their way towards the car, he couldn't help but speak what was on his mind. 'Fuck Vickers. I told you from the off not to get involved—'

'It's not about Jason Vickers, it's about his brother.'

'Who, what's his name?' Snapping his fingers together several times, hoping that the action would help to somehow jog his memory, Jonny racked his brain. 'I know who you mean. I met him once. I was probably around your age at the time. I think your grandad Tommy had done some business with him. Or maybe they were thinking about doing business together. I dunno, I'm not really sure what was going down. What was his fucking name?'

'Colin,' Tommy Jr volunteered.

'That's it, Colin. So, what about him?'

'I know how he died.'

'Even I know that,' Jonny groaned. 'He was smashed out of his nut and decided to get behind the wheel of his motor. The only one to survive was his kid. Well, not even a kid, he was still a baby at the time, a toddler.'

'You mean Vinnie Vickers.'

Taken aback, Jonny paused. 'You mean that little fucker who tried to run you through with a blade?'

'That's the one.'

Jonny blew out his cheeks. 'Fuck me,' he said with a shake of his head.

'Yeah, well,' Tommy Jr continued as he swung his backside on the edge of the car seat before attempting to actually turn his body and get into the car. 'Like I said. I know how he died. And I can tell you right now that he wasn't pissed that night.'

'And how would you know something like that? You weren't even born when Colin Vickers kicked the bucket.'

Tommy Jr paused and as he began to manoeuvre his injured leg into the car, he gritted his teeth. By the time he'd actually made it into a sitting position, sweat lined his forehead. 'Because,' he said in between taking deep breaths, 'I know exactly who killed him.'

* * *

Jason Vickers was raging. Even as a little girl his daughter had been independent. She took after her elder brother in that respect. And so to hear her so distraught had made the hairs on the back of his neck stand upright. Demi would never have called him, not unless she was desperate or... He swallowed deeply, not wanting to think about the possible scenarios that had been running through his mind on the drive to her home. The only thing he knew for certain was that if Gio, the useless ponce that he was, had hurt his baby in any way, shape, or form, he would kill the bastard stone dead. And that was no empty threat. He would take pleasure in hurting the cunt. It had been a long time coming in his eyes.

'She should never have married him,' Damien spat. 'I could have told her from day one that he was nothing but a lairy prick.'

'And you think I didn't try?' Jason exclaimed. 'I even offered her a substantial sum of money not to turn up at the church.'

Damien blew out his cheeks. 'I didn't know that.'

'Well, I was hardly going to make it public knowledge, was I,' Jason declared. 'The whole fucking fiasco was embarrassing as it was. There were a lot of faces at the wedding, and some well-known families. And that prick Gio was pissed out of his nut before they'd even had the first dance. Demi had to prop him up. I should have known it would be a disaster the minute I watched him and his family pull up outside the church. His mother had a face on her that could curdle milk, and as for his old man, he stank to high heaven, and don't get me started on the state of his suit, not only was it stained but it also looked as though he'd had it stuffed at the back of his wardrobe for decades. And I wouldn't mind,' he said as he flicked the indicator. 'It wasn't as though any of them had had to put their hands in their pockets and pay for the wedding. The church, the reception, the cars, the food and drinks, the whole fucking shebang was footed for by me.'

Letting out a low whistle, Damien shook his head. 'He's a fucking snake. And that's another thing,' he said, turning his head. 'I wouldn't be surprised if he was in on this thing with Dylan and Arthur. More than once I've seen Gio and Arthur having cosy little chats. And you can't tell me that that isn't suspicious. Gio's conversation is hardly made of riveting stuff, is it?'

Jason fell silent. 'Me and Arthur had a punch up once,' he said. 'It was long before you were born,' he added as Damien snapped his head towards him. 'Me, your uncle Colin, and Arthur had gone to this strip club. I hadn't even wanted to go out that night, but we'd had a good day and we'd also made quite a bit of cash. In the end Colin convinced me to come out and celebrate our good fortune, and that's where I met your mum.'

Damien screwed up his face. 'Are you saying that my mum was a stripper?'

'No I'm fucking not,' Jason growled. 'She just happened to be there sitting at the bar. What I didn't know was that she was actually waiting for her dealer to show up. Anyway, I'd thought she was the most beautiful girl I'd ever laid my eyes on,' he said with a soft smile. 'And so I went to chat her up. I was a bit of a jack the lad back in those days. I thought I was God's gift to women. And believe me when I say this, your mum soon brought me down a peg or two. She ended up conning me out of twenty nicker, and twenty quid back in those days was a lot of dough. Well, obviously I was pissed off and so the next week I went back hoping I'd see her again, even if it had been on the pretence of getting my money back. And do you know what the saucy mare did?'

Damien shook his head.

'As bold as fucking brass she had the front to tell me that she had no idea of who I was, that she'd never laid eyes on me before.'

Letting out a chuckle, Damien lifted his eyebrows. 'Why doesn't that surprise me.'

'I should have known then that she'd cause me nothing but trouble,' Jason continued. 'But what can you do. From the very moment she'd caught my eye I'd known she was the one for me. And not just the one, but the only one. That was the same night that me and Arthur ended up going at it toe to toe. He'd said something derogatory about your mum. I can't even recall what it was he'd said now.' He shrugged. 'But whatever it was it had got my back up, I remember that much.'

Damien fell quiet and as Jason glanced towards him, he continued.

'I suppose deep down I've always known that he didn't like your mum,' he said, giving another shrug. 'But I thought that after all of these years he'd learned to accept her. We barely even talk about her,' he said, screwing up his face. 'Or at least we haven't done for quite some time.'

'And you don't find that weird?'

'Not really,' Jason replied as he flicked the indicator in order to turn into Demi's road. 'I never ask how Gio is. To be perfectly honest I couldn't give a flying fuck about the prick. All I care about is my daughter and as long as she is okay, I'm okay too.'

'Yeah, I get that,' Damien answered as he nodded towards where his sister was waiting for them outside her house. Narrowing his eyes, he jumped out of the car before Jason had the chance to even take the keys out of the ignition.

'What the fuck is going on?' Jason asked once he joined his son and daughter on the pavement.

Demi's expression could only be described as crestfallen, and for the tiniest of moments Jason was taken aback. His daughter had always been tough; she'd had no other choice seeing as she'd grown up with two brothers. And as much as he'd had the money to be able to buy his children everything their hearts had desired, he'd never spoiled them, his daughter included. For her eighteenth birthday he'd bought her a designer handbag, the same one that she still used today, despite how tatty it had become in recent years. He'd even offered to buy her a new one but she'd waved him away, refusing the offer, telling him that the wear and tear gave the bag character. Even the house he'd bought her as a wedding gift was quite modest compared to what she could have asked for.

'Dad,' she cried, shaking her head.

The hairs on the back of Jason's neck stood upright. 'What's he done?' In any usual circumstance Demi would have defended her husband until she was blue in the face, and as he waited for her to correct him, a ball of unease began to grow in the pit of his stomach. The excuses didn't come, and if he'd been worried before, Jason was even more concerned now. His lips curling into a snarl, he snapped his gaze towards the house. 'Where is he?'

'Dad, please.'

'I asked you a question,' Jason hissed. 'Where is he?'

Pressing her lips together, Demi shook her head. And for the first time since his arrival, he could actually see fear in her eyes. This was no lovers' tiff, nor a minor disagreement that would soon be rectified by the two of them kissing and making up. This was something serious.

'I can't, Dad,' she croaked out. 'You'll kill him. And you can't do that. Mum needs you.'

Holding his daughter at arm's length, Jason cocked his head to the side. Taking note of just how pale she was, he was beginning to feel even more worried. There was only one reason he would actually kill Gio and that was if he had harmed his daughter. 'Has that bastard hurt you?' he asked.

Again, Demi shook her head and he could see the hesitation in her eyes. 'Damien, please,' she cried, turning to look at her brother. 'Promise me that no matter what, you won't let him kill Gio.'

Damien screwed up his face. Like Demi, his skin had also become pale, although Jason had a feeling it was more because he was becoming increasingly frustrated with his sister than for any other reason. 'Nah.' He shook his head. 'Cut the crap. And start fucking talking before I hunt that fucker down and do him in myself.'

Demi swallowed and as her hand slipped into her pocket, Jason followed the movement. After a few moments, she pulled out a mobile phone, one that Jason recognised immediately. The image of a large cannabis leaf on the phone case was a dead giveaway as to who the owner was. He'd told Gio enough times to replace the phone case; it was hardly professional or the kind of image he wanted the casino to be known for. And yes, he knew that drug-taking took place on his premises, but at least it was discreet. Jason's gut began to churn and as a sense of dread engulfed him, he sucked in a breath.

'I'm sorry, Dad,' Demi began as she held the phone out towards him. 'I...'

Jason had stopped listening, and as he stared down at the image, his heart began to beat so hard and so fast that he actually thought he would collapse. Either that or the organ was going to burst out of his chest and give out on him. 'What the fuck is this?' he hissed.

When he received no reply from his daughter, Jason turned his head. His expression was one of complete and utter hatred as he stared at his daughter's home.

'I'm going to kill him,' he muttered with a calmness that was as chilling as it was terrifying. 'I'm going to string him up by his fucking bollocks and then tear the cunt limb from fucking limb.'

21

Jonny Carter looked across to Jason Vickers' casino and groaned. He'd already had an inkling that the place would be locked up for the night. Taking a quick glance at his watch, he began tapping the steering wheel with his thumb.

'What do you wanna do?' he finally asked as his gaze fell on Tommy Jr's knee. Even through the jeans he wore, Jonny could see just how swollen his nephew's kneecap was. 'Surely it can't be that important,' he continued. 'Because I really think you need to get that leg seen to.'

'Yeah, and I will do,' Tommy Jr confirmed. 'Once I've seen Jason Vickers.'

Rolling his eyes, Jonny gave an agitated sigh. 'You're too fucking stubborn, do you know that?'

'Yeah, and I wonder who I get that from?' Tommy Jr retorted. Shifting his weight, he couldn't help but grimace. He wasn't fooling anyone, least of all his great-uncle.

As Jonny went back to tapping the steering wheel again, he chewed on the inside of his cheek for a moment. 'I suppose we could rock up at his house again,' he said as he took another sneaky glance at his watch. 'Will be one way to piss the fucker off I suppose. Because let me tell you right now,' he said, glancing over his shoulder at Tommy Jr. 'If someone turned up at my gaff at this time in the morning I'd swing for them.'

Tommy Jr cocked an eyebrow. 'Like I said already, he's going to want to hear this, and believe me, it won't be us he starts swinging for.'

Jonny wasn't so sure, and even as he turned the key in the ignition, he was having second thoughts. Jason Vickers wasn't the kind of man you wanted to piss off. That wasn't to say however that Jonny was afraid of him, because he wasn't, it was more the fact that it was added aggravation that he could do without. Going to war with Jason Vickers was bound to cause an inconvenience. Not only would his brothers end up getting themselves involved, but also his nephews. Nah, fuck that, he decided. He was barely functioning as it was all thanks to having a newborn baby in the house. He checked his watch again and cursed under his breath. His girlfriend Terri would more than likely have his head on a stick if he didn't head home soon. As it was she was beginning to get ratty with him through lack of sleep, and as much as they were both in love with their baby boy, James, neither of them had realised just how much work having a baby would entail. Especially when you took into account that his chosen career wasn't exactly a nine-to-five job.

He gave a sigh. 'I'll do you a deal,' he said, checking his wing mirror before pulling out into the road. 'We'll stop by Vickers' gaff and if he's not there, I'm gonna drop you off at the nearest accident and emergency to get that leg seen to.'

'And what if he is there?'

Thinking the question over, Jonny rubbed his hand over his jaw. He could see this going tits up, and Tommy Jr was hardly in a position to go toe to toe with someone, especially when that someone happened to be Jason Vickers. And as much as his great-nephew may have had a wicked righthander on him, it meant fuck all if he was unable to even stand up unaided. 'Then we play it by ear.' It was a copout of an answer and as soon as the words left his mouth, Jonny wanted to take them back.

As though he hadn't noticed, Tommy Jr nodded. And changing the subject, Jonny cleared his throat before giving Cameron a surreptitious glance. 'Make sure he gets that seen to,' he said, lowering his voice slightly. 'Because if he doesn't want to listen to me, let's hope he's gonna listen to you.'

Even as Cameron gave a nod, Jonny wasn't so sure that Tommy Jr would listen to anyone. It wasn't in his nature to take orders, hence why he'd often needed to come down hard on his great-nephew. Tommy was a law unto himself and was like the spit out of his grandad, Tommy Snr's mouth. In fact, the two were so alike that at times it took Jonny's breath away. Tommy Jr could be charming, respectful, fun to be around, and was basically the kind of kid that everyone liked. But there was also another side to him. One that even Jonny himself was wary of. Tommy Jr was more like his grandad then any of them had ever given him credit for. Not only was he a tough little bastard, but he was also ruthless. His mind both sharp and calculated. Jonny was actually interested to see if Tommy Jr had what it took to plan out an armed robbery, because if he truly was anything like his grandad, Tommy Snr, then he had a feeling that his great-nephew could very well end up becoming even more of a legend than his grandad was.

* * *

Demi's heart was thumping so hard that she placed her hand on her chest, praying that the organ wouldn't actually stop altogether.

'Dad,' she screamed as she chased after her father. 'Stop, I'm begging you.' Just as she had known they would, her words fell upon deaf ears. There was no one in the world who could ever get away with disrespecting her mother, and as much as it would be safe to say that Carmen wasn't perfect, her dad more than just loved her, he idolised the very ground she walked on. Carmen could commit murder in front of his eyes and Jason would swear blind that it hadn't been her.

Tears rolled down Demi's cheeks and as fear began to get the better of her, she tugged on her elder brother's arm. To her dismay, Damien swatted her away as though she weighed nothing more than a fly. Damien hadn't even seen the image, or rather he hadn't had a clear view of the photograph like their dad had. It was their father's reaction that had made him bolt into the house after him.

Demi had never seen her dad so angry. Even when he and Damien had torn chunks out of one another, he had never been as livid as this.

The squeal that came from Gio was loud. And as Demi charged into the lounge, she witnessed her dad slam her husband against the wall, one hand wrapped tight around his throat and the other clutching a handful of his shirt in his fist. The grunt that came from Gio as his back collided with the wall was enough to tell her that he'd been winded, and as his chest heaved in and out, a look of shock was etched across his face. 'What the...' he began.

Jason snarled. 'Say one more word, just one,' he roared, 'and I'm going to rip that bastard tongue out of your mouth.'

The colour drained from Gio's face, and snapping his lips closed, he gave his wife a pleading look.

'Dad, please,' Demi began as she stepped forward. 'This isn't the answer…'

The look that Jason shot towards her was enough to make Demi slam her lips closed.

'My wife,' Jason spat as he directed his rage back to his son-in-law. 'My fucking wife.'

It was then that Demi watched the realisation take hold, and as Gio's skin became ashen, she could see the panic in his eyes. She was no fool and as much as she hadn't wanted to look too far into the image, it was pretty obvious what had taken place. Gio had sexually assaulted her mother. Something she had a feeling that her father was also more than aware of. It was in that instant that Demi came to realise that Gio's life was over. That no matter how much she might plead with her dad not to kill him, Jason was going to do just that.

The next thing she knew, Gio was being hauled out of the house, his screams muffled by her dad's hand clamped over his mouth. But it was the look that Damien directed towards her that scared her even more. It was a look of warning, his eyes wide, and his expression one of concern. An emotion she would never have believed her brother to be capable of if she hadn't witnessed it with her own two eyes.

'Damien…' she began before her brother lifted his hand in the air, cutting her off.

'I won't be able to stop him,' he answered as he ran around to the driver's side of the car. 'Not when he's like this. Get Win on the blower. Tell him to be ready and waiting for me to pick him up.' He began to climb into the car, then paused. 'Oh,' he added, 'and tell him to be tooled up.'

Demi nodded, her heartbeat picking up pace. If it wasn't bad enough already then adding Winston plus a weapon to the mix was bound to make matters even worse. She turned then to look at her husband as her father began the process of bundling him into the car. She should have felt something, she was sure of it. And other than fear of the unknown, or rather the consequences of her dad's actions, she felt very little else. She certainly didn't view the demise of Gio to be devastating. She'd not loved the man for years; she didn't even like him, and if she was being even more honest, he made her skin crawl. Just one glance in his direction was enough to irritate the life out of her. She'd put on the act of being happy for so long that it felt almost freeing to finally be shot of him.

Calmly, she walked back down the pathway, her gaze flitting left then right. She was pretty certain that none of her neighbours had witnessed the interaction, but you could never be too sure. Satisfied that none of her neighbours' curtains were twitching, she walked into the house and as though on autopilot, she made her way through to the kitchen. From under the sink she took out a roll of bin liners, then making her way upstairs, she paused in front of her husband's bedroom. The fact they had not shared a bed since their honeymoon should have been the first indication that there was a serious problem within their marriage.

Pushing open the bedroom door, she paused again, the scent of her husband invading her nostrils. As she'd expected, the room was a mess, clothes strewn across the floor, the bed unmade and the duvet rumpled. She couldn't actually remember the last time he'd cleaned his bedsheets. She had certainly never offered to do it for him. Wrinkling her nose, she stepped inside. Considering just how important he believed himself to be, Gio didn't appear to own very much. There were no personal items, no knickknacks to indicate the kind of person he was. And other than his clothes, a few pairs of trainers lined up on the floor and a chest of drawers with a couple of bottles of cheap aftershave and toiletries placed on top, there was very little else.

Methodically, she began to place Gio's belongings into the bin bags. She wanted all trace of him erased from her life. As far as she was concerned, he was a monster. The fact he'd abused her mother, a vulnerable woman, was testament to that.

Within twenty minutes, the room had been cleared, even the bedding, which just as Demi had rightly suspected, was filthy. After a final glance around the room, she dragged the bin bags into the hallway then tied them up. At the top of the stairs, she looked from the bags down to where the front door was, and without giving the moment a second thought, she placed her foot on the first of the bags and then pushed it. As the bag tumbled down the stairs, she lined up the second bag. It wasn't as though Gio would need his belongings, especially not where he was going, so who cared if his bottles of aftershave were smashed to smithereens in the process?

A small smile tugged at her lips and as she slowly descended the stairs, she suddenly felt lighter, almost as though a heavy burden had been lifted from her shoulders. Perhaps she should have got rid of her husband years ago, or better yet, never married the man in the first place.

With the bags now placed outside the front door ready for the bin men to collect them, she slipped her hand into her pocket and pulled out Gio's mobile phone. For the briefest of moments, she considered untying one of the bags and placing it inside. No, she decided. She would pass it to Damien. He would know exactly what to do with it.

* * *

Bringing the car to a screeching halt, Damien leaned across the middle console and shoved open the passenger door.

Winston's expression was what could only be described as wary, and as he snapped his gaze from Jason and Gio on the back seat, he turned to look at Damien.

'What the fuck, D?' he muttered as he climbed into the car.

Damien gritted his teeth and as soon as Winston had slammed the car door closed, he sped away from the kerb. Moments later, he could feel his best friend's accusing stare boring into the side of his face.

'Do you wanna explain to me what the fuck is going on?' Winston asked as he gave both Jason and Gio a surreptitious glance. 'Because right now I'm confused as fuck.'

Damien swallowed. He didn't even know where to begin. Glancing up at the rearview mirror, he locked eyes with his father. As angry as his dad was, Damien could also see the devastation written across his face, and he had a sneaky suspicion that this was the only reason Gio was still breathing.

Tearing his gaze away from his dad, he gave Winston a sidelong glance. He hadn't even seen the image of his mum, at least not properly anyway, and if he was being honest he didn't want to see it either. As far as he was concerned it was an image that no son should ever see of their mother. 'That cunt,' he growled, indicating over his shoulder to Gio. 'He...' Damien swallowed again. He couldn't say it; no matter how much he might want to spit the words out, he couldn't bring himself to do so.

Winston heaved his body around so that he could look at Gio. 'He what?' he asked, screwing up his face. When he received no reply, he snapped his head in Damien's direction. 'D,' he hissed. 'What the fuck is going on, man?'

The look across Damien's face was enough to make Winston

reel slightly away from him. And turning his head to look at Gio again, his lip was curled into a snarl. 'What did you do?' he hissed.

Damien glanced up at the rearview mirror again. Gio wasn't only pale, but he was also sweating, his forehead slick and his hair damp. He stank too, Damien noted. 'Well, go on,' Damien spat. 'Tell him what you did.'

Gio was shaking, his hands trembling so much that he had to clasp them together. 'I didn't do anything.' The jab to the side of Gio's face was as unexpected as it was hard. And as he began to howl from both the shock and the pain, the look across Jason's face was murderous.

'I saw the photo,' he roared, punching Gio's face a second and third time in quick succession. 'I saw what you did to my wife, you dirty, no-good fucking cunt.'

Winston slumped back onto the seat, his eyebrows scrunched together as though he were trying to make sense of what was going on. Finally he turned his head to look at Damien again. 'Tell me this isn't what I think it is?' he pleaded.

Damien licked at his top lip. It was a reaction that Winston had witnessed many times over the years. Some had wrongly assumed it was because he was nervous or maybe even worried, but Winston knew differently. He'd likened it to being the calm before the storm. In that instance, no words were needed. In fact, Damien's reaction had been the only confirmation Winston had needed. As quick as a flash he'd turned in his seat again, his heavy fists raining down punch after punch upon whichever part of Gio's face and upper body he could reach. And even as Gio screamed and brought up his hands to protect his head, it did nothing to deter Winston; if anything, the attack became all the more ferocious, especially once blood exploded from Gio's nostrils. It was only when he was out of breath that Winston finally stopped punching. And as his chest heaved from the exertion, his expression was one of contempt as he slumped back in the seat.

'Where are we gonna take him?' he asked, still breathing heavily.

Damien thought the question over, and as he looked up at the rearview mirror again and locked eyes with his dad, he finally answered. 'Do you remember that shed down at Leigh on Sea?'

Winston nodded. Although to call it a shed was a bit of an understatement. It was more of a concrete outbuilding, one that had once been used by the local fishermen and where they had brought their hauls to be sorted out and then sold on to fishmongers. For some reason, Damien had been thinking about buying it. Why, Winston wasn't so sure. As far as he was aware, Damien had never even stepped foot on a boat let alone had an aspiration to actually go out sea fishing. 'Yeah, what about it?'

'Well.' He shrugged. 'It's empty, secluded, and has easy access to the sea.'

'Small problem,' Winston said, stifling a grin. 'You don't have a key to get into the place.'

'Since when have we let something like that hold us back?' Damien winked. 'And what's more, the geezer looking to sell up is so desperate for the cash that if I was to tell him I'd be willing to sign along the dotted line in return for a favour, I can guarantee you he'd bite my hand off.'

Winston narrowed his eyes. 'What kind of favour?'

'Think about it,' Damien answered, tapping the side of his head. 'The man owns a boat and seeing as we're gonna have a body that will need to be disposed of, you shouldn't need a genius to understand the logic behind my thinking. Besides,' he growled as he observed his brother-in-law in the rearview mirror, 'after what that bastard did to my mum, he deserves to disappear off the face of the earth. He certainly doesn't deserve a burial, I know that much.'

'Too fucking right he doesn't,' Jason growled. 'Let the fish scavenge on whatever is left of his corpse.'

Damien smiled, although it would be fair to say it was one that didn't quite reach his eyes. And as he concentrated on the road ahead of him, the sound of Gio's groans were loud in the confines of the car. The anger that bubbled within him was beginning to intensify. He hated to say I told you so, but he'd known from day one that Gio was nothing more than a spineless rat. His mum weighed little more than a child; she was tiny, even compared to his sister, who would be considered petite. And yet Gio had abused her. Damien gritted his teeth, and gripping the steering wheel, he forced himself to calm down. He was more than prepared to kill; in fact, he *was* going to kill and there was no getting away from that fact. An image of Natasha crossed his mind. No matter how much he loved her – and he really did love her; he would even go as far as to say that she was the only woman he had loved, other than his mum and sister of course – she was going to be disappointed in him. After all, her chosen career didn't exactly view murderers as pillars of the community. But in the circumstances, what other choice did he have? Gio had violated his mum, and that right there was enough to warrant a death sentence.

'How far away is this place of yours?' Jason asked.

'Roughly another fifty miles.'

Jason nodded. 'Well, do me a favour,' he growled, 'and put your foot down before I do this cunt in here and now.'

Doing as he'd been told, Damien pushed his foot down on

the accelerator. If the circumstances were any different, he may have felt sorry for Gio, because with his dad on the war path he had a feeling that Gio's demise would be neither quick nor easy. To be more precise, Gio was going to wish that he'd never been born.

22

As Vinnie Vickers made himself comfortable on his uncle's sofa, he flicked on the television then muted the sound. He had no interest on the actual programme being shown, he just didn't like sitting in total darkness. Of course, he could have always switched the main light on, but he didn't want to do that either. All he wanted to do was to sit in silence and go over what had taken place in the last twenty-four hours, to somehow make sense of it all.

One thing he did know was that he wished he'd had the chance to chin Gio. He turned his head then. From where he was sitting, he could see into the kitchen, hence why he'd chosen this spot. Carmen sat at the kitchen island, her head bowed. She looked so small and so vulnerable that Vinnie's heart went out to her. As much as he knew first hand that Carmen hadn't been the greatest of role models when he'd been growing up, he was eternally grateful to both her and his uncle. If they hadn't have taken him in after the death of his parents, he would have more than likely ended up in the care system. The mere thought was enough to make him shudder.

Momentarily he closed his eyes, and pinching the bridge of his nose, he took a deep breath. He wanted to berate himself. He should have watched Dylan more closely, should have paid attention to his behaviour. He'd already known that he spoke to his mum abysmally; he'd even pulled him up on it once or twice. But not for a single second had he thought that he would actually go that one step further and lash out at his mother. The mere thought of anyone actually physically harming Carmen was abhorrent to him. As much as she could have a sharp tongue at times, there was also another part of her that made you want to look after her. She was easy to love, he supposed, and he could see exactly why his uncle adored her so much.

The sound of breaking glass made Vinnie snap his attention towards the kitchen, and as he jumped up from the sofa, the piercing scream that came from Carmen made his blood run cold.

'What the fuck,' he shouted as he surveyed the French door that led out onto the patio. 'How the hell did this happen?'

Carmen's eyes were as wide as saucers, and as she shook her head, Vinnie narrowed his eyes.

'How could you not know?' he asked, throwing up his arms. 'You were sitting right here.' Turning his head again, he took in the shattered glass. This was no accident, it couldn't be, and unless he was very much mistaken, French doors didn't spontaneously shatter into pieces. No, this was deliberate. The hairs across the back of his neck stood upright and as he glanced towards his aunt, fear was etched across her face.

Still, it made no sense to him. The house had even more security than the casino and he knew for a fact there was little chance of anyone breaking into the property. For a start, there were the security cameras surrounding the house, and that was without the alarm system that his uncle had paid a small fortune for. Vinnie tilted his head to the side. That was a point actually. Why weren't the alarms sounding?

The sound of footsteps made Vinnie snap his head back to the broken door and seeing Arthur Brennan come into view, his shoulders relaxed. 'Thank fu—' The words died in Vinnie's throat, and narrowing his eyes, he took a step back. Why hadn't Arthur used the front door, and more to the point, why was he carrying a hammer?

Before Vinnie could even process those thoughts, Arthur swung the hammer through the air. Vinnie didn't have time to process the pain as the hammer collided with the side of his head, neither did he have any recollection of landing face first on the kitchen floor.

* * *

Just as Damien had predicted, finding a way inside the concrete shed had been a piece of piss. Moments later, he hauled Gio into the outbuilding, not caring one iota if he pulled his brother-in-law's hair out by the roots as he dragged him inside.

A thin stream of what was obviously urine trailed across the floor behind them, and as Damien shoved Gio to the ground, it became all the more obvious that Gio had urinated himself.

'Please,' Gio sobbed as he looked up at them. 'I didn't mean to.'

Jason's eye twitched, the only indication he gave away to show just how livid he actually was. 'You didn't mean to do what?' he spat.

Gio visibly swallowed, his entire body trembling.

'I asked you a fucking question,' Jason roared, stepping closer, his fists clenched into tight balls. 'What exactly didn't you mean to do?'

Gio's face was so pale that for the briefest of moments, Damien thought he might pass out. Which, when he thought about it, shouldn't have come as a surprise. Gio was only able to throw his weight around when he was amongst women, but up against men he'd proven himself to be nothing other than a coward. Not that Damien had suspected any different. Gio liked to give it the mouth, he liked others to think he was something special, that he was some kind of tough man, and yet in reality he was weak.

'I wasn't thinking.' Gio began to sob, and as tears and snot mingled together, he dragged his hand over his face. 'We all make mistakes,' he said, looking up with a crafty gleam in his eyes. 'Isn't that right, Damien?'

Damien narrowed his eyes and as both his dad and Winston turned to look at him, he cocked his head to the side. 'What the fuck is that supposed to mean?'

A smirk tugged at Gio's lips. 'I saw you,' he said as he reached up to gingerly touch the bridge of his nose. 'It looked as though you were having a nice friendly chat with the filth. I even thought you were going to kiss her at one point. You were all over her and more or less had your tongue down her throat.'

The colour drained from Damien's face, and as much as he didn't want to appear guilty, he couldn't help but think that his father and Winston, especially Winston, would be able to see straight through him.

'What's he going on about?' There was a hint of amusement in Winston's voice.

'Maybe you should ask your sister,' Gio piped up before giving Damien another crafty glance. 'Because that's who you were in the car with, wasn't it?'

It took several moments for Gio's words to actually sink in, but once they did, the amusement faded from Winston's eyes and was replaced with shock, then betrayal, before finally being followed with anger.

'Win.' Damien shook his head, and taking an involuntary step backwards, he held up his hands. 'I can explain. It's not what it seems.'

'Then explain it to me,' Winston spat, his voice barely louder than a low growl.

Damien dropped his hands to his sides. 'I'm not going to have a tear up with you,' he said, shaking his head. 'We've been mates for far too long for it to come to blows between us.'

'Mates?' Winston snorted out a laugh. 'Is that what you were thinking about when you were sniffing around my sister, or how about when you were screwing her behind my back? Because let's be honest here, D, you've been acting shifty for months.'

'Win,' Damien warned, his voice becoming serious. 'Don't talk about her like that.' On seeing the look of disgust that flashed across Winston's face, Damien held up his hands again. 'Come on, mate, she's your sister, not some slapper.'

In that instant, Winston bounded forward, and shoving Damien roughly into the wall, his eyes were hard. 'I know exactly who she is.'

Damien nodded. 'I know you do,' he said as he grasped hold of Winston's forearms in an attempt to push him off.

'How long?'

Damien swallowed. It was on the tip of his tongue to lie. Thinking better of it, he chose to tell the truth. 'Six months.'

Winston's eyes widened. And as much as the revelation had come as a shock, it was the hurt in his eyes that Damien likened to a kick in the gut.

'You'd better be kidding me,' Winston hissed. 'Because six fucking months, D, that's a long time.'

'I know it is,' Damien repeated, his voice equally low. 'I didn't mean for—'

Shoving Damien back against the wall, Winston pinned him in place. 'Do you wanna know something? Not once did I ever think that you of all people would betray me. Neither did I take you for someone who would creep around behind my back, but I suppose it just goes to show you never really know someone.'

As Winston clenched his fist, Damien squeezed his eyes shut. 'I love her,' he blurted out. 'And you can beat the crap out of me if that makes you feel better, but it won't change anything. I won't give her up.'

The snarl Winston gave would have been enough to terrify most men. 'What do you mean, you love her?' he spat. 'You don't even know her.'

'Leave it out,' Damien countered. 'I've known her since we were kids and I've been seeing her for more than seven months.'

Winston's eyebrows knotted together. 'I thought you just said it's been six months?'

Damien paused, and shaking his head, he screwed up his face. 'I don't know.' He shrugged. 'I've not exactly been keeping count. It's more or less six months, give or take a few weeks.'

'I can't believe this,' Winston hissed. 'You've been lying to me for more than half of the year.'

'I'm sorry, mate.' Cautiously, he stepped away from the wall, his hands held up in front of him as though he were surrendering 'It just happened and...'

From behind them, Jason cleared his throat. 'When the pair of you are ready, there's a more pressing issue to be taken care of other than your love life.' Shaking his head, he addressed Winston. 'How the fuck you didn't see that coming I'll never know. Talk about burying your head in the sand. Even when you were nothing but kids, there was something going on between them. And if I noticed it then it just goes to show how blatantly obvious it was.'

Tearing his gaze away from his father, Damien nodded again, and resting his hand upon Winston's shoulder, he gave it a reassuring squeeze. 'I meant what I said.' He gave a small smile. 'And you know me.' He winked. 'You know exactly how hard it is for me to admit when I'm in the wrong. If I could turn back the clock I would tell you from the off.'

Winston lifted his eyebrows. 'Or how about you would have steered clear of her instead.'

'What, you don't think I tried? She's your sister, you should know just how determined she can be when she sets her mind to something.'

Winston sighed, and in that instant, Damien knew his words had had an impact. And it was true. Natasha wasn't only ambitious when it came to her career; if she wanted something, she went all out in her attempt to get it, and as it just so happened it had been him she had wanted. She had been the one to do the chasing, and she hadn't been prepared to take no for an answer. 'And as for you,' Damien continued as he turned his attention back to Gio, 'just goes to show how much of a slimy bastard you really are.'

As much as Gio attempted to scoot away from them, a smirk still lined his face. 'And what about Dylan, eh?' he goaded. 'Did you think he was a slimy bastard an' all?'

Damien's left eye twitched.

'You know fuck all,' Gio continued with a laugh. 'The so-called golden boy was laughing at the lot of you behind your backs.'

Jason bounded forward, ready to lay into Gio, to shut him up for once and for all.

'No.' Damien shook his head, and pulling on his father's arm, he lifted his eyebrows. 'Not yet.' Call it intuition but he had a feeling there was more to come.

'He was a genius,' Gio continued. 'Or at least that's what I thought of him. He had all of yous fooled.' He gave a small laugh, his eyes twinkling with amusement. 'He hated all of you, but you,' he said, nodding towards Jason, 'oh, he hated you the most. You should have heard the things he called you.' Laughing even harder, Gio clutched at his stomach. 'He used to say that you'd lost your nerve, that you'd grown soft, and that you wouldn't know a good business deal if it was to jump up and bite you on the arse. Why else do you think he propositioned Arthur? Because I can tell you right now other than the fact he was loaded, there was no other reason why he would have needed to bring him in. No.' Gio shook his head. 'It was all part of Dylan's masterplan. He was going to kill you and to prove just how sick in the head he was,' Gio added, tapping his temple. 'He wanted to do it himself.'

The colour drained from Jason's face.

'But before then,' Gio continued, 'he needed to get into the safe. He needed the deeds to the casino so that once he'd bumped you off, that only left Arthur to be got rid of.'

'And is that where my mum came into it?' Damien growled.

Gio turned his head, his eyes ever so slightly narrowed. 'If you're talking about the crack.' He shrugged. 'I don't think Dylan had a plan, not as such anyway, or at least not at first. It was all a bit of an accident the way it came about. Carmen had threatened to inform yous about his behaviour, the threats and the violence. And, well, he couldn't have that, could he, so he introduced her to crack, more so to keep her quiet than for any other reason. But then he realised he could use it to his advantage, and so he started blackmailing her. She either did as he asked or he would inform you about the crack.'

'The sly bastard,' Damien muttered under his breath.

'No.' Jason shook his head. 'I don't believe it. That wasn't my son…'

'Dad,' Damien warned.

'No,' Jason shouted. 'This wasn't what Dylan was about and you know it.' As he made to charge forward again, Damien hauled him back a second time.

'You heard what Mum said about him,' he hissed in his ear. 'And this prick,' he said, flicking his head in Gio's direction, 'has all but confirmed it. Whether you like it or not, Dylan played us like a fucking fiddle, all of us. We made it easy for him, because not once did we ever think that he of all people could ever be capable of treachery.'

Walking to the far side of the outbuilding, Jason crouched down and held his head in his hands. Even from where he was standing, Damien could see the devastation in his father's eyes. Dylan had been the one who would one day have taken over their father's business. A thought suddenly occurred to him and he snapped his gaze towards his brother-in-law. 'What about Vinnie?'

Gio narrowed his eyes. 'What about him?'

'Where does he fit into any of this?'

'He doesn't.' Gio shook his head. 'Dylan didn't trust him. Said that he was too loyal to the family and that he'd betray him the first chance he got.'

Damien sighed and as he rubbed his hand over his jaw, he gave Winston a sheepish glance. Time and time again he'd berated his cousin. He'd been convinced that he couldn't be trusted and that if anyone was bound to betray the family then it would be Vinnie. Only he couldn't have been more wrong; his own brother had been the one who couldn't be trusted. He was the wolf in sheep's clothing, the one they should have all been wary of, not Vinnie.

'Dylan could have had everything,' Gio continued. 'He could have been someone. Only he showed his cards too early. He had Arthur running scared, not that he'll ever admit that out loud. Why else do you think he had him taken out?'

Jason's head snapped up, his eyebrows scrunching together. 'What did you just say?'

Gio was on a roll, and as he smirked, he prodded his jaw. 'Arthur was the one who organised the hit. He's got mates in high places, but then you should already know that seeing as you're his business partner.'

Jason's skin paled, and as Damien looked towards Winston, his eyebrows shot up. Hadn't Winston suggested as much, that whoever had put out the hit must have had connections? How could they have all been so blind? Arthur didn't only have the odd person in his back pocket, he had judges, high-ranking police officers; he even had a coroner.

Damien's eyes were hard as he held out his hand to Winston.

Without hesitation, Winston slipped his hand into his jacket pocket and pulled out a small handgun, or to be more precise a Glock 19.

The colour drained from Gio's face, his eyebrows shooting up in surprise. 'Nah,' he cried as though the situation had just become all the more real. 'Come on, you can't do this.'

'I can do whatever the fuck I like,' Damien roared back at him. Turning the gun over in his hand, he made to take aim at Gio's head then paused. Giving his dad a sidelong glance, he offered him the weapon.

Jason took the gun. His lips were curled into a snarl as he

aimed the shooter at his son-in-law's head. When he spoke, his words were a low growl. 'Where's Arthur?'

Sweat glistened across Gio's forehead. Even as he tried to push himself back and away from them, there was nowhere for him to actually go.

'Answer the fucking question,' Jason shouted. 'Where is Arthur?'

Gio visibly flinched. 'I don't know,' he cried as tears and snot mingled together. 'Come on,' he pleaded with them. 'Don't do this. I'm begging you. I don't want to die.'

'They never do,' Jason answered as he took aim then squeezed the trigger.

The gunshot was loud and as Gio fell onto his side, blood oozing from a bullet-size wound in the middle of his forehead, Jason sneered. 'Good riddance to the fucking ponce. I should have done that the very first time I laid my eyes on him.' He turned then to look at his son, and as he held out the gun, he cocked his head to the side. 'I take it there isn't a second bullet with my name on it?'

Damien fell quiet. Not so long ago he would have given anything to be in this position with his father. Especially somewhere so secluded. The loathing they shared for one another had been on another level and had been so intense that not for a single moment had Damien ever imagined that they would be able to put their differences behind them. And maybe they still couldn't. Perhaps the situation was so bad between them that they would never actually come to an understanding. He shook his head, and passing the gun across to Winston, he nodded down at Gio's corpse. 'I'm going to get on the blower and arrange getting him disposed of.'

Jason nodded and just as Damien was about to pull his phone out of his pocket, he narrowed his eyes. 'Why were you looking into buying this place?' he asked as he gestured around him.

Damien lifted his eyebrows, and as he gave a small grin, he motioned down towards Gio. 'Why do you think?'

Jason couldn't help but smile. Perhaps his eldest boy was a chip off the old block after all.

23

Call it an inkling, or maybe even the fact that she had the nose of a copper, but Natasha had a feeling that something was wrong. Not only had Damien bolted out of the house this morning, but she'd not heard from him since, except for one text message to tell her that he would be home late. But she had also not heard from her brother either, despite calling him more than ten times and him not picking up. Which wasn't entirely unusual for Winston, and in any normal circumstance she wouldn't have been too concerned about his lack of communication. He tended to check in with her sporadically, more often than not at the most inconvenient of times, such as when she was in the bath, or in a meeting at work. But again, it was that gut feeling telling her that something wasn't right.

Pulling up outside Demi's house, she switched off the ignition then sat for a few moments chewing on the inside of her cheek, unsure whether or not she was doing the right thing. Of course, she could have driven straight to Damien's parents' house; after all, that was where he had headed to this morning. But she didn't like to intrude, especially as no one knew that they were an item; well, other than Joanie, but even that had been by mistake. It was their own fault; they should have been more careful. Except this morning they had both woken up late, and Damien had been more out of it than usual, no doubt because he'd got home so late the night before.

After a few moments she stepped out of the car, locked up, then began walking down the street. Seeing as she had met with Demi at the pub the evening before, it shouldn't be too odd that she'd turned up here out of the blue. They had been close once, and it was only when Natasha had joined the police force that they had begun to drift apart. She was ambitious, that was half the problem, and ever since she'd become a detective constable, she'd found herself becoming even more immersed in the job. She was aiming for the top and chasing promotion to detective inspector.

Outside Demi's front door there were several bin bags, stacked on top of one another.

'Jesus Christ,' Demi squealed as she exited her house, her hand clutching at her chest. 'You nearly gave me a fucking heart attack.'

Natasha laughed. 'I'm sorry,' she said as her gaze drifted back to the bin bags. 'I didn't mean to give you a fright. Are you having a clear-out?' she asked, nodding down at the bags.

Demi immediately clamped her lips together. 'Yeah, something like that,' she finally answered as she delved inside her handbag and pulled out the keys to the house. Locking up, she motioned down the pathway. 'Sorry, Tash, I'm in a bit of a hurry.'

Natasha's forehead furrowed. 'There's nothing wrong, is there?'

'No,' Demi answered, laughing off the question. 'I'm going to see my mum. Why would something be wrong?'

Natasha shrugged. And there it was again, that niggling gut

feeling. 'Do you mind if I tag along? I've not seen your mum in ages.'

Demi came to an abrupt halt, anger flashing in her eyes. 'Look, I'm not being funny, Tash, but you haven't seen my mum in years. I doubt she would even recognise you if I'm being honest.'

Natasha lifted her eyebrows. Maybe it was true, but somehow she highly doubted it. Up until she'd joined the force she'd spent a lot of time at Demi's parents' house. She often referred to it as being her second home. 'It was only an idea.'

A sigh escaped from Demi's lips and as her shoulders sagged, she shook her head. 'Now isn't a good time. My mum, she…' Biting down on her lip, she glanced away but not before Natasha saw the tears in her eyes.

'Maybe I could help,' Natasha answered, her voice gentle.

Demi gave a small, almost bitter laugh and as she swiped the tears from her eyes, she shook her head again. 'Come on, Tash, you're not an idiot. Do you honestly think that I'd take a copper to my parents' house? My dad would go fucking mental.'

As Natasha pulled herself up a little taller, her expression was serious. 'I might be a copper, but I'm also a Baptiste. I came from fuck all. And you're right, I'm not daft. I know exactly what our families are capable of. You're not the only one to have had a brother serve time.'

'Yeah,' Demi agreed. 'I know.' Looking into the distance, she bit down on her lip again before swallowing.

'It's okay,' Natasha reassured her. 'You can trust me.'

Demi looked as though she were going to refuse when tears sprang to her eyes again. 'I think that my husband sexually assaulted my mum,' she blurted out.

Of everything Natasha had been expecting, she could hand on heart say it hadn't been this. Her mouth fell open, and grasping hold of Demi's hand, she held on tight. 'I...' Lost for words, she shook her head.

'I found an image on his phone.' Unclasping her handbag, she took out her husband's phone, unlocked the device, then passed it across.

Natasha's eyes widened. 'Demi, you need to—'

Demi snatched the phone back. 'I don't need to do anything.'

'But—'

'You heard what I said.' Demi lifted her eyebrows. 'My dad and brother are taking care of it.'

Natasha's jaw dropped a second time and as a shard of ice made its way down her spine, it took everything inside of her to outwardly appear calm. How could Damien be so stupid? How could he put their future in jeopardy?

'Can I at least come with you and check that your mum is okay?' She held up her hands. 'Please, Demi. I'm asking as a friend, and no other reason. I promise, no hidden agendas, I just want to make sure your mum doesn't need medical help.' Although to be fair, perhaps she did have an ulterior motive. She wanted to know what was happening and she knew for a fact that Damien wasn't going to tell her outright that he and his father had taken matters into their own hands.

Demi looked to be thinking the question over.

'Please,' Natasha asked again.

'Okay.' Even as she answered, Demi didn't look quite so sure. 'But anything you see or hear stays off the record, are we clear on that?'

Natasha nodded.

'Because don't underestimate me, Tash. I'd kill you stone dead and not give a flying fuck about the consequences.'

Natasha nodded again. Somehow she had a feeling that Demi was telling the truth.

***

The scream that escaped from Carmen's lips was loud and for a moment or two she was paralysed with fear. As she came to her senses, her gaze snapped down at Vinnie. Her nephew was out cold. Perhaps even dead. Tears sprang to her eyes and as she made to move forward and check on him, Arthur shook his head, forcing her to back away.

'Do you know how many times I've fantasised about doing that?'

Carmen shook her head, her eyes wide.

'He's a mouthy little cunt, just like his old man.'

As much as it was true that Vinnie took after his father, he was a good boy, decent, kind, and what's more, she loved him as much as she loved her own children. 'I need to check on him,' she pleaded, taking a tentative step forward. 'I need to know that he's okay.'

Arthur's lips curled into a snarl. In that moment he had never looked more evil. 'Leave him.'

'But—'

'I said leave him,' Arthur roared as he bounded forward and shoved Carmen against the kitchen worktop.

The squeal that came from Carmen was animalistic. It was more than panic, but also a raw fear that could only come from somewhere deep inside of her.

'I should have fucking killed you all those years ago, I should have slit your throat and left you for dead.'

As Carmen snapped her eyes shut and turned her head to the side, she could feel Arthur's hot breath fan out across her cheeks, and as his hands began to pull at her clothes, she cried out in terror.

'You've been nothing but the bane of my life, did you know that?' he continued to shout.

Shaking her head, Carmen pulled at his hands in an attempt to free herself. Not that it did her any good; he was far too strong. She didn't stand a chance against him. 'Please,' she begged.

'I should have let Dylan finish you off.' He gave a sinister laugh. 'He had offered but I'd told him to wait it out, told him to find a way to keep you quiet instead. Why else do you think he offered you the crack?'

In that instant every inch of Carmen's body stiffened and as her heart began to beat even faster, she had never felt as much hatred as she did in that moment. 'Like father, like son.'

Arthur narrowed his eyes.

'Oh, come on.' As terrified as she was, Carmen wasn't prepared to back down. Not this time. Arthur could kill her; he more than likely would. But that wouldn't be enough to stop her from spilling out a secret she had held close to her chest for almost twenty years. 'You raped me, Arthur. Surely you must have put two and two together and been curious when nine months later I gave birth to Dylan.'

Arthur's mouth opened and closed in rapid succession. And as a flurry of different emotions swept over his face, he took a step backwards. 'You're lying,' he spat.

Carmen snorted out a laugh. 'I've no need to lie. Dylan's dead and I've left it a bit too late to come after you for child support, haven't I.'

As his eyebrows knotted together, a new wave of anger engulfed Arthur. 'You should have told me,' he screamed in Carmen's face, spraying her in spittle as he did so.

No matter how afraid she was, Carmen refused to back down.

For the past twenty years she had lived a lie. When he'd been a newborn baby, she had watched her husband fall in love with her youngest son. She'd watched him smile as Dylan at just a few hours old had wrapped his entire hand around one of Jason's fingers. And then she had watched as her husband had continued to shower Dylan with love. He'd spoiled him too, much more than he ever had Damien or Demi. The guilt had eaten away at her. Especially when sometimes she could see Arthur in Dylan. It was their eyes; they both had a knack of being able to look straight through you.

'It's because of you,' he screamed as he gripped her around the throat, 'that I killed my own son. My flesh and blood.'

Carmen's eyes widened, and not only because Arthur's fingers were cutting off her air supply. Had he just confessed to being behind Dylan's murder?

Gasping for air, she clawed at his hands. He was going to kill her, there were no two ways about that. Frantically she reached behind her, her hand searching for something, anything that she could use to stop the attack.

Finally her fingers skimmed over something hard. She wasn't even sure what it was, but gripping the object, she slashed it blindly through the air.

Her vision was beginning to turn black and as Arthur leaned over her, his expression one of pure concentration as he attempted to throttle the life out of her, she knew she had one last chance to defend herself. It was then that she used what little she had left of her strength to thrust the object deep into whichever part of Arthur's body she could reach.

The hiss that came from Arthur was loud and he immediately released his hands from around her throat, then took a stumbling step backwards. The fine mist of blood that coated her face and upper torso made Carmen audibly gasp. Taking in large gulps of air, she continued to cough and splutter, the iron scent that invaded her nostrils making her feel nauseous. She could barely believe that she was still alive and that all thanks to the pair of kitchen scissors in her hand, she now held all of the cards.

'You cunt.'

Despite his obvious injury, the anger inside of Arthur had not diminished. And even as the blood continued to spurt, coating Carmen, the floor, and the ceiling, he still looked determined to end her life.

In that moment, Carmen once again looked down at the scissors that were also stained with blood. The entire length of the steel was smeared with claret, bringing further testament to just how far she had plunged them into Arthur's neck.

'You...' Arthur's voice sounded weaker, as though it were taking all of his strength just to talk. 'You...' He took a step closer, one hand clutching his neck.

Carmen realised that she now had the upper hand, and her eyes were hard. 'I hated him,' she snarled. 'Did you know that? When I was pregnant I willed for a miscarriage, prayed for it in fact.'

Arthur's eyes widened.

'How could I ever love anything that had come from you? Something you had forced upon me? You're evil, a monster.'

As Arthur's skin became even paler and a blue tinge spread across his lips, Carmen continued.

'He could have been a nice kid if your genes hadn't tainted him. But at the end of the day he didn't stand a chance, did he? How could he when it was your blood that ran through his veins?'

Arthur sank to his knees, and with one hand clutched at his throat he slammed his free hand onto the floor in an attempt to stop himself from falling face first. He let out a long groan, and when he finally spoke, his voice was nothing more than a strained whisper. 'I have a son.'

Disgust curled at Carmen's insides. It had been no lie when she had stated that she had prayed for a miscarriage, because she had, night and day. Ever since Dylan's birth, she had been on edge. Terrified that Jason would look at him a little too closely and see the resemblance between the child he often called his number one boy and his business partner. She couldn't bear to see the hurt upon her husband's face, the devastation when he came to realise that he had been raising another man's child.

Sidestepping around him, Carmen continued to look down at Arthur, her eyes full of loathing. And as he began to gurgle, it suddenly occurred to her that she was watching a man take his last breaths. There was no remorse for what she had done. She felt as though a heavy weight had been lifted from her shoulders. She was finally free.

The groan that came from Vinnie made her jump, and rushing to his side, she crouched down and placed a bloodstained hand upon his cheek.

'Vinnie, sweetheart,' she cried as she took in the blood coating his scalp and hair. 'I'm going to get you help, darling.' In that instance she glanced across to Arthur. How on earth was she going to call for help when she had the body of her husband's business partner laid out on the kitchen floor?

The reality of what she had done finally hit Carmen with the intensity of a sledgehammer. She was responsible for the death of a man. She would go to prison. And even worse than that, she would need to find a way to explain to her husband why she had killed his closest friend of more than thirty years. Her hands began to tremble, and as she got to her feet, she located her mobile then fumbled to unlock the device. She forced herself to take a deep breath; her hands were shaking so violently that she was unable to press down on the keypad. Tears slipped down her cheeks, blinding her vision. She needed to calm down, or to be more precise, she needed something to calm her down. Spotting the vodka bottle next to the sink, she stepped across the kitchen, but as she unscrewed the lid, she hesitated. Vinnie should have been her top priority, her only priority. Bringing the bottle up to her lips, she took a long sip, swallowing down the vodka neat. And so he would be, she decided. Once she'd had a drink to settle her nerves.

* * *

Jonny Carter switched off the ignition then settled back in the seat. The fact Jason Vickers' house was still lit up had to be a good sign. Not that he actually believed they were doing the right thing by turning up at this time of the night. Glancing over his shoulder to look at Tommy, he jerked his head towards the house. 'Wait here a minute. Once he answers, me and your dad will come back for you.'

Tommy Jr screwed up his face. 'I'm not waiting here,' he said as he pushed open the door and began to shuffle his backside over.

'Leave it out,' Jonny chastised. 'You can't even fucking walk. For once in your life do as you're told and wait here.'

Tommy Jr groaned. Although he had to admit he could see his uncle's point. Even shuffling a few inches over had caused him a great deal of pain. And if it turned out Jason Vickers wasn't home then he would have put himself through a great deal of agony for no reason.

* * *

Striding across the forecourt, Jonny was still complaining. 'How many times did I tell him not to get involved?'

Cameron sighed. 'More than once,' he agreed.

'Exactly,' Jonny answered. 'But did he listen? Did he fuck. And now look at what has happened. He'll be lucky if he ever walks again without the aid of a crutch.'

Cameron snapped his head around to look at his uncle, his eyes wide and fearful.

'Well,' Jonny continued as he rang the doorbell. 'Obviously I'm not a doctor, but you can't tell me that it doesn't look bad. And you and I both know it's a lot worse than what he's actually letting on.'

Before Cameron could answer, Demi Vickers, or rather Demi Ferrari as she was now known, made her way across the courtyard with another woman beside her.

As he ran his tongue over his teeth, Jonny narrowed his eyes. He knew old bill when he saw one and he'd bet his knob on the fact that the woman beside Demi was a copper. Giving Cameron a surreptitious glance, he ever so slightly jerked his head in the women's direction.

Taking the warning on board, Cameron nodded and as he glanced across to where his son was sitting in the car, he cleared his throat.

'Just let me do the talking,' Jonny said in a low voice.

As the two women approached, he gave them a wide smile. 'Jonny Carter,' he said, holding out his hand. 'We met earlier at the casino.'

Demi shook his hand and as she returned the smile, there was a slight nervousness about her, he noted.

'I wanted a word with your dad,' Jonny piped up. 'Or rather my nephew does,' he added, jerking his thumb in the direction of his car.

Demi followed his gaze. 'I'm not sure if my dad's home.'

Jonny nodded. 'Only one way to find out.' He winked, motioning to the key in her hand.

Demi looked towards the woman with her, then heaving out a sigh, she pushed the key into the lock.

'Wait here a moment and let me see if he's in.'

Jonny nodded and stepping aside, he glanced at his watch. It had gone midnight and as he shot Tommy Jr a glare, he shook his head. All thanks to his great-nephew, he had a feeling that he'd be spending the night on the sofa. The last thing he wanted to do was wake the baby, who rarely slept through the night as it was. He was just about to tell his nephew as much when he heard shouts coming from inside the house.

Both his and Cameron's eyes widened and without giving the matter a second thought, Jonny pushed open the front door and stepped across the threshold. Following the commotion, he made his way forward with Cameron beside him.

The scene that greeted him was enough to make him rock back on his heels. And as the woman he assumed was Jason Vickers' wife let out a blood-curdling scream, he immediately held up his hands, hoping if nothing else but to prove to her that he wasn't a threat, nor that he intended to cause her any harm. Although if the amount of blood that covered her was anything to go by, he had a sneaky suspicion that the actual threat had been that of the body laid out on the floor. The very same body that, unless he was very much mistaken, held a striking resemblance to that of Arthur Brennan.

24

Just as Damien had predicted, the man who had owned the outbuilding had all but bitten his hand off to make a deal, and it was a rather generous deal in Damien's opinion. He'd secured the outbuilding itself for just under the asking price and then had added on an extra 20k for Gio to be dumped out at sea. And luckily for them, the tide had been in, meaning there had been no delay in getting rid of the body. As for the legalities, he'd worry about that part of the deal later down the line. It might seem like an odd way to do business, but it was a lot more common than people realised, especially amongst those who lived their lives as villains or gangsters.

Once he'd been handed the keys to the premises, Damien had felt a stab of pity for the previous owner. Gambling had been what had led to his misfortune, or rather gambling debts. And as a result the business which had once belonged to his late father and then grandfather before him had now come to an end. In a way he supposed it was a lesson well learned, and one that he had a feeling would sting for the remainder of the man's life.

Now that the building had been cleared of Gio's body, Damien was still unsure of what exactly he was going to do with the building. It was fairly large in size, the concrete walls bare and whitewashed. He'd sit on it, he decided. If nothing else it was in an ideal location to dispose of anyone who'd pissed him off on a major scale.

Flicking the indicator, he glanced up at the rearview mirror. His old man had been quiet the entire journey back to South London. In a way he didn't blame him for not wanting to strike up a conversation. He was more than likely in shock still and trying to process what the hell had gone down and where it had all gone so wrong. They'd been given some home truths and at some point in the near future, they would need to discuss Dylan. Not only how they'd been deceived by him but also how they were supposed to move on with their lives knowing that he'd despised them so much that he'd actually been prepared to kill them.

Eventually, Damien cleared his throat. 'What do we tell Demi?'

Anger flashed across Jason's face. 'We tell her the truth. That the cunt is now residing somewhere between Southend on Sea and Kent.'

'What, and you don't think she's gonna kick off?' Winston asked. 'He was her husband.'

Damien turned his head. 'The minute she got on the blower to my old man she knew it was game over.'

'Yeah.' Winston shrugged. 'I suppose so.'

'There's no suppose about it,' Damien persisted. 'She knows the score. Besides, it's hardly what you'd call a great loss to society, is it? Gio,' he said, screwing up his face, 'was a waste of space from the get-go. He was a prick, and if you want my opinion, he got off lightly after what he did to Mum.' Glancing up at the rearview mirror, he took note of the fury reflected in his father's eyes. He himself felt nauseous whenever he allowed himself to dwell on what his mother had been subjected to. And as much as he hadn't taken a good look at the image saved on Gio's mobile phone, he could only imagine that it had been harrowing. Maybe the less said about what Gio had done the better it would be for them all. Although he had a sneaky suspicion that it was yet another situation that would need to be addressed sooner rather than later. And to top it off, there was Arthur and the part he'd played in all of this to contend with, too.

With his elbow leaning against the car window, Damien massaged his temples. He'd had a gutful, he knew that much. He could only assume that his dad was feeling the same, especially as Dylan had been his son, and Arthur was not only his business partner but also one of his closest friends. The betrayal must have been a lot for him to get his head around; after all, it was the equivalent of a mind fuck. His dad had trusted Dylan, Arthur too; he would have had no reason not to and certainly would have never guessed that the two of them would have formed an allegiance, one that was to have deadly consequences.

A short time later he turned into the road where his parents lived, and narrowing his eyes, he motioned ahead of him. 'Who does that car belong to?' he asked, referring to the Mercedes parked on his parents' driveway.

Jason craned his neck to look through the windshield. 'That's Jonny Carter's motor. And I know that to be a fact because I was sitting in it this morning, or rather yesterday morning,' he corrected as he took a peek at his watch.

Damien's forehead was furrowed. Why the fuck would Jonny Carter be at his parents' house, especially since his dad wasn't even home?

* * *

Natasha Baptiste's heart began to beat faster. She'd been trained for incidents like this, only now that it had become her reality, her mind had gone completely blank. As she tried her utmost to process the situation, her gaze fell upon each of the casualties. She had just seconds to prioritise them. One she was pretty certain was already deceased, the second appeared to be traumatised but physically unharmed if the scream that had escaped from her lips was anything to go by. And the third was groaning and doing his utmost to pull himself into a sitting position, and other than the blood seeping from a headwound, he appeared to have no other injuries.

Making a split-second decision, she crouched down beside Vinnie Vickers, her eager gaze raking over his body on the lookout for any signs of visible trauma. 'Can you hear me?' she asked.

Vinnie nodded and as he whipped his head around to look for Carmen, his eyes widened. 'What the...' he began as he tried to get to his feet.

Natasha put out her hand. 'She's fine,' she said as she too glanced in Carmen's direction. 'From what I can tell it isn't her blood.'

It was then that Vinnie cast his gaze upon Arthur, and blowing out his cheeks, he flopped onto his back. 'This is fucked up,' he said, staring up at the ceiling.

'Yeah,' Natasha agreed. And he could certainly say that again. The whole situation was fucked, and even more than that, when they eventually alerted the emergency services, she had absolutely no idea how she was going to explain how she'd somehow managed to stumble upon the crime scene. Even in her own head it sounded suspicious, so how the hell was she supposed to convince the first officers on the scene that this had actually been the case?

* * *

As Damien strode across the driveway, he narrowed his eyes at the sight of Tommy Johnson sitting in his uncle Jonny's car. He was trying to gain their attention and had even shoved open the car door and called out to them. And maybe if it wasn't for the fact that his parents' front door was wide open, they would have stopped. Instead, all three men charged forward as they headed for the kitchen, Jason calling out his wife's name, the tone of his voice filled with panic.

At the threshold to the kitchen, they came to a shuddering halt, their eyes wide and their foreheads furrowed until finally Jason stepped into the room, his hands clutching at the back of his neck.

'What the fuck?' he cried as he automatically searched out his wife. 'What in the actual fuck is going on here?'

As Damien too stepped into the kitchen, he took in the carnage, fear curling around his insides. There was so much blood that for a split second he wasn't so sure who had been injured. He'd thought it was his mum at first considering the amount of claret she was covered in. But much to his relief he'd soon come to realise it wasn't her blood, but Arthur's.

It was only then that he caught Natasha's eyes. Until now he'd tried to avoid her. She was a copper and at the end of the day there was no getting away from that fact.

'Tash...' he began.

Natasha shook her head, and averting her gaze, she got to her feet. Her hands were smeared with blood and in that instant, he took a wild guess that it belonged to Vinnie.

'Tash...' he tried again.

This time she looked up. He could see the unease written across her face and he watched her visibly swallow. 'I can't,' she said quietly with a shake of her head. 'You know I can't.'

Damien too swallowed. 'Tash.' He came forward and took her hand in his, not giving a single fuck about the blood coating her hands. 'This is my family.'

'I know it is.' He could see the dilemma then in her eyes. A sense of knowing what was right and what was wrong. 'Damien,' she whispered as she shook her head. Before he could answer, her gaze swept over the room. He could almost see the cogs turning in her head, as though she were weighing up her options.

'I'll get rid of him,' he said, jerking his head towards Arthur. 'We'll get this place cleaned up. And no one will be any wiser.' He glanced then towards Jonny Carter and Cameron Johnson. It wasn't ideal that they were witnesses but at the same time he had a gut feeling that he had nothing to worry about where they were concerned. Besides, if the rumours about them were true, they had more than enough secrets of their own to keep schtum about.

Still, Natasha didn't look too sure, and as she bit down on her bottom lip, her hands ever so slightly trembled. 'Damien...'

Before she could continue, Damien pulled her into his arms. 'Do the right thing for my family, Tash,' he pleaded with her. 'And not just my family but your brother too. If we end up getting nicked then it'll be game over for all of us, you know it will be.'

'But you and Win weren't here when it happened.' Natasha's gaze flicked towards her brother, her eyes filled with a sense of righteousness.

'It won't matter,' Damien protested as he too looked in the

direction of his best mate. 'Me and Winston both have records. We will both be carted off to the nick.'

Heaving in a breath, Natasha took a final look around her before finally nodding. 'My arse will be on the line for this,' she sighed. 'But...'

'You don't need to say it,' he said, kissing the top of her head. 'I already know what you're sacrificing. Oh.' He made to pull away then paused. 'By the way, Winston knows. About us, I mean.'

Natasha's eyes widened, her cheeks flushing red.

'So no more creeping around.' He winked.

As she gave her brother a surreptitious glance, Natasha nodded.

Releasing Natasha, Damien looked down at his cousin. 'You all right?' he asked.

Still blurry eyed, Vinnie nodded. 'Yeah, I think so,' he said, tentatively reaching up to touch his head. 'I think I was out cold for a while.'

Damien nodded. He'd guessed as much. He'd even go as far as to say that his cousin could possibly have concussion. 'What happened?'

Vinnie screwed up his face, as though he were trying to recall what had taken place. 'I don't know,' he finally answered. 'I remember Arthur smashing the window, then he came at me with a hammer. The rest is all a blur.'

It was definitely what Damien had suspected, and walking across the kitchen, he stood in front of Arthur's lifeless form. He had never felt such hatred for anyone in his life. And as much as he was glad that the man was dead, it wasn't enough to satisfy him. He wanted to watch Arthur suffer. And even more than that, he had wanted to be the one to dish out the final blow.

He cocked his head to the side then. 'Where's Joanie?' he asked, turning his head from side to side.

Jason too looked around him, his expression one of bewilderment. 'Where is she?' he asked his wife.

Carmen shook her head, her wide eyes darting down to Arthur's body. 'I don't know. She was here before...' As she shook her head again, she turned to look at the smashed patio door. 'She was here; she was pottering around. Doing what she always does. I was barely taking any notice of her.'

The hairs on the back of Damien's neck stood upright and bolting out of the house, with both Winston and Natasha close behind him, he came to stand on the vast lawn. 'Where the fuck is she?'

It was Natasha who began to run in the direction of the pool house, and just moments later they were banging their fists on the locked door.

'Joanie,' Damien called out before backing up then planting his size eleven boot in the centre of the wooden panel. Just as he'd expected, the wood splinted, and kicking out again, the door almost came off its hinges as it sprang open.

'Joanie,' he called out a second time.

'Damien.'

In that instant Damien's heart lurched, and following where the voice was coming from, he found Joanie in the main pool area, her cheeks red and her eyes red rimmed.

'Oh my God,' she cried as she clung to him. 'Your mum?'

'Mum's okay,' he reassured her. 'Everyone is okay; well, other than Arthur that is.'

As she sniffed back her tears, Damien could see the terror in Joanie's eyes. She was a tough old bird; she had to be, he supposed, when you took into account the family she worked for, although she was more like family than the housekeeper.

'He said he was going to come back and finish me off. He said that once he'd dealt with your mum, I would be next. I've been here waiting for him to come back for me. I've never prayed so bleedin' hard in all my life, I know that much.'

Damien couldn't help but laugh. Joanie had never struck him as being a particularly religious person.

'And your mum is okay... He didn't harm her in any way. You're sure about that?'

'She's okay,' Damien said as they made their way back to the main house. 'Or at least as well as she can be.'

* * *

Talk about revelations. If the Vickers' heads weren't reeling enough by the time Tommy Jr had dropped his bombshell on them, they were positively mind blown.

'I knew it,' Jason declared. 'I always knew that Colin would never have driven under the influence. He barely drank alcohol and not only that, he loved his wife and son too much to ever put them at risk.'

All heads turned to look at Vinnie, and he gave a small smile. As much as he knew that his parents were never going to come back, growing up he'd harboured feelings that perhaps his dad hadn't loved his family enough. That perhaps he hadn't cared if he were pissed out of his nut when he'd driven them home that night. And to know that this wasn't the case eased the loss he felt somewhat.

He turned then to look down at Arthur's corpse. A short time before Natasha and Demi had led Carmen out of the kitchen, someone had thrown a coat over him. Not that it disguised the fact a dead body was laid out on the kitchen floor. 'What are we going to do with him?'

Damien opened his mouth to answer before pausing. 'Do you know what,' he said, giving the body a customary glance. 'Why don't you do the honours. You choose how we dispose of him.'

'Me?' Vinnie was taken aback, and his jaw dropped.

'Yeah, you,' Damien replied. 'He murdered your mum and dad. So you choose.'

Vinnie's face lit up. And rubbing his hands together, he turned to look at Jonny Carter. 'Has your scrapyard got one of those machines that crushes cars?'

Jonny tilted his head to the side. 'No. But I know someone who does.'

Vinnie grinned. 'That's what I want done with him. The high and mighty Arthur fucking Brennan crushed down to a pulp. And then I want whatever is left of him to be thrown in the Thames.'

'Right.' Damien nodded. 'You heard him. Let's make sure this no-good cunt is obliterated.'

'I don't just want him just obliterated,' Vinnie added. 'I want to make sure there is nothing left of him, that he'll never be found and given a proper burial. Because as far as I'm concerned, the bastard doesn't deserve one.'

For a moment both Jason and Damien were thoughtful until finally Jason slung his arm around Vinnie's shoulders. 'Trust me,' he said as he eyed his former business partner. 'There won't be anything left, I'll make sure of that. If nothing else, I owe that to your mum and dad. In fact, I'll even go one better and stay there throughout the entire process just to make sure the deed is done.'

Vinnie gave a satisfied nod. It could never bring his parents back, but at least they had the justice they deserved. At least now they could rest in peace.

EPILOGUE

Jason had been true to his word and packed Carmen off to rehab. She hadn't even protested and had willingly walked out of the house and into his car. Even when she was being shown around the facilities, she didn't complain or refuse to engage with the staff. It was almost as though she had known from somewhere deep down inside that the time had come for her to seek professional help. And of course money had been no object. Only the best would do for Jason Vickers' wife, and as a result, her treatment programme was one of the best the country had to offer.

As he relaxed on a chair, Vinnie tilted his head to the sky and closed his eyes. He could get used to this, he decided. And from what he could see, rehab was a doddle. His aunt had it made – freshly cooked meals, activities to stop her from feeling bored, and what's more, she could sit out in the garden doing fuck all for as long as she wanted.

'Hello, darling.'

Vinnie snapped his eyes open and as he got to his feet, he

offered a bright smile. 'How are you?' he asked after kissing his aunt's cheek.

'Good.' Carmen smiled.

And it was true, she did look good, Vinnie decided. She'd put on some weight and her hair looked clean and glossy. And what's more, she actually looked a lot more alert than she had in previous years.

As he took a moment to study her, Vinnie's heart swelled with love. He couldn't remember his mother, other than one vague memory he had of her tucking him into bed one night. In a way, Carmen had been the only mother figure he'd ever known. And so to know that Arthur had violated her broke his heart.

He'd never told anyone what he'd heard that night. He'd pretended that he'd been knocked out cold, which of course he had, seeing as he'd had a hammer blow to the head. But he hadn't been unconscious the entire time. He'd heard Carmen confront Arthur, had heard her tell him how the rape had resulted in a pregnancy, and that Dylan had been the result. At first he'd thought he was hallucinating, that perhaps his mind was playing tricks on him. But no, to his despair he realised it was all true.

He would never breathe a word of what he'd heard. He would take Carmen's secret to the grave. His family were trying to heal; why cause them even more grief? And in this instance just maybe what they didn't know wouldn't hurt them.

Turning his head, he watched as his uncle Jason and Damien came into view carrying mugs of tea and what looked suspiciously like a packet of biscuits, no doubt chocolate chip cookies, his aunt's favourite. And as Jason kissed Carmen's forehead before taking a seat, he couldn't help but catch Damien's eyes. Once upon a time he would have seen hatred in them, but now the only thing he saw was acceptance. At the end of the day they were cousins, and thanks to the disposal of Arthur's body, they now shared something in common. Or maybe it was the fact that Damien had stopped viewing him as the enemy, especially when the only real enemy had been his actual brother.

As the conversation began to flow, Vinnie relaxed back in his seat. He enjoyed the trip out to see Carmen and as much as she wasn't quite ready to come home yet, she was on the right path. Besides, it was also nice to just put his feet up for a while. Since the demise of Arthur, Jason had been training both Vinnie and Demi on how to run the casino in his absence, and he was a strict taskmaster too. Vinnie also had a feeling that once Carmen was out of rehab, Jason intended to spend a lot more time at home with her, hence why he was coming down so hard on both him and Demi – they had to be ready to take over from him.

As he caught Damien's eyes again, Vinnie's body became slightly tense. And as Damien tilted his head to the side, there was a look of warning in his eyes. Not that this was enough to deter Vinnie, and without even giving the matter a second thought, he lunged forward and swiped the last cookie.

'Fucker,' Damien muttered under his breath, although there was no hint of malice there, Vinnie noted.

As Carmen and Jason laughed, both Damien and Vinnie joined in. It may have taken a bit of time, but they were actually beginning to feel like a family again. And if there was one thing that Vinnie knew, it was the fact that he would kill for his family. And who knew in the future, that may very well be the case. Either way he was ready for it and as he looked between his uncle and cousin, he had a sneaky suspicion that he wasn't the only one.

* * *

Tommy Jr could feel his cheeks turn red. He'd never really been one for hogging the limelight, and despite the fact he'd spent the majority of his life at the centre of his parents' world, he'd never really felt comfortable with the way they fussed over him, especially his mum. He was an only child, and to a certain degree it was to be expected, he supposed, that she would want to cater to his every need. But when you took into account that he was also Tommy Carter's eldest grandson and namesake, it would be safe to say that the amount of attention he received was on another level. Reece used to tell him to suck it up, that if nothing else, the fact he and Tommy Snr looked so alike meant that he could get away with blue murder. Which to be fair was the truth. Not so long ago he and Reece had been a right pair of scallywags, getting up to all sorts of trouble. Funny how times change. He was about to become a father, and as much as he didn't think he'd overly changed, he could sense that there was something different about himself. He'd grown up a bit, he supposed.

Aimee rested her hand on the small of his back. She was probably one of the few who knew just how much he disliked occasions like this. After he had a few drinks inside of him he'd be okay, as right as rain, not that he was supposed to drink on the painkillers. Fuck it, he decided. One or two drinks wouldn't hurt. It wasn't as though he had to get up and go to work in the morning. His uncle had very generously given him a couple of weeks off work; after all, he couldn't exactly chase up debts on crutches, could he? He'd become a laughing stock. As for his knee, he'd been right when he'd said he thought the kneecap was broken, because it was. His knee had been so swollen that the hospital staff had had to cut his jeans off him, and surprisingly, there had only been one fracture rather than the multiple fractures that he'd been expecting. Still, the recovery time was expected to be between three and six months, a lot longer than he'd been hoping for.

'Are you okay, babe?'

Tommy Jr looked up and, seeing the expression across Aimee's face, he gave her a wide smile.

'Yeah,' he answered. 'I'd much rather they hadn't done this though,' he said, nodding towards his nan's house and in particular the amount of cars parked on the driveway. 'I can't stand all of this shit.'

'I know.' As she followed her boyfriend's gaze, Aimee bit down on her bottom lip. 'It's just for a couple of hours though. If it gets too much you could always say that your leg hurts too much and that you want to go home.'

Tommy gave a light laugh. 'You've met my family,' he joked. 'There ain't a chance in hell they'll let that happen. They'll stick me in a corner somewhere and ply me with even more booze.'

Aimee lifted her eyebrows. 'I doubt it,' she remarked. 'Your mum would have their guts.'

'Yeah, fair point.' Knowing his mum she would go garrity if she so much as saw an alcoholic drink in his hand. And she'd warned him as much that afternoon. She'd even shoved the bottle containing the painkillers underneath his nose, telling him to read the fine print, where it stated that alcohol wasn't advised. Still, he decided she couldn't watch his every move and with so many family members, she was bound to lose track of what he was getting up to.

Taking a deep breath, Tommy Jr adjusted the crutch underneath his armpit then took a tentative step forward, all the while resisting the urge to screwup his face. He was still in a lot of pain; a lot more than he was ever willing to let on.

Amid a chorus of cheers he entered his grandmother's home. His nan had gone all out and the lounge had been decorated to the max. Get well soon banners adorned the walls and beside the large brick fireplace were a cluster of weighted balloons.

'Here he is,' his nan called out as she rushed up to him, took his face in her hands and kissed each of his cheeks.

Tommy Jr squirmed. 'Nan,' he protested.

'Oh, shush you.' Stacey laughed as she went on to kiss Aimee's cheek. 'It's not every day my firstborn grandchild survives the kind of ordeal that you did. You deserve this, my darling, and despite not being one to promote violence in this instance, I'm bloody proud of you.'

Tommy rolled his eyes. He'd hardly done anything at all, at least nothing that warranted his family to be proud of him, and if it hadn't been for the dog walker who'd then disappeared off the face of the earth, he had a feeling the outcome would have been very different.

Gratefully taking the drink offered to him, Tommy gulped it down before his mum had the chance to berate him, and as a second one was pushed into his hand, he gripped hold of the glass while doing his best to manoeuvre around his grandmother's lounge, stopping here and there to talk to his family members. As much as he might have complained about them, he couldn't wish for a better family. Not only were they tight, but they were also loyal to one another, and even more than that, he knew he could count on them to have his back if needed. And when you took into account the amount of lies and deception within the Vickers family, that was saying something.

* * *

Caleb Carter, or Cal as he was more frequently known, lounged back on the sofa and resisted the urge to roll his eyes. Tommy Jr got on his wick. He wasn't even a Carter, not really. He was a Johnson and there was no getting away from the fact, yet the way the family fawned all over him you'd think he was something special. He glanced towards his brother, Reece. He was another one, constantly following Tommy Jr around, a yes man if ever he'd seen one. He wouldn't mind but Tommy Jr was a year or two younger than himself and the little prick actually had the gall to think he could boss him around, act the Billy big bollocks and throw his weight around.

Fucking arsehole. Pulling out his mobile phone, he scrolled through his contact list then shot off a text message. Just moments later, a reply pinged back.

A smile spread across Cal's face and downing his drink, he got to his feet and stuffed his mobile into his back pocket. He highly doubted that anyone would notice him missing, other than perhaps his dad, but even then he probably wouldn't bother to give him a call and check in with him.

Slipping out of the house, moments later he jumped into his car and started the ignition. Giving his aunt's house a scathing look, he pushed his foot down on the accelerator then sped off the drive. A short while later he brought the car to a screeching halt and as his best mate Tjay Nixon climbed in, he gave him a bright grin.

'I take it you'd had enough,' he said, referring to Tommy Jr's get well soon party.

'If you're asking if I'd had enough of hop-along Cassidy taking centre stage as per fucking usual, then yeah, too fucking right I did.' He scowled. 'He pisses me off. Just seeing that smug face of his riles me up. Telling me what I can and can't do.'

Tjay frowned. 'He is your cousin though…'

'Cousin once removed,' Cal interrupted as though it made a huge difference in the grand scheme of things.

'You're still family though,' Tjay persisted.

It was Cal's time to frown, and as he turned his head, his lips were curled into a scowl. 'Whose side are you on?'

Tjay sighed. 'Yours, obviously.'

'Good,' Cal answered as he allowed his shoulders to relax. Flashing a wide smile, he turned his head. 'You got the dough on you?'

Tjay patted his pocket. 'What do you think?' he asked as he went on to rub his hands together. 'Not that he ever asks for it.'

Cal laughed. He'd been keeping a secret from his family, one they were bound to be upset over, especially his mum and dad, maybe even his brothers and uncles. Not that this was enough to deter him.

Pulling up beside the kerb, Cal climbed out of the car, locked up, then stuffing his hands into his pockets, he looked up at the block of flats before him. His bird, Shannon, lived on the eighth floor. She was a right little goer and exactly what he looked for in a woman. Big tits, nice firm arse, and legs up to her armpits. She also knew how to look after herself – hair extensions, fake tan, lip filler, the works. She got a lot of attention when she was out and about too, but he'd been the one who'd bagged her.

He threw Tjay a sidelong glance. 'With a bit of luck, Shan will have some gear.'

As he contemplated this, Tjay chewed on his bottom lip. 'And what if she hasn't?'

'Then she'd best get some.' He chuckled. 'Otherwise we'll fuck off and find someone who does.'

A smile tugged at Tjay's lips. 'Now you're talking.' He grinned.

A few moments later they were in the lift, and as it slowly

made its way up to the eighth floor, Cal ignored his mobile phone. The constant ringing was beginning to get on his tits. He didn't even need to pull it out of his pocket, he knew exactly who it was. Either his dad or his brother Reece. They would more than likely demand to know why he'd left hop-along Cassidy's party, and then because they were nosy bastards, they would want to know where he was. Well, fuck that. Shannon was his best-kept secret; well, other than the other little secret of course, but as the two were closely linked it was all the same to him.

It had been Shannon who'd introduced him to heroin, or rather it had been her brother, Jordon. But in the grand scheme of things who actually cared, because he sure as hell didn't.

All he wanted to do was fuck his bird and get stoned, even if it meant giving out some of his family's secrets in the process. Not the big secrets of course, but some of the smaller ones, or rather some of the smaller bank jobs they'd taken part in. Jordon had lapped it up and hung on to his every word as though he were telling some of the greatest stories known to man. He'd even produced a tape recorder the last time he'd brought along the brown. He'd said that he liked listening to the things the Carter family got up to when he was alone. Weirdo. Still, Cal decided. Who cared. Jordon was a top bloke, he'd barely, if ever, charged them for the heroin he'd provided. He never even said anything when him and Shannon would disappear into the bedroom for hours on end. He'd just sit it out in the living room with Tjay for company and his little tape recorder recording everything that was going on around him.

Cal's mobile phone began to ring again and staring down at the device, he saw Reece's name flash across the screen. Switching the phone off just in time as the lift doors opened, Cal stuffed the phone back into his pocket. A combination of mould and stale air hit his nostrils. It had become as familiar to him as his own home. Moments later, he was striding across the communal hallway and thumping his fist on the front door. It took just seconds for Shannon to pull the door open wide, and as she gave him a seductive smile, he copped a feel of her arse as he made his way past.

As usual, Jordon was in the kitchen. On the counter he took note of the spoon and makeshift tourniquet ready and waiting for him, and then the tape recorder beside it. Briefly it crossed his mind to ask why Jordon wanted to record his every visit. It wasn't as though he had anything interesting to say, at least not unless it involved his family. He was just about to say as much when Shannon pulled on his hand, her eyebrow cocked as she indicated towards the bedroom.

Another time, he decided. It wasn't that much of a big deal, he supposed. Not really. It certainly wasn't life altering. Or just maybe it was.

* * *

MORE FROM KERRY KAYA

Another book from Kerry Kaya, *Betrayal*, is available to order now here:

https://mybook.to/BetrayalBackAd

ACKNOWLEDGEMENTS

Thank you to the team at Boldwood Books for your continued support. And a special thank you to my editor, Emily Ruston, for everything you do. Thank you to Jennifer Davies and Arbaiah Aird.

Thank you to my girls, Joana, Thanu, Liz, Katie, and Chantel, your support and encouragement means everything to me.

Thank you to Deryl Easton and NotRights Book Club. You have been there from the very beginning, and your support is invaluable.

And lastly, a special thank you to my family for continuing to believe in me.

ABOUT THE AUTHOR

Kerry Kaya is the hugely popular author of Essex-based gritty gangland thrillers with strong family dynamics. She grew up on one of the largest council estates in the UK, where she sets her novels. She also works full-time in a busy maternity department for the NHS.

Sign up to Kerry Kaya's mailing list for news, competitions and updates on future books.

Follow Kerry on social media here:

- facebook.com/kerry.bryant.58
- x.com/KerryKayaWriter
- instagram.com/kerry_kaya_writer

ALSO BY KERRY KAYA

Reprisal

The Fletcher Family Series

The Price

The Score

Carter Brothers Series

Under Dog

Top Dog

Scorned

The Reckoning

The Carters: Next Generation Series

Downfall

Retribution

Dishonour

The Tempests Series

Betrayal

Revenge

Justice

PEAKY READERS

GANG LOYALTIES. DARK SECRETS. BLOODY REVENGE.

A READER COMMUNITY FOR GANGLAND CRIME THRILLER FANS!

DISCOVER PAGE-TURNING NOVELS FROM YOUR FAVOURITE AUTHORS AND MEET NEW FRIENDS.

JOIN OUR BOOK CLUB FACEBOOK GROUP

BIT.LY/PEAKYREADERSFB

SIGN UP TO OUR NEWSLETTER

BIT.LY/PEAKYREADERSNEWS

Boldwood

Boldwood Books is an award-winning fiction publishing company seeking out the best stories from around the world.

Find out more at www.boldwoodbooks.com

Join our reader community for brilliant books, competitions and offers!

Follow us
@BoldwoodBooks
@TheBoldBookClub

Sign up to our weekly deals newsletter

https://bit.ly/BoldwoodBNewsletter

Printed in Dunstable, United Kingdom